BECAUSE I'M WATCHING

ALSO BY CHRISTINA DODD

Obsession Falls

Virtue Falls

Love Never Dies

The Relatives

The Listener

Candle in the Wind

Treasure of the Sun

Castles in the Air

Priceless

Greatest Lover in All England

Move Heaven and Earth

Once a Knight

Outrageous

A Knight to Remember

That Scandalous Evening

The Runaway Princess

Someday My Prince

Rules of Surrender

Rules of Engagement

Rules of Attraction

In My Wildest Dreams

Lost in Your Arms

A Well Pleasured Lady

My Favorite Bride

Scandalous Again

Just the Way You Are

One Kiss from You

Almost Like Being in Love

A Well Favored Gentleman

Some Enchanted Evening

Close to You

The Barefoot Princess

Dangerous Ladies

Trouble in High Heels

The Prince Kidnaps a Bride

Tongue in Chic

My Fair Temptress

Scent of Darkness

Touch of Darkness

Thigh High

Into the Shadow

Into the Flame

Danger in a Red Dress

Storm of Visions

Storm of Shadows

In Bed with the Duke

Chains of Ice

Chains of Fire

Taken by the Prince

Secrets at Bella Terra

Revenge at Bella Terra

Betrayal

The Smuggler's Captive Bride

Last Night

Kidnapped

Wilder

Wild Texas Rose

Stone Angel

Lady in Black

BECAUSE I'M WATCHING

CHRISTINA DODD

ST. MARTIN'S PRESS ❧ NEW YORK

BECAUSE I'M WATCHING. Copyright © 2016 by Christina Dodd. All rights reserved. Printed in the United States of America. For information, address St. Martin's Press, 175 Fifth Avenue, New York, N.Y. 10010.

www.stmartins.com

Designed by Omar Chapa

Library of Congress Cataloging-in-Publication Data

Names: Dodd, Christina, author.
Title: Because I'm watching / Christina Dodd.
Other titles: Because I am watching
Description: First edition. | New York : St. Martin's Press, 2016.
Identifiers: LCCN 2016012736| ISBN 9781250028457 (hardcover) |
    ISBN 9781250028440 (e-book)
Subjects: | BISAC: FICTION / Romance / Suspense. | FICTION / Suspense. |
    GSAFD: Suspense fiction.
Classification: LCC PS3554.O3175 B43 2016 | DDC 813/.54—dc23
LC record available at https://lccn.loc.gov/2016012736

Our books may be purchased in bulk for promotional, educational, or business use. Please contact your local bookseller or the Macmillan Corporate and Premium Sales Department at 1-800-221-7945, extension 5442, or by e-mail at MacmillanSpecialMarkets@macmillan.com.

First Edition: September 2016

10 9 8 7 6 5 4 3 2 1

Because I'm Watching is fondly dedicated to retired
Air Force Major Roger B. Bell, who critiques and edits,
who advises me on cars, planes, firearms, and the military.
Virtue Falls is alive because of you.

And to Joyce Bell, a wonderful writer and a friend forever.

Thank you both!

ACKNOWLEDGMENTS

Some publishing companies and some editors would flinch when I say I'm writing a story that melds two great classic suspense movies, *Gaslight* and *Rear Window*. St. Martin's Press and Jennifer Enderlin greenlighted the project and encouraged me to produce *Because I'm Watching*, a creepy, charismatic tale of two broken people and the terrors that haunt them. Thank you to SMP and Jennifer.

To Anne Marie Tallberg, Associate Publisher, and the marketing team of Jessica Preeg, Brant Janeway, Angela Craft, and Angelique Giammarino, thank you for your enthusiasm for *Because I'm Watching* and the whole Virtue Falls series.

The art department, led by Ervin Serrano, captured my vision of a terrifying story with this groundbreaking cover.

To everybody on the Broadway and Fifth Avenue sales teams: thank you for placing *Because I'm Watching* in just the right places and at just the right times.

A huge thanks to managing editor Amelie Littell and Jessica Katz in Production.

Thank you to Caitlin Dareff, who keeps me up to date and on time.

Thank you to Sally Richardson, St. Martins's president and publisher. I am so glad to be part of St. Martin's Press.

CHAPTER ONE

Two years ago
Old Broadmoor neighborhood of Colorado Springs

Upstairs at her desk, Madeline Hewitson heard the back door open and close. She stopped typing.

"Hey, honey, it's me!" he called.

She smiled. "Welcome back!" she answered.

He was home.

Easton Robert Privet was the best thing that had ever happened to her, and he was home. His law office was in downtown Denver; after they got together she had offered to move into his high-rise condo and spare him the commute to the suburbs. But without being told, he had understood that to write interesting, riveting novels she needed to concentrate. She needed space around her, the sounds of birds, the smell of grass, a place to plant some flowers. He had bought an estate in a gated community with a guard and hourly security patrols because again, he understood she needed to feel safe.

What he didn't understand was that *he* made her feel secure.

Her brother Andrew was a good guy, but he'd grown impatient with her. He had told her to grow up, to get over her depression and her terror.

Not Easton. When she woke at night, rigid with fear, he was there to cradle her, to whisper encouragement: *The monster is gone. You were brave. You risked your own life to try to save them . . . because of you, the monster is dead.*

Maddie traced the dark stain that marred the smooth grain of her walnut desktop.

Blood.

It wasn't surprising that it was there; it was surprising there wasn't more.

Andrew said she should have the desk refinished, have the bloodstain removed. But to Maddie, that would be a desecration, so every day as she wrote, she would touch the stain, acknowledge the passing of her friends, and try very hard to forgive herself for not dying, too.

After witnessing those deaths, she had not imagined she would ever find the courage to live again. But Easton had given her that courage. He saw past the brave front she presented to the world, to the cowering girl caught in a cycle of fear and self-loathing, and he loved her. He had helped her break free of the past. With him, she was learning to move forward.

She shut her laptop and stood, ready to head downstairs. Easton had left early this morning on a business trip, one of those fly-out, fly-in things that he did on a regular basis. He seldom talked about where he was going; he took his pledge of client confidentiality seriously, and this morning when he woke her to kiss her good-bye, he had looked unusually grave. So it had been one of *those* cases, probably an ugly child-custody situation.

He'd landed at Colorado Springs Airport about an hour ago, called, and told her he would pick up dinner somewhere. They would eat, he'd ask how the book was coming, she'd ask how his day had gone. He would say, "Fine," even when it hadn't, and she would keep it light and cheery. Everything about living with Easton was so normal, so all-American white-bread average, and so much more than she had ever hoped for.

Downstairs, she heard him speaking to someone in that special, soothing tone he used when addressing a frantic client.

She sat back down in her chair. When he was on the phone, he didn't want her listening in. She put her fingers on the keyboard and prepared to sink back into the story.

He gave a half shout followed by an odd, off-pitch squawk.

She found herself on her feet, staring toward the stairway. "Easton?" she called.

No answer.

"Easton?" She owned a pistol. Easton had bought it for her twenty-fourth birthday. Easton had said it would make her feel secure to own a pistol, to learn how to use it. She had learned, and she kept it . . . close. She groped in the desk drawer and brought out her Smith & Wesson 642 revolver.

She didn't feel secure right now.

She released the safety and edged toward the door. "Easton? What's wrong?"

Still no answer.

The outer door opened again. It didn't close.

It was winter in Colorado Springs. Easton might go back out to his car. But he would never forget to close the door after himself.

Call the cops. Call the cops. Call the cops call the cops call the cops.

She scurried back to the desk. Without looking away from the door, she picked up the phone, fumbled it, caught it. She pressed the top entry on the autodial and when the 911 operator answered, she said, "I think there's something wrong with my fiancé."

"Who is this?"

"Maddie . . . Madeline Hewitson."

"Can you tell me more, Madeline?"

Maddie stood, listening to the silence.

"Madeline! What do you think is wrong?"

As it was meant to do, the snap in the operator's voice brought Maddie's attention back to the call. "He made a funny noise. Now he's not answering me. I think . . . I think there might be an intruder."

"Is your address—"

Maddie put the phone down on the desk, raised the pistol to the fist-in-palm position, and using the gun as a pointer, again started to move toward the door. But a movement in her peripheral vision caught her attention, made her glance out the window. A man hurried down the sidewalk. She could only see him from above; he wore a broad-brimmed black hat and a long, dark, businessman's coat. But the coat was open. It was flapping in the wind.

That wasn't right. In this weather, everyone huddled into themselves, their coats securely fastened.

That wasn't right.

Then he was out of sight.

She stuck her head out the doorway, glanced down the hallway, pulled back, and leaned against the wall. Her heart pounded painfully. Tears gathered in the corners of her eyes. Her hands shook in violent tremors.

She had to go down. She had to reassure herself that Easton . . . that he was okay.

She edged out of her office and with her back against the wall, she slid toward the stairs.

Easton was okay. Maybe he'd fallen and hurt himself. Maybe he'd forgotten the food in the car. Maybe . . . maybe there was a reason the cold north wind blasted through the open door and up the stairs, ruffling her hair and taking her breath.

Hurry! She needed to hurry!

But it was all she could do to lift one foot, then the other. She descended to the short landing near the bottom. She stopped there. The steps loomed as if they went up instead of down. Beyond was the kitchen where Easton was . . . had been . . .

She stopped to quiet her breathing.

Everything was fine. She was overreacting.

She sidled over to the entry and peered into the sleek kitchen.

The room was empty. She didn't see anything unusual. Except the outside door was open. And a crimson stain on the tile floor . . . was moving, filling the lines of grout, and flowing toward her.

And that odor. She recognized the odor. It smelled like nighttime, like dust under her bed, like broken pleading and a man's smooth voice, oozing with pleasure as he vivisected her friends.

She heard a noise, a scratching.

She froze in place, her breathing silent and shallow.

He was going to find her. He was going to kill her.

Then a thump.

She jumped.

Another thump. A movement from behind the island. Red-stained fingers groped the corner of the cabinet as if seeking her.

She recognized the ring. His ring. Easton's ring.

Yet still, for one long terrible moment, she hesitated.

The door was open.

She was afraid.

She didn't want to see . . .

Then she ran toward him, rounded the corner of the island, saw her friend, her lover, stretched out on the floor in a spreading puddle of blood, his throat cut.

His eyes were open, but death's gray blanket had already covered him.

She knelt. She took his hand. "Easton," she whispered. "Easton."

But she didn't speak too loudly, in case the killer was still nearby.

When the police arrived, she still held the pistol in her hand.

Electronics are working. First test run. Subject afraid,
insane, malleable.

CHAPTER TWO

Today

Virtue Falls, Washington

Jacob Denisov sat in his upright chair in his living room, staring into the dark. If he kept his eyes open and stared with precisely the right concentration, without movement or thought, the pain didn't break through. It took work, but for months now, he had practiced, and he had gotten pretty good.

No pain slashing at his skull, trying to get out, to explode, to manifest itself in wild screams and violence that never stopped until he broke everything . . . especially himself . . .

No North Korea. No deaths. No fault. The world beyond the dark did not exist. He floated in bleak eternity and only the stench of guilt lingered, ceaseless . . .

The phone rang.

He jumped.

It rang again.

Thought returned.

Five rings and the answering machine picked up.

"Jakie." It was his mother's voice, loving, but with a sprinkling of fear and a dollop of exasperation. "I know you're there. Pick up the telephone."

His mother was a morning person. That was when she did her best nagging. So the sun must be up.

She continued, "Just tell me you're all right. That's all you have to do, tell me you haven't died sitting in the dark in that house, brooding about a past you cannot change."

A pause.

He waited.

"Jakie, are you eating right? You are a big man, like your father. You should be eating right."

Another pause.

Jacob knew she wasn't done yet.

"Jakie, on Sunday, Father Ilovaiski asked about you. He said he was praying for you. Doesn't that feel good, to know he's praying for you?" As it did when she grew excited, her Russian accent strengthened. "When you come home to Everson and go to church with me, you will be healed. I'll fix you your favorite meal—the black bread, the stroganoff, the pirozhki—and the family will rejoice at the return of the prodigal son."

Oh, no. She was trying her patented *Trust in God and family* routine and throwing in a food bribe. She didn't understand that the idea of being out in the sunshine with people would break him. She didn't understand he had lost his faith in God. He didn't care about his family. Food meant nothing to him. And he could never be healed.

How could she comprehend? She was his mother, she remembered the boy he had been, and she would love him and believe in him forever.

That boy would never return. He had drowned in an ocean of blood and come to life only to die again. Soon, he hoped.

Her tone of voice changed, and her rising temper crackled across the wires. "Jakie, if you don't pick up the telephone soon, I will come down there and break down the door of your pitiful little hiding place. Don't think I won't!" She ended the connection so violently she cut off her own voice.

He closed his eyes. He knew she would. Nothing his father could say would stop her. His mother was a force of nature.

So next time when she called, he would answer, and he would talk to her. To relieve her mind he would pretend he was fine, that he had been outside working on some unspecified and manly project and couldn't make it to the phone . . . for the last week . . .

His parents lived in Everson, up by the Canadian border, and he had deliberately moved here, to this location on the Olympic Peninsula, so he could feel at home and at the same time be far enough away from his large family to avoid their well-intentioned intrusions.

It worked . . . mostly.

He never knew when the sun rose or set; no light leaked through the blackout shades on the windows. He'd made sure of that. He hadn't eaten since . . . he didn't remember. Yesterday sometime. He should go into the kitchen and get something out of the refrigerator. A piece of pizza. A sandwich. Whatever he had in there.

How long had it been since he'd had a grocery delivery?

He groped for the lamp on the end table, found the switch, and turned it on. Even the pitiful amount of light the twenty-five-watt bulb produced made him blink. When his vision cleared, he looked at the marks he had scratched on the wall.

Five days since the boy rang the doorbell, took the check Jacob had taped to the window, and left two grocery bags of canned soup, prepared food, and milk.

That meant every bit of food in this house was stale or rotting, or needed a can opener, a clean pan, and the will and energy to prepare it for consumption.

Only two more days until he received groceries again.

He turned off the light.

He could wait.

At the camp, he had learned to wait for the right moment. He had learned . . .

He pushed his spine hard against the chair, braced himself for the wave of pain—

And with a high screech of jagged wood against paint and metal, a gray Subaru Forester shot up the concrete steps of his front porch and exploded through the wall of his house, front wheels in the air, headed right for the heavens—and then, as it tilted toward earth, at him.

CHAPTER THREE

Jacob blinked and squinted against the assault of sunshine. He lifted his arm to protect his eyes while around him the house disintegrated. Brittle glass blew out of the old single-hung windows. Lath and plaster from the walls blasted into a dry, choking dust. Rock wool insulation dropped from the jutting ruptures in the ceiling.

The front of the small SUV slammed down hard onto the hardwood floor, ate the old TV, the decrepit wooden stand, and the low coffee table. With the roar of a revved-up engine, at last death had come for him.

About damned time.

He sat unmoving, waiting to be obliterated.

Then snap, boom! The left front tire from the small SUV broke through the hardwood floor. With a screech, the vehicle stopped abruptly . . . three feet from his knees.

He said the first unrehearsed words he had said in three months: "Oh, come on!" The car couldn't have driven another six feet and flattened him?

The house creaked and moaned, distressed by the violence.

The engine idled and died.

A hush fell over the surreal wreckage of his home.

The car sat tilted forward and to the side, with the left side of the bumper resting on the old braided rug. A white-painted, splintered rail from the front porch pierced the hood. Wood shards and dust covered the windshield, but the glass was miraculously unbroken. A white air bag filled the driver's side of the car . . . slowly it deflated, revealing a wide-eyed young woman in her twenties.

She stared at him in horror and disbelief.

He stared back.

She had black hair tucked into a messy bun and startled blue eyes. Her skin was the color of parchment. Blood trickled from her lower lip. She groped around and opened her door. The edge slammed into the splintered remains of the hardwood floor, leaving a gap of only inches.

She looked puzzled, started the car again. The motor gasped. Then, because she was damned lucky, it turned over. She rolled down the window.

Coolant and oil blew past that porch rail like blood from a perforated artery. The motor died.

She watched until the gusher dwindled, then crawled out.

She was short, he realized, and thin. Too thin. Was he wrong in his assessment of her age? Was she a skinny adolescent, someone who had recently learned to drive?

Then she scrambled to her feet and faced him, and he knew his first impression was right. She was in her midtwenties, maybe a little older, dressed in a blue short-sleeve T-shirt, yellow cropped sweatpants, and one flip-flop. Damp brown stains splattered her shirt and sweatpants.

Made sense. If he'd driven his car into someone's house, he'd have brown stains in his sweatpants, too.

Somehow, since he'd moved to Virtue Falls, winter had turned to summer. A bright, sunshiny, contemptuous summer, glaring down on the concrete sidewalks, the narrow asphalt road, the neighborhood of cheap houses built in the 1920s; all appeared through the gaping hole in his living room wall.

He looked at her again.

Her. This person who had ripped off the fifteen-foot-wide front wall of his house, exposing him, in his boxer shorts and T-shirt, to the sight of the world—and was apparently oblivious to her mistake.

She stuck out her hand. "Hi, I'm your neighbor Maddie Hewitson."

He stared at her outstretched fingers.

"I live across the street."

He glared at her.

She smiled, winced when her lip split wider, and touched the trickle of blood. "Ow!" She stared at the red on her fingers and looked confused, surprised to find herself here. At the sound of sirens, she glanced around, saw the neighbors gathering, peering in, and in a tone of despair said, "Oh, God. Not again."

Not again? "Do you make a habit of driving into people's houses?" His voice was rusty with disuse.

"No. Of course not! This is my first time."

The way she said it, she didn't sound sure it would be her last.

"I'm . . . I'm sorry," she said. "I didn't mean to . . . um . . ."

The sirens were getting louder.

She stopped stammering out her feeble apology. She bent and

scrutinized his face. Going back to the car, she wriggled through the window until only her feet stuck out, and hung almost upside down to get something off the passenger's side floor.

He couldn't remember the last time he'd noticed a woman's ass.

But . . . *nice ass.*

She hand-walked herself back out of the vehicle, returned to him, and offered a brown cardboard to-go box, tied with a sparkly blue ribbon. A plastic fork was stuck into the bow.

What the hell?

"Go ahead," she said. "I bought it for my lunch, but you look like you need it worse than I do."

Nice ass or not, he was suddenly and completely sick and tired of her. Leaning his hands on the arms of the chair, he pushed himself to his feet.

She watched him rise, her eyes widening in alarm, and as if realizing he could be hostile, she stepped backward—toward the jagged hole her tire had ripped in his floor.

He caught her upper arm and half-lifted her to safety.

She squeaked.

Three vehicles pulled up to the curb, lights flashing, two from the county sheriff's department and one from the Virtue Falls city police force. A fire marshal and a fire truck arrived and parked by the hydrant.

Jacob's gaze shifted to Maddie's alarmed face, to the cops, and back to her. "You started a circus."

"I'm really sorry." She glanced toward his crotch and lowered her voice. "Do you think you ought to go put on some pants?"

He wanted to tell her he would, but only if she managed not to create another disaster. But he'd already said three sentences today.

He looked out at the law enforcement officers facing off on the sidewalk. City cops vs. the sheriff's department, fighting over what was probably the spring's most interesting mishap.

With all this going on, it seemed inevitable he would have to say more. Turning on his bare heel, he started across the kitchen's warped old linoleum floor.

"Be careful of the glass!" Maddie said. "Watch where you step; you don't want to have to go to the hospital."

No. He did not.

He watched where he stepped.

As with about half the houses in the neighborhood, Jacob's one-bedroom shotgun house was stacked, room by room, on a narrow lot: the living room and the tiny kitchen in one big room. Then the bathroom, with a door into the kitchen and one into the bedroom. The bedroom faced onto the back porch, which faced into a weedy, overgrown backyard, which led to the alley.

He shuffled into the bathroom and shut the door behind him. He used the toilet, washed the dust off his hands and face, stared into the mirror.

He looked like shit: pasty white, sunken eyes that looked like two piss holes in the snow, three months' worth of dark hair curling wildly around his neck and ears, and five-day-old thick, black beard stubbling his chin. If his drill sergeant could see him now, he would feed him his balls on a shingle.

Jacob had a razor. He needed to shave his head.

No time.

He had a situation out there.

In the bedroom, he pulled on a worn pair of jeans and his athletic shoes with no socks, and headed back out to the scene of the crime. As soon as he opened the door, he flinched at the brilliant sunshine thundering into what remained of his sanctuary. Brilliant light, where before there had been deep, black, comforting darkness.

He didn't want to do this. He didn't want to face these people. He didn't want to talk.

He had come here to hide. To die.

Goddamn Maddie Hewitson. Goddamn her all to hell.

CHAPTER FOUR

Three cops, one city and two county, had climbed up broken steps and over and around piles of splintered and shattered lumber, all that remained of the railing of Jacob's porch. They stepped onto the broken remains of Jacob's floor.

Firemen in full gear stood arguing over a cluster of broken electrical wires. One of them, the fire marshal, looked at Jacob. "Mr. Denisov, this is a dangerous situation and we've turned off your power."

"Okay."

"You realize you're not going to have lights or electricity to run your refrigerator or water heater."

Jacob shrugged.

The firemen exchanged glances.

Clearly, they thought he didn't understand the gravity of the situation.

Clearly, they didn't know his refrigerator was mostly empty and he never showered. Although, if they got close enough, they would be in no doubt about the shower.

Three more cops were on the sidewalk, interviewing the gawking witnesses. Those gawking witnesses were Jacob's neighbors, he supposed, although he could see a few people standing around in exercise clothes and running shoes, and a sunburned couple who looked as if they'd come up from the beach.

All these people, staring at him as if they knew what he had done.

A Virtue Falls policeman and a deputy sheriff were talking—and scowling—at Maddie Hewitson.

The county sheriff was standing, hands on her hips, examining the car that had invaded his sanctuary. When he picked his way across the rubble on the floor, she turned to face him. "Mr. Denisov? Mr. Jacob Denisov?"

He nodded.

"I'm Sheriff Kateri Kwinault."

He could see that from the name on her pocket.

She continued, "May I ask you some questions?"

He wanted to ask her some questions, too, like how a Native American in western Washington had managed to win the election to become sheriff. Prejudice in this part of the state was quiet and pervasive. But any inquiries would indicate curiosity on his part, and he didn't care that much, so he nodded again.

She flipped open a worn notebook, opened her mouth, looked around at the wreck of his home, and shook her head as if she didn't know where to start.

"She drove into my house," he said.

"I see that. You own this home?"

"Yes."

"Did you previously know Miss Hewitson?"

"No."

"You've never met her before?"

"No."

"She lives across the street."

He shrugged. He knew Sheriff Kwinault had seen the aluminum foil at the one remaining living room window. He didn't know what conclusions she had drawn. He didn't care.

"So she has no grudge against you?" Sheriff Kwinault asked.

He was beginning to get irritated. "I've never laid eyes on her before."

"Then why did she drive into your house?"

He was becoming even more irritated and was already fed up. "Woman driver."

Sheriff Kwinault gave a laugh. "Of course. What other reason could there be?"

The more he observed Sheriff Kwinault, the more of an oddity she was. Native American. Female. Pretty woman, early thirties. But twisted, like a tree that had been warped by a great wind. One shoulder was higher than the other. Thin white scars covered her hands. Her brown eyes looked like those of some of the guys he'd met overseas, like she'd looked death in the face.

A long time ago, he would have been interested in sitting down and having a conversation with her. Now . . . she was a reminder of who he used to be, and what he had become.

Conversations were for people who still walked and breathed and hoped and dreamed. Not for him.

Dust drifted and swirled in the sudden onslaught of outdoor air currents and intrusive rays of sun, settling on his ugly-ass furniture, the stuff that had been left in the house when the old lady had died and her lousy unsentimental son had sold everything, lock, stock, and barrel, so he didn't have to fool with it. As he had said, *It's not like Mother had anything of value in here.*

More and more people were gathering on the sidewalk. He could hear the buzz of their voices now, like killer bees swarming, preparing to attack with questions and conversations and nosiness masquerading as sympathy.

A line split the floor; on one side was sunshine, on the other, shadow.

He moved farther back, into the shadow. He would not come out. He would not expose himself to the light.

Then he heard Maddie say, "But I don't want to take a blood test. I'm not drunk, and I'm not on drugs!"

He wanted to smack someone. "Wait a minute," he said to Sheriff Kwinault. He turned toward the two cops who had Maddie cornered against his recliner. "She's not on drugs," he said.

Both cops and Sheriff Kwinault viewed him with interest.

Sheriff Kwinault said, "I thought you said you didn't know her."

"I don't have to know her to know she fell asleep at the wheel. Look at her. Lack of coordination. Dark circles under her eyes. Pupils are normal, but can't stay on track with any thought." He gestured stiffly. "I don't know when she slept last, but it's been a long time."

Maddie blinked at him. She did that a lot, to keep her eyes focused.

He knew what he was talking about. He did that most days, himself. Waking hallucinations were better than nightmares. Usually.

"Those are also symptoms of drug and alcohol use," Sheriff Kwinault said.

He didn't care. Abruptly, he replied, "Fine. Do the goddamned blood test. It's your money you're wasting."

The cops exchanged glances.

Jacob conceded that he might have sounded hostile.

The Virtue Falls policeman, Ed Legbrandt, seemed to realize he was facing a losing proposition and backed away from the scene. "You know, Kateri, you are right. Dogwood Blossom Street is past the city limits sign and into the county. It's your jurisdiction. It's your case." He opened up his computer tablet and tapped it a few times. "I sent you a file with all the evidence I've collected." He jumped down from the remnants of Jacob's porch onto the small, rutted, overgrown lawn. "Have a nice day."

"Coward," Sheriff Kwinault muttered. To her cohort, Deputy Sheriff Gunder Bergen, she said, "Go give the guys a hand interviewing the witnesses."

Bergen nodded, a brief, antagonistic acknowledgment, and followed the city cop out of the house—or rather off the floor—and onto the street.

Ah. *There* was the antipathy Jacob expected.

Sheriff Kwinault seemed oblivious to her deputy's attitude. All of her focus was on Maddie. "Okay, let's assume Mr. Denisov is right and you're sleep deprived. Why are you sleep deprived?"

Maddie brushed her overgrown bangs off her forehead. "I'm . . . I don't sleep well at night."

"Then why did you get into a car and drive?" Sheriff Kwinault asked. "Surely you know it's dangerous."

"I was desperate. I was out of food. And toilet paper. And"— Maddie's voice got very quiet—"feminine hygiene . . . um, products?"

In unison, Sheriff Kwinault and Jacob said, "Oh."

Maddie acted like this monthly thing was excruciatingly embarrassing, and for a woman her age . . .

"How old are you?" Jacob asked.

"Twenty-six."

"Twenty-six. Yeah, well, I'm thirty-four. Do you think I don't know that females—"

Sheriff Kwinault gave Jacob the stink eye.

Impatiently, he said, "I've got two older sisters. And a mother."

Sheriff Kwinault gave him the sterner stink eye.

He shut up. He sat down on his chair, the one sitting like a throne in front of the hole in his floor, which was occupied by the Forester's front tire. He picked up the brown box with the sparkly blue ribbon and the fork.

"Where did you go?" Sheriff Kwinault asked Maddie.

Jacob held the box in both his hands. Something smelled good inside.

Maddie said, "I went to the grocery store and the sporting goods store and to the Bayview Convenience Store for lunch."

He untied the ribbon and opened the box. Inside was some kind of sandwich, some kind of pasta salad, and a giant cookie. Smelled like ginger. "She's telling the truth about lunch, anyway."

"I've got groceries in the back of my . . . um . . ." Maddie looked at the SUV, really looked at it, at the building's timber that had pierced the hood, and the puddle of oil and transmission fluid seeping from under the front end, and she sagged. "My brother is going to kill me."

"Your brother? The writer? Why would he care?" Sheriff Kwinault asked.

"He bought me the car." Maddie looked embarrassed.

As she should. Any twenty-six-year-old who had to have her brother buy her a car needed to grow up and go to work.

"He lives near Denver, right?" Sheriff Kwinault asked.

"Yes. In Colorado Springs in our parents' home," Maddie confirmed.

"You moved to Virtue Falls from there?" As if she knew the answers, Sheriff Kwinault was fiddling with her pen and watching Maddie, waiting to see if the story had changed.

"Actually, I moved out when I went to college and after . . . after college I lived with my fiancé in Colorado Springs." Maddie's eyes looked bright and luminous, as if she were holding back tears.

"When you speak with your brother, please tell him how much I enjoyed his last book," Sheriff Kwinault said.

Maddie beamed. "I will. Thank you. There's another book coming out in a few weeks. Its title is *Sacrifice!*"

Sheriff Kwinault made a note. "I'll order it."

Jacob took a bite of the sandwich.

He would have thought a puny-looking girl like Maddie would get some wimpy vegetarian sandwich. But no, this was pork barbeque with ham and swiss cheese, some lettuce and garlic aioli on a whole grain baguette. Best damned thing he'd put in his mouth since he'd returned to the States.

Sheriff Kwinault looked in the back window of the Subaru. "Groceries," she confirmed. "Scattered all over the back. And a sleeping bag?" She straightened. "Are you going camping, Miss Hewitson?" For whatever reason, Sheriff Kwinault made camping sound like a crime.

Maddie's gaze dropped, and by God if she didn't look guilty. "Maybe?"

Interesting. Jacob finished half of the sandwich and ate the cookie. What did Sheriff Kwinault suspect Maddie would do when she went camping?

Did people who committed crimes here go on the lam into the wilderness and escape justice?

Why was he thinking like a cop? He was not curious.

He pried the lid off the pasta salad.

Sheriff Kwinault leaned in close to Maddie. She sniffed at her, looked into her eyes, had her display her inner elbows. "I believe you. But at the least, we're going to have to give you a ticket for reckless driving and endangerment."

"Okay." Tears rose in Maddie's eyes and trickled down her cheeks.

"Perhaps Mr. Denisov wants to press charges for attempted vehicular homicide?"

"No." Like he wanted that kind of attention.

Undaunted, Sheriff Kwinault continued, "He might also bring a civil suit for damages."

Right. Make *that* clear. With the plastic fork he gestured around at the house. "You're going to have to pay for this." As if on his signal, the cornice fell off the wall and disintegrated in a puff of ancient wood and plaster.

Maddie flinched. "I'm sorry."

Jacob didn't care whether she said she was sorry. Jacob didn't care whether she cried or not.

He put the fork back, shut the box, and put it down beside his chair.

He wanted her—all of them—to go away.

Sheriff Kwinault was oblivious, or maybe indifferent, to what he wanted. She asked, "Miss Hewitson, have you got a driver's license and proof of insurance?"

Maddie nodded and crawled into the car again. She searched in the glove box and center console.

Still a nice ass.

She crawled out with her purse on her arm and a long slip of paper in her hand. She handed Sheriff Kwinault her information.

Sheriff Kwinault scanned everything into her phone and handed them back. "You might want to call your insurance agent and get him out here."

"Right." Maddie pulled her phone out of the pocket of her sweatpants and headed toward the back of the room.

Sheriff Kwinault put her phone in her breast pocket. "If this wasn't *actually* in my jurisdiction and if I wasn't *already* caught in a pissing match so violent it's like being caught in a monsoon, I would have let the city boys keep this case."

"Pissing match? Because you're a woman?" Jacob didn't know why he was asking. He didn't care.

"That, and this is my first post in law enforcement. The former sheriff had to take medical leave to be with his wife who suffered through a difficult pregnancy—she required hospitalization—and he strongly suggested the county commissioners appoint me." A dimple briefly flashed. "Against their better judgment, they did."

"Right." That explained how a Native American woman had gotten elected.

She hadn't.

Kateri said, "None of the men in area law enforcement have taken kindly to the change. They think Bergen should have gotten the post."

Bergen looked perfect for the job. Midthirties, tall, rugged, in shape, with sharp eyes that saw everything. He was white, and he was a *he*. "Right."

Sheriff Kwinault looked him right in the eye. "Do you mean, 'Right, Bergen should have gotten the post' or 'Right, now you understand'?"

Jacob looked right back at her. "I mean, 'Right, I don't give a shit.'"

"That's okay, then." She glanced at Maddie's back. "She's got worse problems than driving into your house."

He muttered, "I don't give a shit about that, either."

"The real reason I didn't bother to get a blood test was because when we've tested her before, she's never come back with a positive result."

CHAPTER FIVE

Now Jacob did give a shit. "Before?"

Sheriff Kwinault inclined her head. "On previous occasions, we've tested her drug and alcohol level."

The silence that followed was long. Sheriff Kwinault was content to wait for Jacob to decide what he *really* wanted to do.

He *really* wanted to end the conversation. He didn't want to be involved. He wasn't curious. He damned well wasn't concerned about his crazy neighbor. Yet the question popped out of his mouth. "Why did you test her?"

"Apparent hallucinations. Public scenes. Illegal use of firearms."

"What's wrong with her?"

"I don't know that I would say there's anything *wrong* with her. A couple of things happened to her. When she was in college, she was the sole surviving witness of a massacre in her dorm room. Crazy guy—the janitor—with a knife and a fingernail filed to a point. Four girls—friends—dead. You might have heard about it?"

He shook his head. "Out of the country, probably. How did she escape?"

"She hid under the bed and called campus security. The call gave away her position. The nutcase knocked over the bed and went for her. Campus cop arrived and shot him. Killed him."

"Jesus."

"A couple of years later, her fiancé was murdered, his throat cut." Based on the concise way Sheriff Kwinault gave her report, she *must* have been in the military. "Assuming she had an unstable mental state, and given the security of the premises and the fact that she was holding a pistol, law enforcement believed she did it."

"You said his throat was cut."

"She didn't save him. Maybe she held him at bay while her accomplice finished him."

Jacob closed his eyes. "People are stupid."

"Agreed. Seemed unlikely to me. Lack of evidence led to her release."

"Case never solved?"

"No."

He looked back at the skinny, short girl talking, gesturing to her insurance agent over the phone. "Everyone in Virtue Falls knows that?"

"Gossip circulates." Sheriff Kwinault waited while he processed the information.

This sheriff was an irritating woman. Good cop, though. He recognized those tactics. He could end the conversation, and she would be satisfied. She would have delivered her warning packaged as common knowledge. Or he could ask more questions.

He didn't want to ask more questions.

But Maddie was still talking, the deputies were headed toward the house, and if Jacob wanted to know, he didn't have much time. Inevitably, his mind moved into the familiar pattern of inquiry.

"She's violent?"

"Not at all. Well . . ." Sheriff Kwinault gestured at the vehicle parked in his house. "This."

Deputy Sheriff Gunder Bergen and a young redhead wearing a badge that identified him as Officer Rupert Moen joined them.

Sheriff Kwinault turned to them. "What did you find out?"

Bergen said, "Quite a lot. Lots of witnesses. A couple of them are even credible. Mrs. Butenschoen was out watering her new rhubarb starts."

"Mrs. Butenschoen saw the whole thing . . . that's a stunner," Sheriff Kwinault said. To Jacob she said, "Nosy neighbor."

"She said she noticed Miss Hewitson because she was driving erratically. Miss Hewitson's head was nodding. She almost didn't make the turn onto the street. At the last minute, she corrected, then over-corrected, then hit the gas. . . ." Like Sheriff Kwinault, Bergen gestured at the vehicle.

They all looked at Maddie.

She was making a second, rather tearful phone call.

Officer Moen said, "Hey, Kateri, did you tell Mr. Denisov that Madeline Hewitson has a history of erratic behavior, and she was accused of murder?"

Sheriff Kwinault turned to face Moen. "I didn't put it quite so bluntly. The sheriff's department would not like to be accused of slander."

"Oh. Right." Moen had that fair complexion that turned blotchy when he blushed, and he blushed now.

Jacob recognized the weak link in the chain, and with the full weight of authority in his voice, he asked, "What kind of erratic behavior?"

In a panic, Moen looked at Sheriff Kwinault.

She inclined her head and pushed her hand toward the floor. *Not too much,* she meant.

Even with Jacob throwing his weight around, even with Bergen being annoyed at the role of second-in-command, she was in charge. This might be her first post in law enforcement, but she'd had military training, or she was a natural, or both.

Moen said, "Miss Hewitson has done some pretty crazy—"

Sheriff Kwinault shook her head.

Moen started again. "The sheriff's department has had to come to Miss Hewitson's home several times to check for intruders that do not exist and open doors that are already unlocked." He looked to Sheriff Kwinault.

She nodded approvingly.

Jacob kept his attention on Moen. "What kind of intruders?"

He answered, "They—or rather he, she is quite specific that it is a he—moves her furniture, eats her food, and occasionally wakes her out of a sound sleep to threaten her with a knife."

"No evidence?" Jacob asked.

"None." Sheriff Kwinault silenced Moen with a glance and took over the answers. "The first incident included a shooting." Sheriff Kwinault had obviously saved the best for last.

"She shot at this nonexistent intruder?"

"Yes."

"She owns a gun?" Jacob clarified.

"A pistol."

"It's registered to her?"

"Yes, and in Colorado she took classes in how to use it as well as gun safety."

"Didn't take, huh?" Amateurs with firearms made Jacob jumpy.

"Miss Hewitson's night in jail, the judge's stern lecture, and the fine for firing said weapon within the city limits impressed upon Maddie the importance of not firing said weapon at dark, man-shaped shadows who appear out of nowhere and swoop down on her." Sheriff Kwinault smiled tightly.

"Huh." It was a thin line between PTSD and certifiably crazy. It sounded as if Madeline Hewitson had crossed that line. The sheriff's department believed that at best she was a nuisance and at worst a killer.

ssiping.

ark was

nly had

blocked

e corner

was that she'd driven when she shouldn't

s in the area?"

from Connecticut."

ected.

Colorado."

Jacob asked.

Kwinault countered.

e.

"Just . . .

walk down to the end of this street and

r ocean. "This picturesque tourist town

st glorious is irresistible."

t his blacked-out windows. "I can see

vanted to

light, on

t squall that worked like a live electric

b's spine. All three law officers groped

e text.

hed." She

ff Kwinault said, "Damn it."

d. Looked

n toward their vehicle.

e away and said to Jacob, "Mr. Deni-

r end of the county. Is it possible for

oor beside

norrow?"

n if all three of them were headed

e Hewitson. "Sure."

he cookie."

ow what he was thinking. "I've seen

Do you have

violent, and I promise you I would

ught she could or would hurt you."

the dash."

, then pointedly at the SUV's hood.

headed into

und to put-

ure she understands she cannot

djuster has made an assessment."

t the people

things, but clearly she had already

She walked toward Maddie.

ctation that

s getting thicker.

Jacob needed to escape. Sun shining. People talking. Go
Staring. He wanted to sit in the dark in his chair. But the d
gone. He could escape to his bedroom. It was so small he o
room for a queen-size bed and a dresser. But aluminum foil
those windows, too, and he could curl up on the floor in th
and—

Maddie put her hand on his arm.

He jumped. He turned on her, hand upraised.

As if by instinct, Maddie lifted her arm to protect her fa

That brought him to his senses. "Don't touch me," he said.
don't."

"No. I won't." She licked her lips as if they were dry. "I
say . . . the insurance adjuster is on his way."

"Shit." Jacob was going to have to stay out here, in the
display.

"When I told Mr. Wodzicki what happened, he laug
looked like she was about to shrivel from shame.

"Shit." Now he was feeling sorry for her. He looked arour
for an escape.

"My brother said . . . he said it just figured."

Jacob's gaze lit on the small brown box sitting on the f
his chair. He picked it up. "Here." He handed it to her.

She stared like she didn't recognize it.

"The sandwich is good. The pasta salad's okay. I ate t
She was pale. Probably in shock. Maybe she needed sugar. "I
anything to drink?"

"I had a Dr Pepper in the cup holder. It blew all over

That explained the brown stains on her clothes. He
the kitchen, got a Coke off the counter—he never got arc
ting them in the fridge—and brought it out.

She was still standing there, holding the box, staring
who were staring back at her.

"Sit!" He barked out the order with every expe
she would obey.

She did, abruptly, in his straight-back chair.

"Eat!" He was still in command mode. Old habits die hard. He popped the tab on the can and put it on the scarred table beside the chair and stood there, waiting.

She put the box in her lap, opened it, and pulled out the half sandwich. Her fingers had that fine tremble that proved she was low on carbs. She took a bite.

Okay, he had done his good deed for the day, and for the very woman who had crashed into his house. Yay for him. If he kept this up, he would almost be human.

He headed for the back of the house. Now he would lock the bathroom door and sit in the dark . . .

A car drove up.

Maddie whimpered.

His hand hovered over the doorknob.

He didn't care. He didn't care. He didn't care.

He turned, and saw why she was distressed.

A middle-aged man in a dark suit, white shirt, and blue tie had pulled up in a white car. A sign on his door proclaimed WODZICKI INSURANCE. The guy got out, chatted with the crowd, called a few by name, then turned toward the house and did a staged double take.

The crowd laughed. A few applauded.

Jacob looked at Maddie.

She sat frozen, pale, staring fixedly at the street, as if it had occurred to her she had made his house, his asylum, into a stage that opened onto the street. The fork loaded with pasta salad shook, spilled cooked macaroni and mayonnaise back into the box.

"Drink the Coke!" he barked.

She startled, then blindly reached for the can.

He picked it up and stuck it in her hand. "Do not spill it. We're already involved in a farce that guarantees the front page of the *Hayseed Herald*."

"The *Virtue Falls Herald*."

"What?"

"The newspaper. The *Virtue Falls Herald*. It's online only, so it's a virtual front page."

He examined her to see if she was mocking him. She seemed quite serious. "Drink. Your. Coke," he said.

As she took a swallow, the can rattled against her teeth, but when she pulled the can away, her hand was steadier, her face a little less strained.

The insurance agent followed the same route as the cops, climbing the debris into the house. He headed right for Jacob. "Mr. Denisov, I'm Dennis Wodzicki." He took Jacob's reluctant hand and shook it heartily. "I heard about you on the news. It's an honor to meet you, sir. A returning veteran. A national hero. We shall never forget!"

Jacob yanked his hand free.

The insurance man was oblivious. He fumbled for his phone. "Can I get a picture with you?" He glanced at Maddie, then dismissed her, stepped close to Jacob, and extended his arm.

A selfie. The stupid bastard wanted a selfie to put on his social media and slap in his advertising, mouthing patriotic crap about how he loved America, and all the while buying dog food from China and cars from Germany.

This son of a bitch had worn a tie to keep the foreskin from flipping over his head. "Save that crap for someone who believes it." Jacob shoved him aside and walked away, through the kitchen and the bathroom, and into the bedroom. He slammed the door behind him and realized—the old-fashioned lock required a key and he didn't have any idea where that would be. So he pushed the chest of drawers against the door—it took all his feeble strength. And in case the fatuous insurance POS didn't get the message, he picked up his glass and flung it at the door.

Goddamn thing was plastic. It bounced back and hit him in the face.

Abruptly, rage became anguish and depression. He sank down on the floor, curled into a little ball, and waited for the pain to batter him again.

It always came back.

It always would.

She's afraid to go to sleep. It's better than a movie, watching her struggle to stay awake.

CHAPTER SIX

Monsters live in the real world. Monsters and ghosts and ordinary human beings capable of incredible cruelty.

I am a warrior of the night. I hunt them all.

Maddie used pen and ink in the slow, meticulous re-creation of the heroes and horrors that lived in her mind. Black ink stained the side of her finger and slid under her nail, and she frowned ferociously as she imagined her alter ego, a woman-warrior who trembled with fright yet fought to avenge lives lost and innocence slaughtered.

Then she delved deeper into the old, terrible memories to bring forth the soft-spoken man who started out so normal-looking, then, as the blood began to flow, transformed himself into a monster: hideous, warped . . . and in that moment, happy. So happy to bring forth fear and loathing, pain and death. Seared onto her mind was that moment when he pulled the leather glove off his left hand and she saw that long nail, pointed and—

Long, skeletal fingers scraped at her window.

Maddie started. Her heartbeat surged.

Logically, she knew the bush outside swayed in the breeze and scratched at her house. No pointed fingernails waved in slow, crooked circles, taunting her, threatening her.

Abruptly, she was outside, a ghostly watcher who drifted above the lawn, and glimpsed the hunched and decayed form dressed in a long black businessman's coat and a wide-brimmed hat, risen from the grave . . .

With a gasp, Mad Maddie Hewitson lifted her head from her desk.

She was awake.

She was inside. And awake. Wide awake.

She had fallen asleep, that was all.

She wasn't crazy.

She was *not* insane.

But she reached trembling fingers toward the window, making

sure the blinds were real and closed. She traced the outline of the blood spatter that marred the corner of her walnut desk. She looked at the clock: 3:24 A.M. Only a few more hours of darkness. Surely she could keep herself awake until the sun peeked over the horizon at 5:32 A.M.

When night pressed in and the world filled with slithering darkness, sleep was the enemy. Like a vampire, she always knew what time the sun set and what time it rose.

In daylight, the window looked out over her lawn and the street and, after yesterday's ordeal, right into Jacob Denisov's house. In daylight, she kept the blinds open, reveling in every second of cloudless sun and vanquished fear. In daylight, she worked at her desk, the desk her mother had left her, building worlds, creating emotions from words, and crafting pictures that told the stories of her heart.

Her psychiatrist, the good one, had suggested she draw the monster that haunted her. He said getting the beast out of her head and on paper would help exorcise the ghost.

Her brother had agreed that was a good idea, had liked that she could put those art classes she had taken in the sanitarium to use. He pointed out graphic novels were extremely popular with readers and would be great companions to the horror novels she wrote and that they published under his name.

She had refused to draw the monster. She feared to give him form.

Andrew said it was time for Maddie to stop being such a coward.

He hadn't always been so impatient with her. Yet recently he snapped more easily.

She did try to be brave. She really tried. She used all kinds of coping mechanisms. But she saw things that weren't there. Of their own volition, pieces of furniture moved in her house. Bowls of rotting food appeared in her refrigerator or on her desk. Worst of all, her lights flickered; she was always afraid they would go off completely, and leave her at the mercy of the demon who took form and sustenance from darkness.

So she didn't admit to anyone, not even Andrew, that she had finally started experimenting with pen and ink. In the daytime, she wrote on the computer and turned in her allotment of words. When the sun set, she closed herself in. She lowered the white accordion blinds that protected her from ambush by the fiends that hunted, not her alter ego, but *her*. And she drew.

A metal folding chair like the ones set up in school auditoriums served as her desk chair. It was cold and uncomfortable, but it kept her awake long past the hour when her forehead would have hit the paper.

She looked around the bright living area. Before she had moved in, she had remodeled; throughout the house she'd stripped away the wall-to-wall carpet to reveal the antique maple hardwoods. She'd had the floors refinished; some people would have placed area rugs, but she figured she was more likely to hear the click of a boot heel on a hard surface.

A large-screen TV occupied the sidewall, well-placed lamps illuminated every corner of the living room, and her slate-blue leather sofa and easy chair were deeply padded and comfortable for those moments when she worked away from her desk.

In the kitchen, she'd replaced the old appliances and invested in undercabinet lighting and elegant copper lamps over the scarred wooden table. The furniture saleslady had called it distressed, but Maddie knew scarred when she encountered it, in her furniture and in her mind.

The former residents had remodeled the bathroom and the bedroom in a half-assed way, and Maddie had done more, taking special care to create a secure environment.

The branches scraped at the window again.

She ignored them, leaning over her work, studying each detail to see if she had exactly re-created *him*. She needed to concentrate, but . . . man, what a crappy day yesterday had been.

Usually in the afternoon, if it wasn't raining—it did that a lot on the coast—she headed outside, dragging her chaise into the sun, and grabbed a few hours of sleep. Not yesterday, though, because she had fallen asleep at the wheel and broken open the front of Jacob Denisov's home and revealed a hermit, filthy, gaunt, and hostile.

Not that she blamed him about the hostile part. She would never forget waking up behind the wheel, her vehicle out of control, climbing the stairs, ripping through the wall—and seeing that face, brown and bleak; the eyes, blinking against the light; that filthy matted hair; the bony body; the grubby shorts. He looked like some Asian yogi who lived high in the Himalayas on roots and berries and whatever gifts his disciples brought him.

She had thought she was going to run over him.

She had thought he would try to move.

She hadn't.

And he hadn't.

The car had dropped into a hole, slammed to a stop. The air bag inflated, then deflated. She and Jacob Denisov had stared at each other through her windshield like two opponents sizing up the competition.

The only competition they could be in was who was more damaged by life.

She thought he would win. At least *she* wasn't starving herself to death.

Jacob Denisov had been caustic in his comments about her driving.

But nothing like her brother. And nothing like Mr. Wodzicki, who'd proved once again he was a misogynistic jerk. She would have taken her business elsewhere, except Andrew handled this stuff for her. She didn't want to take the time to do it herself . . . and Andrew got so cranky when she suggested a better method of doing . . . anything.

If Andrew had a fault, it was that his way was always best. And she depended on him—like most writers, she wasn't making enough to support herself, and he kindly supplemented her income. She needed Andrew, she had been an awful disruption in his life, and most of the time he was a good, thoughtful brother. But not when she insinuated he was wrong.

No one had known why, after the investigation of Easton's death, she'd fled to Virtue Falls. As Andrew said, it was a Podunk town on the edge of nowhere, famous for one thing—the massive earthquake and tsunami that had been meticulously documented by the on-site Banner Geological Study.

That was what had appealed to Maddie. She had been captivated by the tsunami video, had dreamed of visiting such a spot so remote that, in this day and age, it could be cut off by a natural catastrophe. When her own unnatural catastrophe destroyed her life—again—she had fled urban Colorado and bought a tiny house on a tidy street. She had hoped to be anonymous.

Of course, that hadn't happened. To be anonymous, she probably would have had to change her name and have a plastic surgeon alter her face. Frankly, any kind of surgery freaked her out. The idea of someone leaning over her unconscious body, holding a knife . . .

Something scraped at the window. Softly, gently. With intent.

Her head fell to her chest.

I am a warrior of the night. I hunt them all. I move through the tendrils of bleak fear, tearing them asunder, seeking the monsters who disguise themselves as plumbers or delivery men or cruel nurses—oh, my God, what looms at the edge of my consciousness?

Maddie jerked awake. She rubbed her forehead, then looked at her hands and hoped she hadn't smeared ink on her face. Not that it mattered; nobody saw her. But she had already discovered pigment ink was a bitch to clean off.

During her time at the mental institution, she had suffered nightmares about her friends' massacres and her own mutilation. She had been cowering, afraid, and with the help of a few good therapists, she had discovered it was up to her to move away from her fear and live again.

After her year in the asylum, her nightmares changed, became long green corridors stretching forever and going nowhere, drugs that affected her too much, kind caregivers who changed into cruel predators who mocked her grief, intensified her fear, administered painful injections that plunged her into a whirlpool of guilt and fear.

Taking a deep breath, she put down her pen.

Barbara Magnusson and Gary Alexander, nursing assistants in the mental institution . . . those two had despised and tormented their patients. Eventually they had been caught and dismissed, but until that moment, they had exercised and abused their powers.

Maddie had learned one thing during those years of murder and her resulting breakdown: monsters walked this earth in human form.

She stood, stretched with her arms behind her and overhead, then with her feet planted hip-width apart, she rotated from the waist. A little exercise helped keep her limber and awake. Caffeine would help, too, but she hesitated to drink caffeine now, and take the chance it would keep her awake in the daylight.

Besides—she shuffled through the sheets of paper—she had made good progress tonight. No drawing could ever convey the horror of the monster, but these were close. Close enough to make her skin crawl.

She seated herself and picked up the leaky pen.

The branch scratched at the window again. "Oh, shut up," she muttered, and started another panel, placing a wide-brimmed hat on the monster's head.

Lack of sleep+stress=a solid case of the crazies.

CHAPTER SEVEN

Jacob came out of his doze and lay rigid on the floor, listening desperately for the sound of a soft silk slipper against the concrete floor, the signal that *he* was back and the torment would begin again.

Jacob heard nothing. Nothing. But that didn't mean *he* wasn't standing over the top of Jacob, waiting with sadistic pleasure for Jacob's cramped muscles to twitch . . .

On the street, a car cruised slowly by, taking its time . . .

A car.

Jacob opened his eyes. He was in his house. In Virtue Falls. In Washington. He rested on a hard floor, yes. But thin carpet over warm wood, not cold concrete. There were no footsteps. He was by himself in the place where he endured, marking time until the end.

He pushed himself onto his hands and knees, groaning as the stiff joints protested being motionless for so many hours.

He remembered the earlier fracas, the crumpling front wall . . . Was he alone? They couldn't still be out there, could they? The curious crowd, the obsequious insurance man, the girl with the nice ass?

What time was it? In here he had no clock. Normally he didn't care. He moved from bedroom to bathroom to living room on some irregular cycle.

Uncle Decker, his gung ho let's-go-to-war uncle who had never served in the military, called him self-indulgent.

Jacob thought a better word would be "cowardly."

But today—or tonight—he had to worry about the time, because earlier, Madeline Hewitson had knocked the front wall out of his house, and when he walked out there, he would be revealed to the world.

Crawling over, he pushed the chest aside, then peered through the crack under the door. No light.

He turned the knob and peered out at the weird scene: the wreck of his house with its dangling trusses, catawampus studs, and exposed electric cables, and beyond that, the blessedly empty night dimly lit by the yellow streetlight at the corner.

Maddie Hewitson's vehicle had been removed.

Cautiously, he shuffled out, half-expecting some stranger to pop out and try to snap a photo. But it was *really* quiet. He didn't know what that meant; he didn't know the rhythm of this neighborhood, when people rose, when people slept, who came and went. He didn't want to know, but right now, knowledge would be convenient.

He peered at the clock on the stove. It was blank.

Then he remembered—the firefighters had turned off the electricity.

He groped around, found the battery-operated alarm clock on the kitchen shelf, peered at its glowing hands. Three thirty-two in the morning. He had a few hours before sunrise, before the curious came back to gawk at his house and, if they could, at him.

He hadn't realized anyone knew who he was. He had thought he'd left that hero crap behind. But no. Someone had recognized his face or his name—the lady at the title company, the kid who delivered his groceries—and word had spread. Probably not to everyone, but to the nosy people and the people who wanted to use him to make themselves look good. Like Wodzicki the insurance creep.

Going to the sink, Jacob got a drink of water, then looked in the refrigerator. The lemon sitting on the shelf had been here since he moved in, and it was as wrinkled as Uncle Decker's face. He opened the freezer to find a package of thawing peas.

He *hated* peas. He took them out, tore the end off the box, and shook a handful into his palm. One by one he flung the shriveled green knobs down his throat. When he couldn't gag down any more, he tossed the package at the garbage and walked toward the exposed front of his house.

Someone had put a piece of plywood over the hole in the floor and tried to wipe up the oil. Half of his porch roof had been splattered across his yard, leaving the other side hanging at a jaunty half wink. His front door had somehow come to rest on the hydrangea. His mother would cry at the damage to the bush.

His street, Dogwood Blossom Street, was nothing but a stub; ten houses on one side, nine on the other, starting on the intersection of Elm Street and ending in a battered guardrail that protected cars from an accidental plunge off the cliff and into the ocean. A wooden sign in the corner yard proclaimed this was the Dogwood Blossom Historical Neighborhood. When Jacob had first come to look at this house, he had thought that the sign was vain and stupid. But he thought pretty much everything was stupid, so no surprise there.

At the house across the street, every window was covered by pale yellow blinds, yet even so late at night, light glowed, defying the night.

Maddie Hewitson's house. He'd hate to pay her electric bill.

He inched forward, staring, tripped on a chunk of broken ceiling plaster, and barely caught himself before he went headlong across his threshold and into the broken pit of his porch.

He ought to keep going. He ought to make his way through the scattered boards, walk down to the end of the street, over the cliff, and into oblivion.

He ought to. But like he said—a coward.

He turned back to his living room, to the upright wooden chair where he sat and suffered and waited for courage.

But his chair was smashed to splinters, crushed beneath an ancient steamer trunk that had fallen through the crumpled ceiling. When the hell had that happened? . . . Sometime after he left the scene, he would guess.

If he had stayed, that trunk would have killed him for sure.

"Son of a bitch!" Death kept missing him by minutes and inches. He had the worst luck of any man he'd ever known.

Well. Some of his kids would disagree with him. The ones who were dead. The ones who lived with pain and mutilation . . .

He squatted, bent his head, held his belly, writhed as he rode out the memories.

A car drove by on Elm Street. A car. People might see him.

He lifted his head. He crawled to the recliner, knocked the worst of the rubble off the seat, and dragged his butt onto the sagging cushion. The whole thing smelled like dust and funky old lady; the former owner must have slept in it, too, and maybe died in it. He looked at the ceiling and wondered if the old lady had stored any more heavy trunks up there that would blast through the weakened rafters to crush him. But no—the plaster was gone overhead and he could see all the way through to the cracks in the damaged roof.

Madeline Hewitson had even screwed up his roof. He'd bet Wodzicki's wallet would shriek when it heard about that.

The old Jacob would have felt guilty for making Maddie handle Wodzicki alone. But she'd brought it on herself, and besides, he didn't have room for one more scrap of guilt. His soul was already booked up. When he thought of what had been done to him, and what he had done . . .

The pain came, blasting him with agony, taking him to the edge of self-loathing and . . .

A car turned onto Dogwood Blossom Street. Headlights flashed into his living room. The driver slammed on the brakes; Jacob couldn't see who was inside, but he knew whoever it was, was staring at the open-face house and probably at him.

The car parked along the curb. A man about Jacob's age got out and walked determinedly across the yard.

Yay. Jacob was about to meet another new friend.

The guy stopped by the concrete steps that now went to a porch that didn't exist. "I'm your next-door neighbor, Dayton Floren." He paused and waited for Jacob to introduce himself.

Jacob didn't tell him to fuck off.

"You must be Jacob Denisov." Floren's voice carried in the quiet of the night. "What happened to your house?"

"Your neighbor invited herself in. With her car."

Dayton Floren turned and looked right at Madeline Hewitson's house. So he knew who Jacob was talking about. "That woman is a walking wrecking ball. Ever since she moved in we've had double police presence, county and city. That's good, I guess." He paused, waiting for Jacob to respond. When Jacob didn't, Dayton asked, "How long before insurance moves in to fix it?"

Jacob shrugged.

"Exactly. With insurance companies, who can say? Home owner-ship is a pain. You should do what I do: rent. Then you don't have to worry about the ugly details."

Jacob dredged up some vestige of grim humor. "Who's going to buy this place?"

"Very true. Very true." Dayton nodded, then brightened. "I would! I could add your lot to mine and have a nice yard."

"I thought you rented."

"If I could buy them both, it might be worth it. If I did that, you wouldn't have to bother with rebuilding." Dayton kicked at a pile of lumber. "It's going to be a painful process. You'll have to move out."

Like hell. "No."

"But—" An ungodly shriek of terror cut him off. He whirled to face Maddie's house.

There, silhouetted against the white accordion shade, Maddie stood swinging a baseball bat at nothing and screaming, a high, shrill, pri-mal sound that recalled torture and terror and death. Her shadow whirled and swung, caught the blind, and ripped it halfway off the win-dow. Then they could see her, dodging, dancing, her face a contorted parody of fright. She stumbled, swung, blasted her desk lamp across the room.

Glass shattered.

The screaming stopped.

She stood, holding the bat, chest heaving, her head turning from side to side as she sought her invisible attacker.

"Wow," Dayton said in awe. "Just wow. She's really nuts."

As opposed to Jacob, who sat here in the same wrinkled pants and grubby shirt he'd worn earlier, his hair and beard a hive for any vermin that chose to nest there. Apparently being quietly nuts was more respectable than being outgoingly nuts. Or maybe it was just the dif-ference between being a nutty male or a nutty female. As his sisters always informed him, gender bias was a bitch.

"At least this time she's not shooting at anything. Hey, if you sell me your house, you won't have to worry about *her* anymore."

"I don't worry about her now."

Hostility might have leaked through Jacob's tone, for Dayton backed up. "If you change your mind about the sale, let me know."

Jacob stared at him. Just stared.

Dayton lifted a hand. "Good to meet you!" He headed toward his car, drove forward a few feet to park in front of his house, and headed inside.

Maddie's frenzy had made a few lights switch on in the neighborhood, but nobody came out to see what was wrong.

Not real caring folks here. Or they'd been suckered by her a little too often.

Or maybe they really did believe she was a killer, and they were afraid.

She's afraid of her own shadow now. You should have seen her fighting w/ nothing. LMAO

CHAPTER EIGHT

Jacob sat in the recliner until the sun came up.

He observed Maddie drag her sleeping bag and baseball bat out of the house and scurry toward the overgrown rose garden in the corner by her front fence. There she got on her hands and knees, shoved the sleeping bag and the bat between the bushes, and, after a few muttered exclamations—mostly *ouch!*—she settled down out of sight.

Not long before dawn, the elderly lady next door to Maddie let her dog out. It was one of those fat, nasty, miniature dogs that snarled at the molecules in the air. When the old lady shut the door on it, the little beast stalked stiff-legged across her lawn, fought its way through the picket fence to the well-manicured yard on the corner, and did its business. Then it wiggled back through the pickets and stood sniffing the air. Its head turned; the dog focused its beady eyes on Maddie's refuge. It prowled toward her fence, pushed through, and went right for the rosebushes.

Jacob braced for another round of screaming.

He got a series of sharp, hostile barks that died away under a barrage of conciliatory murmurs.

Apparently Maddie was trying to befriend the hostile little fiend.

The old lady stepped out on the porch and called, "Spike! Come inside, sweetums, I've made your breakfast!"

The dog, presumably Spike, trotted out of the rosebushes, through the fence, and up to its owner, who held onto the porch railing, laboriously leaned down, picked up the dog, and carried it inside.

More light brightened the sky.

The house on the corner, the one with the Dogwood Blossom Historical Neighborhood sign, lit up. The shades on the kitchen windows were raised, and he caught a glimpse of a dimple-cheeked darling of a woman with dyed ash-blond hair, a wholesome demeanor, and a cheerful pink bathrobe. In the background, he could see a small dining area with flowered teapots wallpaper.

She looked out, admired her yard, nodded with pleasure, and turned away.

Obviously she hadn't yet spotted the dog poop.

Across the street and toward the west, lights came on, a woman's voice called, children answered, a man grumped. The father came out first, dressed for work, two grade-school-age kids trailing him. They got in the car parked in the driveway, waved at the mother, and drove off. Next the mother came out, dressed for work, carrying a toddler. She tucked the kid into the car seat and left.

They looked normal. So the street wasn't full of only retirees and crazy people.

The tiny house on the other side of Maddie—it looked identical to his, except recently painted—remained silent and dark. Whoever it was either wasn't awake yet or wasn't home.

Jacob stood. The sun was up. The light hurt his eyes. He had to get out of here before someone saw him. In the bedroom, darkness—and pain—awaited.

Someone knocked.

Jacob's eyes slammed open.

Where was he? What was he seeing? Had he been asleep?

No. No sleep. The nightmares came when he slept . . . only they weren't nightmares. They were the truth.

Someone knocked. Again. On his door. His bedroom door. In Virtue Falls. In his wrecked house.

"Goddamn it." He spaced the word carefully, making each syllable count. Bracing his back against the wall, he inched up off the floor and out of the corner where he had crouched for the past however many hours. "Goddamn it," he said again. How goddamn many people did he have to talk to in one twenty-four-hour period?

He jerked open the door and caught some guy in jeans and a work shirt with his fist upraised, about to knock again. "What?" Jacob snapped.

The guy dropped his hand and backed away. "Hey, Mr. Denisov, I'm Berk Moore. I'm the contractor Mr. Wodzicki sent to bid on your repairs."

"Fine. Do it." Jacob turned away.

Moore said, "I have to ask you some questions."

Jacob paused. "Why?"

"Because I need to know what you want me to do . . . beyond the obvious, I mean."

"Fix. The. House."

"It's not possible to fix it exactly like it was." Moore spoke quickly, trying to keep Jacob with him. "Most of the building materials used in this house—in any house built in the twenties—are no longer available. So we'll have to use substitutes. Plus modern building codes are different. Plus you might want upgrades."

"No."

"Plus, you know"—Berk waved a hand vaguely at the floor—"this linoleum hasn't been used since the sixties and you'll have to pick out new floor coverings to, um—" Jacob may have been glaring, because Berk backed up a little farther. "Really, I have to consult with you about at least some of the items."

"Use your judgment." Jacob started to close the door.

Moore stuck his foot in there.

Damned good thing Berk had work boots on or Jacob would have crushed him like a bug.

"I wouldn't bother you if I didn't have to, and I get it. I'm a veteran, too. Two tours in Afghanistan. Got a belly wound that got me discharged." Berk Moore tugged his shirt out of his belt and displayed the puckered pink scar. "The insurance won't pay unless I get work orders signed by you. Please, have a heart."

Don't appeal to me as a fellow soldier. Just . . . don't. "Come back at night when it's not so bright."

The guy glanced behind him at the sunlit street. "I'm here now. How 'bout I give you my sunglasses?"

Right. Sunglasses would protect Jacob's eyes from the vicious light . . . and give him something to hide behind. "Yeah."

Moore took off his aviators and handed them over.

Jacob put them on and stepped into his kitchen. "Looks worse in the daylight."

"Maddie might have done you a favor. Blow some of the old-house-stink away." When Moore realized what he'd said, he looked alarmed. "Not that I'm saying your house stinks. No more than most old houses on the coast."

Jacob never washed his clothes. He didn't shower. If something smelled around here, it was him.

Moore talked faster. "The house was due for a remodel, anyway, and this will improve your chances of resale."

"I'm not going to sell it." But his mother would, and she would be glad to off-load it quickly. One less thing for Jacob to feel guilty about.

"Right. Don't blame you. Good location. Okay, for starters, we got to talk electrical. The wiring in the house is ancient. It all has to be changed out."

Jacob grunted. He'd figured that, by the way the responding fire-fighters had got the power off so fast.

"We'll do that first, but meantime, you've got no power. The cops told me you want to stay here. Mr. Wodzicki said he'd spring for the cost of a hotel room."

Jacob could hardly speak for loathing. "That *prick*."

"Okay, so you're going to stay here." Moore made a note on his clipboard. "I'll throw every electrician I can find at the project. Now, about the structure in the house and porch. The whole thing was built to last, obviously, or—"

A shriek from across the street stopped Moore in his tracks.

Jacob sighed. *Not again.*

The two men walked cautiously toward the front of the house.

But it wasn't Maddie. This time, the dimple-cheeked darling from the house on the corner stood on her lawn examining the sole of her shoe. She gave another sharp, angry shriek, then whirled and stormed over to her old lady neighbor's. She rang the doorbell, then knocked for good measure.

Inside the house, the little dog started yapping.

While Dimples was waiting, she wiped her shoe on the concrete porch and muttered furiously.

"That's Mrs. Butenschoen. I remodeled her kitchen." Moore's tone told Jacob everything he needed to know about Mrs. Butenschoen.

The old lady answered her front door and looked through the screen.

Mrs. Butenschoen started scolding, pointing at her yard, her shoe, the dog.

The old lady was clearly apologetic.

The scolding continued.

The old lady wrung her hands.

Mrs. Butenschoen jerked open the screen door.

Spike darted out, barking wildly, intent on protecting his mistress.

Mrs. Butenschoen stumbled backward, off the front porch, and down the stairs.

Moore cackled. "That's it, Spike. Take her down."

The old lady called Spike until he returned to her.

When the old lady held the snarling little beast in her arms, Mrs. Butenschoen announced loudly, "I shall call animal control!" She turned, bosom heaving, and spotted the two men watching.

"Uh-oh." Moore eased back.

Mrs. Butenschoen tossed her head and continued toward her own house.

When her own screen door slammed behind her, Moore breathed a sigh of relief. "That was a close one. She's been hunting you ever since you moved in."

Jacob knew what to blame. "Goddamn war hero crap."

"It's not that. I mean, it is, but mostly it's Mrs. Butenschoen. She knows everything that goes on in this neighborhood, and she likes to lay down the law according to Butenschoen. No escaping her. She has *standards,* you know."

"I don't give a fuck about her standards."

"That won't stop her. You watch. Animal control will be out here issuing a citation to old Mrs. Nyback. Mrs. Nyback will call me, crying, to do something about her fence. I'll send some guys in to rig up netting between the pickets, and Mrs. Butenschoen will bitch because the netting spoils the pristine appearance of 'our treasured historic neighborhood.'" Moore used his fingers for air quotes.

Yesterday, Jacob had been alone, in the dark, and he didn't know one thing about Virtue Falls or his neighbors. Now . . . he was hearing gossip?

He must have made a sound or a gesture, because Moore jumped and said, "Oh! You want to get done. What was I talking about? Oh, yeah." He rapped his knuckles on an exposed stud. "This house was built to last or the floor wouldn't have held the weight of the SUV. All oak studs and beams. Can't get wood of that quality anymore, price is prohibitive, so I recommend a steel structure. It'll hold up in the climate and—"

"Fine."

"Right. Fine." Moore wrote on the form and passed the clipboard over.

Jacob signed it, and they went on to the next issue.

There were a lot of issues. Windows were single pane. Pipes were copper and fragile. Nothing was to code.

Jacob said, "Fine," and signed off on everything. Maybe the contractor was padding the job, but Jacob had more experience than most men with government bureaucracy, so when Moore said all this bullshit had to be done to satisfy the building inspectors, Jacob believed him. And signed.

Moore was starting to look less like a mournful basset hound and more like a guy with a hefty profit in his future . . . when the phone rang.

Moore laughed. "Man, I cannot believe your landline survived this disaster."

"Answer it."

The phone rang.

"What? Why?"

The phone rang.

"I came out. I'm signing off on everything. I'm a veteran. Answer it."

Moore went over to the old-fashioned phone and used his sleeve to brush off the dust. "Who is it?"

The phone rang.

"My mother. *Answer it.*"

"You bet." Moore picked up the handset. "Jacob Denisov's residence. Berk Moore speaking. How may I help you?"

Even from where he stood, Jacob heard his mother squawk.

Moore held the phone away from his ear. When the shouting had quieted, he brought the phone close again. "I'm a local contractor. I'm doing some work on Jacob's house . . . Well, Mrs. Denisov, this is an older home and needs repair, so when Jacob had some trouble, he called me in . . . nothing too serious. Some electrical problems, a mushy feel to the living room floor—"

That was one way to describe the hole Maddie's tire had put in the hardwood.

"And he wants to open up the front of the house with a couple of new windows. . . ."

Unwillingly impressed with Moore's ability to spin spur-of-the-moment half-truths, Jacob leaned against the wall and listened.

Moore scrutinized Jacob. "He looks fine. He's skinny. Could use a haircut and a shave . . . Yes, it is hard to believe he used to be clean-cut. . . ." He glared meaningfully at Jacob. "Can you speak to him?"

Jacob sliced his finger across his own throat.

"Right now, he's under the kitchen sink dealing with some old pipes."

Jacob picked up a wrench from Moore's toolbox and pounded on a shattered piece of plaster that disintegrated under his blows.

"You bet, Mrs. Denisov, I'll tell him!" Moore hung up.

Jacob ceased pounding. "Thanks."

"Sooner or later you're going to have to talk to her."

"Later."

"I get it. I really do. I've got a mother, too, and when I came back from Afghanistan . . . God bless her, she meant well." Absently, Moore rubbed the place over his belly wound. "The only cure for battle hangover is time."

"Or death."

Moore gave him one sharp look. "Well, sure. But when you dodge the bullet in battle, it seems surly to seek it out in civilian life. Now, we probably *do* need to look at the pipes under your kitchen sink."

Jacob dropped the wrench into Moore's outstretched hand. "Maddie's car didn't get close to the kitchen."

"Thank God. Can you imagine the mess a broken pipe would have created?" Moore crawled under the sink and rattled around, came out, and wiped his hands on his handkerchief. "You're due for a major break. We'd better replace what we can while we've got light in the crawl space."

Now Moore was definitely padding the job. But Jacob was grateful to him for answering the phone, so he signed off on that, too.

Both men were squatting by the water heater closet, looking at the corroded connections, when a high, cheerful voice said, "Hello, Mr. Denisov."

Moore flinched.

Bit by bit Jacob turned his head and looked.

The woman who had been working in her yard when the accident happened, the one with the pink bathrobe, the one with the dog poop on her shoe . . . was standing behind them holding a pie.

CHAPTER NINE

How had the woman managed to climb through the rubble and remain fresh and clean, the pie tall, pristine, and white with whipped cream?

She was beaming. "Mr. Denisov, I wanted to take this opportunity to welcome you to the neighborhood." Her bright tone changed to dismissive. "Hello, Berk."

"Hello, Mrs. Butenschoen," Berk said weakly.

Jacob rose to his full height.

Moore stayed low.

Mrs. Butenschoen was five-two, 140 pounds. She wore jeans with rhinestones on the pockets, eyeglasses with rhinestones on the corners, and discreet rhinestone earrings. "I made you a howdy-new-neighbor treat." She offered the pie.

Browned coconut crawled through the cream.

She continued, "My pies are famous in Virtue Falls. Aren't they, Berk?"

Moore was on his knees, easing away. He froze like a cornered rabbit and muttered, "Famous."

"I tried to bring a pie over before. More than once, in fact." She waggled her finger at Jacob. "But you didn't answer the door."

"No." If his door had remained on his house, he still wouldn't have answered it.

Mrs. Butenschoen took his hand and wrapped it around the ceramic lip of the pie pan.

A section of the crust crumbled.

She looked stricken. "So few people appreciate the work that goes into a real homemade crust."

He shoved his thumb in. Crust fell like crisp snow.

With a brave lift of the chin, she ignored his antagonism. "But at last I get to meet you, so our little mishap here"—she waved a hand around at his mangled house—"does have at least one happy consequence."

"*Our* little *mishap*?" Jacob stared intimidatingly through Berk Moore's sunglasses.

"It's a tragedy, of course, the way Maddie Hewitson causes trouble. She is certainly incorrigible, and possibly venal."

Moore had scooted far enough out of the line of fire to stand up. "Mr. Denisov, I've got enough to start working up a bid, so I'll head back to the office, then present the bid to Mr. Wodzicki. Shouldn't be any problem—he said anything the insurance disallowed he would pay for out of his own pocket."

"That's so wonderful and kind," Mrs. Butenschoen chirped.

Jacob's hostility was undiminished. "That *prick*."

"Right," Moore said. "This afternoon, I'll get a guy over here to clean up, and I'll be back tomorrow with the electricians. If I can round up enough generators, I'll get my crew to work day after tomorrow."

Jacob moved fast, grabbed Berk's arm. "How long will this take?"

"Couple of months. Maybe a little less, maybe a little more. Depends on what we find when we dig into the walls. If there's mold . . ." Moore shook his head dolefully.

"Two months." Jacob grasped Moore's shoulders firmly enough to make the man wince.

"I'll do my level best to beat the clock," Moore assured him.

Mrs. Butenschoen lowered her chin and glared over the top of her glasses. "I'll keep you to that promise, Berk. We have a nice, clean, normal neighborhood where children play and flowers bloom. We can't have our street disrupted."

"I'll be sure it gets done even if I have to work night and day." Moore shook off Jacob's grip. "Keep the sunglasses, man."

Now Jacob knew how Maddie had felt the day before when he abandoned her. He had seen a sniper with his target in view who looked less determined than Mrs. Butenschoen did at this moment. And a faint memory niggled at him. "You look like someone I know. Someone in black-and-white." From that old TV sitcom *The Andy Griffith Show* . . . He had it! "You look like Aunt Bea."

It took her a minute to figure out who he was talking about. Then she flushed, and he could see her struggling between outrage and nosiness.

He never had a doubt which one would win.

In a soothing, friendly tone, Mrs. Butenschoen asked, "Why don't we sit down and have a chat, get to know each other better?"

"No."

"After all, I own one of the two largest houses in the neighborhood and I feel it's my obligation to help maintain the quality of appearance we all want for our little bit of Virtue Falls historiana. For instance, did you know—"

"Don't care."

"That these houses date back to the days when Virtue Falls was a sawmill town? These smaller houses were built for the sawmill workers, and the larger houses, like mine, were built for the superintendents who—"

"I. Don't. Care."

"I was simply explaining why it's important that we all pull together to maintain trim yards and well-tended homes. I have been caring for your yard. It's the least I can do for one of our honored veterans, but I thought we could pull together and—" This time she interrupted herself. "Would you look at that?"

Mrs. Butenschoen sounded so indignant, Jacob expected to see another car careening toward him. Or a weed in Mrs. Butenschoen's flower bed.

All he saw was Maddie standing up out of her rose garden, disentangling herself from the thorns, dragging her sleeping bag after her like Linus with his blanket. She looked dirty, hollow-eyed, and frightened. As she jerked the sleeping bag free of the branches, she kept her head down and her shoulders hunched. Obviously she knew she was under scrutiny.

Mrs. Butenschoen huffed. "I've tried to talk to her about the pitfalls of an unscheduled existence, but she stares as if I'm speaking a different language. It's not as if she's some kind of undocumented immigrant, you know. She is from Connecticut, a perfectly good East Coast American state."

"Colorado," he said.

"What?"

"She's from Colorado, a perfectly good Midwestern state."

Mrs. Butenschoen ruffled up like a grouse, then subsided under his stare. "If she's going to live off her brother's money, why can't she do what the rest of us stay-at-home ladies do and care for her house?"

"Looks okay to me."

In forbidding tones, she said, "There is moss on the roof, the lawn has dandelions, and let me tell you, I went inside that house once, and it was a disgrace. Why, when Mrs. Kenyon lived there, you could eat off her kitchen floor. Right now, the poor lady is probably spinning in her grave."

"If she's in the afterlife and she's worried about the state of her earthly linoleum, she's probably also got a problem with flames shooting up her ass."

Mrs. Butenschoen seemed not to appreciate that this was the longest speech he'd given since his return from Korea. "Mr. Denisov, I really don't enjoy you using that kind of language around me!"

"What kind of language?"

"You know. The 'A' word."

"Ass?" He could hardly believe this woman. "You're going to be really upset when I say *fuck,* aren't you?"

Mrs. Butenschoen actually lost color. "Mr. Denisov, I understand you are recovering from a trauma."

Recovering? That was news to him.

"So I forgive your crudeness. But"—her head turned again—"oh, my dear heavens."

Mrs. Butenschoen looked so horrified he wouldn't have been surprised to see her head spin in a circle.

Maddie was back outside, dressed in jeans and a wrinkled, long-sleeved T-shirt, and she was hacking at one of the bushes up against the house. With scissors.

"That is not how you trim a rhododendron. I told her . . . but does she listen?"

Maddie stepped back and stared at the bush, then went after the bush with renewed fury.

"I'm going to call the police." Mrs. Butenschoen's head wobbled.

Cool. It really was going to spin in a circle. "Because the neighbor is trimming her bushes?"

"She is a known criminal. She was involved in a mass murder, then she was put in a sanitarium, then she was involved in the murder of her fiancé, then she moved here where nobody knows her, and now she's using scissors!"

Abruptly, he was done with Mrs. Butenschoen. He disliked her more than anybody else he knew. And he didn't like anybody.

He shifted the pie so that he was no longer holding it by the rim.

Instead, he held it balanced on the tips of his five fingers like a TV comedian about to toss the cream pie into her perfectly made-up face.

Mrs. Butenschoen's words faded to nothingness and she lifted her hands to protect herself. She eased backward. "I'm going to . . . to talk some sense into Maddie Hewitson . . . and if that doesn't work . . . I will get the police involved. I'll see you later." She fled.

Not if I see you first.

CHAPTER TEN

The trouble with being a cop was—Kateri couldn't simply park her car, walk into the Oceanview Café, and have a cup of coffee. First she had to cruise the street to make sure everything looked normal. And by normal, she meant—all the jaywalkers seemed properly horrified at the sight of a law enforcement officer, no one was attacking the meter maid over a ticket, and no obvious drug deals were going down in Town Square Park.

Next Kateri had to park in front of city hall in the space reserved for the sheriff. She got out and grabbed her walking stick; she had been working nonstop for far too many hours to think she could keep her balance without it. She walked half a block and crossed the street at the corner, hoping all the while she could get inside the Oceanview Café before a concerned citizen collared her to complain about the jaywalkers, the meter maid, or the drug deals.

Today she made it to the door with only one detour to hustle after Cheryl Morgan's three-year-old when he ran into the street. Kateri and Cheryl reached him at the same minute. Most mothers would say *Thank you.* Cheryl shot her a resentful glance, said "I've got him!," picked up the boy, and huffed away.

Cheryl was nineteen. Like Kateri had had at her age, she had confidence issues and authority issues. Only Kateri had never had a kid to go with them.

She got inside without another incident, and breathed a sigh of relief.

She had been coming to the Oceanview Café, on and off, for most of her thirty-four years, and during that time the place had remained exactly the same . . . until the earthquake. *That* had brought about a forced remodel; the black-and-white-checked linoleum had been changed for red-and-white-checked linoleum, the red Formica tables had become white Formica tables, the overhead light fixtures had become recessed and used energy-efficient LED bulbs. But the breakfast counter hadn't changed and the place still held that same rustic charm that invited people to eat too many fries, drink carbonated colas out of a glass bottle, and say yes to ice cream on their homemade blueberry pie.

The most important accouterment of the Oceanview Café was Rainbow Breezewing, waitress here for more than twenty-five years. In the Oceanview Café, it was Rainbow's personality that brought customers to their knees. She knew everyone. Every Virtue Falls newcomer, every tourist who stopped by for fish and chips, every senior citizen who claimed a special spot at the geezer table.

Plus Rainbow was . . . well. Today Rainbow wore purple-and-pink-striped stockings, brown leather knee breeches with suspenders, and a starched short-sleeved embroidered pink shirt. Kateri wondered if they were celebrating Switzerland National Alpenhorn Day. Yet all in all, for Rainbow, she looked pretty normal.

Rainbow glanced up from taking an order to nod acknowledgment to Kateri, and when she was done she whipped over and said, "I called about Cordelia. She keeps muttering she ought to talk to the sheriff, but the sheriff never believes her."

Kateri turned toward the table in the corner.

Cordelia was either their town weirdo or their town eccentric genius. Or both. She worked for the government doing something top secret security clearance related, and she did it all on her computer while sitting in the Oceanview Café. When she took a break, which she did twice a day at precisely the same times, her hobby was intercepting and reading phone texts sent to and from folks in Virtue Falls. Not that she admitted to that, but once she had solved a crime before it

happened . . . with unexpected consequences. Now there she sat, working on her computer, frowning in concentration.

As Kateri gazed at her, she got that sick feeling in her gut, the kind that warned her trouble loomed ahead. "I don't want to know."

"Yes, you do. But first, you need to remind her there's a new sheriff in town." Rainbow put her hand on Kateri's arm and glanced at the clock. "Hold off for three minutes and forty-two seconds. Then it's time for her pie. Once she's not working, she'll be easier to talk to. Anyway, you've got trouble at the geezer table."

"What?" Kateri glanced over to the table in the other corner where Mr. Setzer, Mr. Edkvist, Mr. Caldwell, and Mr. Harcourt spent their days together, drinking coffee, spying on the customers, and complaining about illegal immigrants, Congress, and kids nowadays. They even called them that—"*kids nowadays.*" Being around them was like a flashback to the sixties—and not a warm, nostalgic flashback, either.

Deputy Bergen sat with them.

"Why is he over there sucking up? Those guys wouldn't vote for me anyway." She was a woman and that was one strike against her. She was half Native American. Strike two. And she was a former Coast Guard commander who had lost a cutter, her reputation, and some said her sanity. That was either strike three, or maybe strikes three, four, and five. But with all-white, clean-cut, hometown deputy sheriff Bergen running against her, she didn't stand a chance with those guys.

"I believe," Rainbow said, "that Mr. Caldwell is Deputy Bergen's campaign manager."

"Really? I thought Bergen's wife was running the show."

"I did, too, and maybe she was, but Sandra was in here a couple of days ago. With school ending and the kids off for the summer, she wants to stay home with the girls and work in the garden. Bergen indulges her as much as he can." Rainbow cast him an affectionate glance. "He's a nice guy."

"A nice guy with Mr. Caldwell as his campaign manager."

"Mr. Caldwell knows his politics. He was a state senator."

"He's a jerk."

"All the more reason you have to go say hello. You can't pretend you didn't see them."

"I sure can!"

"Really? Kateri Kwinault, you can no more back down from a challenge than you can deny your visions."

"Not visions!" Kateri elbowed Rainbow. "They're *insights*. Let's call them *insights*."

"My insight says you're taking the challenge."

Kateri glared into Rainbow's twinkling eyes. Squaring her shoulders, she sauntered over.

As she arrived at the table, Bergen stood up.

She asked, "Going somewhere, Deputy?"

"Standing is a show of respect," he said.

Snarky as ever, Mr. Setzer said, "Respect for the uniform, right, son?"

In a pleasant tone, Kateri said, "Mr. Setzer, it's too bad you're so old I can't pop you a good one without breaking you."

Mr. Setzer reared back, offended.

Mr. Edkvist, Mr. Caldwell, and Mr. Harcourt all laughed.

"You always were a smart-mouth kid." Mr. Setzer was *not* smiling.

Bergen cut in smoothly, stopping the fight before it got started. "Gentlemen, I got to my feet to show respect for the sheriff. It's been a rough couple of days, and Sheriff Kwinault has worked more hours than anyone."

"Damned generous of you, considering you're running against this girl for the office," Mr. Edkvist said.

The geezers nodded.

Nice gesture that turned out well for Bergen. Not that Kateri was cynical.

"Where's Moen?" Bergen asked.

"He was drooping. I sent him home." Because according to the well-known law of physics, a guy who was ten years younger and ten times healthier than she was could whimper one hundred times more than she believed possible.

In one unexpected moment of camaraderie, Bergen said, "God, yes, that kid is a whiner," and offered his chair.

"You'd better sit down, Sheriff. I get shaky when I stand for too long, and I've only had one hip replacement." Mr. Caldwell offered Mr. Setzer a fist bump.

Mean old man. To Bergen she said, "Thank you, I'm on a call."

"The doughnuts called you, Sheriff?" Mr. Setzer asked.

The old guys guffawed again.

In her most pleasant voice, she said, "Mr. Setzer, what I really need to remember is—if I popped you, I'd have to put myself in jail."

Mr. Edkvist nodded and patted her hand. "Good girl. You don't have to put up with trouble from these cantankerous old farts."

Mr. Harcourt said, "You know, Howard . . ."

Howard was Mr. Caldwell.

"Making fun of a young woman who served in the military, and who has had two hip replacements and God knows what else . . . that makes you an obnoxious SOB."

Kateri was so taken aback by this defense, she didn't know what to say.

From the looks of them, neither did Mr. Setzer and Mr. Caldwell.

Rainbow sashayed up with her coffeepot and the kind of benign expression intelligent people found alarming. "Sounds like you boys are giving our acting sheriff a rough time. It would be a real shame if your bottomless coffee cup got cold and your free Wi-Fi was cut off. So maybe you ought to shut the fuck up."

The geezers did shut up. Or they were momentarily speechless, Kateri couldn't tell.

Rainbow grabbed Kateri's arm and steered her away from the geezers' table, leaving four extended coffee cups waving in midair. "It's almost time," she said.

CHAPTER ELEVEN

Rainbow walked to the refrigerator, pulled out the whole milk, poured a glass, and put it in the microwave for fifty-three seconds. While it was heating, she got the pie, measured a width of crust, cut the piece at precisely the right angle, put it on a plate, got a fork and wrapped it in a napkin. She took it to Cordelia and said, "Here you go, hon. The milk is exactly a hundred and forty degrees. The pie is two inches at the crust. It's strawberry today."

Cordelia said "Thank you" in a monotone, and began her ritual of unrolling the napkin, polishing her fork, placing the napkin in her lap, and smoothing the napkin repeatedly. Cutting two bites of pie, she dropped them into the glass, stirred until the warm milk turned pink, then poured one quarter cup of the milk and pie mixture onto the plate. She set her computer timer for one minute, waited, and when it dinged, she began to eat.

At a nod from Rainbow, Kateri walked over and put her hand on the back of the chair opposite. "Cordelia, do you mind if I sit down?"

Cordelia looked up, affronted, then relaxed. "You're Kateri Kwinault."

"That's right. I was in school with you."

"I know. I never forget anything. But I don't usually let people sit with me while I work," Cordelia said.

"You're not working now," Rainbow said. "I asked Kateri to come to talk to you about . . . whatever you saw that made you so uncomfortable."

Cordelia stiffened. "I'm not uncomfortable. I'm perfectly comfortable. Or at least I was, until you interrupted my routine."

Rainbow wasn't going to let her get away with evasion. "You said you needed a sheriff. Kateri is the sheriff. She'll listen to you."

Cordelia rubbed her head fretfully. "The sheriff doesn't listen."

"Sheriff Foster didn't listen. I do." Kateri pulled out a chair and sat without permission. Prying information out of Cordelia could take a while, and whatever else Mr. Caldwell was, he was right. Kateri needed to get off her feet. "Now—if Rainbow says you saw something that makes you uncomfortable, I believe her. If Rainbow says you should tell me what it is, I believe that, too. Because Rainbow is a pretty name, but she really should be named Storm, because she's a force of nature, and I wouldn't dare to defy her. Would you?"

Cordelia thought for a moment. "You are using a simile to describe Rainbow."

"That's right."

"You're trying to create a bond between us by pointing out that we both know Rainbow."

"Again, right."

"I do find it oddly comforting." Cordelia took a long breath. "You know about my hobby."

"Of randomly reading texts."

"I have rules. I only read local texts, and I never know who sends them. I find it entertaining to try to figure out who is doing what to who."

To whom. But Kateri figured Cordelia was smart enough to know that, so she merely nodded encouragingly. "That's how you discovered that . . ." She skidded to a halt. Best not to remind Cordelia of those awful events. "Reading texts is how you discovered the last crime you . . . discovered."

Cordelia seemed oblivious to Kateri's attempts at tact. "Correct. But the last crime was murder, and so much easier to figure out than . . . this. In fact, I'm probably wrong. I shouldn't even be telling you. Except it sounds like someone's in trouble and I'm starting to imagine bad things." Earnestly, she said, "I never imagine *anything.*"

"What kind of things?"

"Like there's a girl out there somewhere who is being kept in a cage against her will."

Cordelia had Kateri's complete attention. "What texts make you think that?"

"I started seeing texts about a year ago, a few texts every few weeks. They were . . . stuff like . . . *She won't get away this time.* And . . . *She doesn't understand what's happening to her.* I never saw a reply, which means the texts were going out of the area. Which is even more fun for me, because it makes figuring out who is texting even harder." With a fair amount of pride, Cordelia said, "I'm getting pretty good at two-sided conversations."

"I would imagine you are." Kateri played with her spoon. "Those texts didn't bother you?"

"In retrospect. But I've discovered a lot of suspicious-sounding texts are . . . harmless."

"Like?"

"Like the time the guy said, *I lost my cock* and I thought, *Oh, no!* The other person said, *LOL! Your cock?* And the guy said, *Stupid auto-correct. My cap. I lost my cap.*"

"Yeah. Stupid autocorrect."

"At the beginning, I didn't know all those texts that sounded sus-picious were coming from the same person. But I've gotten to know her shorthand, the abbreviations she uses, and there's this tone of, I don't know, rage or meanness or . . . it's like she likes being cruel and who-ever it is she's writing to is scared, and that makes her madder."

"Do you know for sure it's a she?"

Cordelia seemed to wrestle with the question. "No. No, I . . . last time, it was a she, so this time I think it's a she again. But there's no reason for that except my own prejudice."

Made sense. "What made you decide to talk to Rainbow?"

"I didn't decide to. She talks to me like she knows me."

"Does she?"

"Does she know me? I guess so, because she knew I was not happy about—" Cordelia got distracted by something outside the window.

Kateri looked, and saw Noah Griffin crossing the street. He was young, handsome, a news reporter turned writer turned her campaign manager.

He had needed a job, and she figured with his news experience, he understood how to run a campaign. Besides, nobody else in town would take the position. Which pretty much told Kateri exactly what her chances of winning were.

Cordelia was looking at him like he was a tasty morsel.

Cordelia had previously been married to a tasty morsel. In an oddly focused sort of way, she was attractive, and she made a lot of money.

Kateri didn't know if she should warn Noah or tell him he had won the jackpot. Probably she would mind her own business.

Kateri tapped her coffee cup with her spoon, and when she had Cordelia's attention, she asked, "About these texts—what specifically made you unhappy?"

"The text that said, *'Electronics are working. First test run. Subject afraid, insane, malleable.'*"

"Wow. Malleable?"

"I thought it sounded like torture and brainwashing. But I thought there could be something I was missing. I don't always comprehend conversations the way normal people do."

"I'm comprehending that text the same way you are."

"Okay. Also, whoever wrote back was cautioning, because the next text from this woman . . . person . . . said, *'Don't back out now. She will make us a fortune.'*"

Kateri felt like she'd stuck her finger in a light socket. "Sounds like a kidnapping."

"Yes!" Cordelia dug a paper out of her briefcase. "I wrote down every text I thought came from this woman. Person. Whoever."

Kateri took it and glanced at the texts and the associated dates. "Is there any way you can discover who is sending the messages?"

"That is against the rules of my game." But Cordelia looked guilty.

"Did you break your own rules?"

"When I got worried, I tried to catch the signal. It's almost impossible, but I had some success, and I discovered the phone, and the service is changing every time it comes into the area."

"Which makes it unlikely the cell companies can chase it down." Kateri thought of the amount of territory in this county, the expensive homes tucked out of the way, the hermits and survivalists who lived off the land, the long stretches of lonely highway and the occasional narrow side road. Then there was the Olympic National Forest, valued for its wilderness . . . "I don't even know where to start." But she did. She focused on Cordelia. "You sit here every weekday, working at this table. You see people come and go. Do you have any idea who this is?"

"No."

Digging her business card out of her wallet, Kateri handed it over. "If you suspect anyone, anyone at all, call me. I need your help. I depend on you."

Cordelia looked alarmed. "You can't depend on me."

"I think I can. In fact, I am." Kateri's phone vibrated and chimed. She pulled it out of her pocket and looked at it. She groaned and stood up. "I have to go. Promise me you'll call me or you'll talk to Rainbow if you hold suspicions about anybody. Promise you won't tell anyone else about this."

Cordelia nodded, but she looked sulky. "I wouldn't have said anything if I had known it would distract me from my work."

Kateri leaned over the table and patted her hand. "You were already distracted or you wouldn't have said anything." While Cordelia was chewing on that, Kateri walked toward the door.

Bergen intercepted her. "Can I give you a hand with anything?"

Cynically, Kateri reflected that Bergen wanted to be seen offering the little lady sheriff a hand. So she pulled out her phone and showed him the text.

He backed away, hands up. "You'll handle this better than me."

"Maybe you ought to come along and learn. After all, you want to be sheriff." Kateri showed all her teeth in a blinding white grin, then strode out of the café, got in her car, and drove back to the neighborhood of shotgun houses, one galloping case of PTSD, one case of sometime sanity and . . . Mrs. Butenschoen.

Kateri was going to have to explain to Mrs. Butenschoen why it wasn't against the law for Madeline Hewitson to trim her bushes with scissors.

If her life were a cop TV show, viewers would use it for a sleep aid.

CHAPTER TWELVE

Abruptly tired, Jacob dropped Mrs. Butenschoen's pie onto the table and seated himself in the crummy recliner.

He had done more today than he had in the past three months . . . or so. Hell, he didn't know how long he'd lived in this house, in the dark and the stink and the silence. He only knew he wanted to go back to yesterday, when he had been alone and nothing assaulted his senses.

Jacob looked across the way.

Maddie was contemplating the bush.

Mrs. Butenschoen was lecturing Maddie.

Without paying a bit of attention to Mrs. Butenschoen, Maddie headed toward the rear of her house.

Mrs. Butenschoen shut up, crossed her arms, and looked impatient.

When Maddie came back with full-sized hedge trimmers, a Pulaski, and a shovel, Mrs. Butenschoen splashed hissy all over her historic neighborhood.

Jacob pushed the chair into the reclining position, crossed his arms over his chest, and considered the situation.

He did long for the safety of yesterday.

But damn, Mad Maddie Hewitson kept him entertained.

Mrs. Butenschoen kept harassing Maddie.

Maddie kept whacking at the branches with the hedge trimmers. Dark green leaves flew onto the scanty lawn.

Sheriff Kwinault drove up in time to see Maddie start hacking at the center of the rhododendron with the pointed end of the Pulaski.

Apparently, Mad Maddie really had it in for that bush.

Sheriff Kwinault clumsily vaulted the fence, took Mrs. Butenschoen by the shoulders, moved her aside, and spoke to Maddie.

Maddie stopped assaulting the rhododendron, put the head of the Pulaski on the ground, and answered Sheriff Kwinault.

Mrs. Butenschoen started in again, yammering at Sheriff Kwinault about Maddie, and her voice was the only voice audible from this distance.

Sheriff Kwinault turned to her, spoke.

Mrs. Butenschoen kept jabbering.

Sheriff Kwinault paced toward her until they were nose to nose.

Mrs. Butenschoen tried, she really tried to retain control, but in the face of authority she visibly wavered, then shut up and flounced off toward her house.

When she had slammed her front door behind her, Sheriff Kwinault spoke to Mad Maddie as she walloped the bush.

Maddie turned, faced her, and answered.

Jacob got a good look at her face.

She didn't look crazy to him. She looked tired. She looked determined. But not crazy.

Apparently, whatever she said satisfied Sheriff Kwinault, for she touched the brim of her hat, walked around to the gate and down the driveway to her patrol car. She was limping as if it had been a long day. She opened the driver's side door, looked across at the roof of the car at Jacob, and gave him a nod.

Like Maddie, Sheriff Kwinault looked tired. And determined.

Jacob started to think Kateri Kwinault deserved to keep the sheriff's job.

CHAPTER THIRTEEN

Jacob had to hand it to Maddie. She hacked at the bush until she was sweaty and dirty, then dragged a chaise lounge out from the back, stretched out in the shade, and went fast asleep.

Jacob watched over her until he realized what he was doing. Abruptly furious, he stood and was headed back toward the dark of his room when a guy in a Ford F-350 drove up, wheeled his truck around, and backed into Jacob's front yard.

Jacob stopped and wavered between safety and knowing who was invading his privacy now.

A tall Native American got out of the driver's seat. He wore jeans, a battered cowboy hat, and a dirty snap-front shirt that would surely send Mrs. Butenschoen into a froth of malice and indignation. He walked up to the porch and in a baritone voice said, "I'm Web. Berk sent me. I'm supposed to clean up the scrap and haul it away."

Jacob sat back down and shrugged.

Web shrugged back and started flinging the pieces of porch railing, plaster, and shingles into the truckbed. He left once for the dump, then returned for another load.

Jacob liked Web. He mostly communicated in grunts. The electricians showed up; he liked them, too. They spoke in low tones, and they worked fast. He thought, by the glances he intercepted, that they were less sanguine about his appearance than Mr. Wodzicki and Mrs. Butenschoen. He thought again about cutting his hair. But thinking about it made him tired. He dozed, and woke up when Web said, "I bought a sandwich at the grocery store. You want some?"

Jacob started to say no.

Web didn't wait, just tore it in half and handed it over. "Trade you for the pie."

"Take it."

"Okay. Where are your cups? I've got coffee."

Coffee. God, coffee sounded good. Hot, dark, bitter. How long had it been since he'd had coffee? "In the kitchen, next to the sink." Jacob sniffed the sandwich. He took a bite. It was pretty crummy; a cold grocery store sandwich on white bread with too much mayonnaise.

Damn Madeline Hewitson. She'd made him remember what good food tasted like. But he was hungry, shaking, so he took another bite.

Web came back with two discolored Melmac cups hanging off one big, hooked finger. He poured coffee out of a thermos and handed Jacob a cup.

Jacob placed the sandwich on the table beside him. He put his nose close to the steam and smelled coffee. Good coffee: toasted nuts, black pepper, a smoky campfire . . . He took a sip. Damn. How had he forgotten this particular pleasure?

Web sat down on the trunk from the attic and ate, and stared across the street.

Mad Maddie got up, picked up her shovel, and surveyed what remained of the shattered rhododendron.

"She the crazy one everyone's talking about?" Web asked.

"No, that's me."

Deadpan, Web looked at Jacob. "She the crazy lady everyone's talking about?"

"Probably."

Maddie started digging at the roots.

"She's lousy with a shovel," Web observed.

She was. She kept hopping on the end and slipping off, and once she got it deep enough under the bush that the blade stuck and she had to wrestle it free.

"I'm taking my lunch hour, right? I'm not charging you now." Web stood up and dusted his hands on his pants. "Can't stand it anymore." He walked over to his truck, got in, drove over to Mad Maddie's, and backed up to the fence. He got a chain out of his crossover toolbox, hooked it to his trailer hitch, jumped the fence, and gently pushed Maddie aside. He wrapped the chain around the base of the bush, got in his truck, eased off the clutch and tore the rhododendron's roots free of the ground.

Maddie smiled.

Jacob stared.

She not only had a nice ass, she had a nice smile, warm as a down comforter on a cold winter morning.

He looked away. He put down the coffee. He stood. He went back into his bedroom, shut the door, and stretched out on his bed.

Mistake.

He slept.

He remembered.

He came awake fighting and screaming, careened around the

room, broke his toe and his face, and only stopped when he knocked himself out against . . . something. When he returned to consciousness, the pain was there, and he welcomed it. He used the bathroom and caught a glimpse of himself in the mirror. He looked like a woolly mammoth with two black eyes and smears of dried blood from the open gash on his forehead.

Damn Madeline Hewitson. He hadn't had an episode like that since he'd shut himself in here, and it didn't take Freud to know what had happened. She had broken open his house and broken open his memories. He couldn't live with this pain.

No, not pain. Call it what it was. Shame. He couldn't stand to look into his own eyes.

He didn't want to go out to the living room. It was light out there. Even at night it was light out there. But two bites of sandwich weren't enough; he had reached the point where he had to eat. If he didn't, he would collapse and not die. Not die, because Berk Moore would come by with more work orders, and when Jacob didn't answer, Moore would break down the door. He'd call an ambulance, they'd take Jacob to the hospital, and then . . . they'd make him undergo more psychological treatment. He was absofuckinglutely never going to do that again. He didn't want to be healed. He didn't deserve to be healed.

CHAPTER FOURTEEN

Jacob trudged to the kitchen.

Apparently he hadn't slept more than a couple of hours, because everyone was still there working.

After one horrified glance, the electricians deliberately avoided looking at him.

Web contemplated him, but said only, "Your groceries showed up." He pointed at the cooler. "Kid put them in there."

Jacob opened the cooler, took out another crummy, flavorless white bread, bologna, and mayonnaise sandwich, and ate. He drank water, then he sat down and waited for the night. Time was marked by occurrences, not by the clock.

Soon the electricians knocked off.

Web drove his pickup away.

The sun sets after ten.

The lights at Mrs. Butenschoen's went off after the news.

This time of the year, it wasn't fully dark until eleven. The lights stayed on at Maddie's. She'd managed to tack her shades back up. He could see her silhouette seated there, facing the window. She was working on something, drawing or writing or both.

About two, her head nodded, and he thought, *Here we go.*

He wasn't being mean. He didn't want her to imagine something was attacking her. Misery loves company, and all that crap, but his face hurt and his toe was swollen and throbbing and he had banged the hell out of his shins. He didn't wish those wounds on anyone. He knew so well what it meant when sleep was your enemy.

Which is why he was surprised when she rose from her desk and calmly walked away. He was more surprised when she came out her front door, dressed for work in jeans, a long-sleeved T-shirt, and tennis shoes, and strolled down her driveway. She didn't hesitate; she turned toward the end of the street, toward the end with the metal traffic guard set up to stop cars from driving over the cliff into the ocean.

Why had he waited so long? Why had he imagined it would be better to be out here and awake and watching Maddie than take a chance on the ghosts in his bedroom?

Because he recognized what she was doing. Exactly what he wanted to do but didn't have the guts for. She was headed over the cliff.

What was he going to do about it?

Every house on the street was dark. He was the only one who saw her, and probably the only one who wasn't scared of her. He could call the cops, but they wouldn't get here in time . . .

He found himself on his feet and limping down the ramp, onto the street, and following Madeline Hewitson, the bane of his life. He called her softly. "Maddie."

She kept walking, not fast, not slow, a smooth, confident stride.

He limped faster, called louder. "Maddie! Stop!"

She pretended he wasn't there.

She passed the last house, the one that tenaciously clung to the edge of the crumbling cliff. She swerved left to avoid walking into the metal traffic barrier.

"Maddie!"

She ignored him.

He broke into a painful run. He caught up with her, grabbed her arm as she was taking that last, long step into the waves twenty feet below. "Maddie!"

She reacted quickly, like someone waking from a dream.

Abruptly, he realized—that was it. She'd been sleepwalking. He shouldn't have woken her like that.

Too late. She looked at him wide-eyed and terrified. She opened her mouth. She screamed.

Damn it! She screamed like a fire alarm. She screamed like he was attacking her. She screamed loud enough to wake the dead—or worse, the neighbors.

Jacob let go and jumped back. "Shh! Shhhh! Stop it, Maddie. Stop!"

She kept up that unearthly shrieking.

The earth was crumbling beneath her feet.

Lights came on in a couple of houses. The house with the kids. Dayton's house. They were probably calling 911.

Nothing to do but to stop her, save her. Stepping close, he wrapped one arm around her body, trapping her arms. He dragged her away from the edge of the cliff. He covered her mouth with his hand. "Shh, Maddie, it's me. It's Jacob. Remember me? You crashed into my house. You gave me a sandwich. I'm not going to hurt you."

She got in a couple of good kicks on his shins—of course, right on his bruises—but with his size and his training, petite little Maddie didn't stand a chance.

At some point she really did wake up and realize what was going on; her tension changed from terror to confusion. She looked around—

at him, at where they were standing—and her eyes held recognition, then, when she looked at the cliff, horror.

"Okay now?" he asked.

She nodded.

Cautiously he took his hand away from her mouth.

She shut it.

Even more cautiously, he took his arm away from around her waist and stepped away.

"What am I doing here?" she whispered. Then she looked at his face. "What happened to you?"

At that moment, some man opened a door and shouted, "I've called the cops!"

"Shit!" Jacob grabbed her arm. "Let's get inside or it's FUBAR all the way."

"Right." She shook off the last of her stupor and headed full speed up the street toward her house.

"*My* house," he said.

He hadn't known she could snap. But she did. "In your *living room*?"

She was right. Damn it. Yesterday he'd been hiding in the dark.

Today he had left his house and now he was going to visit his new friend. What a special couple of days these had turned out to be.

In the distance, they could hear the wail of sirens.

She gave up on her fast walking and sprinted.

He tried.

He should have taped up his toe. But he did have the advantage of longer legs, so he got into her house—she left the door open—only a minute behind her and a good thirty seconds before the first police car turned onto the street.

Good enough.

He shut the door behind him. "What the hell do we do now? Turn off the lights and pretend we're not here?"

She stood in the middle of the room and looked around as if she were still dazed. "They'll suspect me. They will come here. You should hide."

He moved farther into the room.

She went to the window, opened it, and fanned like she was trying to chase a bad smell out. "Hide in the bathroom. Take a shower. With soap. Lots of soap."

He found a moment of grim amusement in her aggression. "Are you insinuating I stink?"

"No, I'm saying it. You stink. I'll handle the cops." She flipped on the light in her bathroom. "You take a shower. Towels are in the cabinet over the toilet. If you use enough soap, I'll let you sit on my furniture."

That seemed like a good deal to him. He went in and shut the door.

He didn't remember the last time he had showered. He sure as hell didn't remember the last time he had showered using sandalwood-scented goat soap and a mint and rosemary shampoo. Washing his face made him wince, and getting the dried blood out of his eyebrows took a couple of rounds of lathering, rubbing, and rinsing. He used a brush for his nails and toes, and a different brush for his back. He found a jar of apple-and-cinnamon-scented oatmeal scrub and used it after the goat soap. He couldn't work the shampoo down to his scalp, so he poured liberal amounts of lavender and thyme conditioner onto his hair until it was slick, then he shampooed it again.

He was in there a long time, and when he came out he smelled like he'd fallen into his mother's herb garden. He found scissors in Maddie's drawer and cut his jagged nails. Inspired by his success thus far, he tried to cut his hair. He got the left half hacked off, his arms got tired, and he gave up. He was using Maddie's razor to shave when, without fanfare, the door opened. He swung around, ready to kill whoever stood there.

It was Maddie. She held an armful of clothes. His clothes.

He was naked.

If she cared, she didn't show it. She put the clothes on the hamper. "Here. After the cops left, I went to your house and found you something to wear." Her lips curled with disgust. "You have perfectly good clothes in the closet, and you were wearing . . . these." With two fingers, she picked up his pants, his underwear, his T-shirt. "I'll take these out to the garbage. You're a pig."

"You sound like my mother."

"That's because we both have vaginas. People with vaginas are smarter than people with penises. If we weren't, we'd live like pigs, too."

His penis apparently heard its name mentioned and took this inopportune moment to remember she had a nice ass. He turned back to the sink to finish shaving.

"When you come out, if you want, I'll give you a hand cutting your hair." She said, "Wow, you're skinny."

He glanced at her.

She was looking at his *face.* "Shaving makes you look even more like a concentration camp survivor. And that bruising. Not a good look. You should put some ice on your nose. And eat something."

For whatever reason, his penis found that exciting, too.

So much for his comforting theory that he was impotent.

He leaned against the cold porcelain sink. *That* knocked back his erection.

Damn Madeline Hewitson. Like he didn't have enough trouble already. Horniness: God's gift for caring whether Maddie walked off a cliff.

When he came out, he was dressed in a pair of his boxers, a worn pair of jeans, and, of all things, a polo shirt. He remembered the jeans— they were his favorites, he'd had them all through his twenties—but his mother must have bought him the polo shirt in one of her periodic attempts to make him more mainstream. Or maybe more eligible. Probably more eligible.

"What happened with the cops?" he asked.

"They asked if I'd heard anything. I said no. I hadn't. Because I was screaming."

Made sense.

"Then they had to go talk to Mrs. Butenschoen, who probably tattled on us because she sees everything. But the cops didn't come back, so maybe she was sleeping the sleep of the self-righteous. I brought your shoes." Maddie pointed at the pair of running shoes and socks.

"I can't wear those. I broke my toe."

"How did you do that?"

"I was kicking someone who wasn't there."

"Oh." She was the only other person in the world who immediately and without question knew about kicking things that weren't there. "Here." She handed him an ice bag and started pulling stuff out of the refrigerator. "Put that on your face while I get you something to eat."

I let her catch sight of me. She knows what's going to happen now.

CHAPTER FIFTEEN

Driven by a curiosity he didn't want to admit, Jacob wandered over to Maddie's desk and looked at her work.

She made drawings in ink, black ink, no color. Disturbing drawings of a young woman, victimized and in anguish, and a monster in a black hat and an open black coat who haunted her, mocked her, drove her to become a superhero.

"You draw comics." He picked up a sketch and looked at it. "Damned gruesome comics."

"Don't look!" She hurried over and plucked the sketch from his fingers. "It's no good."

"Good? No, but it's visceral."

"Really?" She shuffled it together with the other papers scattered over the desk. "No one has ever seen these, so I didn't know . . . but visceral? That's excellent."

He turned his head sideways to look at the sketch on top of the pile. "Are you trying to publish your comics?"

"They're not comics. I'm seeing if I can create a graphic novel." She opened the belly drawer, slid the papers inside, and closed them away from his gaze.

"Comics. Graphic novels." One and the same, his tone implied.

"Graphic novels are more complex, they're set in an already existing universe, and they're bound like a book."

Right. He remembered now. While he was stationed in Korea, one of his kids had avidly read graphic novels. Lydia Adelaide Jenkins's mother had sent them by the boxfull . . . He had called her mother when he got back to the States. He had wanted to pay his respects and offer his wholehearted apology for the death of her daughter while under his care.

Her mother hadn't cared what words he offered in his broken whisper. She despised him. She had hung up on him.

He didn't want to remember. "Why don't you just write a book?"

With a fair dollop of sarcasm, she said, "I've *just* written a lot of books."

"Have you? I thought your brother was the author."

She hesitated, then nodded. "Yes. He's A. M. Hewitson. He writes horror based on . . . stuff."

"Is he good?"

"Sometimes I think so. Sometimes I don't. The books sell well. There's not much money in writing, but I'm not good for anything else." While he was puzzling that out, she walked over to the kitchen table and put her hand on a chair. "Sit down, have something to eat, then I'll cut your hair so it's not so . . . lopsided."

He put his hand up and felt the ragged ends on the cut side, then touched the mats—now conditioned, but still mats—on the other side. He walked over and sat down. "Do you know, while you work I can see you outlined against the light?"

She looked toward her desk in alarm. "When they sold those blinds to me they said . . . no, I didn't know. Thank you for telling me." She brought him a plate.

He looked it over. Vegetables, olives, crackers, thin rolls of cheese wrapped in prosciutto. "You got any coffee?"

"Yes. Yes, I do!" She beamed as if having coffee was an accomplishment. "Do you want me to make some?"

He didn't. He shouldn't. "No."

"I'm going to make myself some, anyway."

As he chowed down, he kept an eye on her.

She got a bag of gourmet coffee out of the freezer. She thought for a minute, then got on her knees, opened the cabinet in the corner, and dragged out a cheap drip coffeemaker. She placed it on the counter and plugged it in, got out the instructions, and read them.

"Don't make a lot of coffee?" he asked drily.

"I don't like it."

"Then why do you have it?"

"It'll keep me awake."

Like her understanding him kicking someone who wasn't there, he understood why she wanted to stay awake.

She loaded the basket with ground coffee, filled the pot with water, filled the cistern, turned on the machine, turned to him, and beamed.

Quickly he said, "Put the pot back under before the—"

A stream of coffee started pouring out onto the hot burner.

She stuck the pot under the stream.

The stench of burned coffee filled the air.

Still, she seemed pleased. "Not bad for my first time."

Nothing much shook this female's composure . . . except for imaginary monsters.

She got the scissors out of her desk.

"Do you know how to cut hair?" he asked.

"No. Sometimes I forget to make a hair appointment, so I trim my own bangs to get them out of my eyes, and they're crooked." She surveyed him critically. "But I can do a better job than you." She went into the bathroom and came back with a comb and brush. She tossed a towel over his shoulders. She moved close to his side.

She smelled nice. Like an apple pie, so he guessed she had been using her oatmeal scrub. He said, "I used up some of your soaps."

"No kidding. How else were you going to get rid of that rancid smell?" She was picking up pieces of his hair. "A rat could live in here and you'd never know it."

"Once you get the length cut off, I can shave my scalp." In fact, he looked forward to it.

She slid the scissors along a thin line of hair and slowly cut. She dropped the shorn part on the floor. She moved on to another section. The sound of the blades shearing off the strands sent a shiver through him. She must have noticed, for she said, "Do you know, you're probably the only person in the world who would let me near them with something sharp."

"Because you might kill me?" He snorted. "You should do me such a favor."

"You want me to kill you?" Another section of hair, and she moved behind him and started work on the back. "Why?"

"Doesn't matter."

She cut some more.

The coffeepot beeped that it was done.

As if that were some signal, he said, "Two people died because of my negligence, young people, one male, one female, and good men were brutalized."

"After we met, I looked you up online and—"

"After we *met*? We didn't *meet*. You turned my living room into a garage."

"You don't have to be unpleasant about it." Placing her scissors on the table, she got out two mugs—ceramic mugs, not Melmac—and poured them full. "I apologized and my insurance is paying for everything." She handed him his mug. "After it's done, you can go back to being a hermit."

He thought longingly about that, about the darkness and the silence, the perfect hours of blank nothingness interspersed with blinding moments of pain . . . then he noticed the warm, savory odor of the coffee. The cup's heat warmed his palms. He watched her take a sip and grimace comically. She made him want to laugh.

Laugh. People were dead because of him, and he wanted to laugh.

Guilt bit at him. He didn't deserve a moment of sensory pleasure. He started to stand.

She put her hand on his shoulder and pushed him back down. "I'm not done with your hair yet. If you want cream or sugar, I'll get it for you."

"No. Black." He took a sip and got a mouthful of grounds. Nasty. That eased his guilt. He swallowed carefully. "You might invest in coffee filters."

"I noticed." She looked doubtfully into the cup. "Do you want me to strain it?"

"No. Give 'em a minute. The grounds will settle."

"I'll finish your hair." She put down the cup and picked up the scissors. "You have scars from being shot."

She'd seen his scars. She'd seen him naked.

He would not get an erection.

She continued, "The online article said you were responsible for saving five lives."

Nope. No erection. "I shouldn't have had to save them in the first place." Maddie's fingers slid through his hair and massaged. He thought she was trying to work the mats apart. But it felt good, and he didn't deserve that either.

"The article said you got five guys out of a North Korean prison, but it didn't say who they were or why they were imprisoned."

"Because they shouldn't have been in North Korea in the first place." He felt his throat began to close. He couldn't talk about this. He refused to talk about this. So he asked, "Tonight. What were you dreaming?"

She didn't answer right away; something about a hunk of hair close to his neckline occupied her so much she muttered about needing a professional. But she must have known he wouldn't allow that, so she kept hacking at it. When she had achieved some measure of success, she said, "I didn't think I was dreaming. I was sitting at my desk writing—I really was, I do that every night—and I could feel the fear begin to creep up on me. I heard noises behind me—"

"What kind of noises?"

"A creaking, like a window opening. A shuffling, like footsteps. The sound of leaves blowing on the wind."

"Go on."

"When I looked, there was nothing there. But I knew he was coming. I knew he was stalking me. I heard laughter, and I had to get out." She put her trembling hand on his shoulder. "Then I was out on a lonely road that stretched forever into the darkness. I wanted to run, to get away from him, but it was so dark, I was afraid of where I was going. Then you woke me and I . . . I'm sorry about the screaming. I thought you were *him*."

CHAPTER SIXTEEN

"Who is he?" Why was Jacob asking? He didn't care.

But he did. He was interested.

Maddie answered. "The man in the coat and the hat with a long fingernail filed to a point. And the knife."

It sounded as if her nightmares contained about the same horror quotient as his. "The police told me about you. They said you've faced two horrific crimes."

"I'll bet they told you more than that," she muttered.

"Not much."

"So you looked me up online."

He pointed at his face. "Do I look like I give a shit?"

She actually came around and stared into his face. "I can't tell."

"If I had Internet, which I don't, your car would have taken it out. So fill me in on the details of your life."

"I thought you didn't give a shit."

"It'll give me something to do while I wait for you to stab me to death." He pointed at his jugular. "Right here."

She gave a half laugh and went back to work on his hair. "When I was a freshman in college, I lived in the oldest dorm on campus. Me and four of my friends from high school decided we could share a suite, three in one room, two in the other, bathroom in between. No one thought we could make it work, but we did. We were really good friends."

So she had lost all her friends at one time.

"The janitor in the building was this guy. We didn't pay any attention to him. He was, you know, in his thirties, skinny, ordinary. We didn't even know his name. I know it now. Chase Billingsly. But he called himself 'Ragnor the Avenger.'"

Jacob caught her wrist. He swiveled to face her. "You are kidding."

"I wish. After he was . . . dead, when the police went through his possessions, they found out he had a thing about old comic books. And they found out that he, um"—she cleared her throat—"he was obsessed with me and my friends."

"Obsessed." His law enforcement brain was already filling in the details.

"The police found photos. He'd cut holes in the wall. Photos of us undressing. Going to the bathroom. Sleeping. He had written love stories about us, bizarre fantasies about how we would all be obedient to him, fawn over him, take turns giving him . . . servicing him." She wasn't blushing. Rather, her forehead and cheeks turned a blotchy red. "But we were normal girls. So he took photos of us with our boyfriends."

"He was a pervert."

She shook her head. "Worse. That night—Saturday night, we were getting ready to go out. Wearing our underwear or a robe or . . . Maggie was just out of the shower. He opened the door and stepped in. He wore a cape. None of us recognized him. We thought it was a joke or something. I mean . . . a cape? My friend, my best friend, Kathy. She was kind of bossy. Tall. Really pretty . . ." Maddie was losing focus, trying to avoid the story.

He pulled her back on track. "What did Kathy do?"

"Kathy told him to get out. He . . . he . . . he locked the door behind him. It clicked." Maddie flinched as if, even now, the sound signaled the start of terror. "He announced we had betrayed him and that he would punish us. At first we were kind of . . . we didn't realize that he was . . . we didn't get it. Stuff like that doesn't happen. We didn't get it until Charlotte reached for her phone and he stabbed her in the shoulder. Then we screamed."

"Didn't anyone hear you?"

"Saturday night. People were out. The ones who heard . . . thought we were watching a movie. A horror movie." The red blotches faded to a ghastly white.

Jacob used his foot to push a chair away from the table. Still with his hand on her wrist, he guided her to sit.

She dropped into the chair.

"How did he control five women?"

"He pulled out two guns. He told us to be quiet or he would shoot us. Which was stupid, because if he had fired maybe someone would have realized what was going on and rescued us."

"Or he could have killed you all."

"That would have been better." Beneath his fingers, her skin grew cold and her pulse faint and rapid. "Kathy handed me her phone and pointed under the bed. She attacked him. He killed her first. He was angry. Because she made him kill her fast."

"Why didn't *she* get under the bed?"

"Dorm beds. Close to the floor. Small space. I fit." Maddie quit talking.

He recognized the finality.

She did not want to remember. She did not want to talk about this. Yet she was caught in the web of memories. She couldn't get out. Not without his help. He had to respond. "Got it."

Not much of a response, but it pushed her to the next memory, the next moment. "I couldn't . . . I was on my belly, arms out. Head sideways. I couldn't see the phone. I had to maneuver. I dialed 911. But he made them be quiet. My friends. He told them to shut up. They were afraid. They did. He didn't seem to realize . . . that I was missing. They didn't . . . didn't remind him. He gagged them. I called 911. I did. But I couldn't . . . couldn't talk. Was afraid to talk. Couldn't tell them what was wrong. Left the line open. They . . . the police . . . didn't realize . . . sometimes they got prank calls from dorms. You know? Until Georgia started screaming. She got the gag out and screamed and screamed. He said he would open us up a new way so he could get satisfaction while he killed us. And he did. I heard him. He raped my friends . . . while they were still warm." Maddie leaped up. She ran for the bathroom.

Jacob heard her retching.

Okay. She had reason to be scared.

She had reason to be nuts, too . . . although some people would say he was the last person able to intelligently make that decision.

He got one of her kitchen towels, wet it, went in, and laid it across her neck.

"Thank you." She propped her elbows up on the seat, held her head in her hands. Her complexion was tinted a pale green.

He leaned against the sink. "How old were you?"

"Eighteen."

Now the inevitable question. "Did he find you?"

"When he was done with the others. He counted bodies. He dragged me out. I saw then that he had grown one of his nails long and filed it to a point. The campus cop started pounding on the door. He—Ragnor—used that nail to slice me from my breastbone to my belly." Now her voice was steady, matter-of-fact. "Then he tried to stab me in the . . . in the uterus. I was kicking at him and screaming. The cop got the door open and shot him. His brains blew . . . they hit the wall. They splattered me. My face. Blood and brains and cruelty I could taste."

"And rescue," he reminded her. Then he realized—he sounded like his military trauma-recovery therapist. Like his goddamn stupid asshole of a therapist, saying goddamn stupid-ass shit that was supposed help.

Apparently it did. Or maybe Maddie had fought her way out of the web so many times she knew what to do, because she continued, "The school had to . . . close the dorm. No one ever stayed in our rooms again. A year later they tore down the building. Because no one would stay there."

"Makes sense."

She started to get up off the floor.

He put his hand under her arm to help.

She flinched away.

He could almost hear her inner shriek. *Don't touch me. Don't touch me. Don't touch me.*

He let her go and walked out to the kitchen. He sat down in the same chair.

She came out, still pale, but steady. She walked over, picked up the scissors, and went to work on his hair again.

So he had the guy with the fingernail. But he wanted to know the whole of the predator who lurked on her drawings and in her subconscious. "Then your fiancé was murdered, too."

She seemed almost cool about this death. "I saw the killer leave the house. He wore a coat and hat. It was Colorado in the winter, so that wasn't unusual. But the viciousness of the crime . . . that was. So the detectives said. That's why they decided it was me. Because I'd spent time in an asylum, so I must be a vicious murderer."

Sarcasm. Good. She wasn't merely a passive victim. "Which killer do you fear?"

"It's not that easy. The thing that hunts me now is not one or the other. He is both. Or neither. He is evil. He thrives on terror. My terror. I fear he will come for me. I fear he will come for anyone who knows me." She put down the scissors. "You shouldn't be here. You should go."

"I would welcome a monster I could kill." Jacob put his hand on her hip and pushed her around to face him. "Have you sleepwalked before?"

"Not that I know of."

"You were headed over the cliff. Are you sure you were asleep? A plunge into that ocean is a pretty solid way to commit suicide."

"I wasn't committing suicide! I don't want to die." Her voice got softer, almost pleading. "But I don't want to live like this, either. When I moved here I thought I had left my demons behind. For six months, I thought the worst thing that could happen to me was being scolded by Mrs. Butenschoen for not deadheading my roses properly. Then things started happening. First my furniture moved by itself. I was working hard and I get absentminded, so I didn't think too much about it. I thought I had done it and forgotten. But then my food disappeared out of the refrigerator. I was still hungry, but I told myself it was more absentmindedness. I lost weight. Then the lights flickered, on and off, on and off, and I knew. I knew someone was after me."

"Someone? Not your monster?"

"At the time, I suspected that someone in town was playing tricks to make me go away."

Now *that* was paranoid. "Why would someone do that?"

She plucked at the neckline of her Rockies sweatshirt. "I couldn't stay in Colorado. After Easton was killed, I was accused of the crime."

"I heard."

"I was acquitted, but no one believed I was innocent. The people in my neighborhood requested that I move. My brother wanted me to get a house close to him. His neighbors petitioned to keep me out." Tears rose in her eyes. "Like I was a child molester. I saw my best friends murdered. Witnessed it. Then the man I loved had his throat slashed in our home. I was grieving, and all anyone could think was that it was my fault. Somehow, my fault because I'd been in the loony bin. That's what one of Andrew's neighbors called it. The 'loony bin.'" In a fierce voice, she said, "Crazy isn't a disease. I didn't catch it from the inmates who lived there because they were schizophrenic or delusional. I was there to recover. And I did!"

He studied her. She made sense. She looked normal. "Then what made you decide it wasn't someone here trying to get rid of you?"

"I saw *him*. The man who killed Easton. In my backyard. He was going out the gate to the alley."

"How did you know it was him?"

"He wore the same hat and coat."

"Could be anybody."

"They never found the man who killed my fiancé."

"So you think the guy who killed your fiancé is after you? Doesn't make sense. Why doesn't he just kill you?"

"Because he feeds on terror. Some people do, you know."

"Yes. I know." The way he saw it, everything revolved around the fiancé's murder.

Maybe the cops were right, and she had been so psychologically destroyed by witnessing her friends' murders that she had killed her fiancé. Maybe her fiancé's murder had nothing to do with her, but she had gone whacko and imagined someone was stalking her. Maybe someone actually was so obsessed with keeping her isolated from the human race that he—she was convinced it was a he—would kill the man she was going to marry. And chase her across the country to torment her here.

But why? Why would someone be obsessed with keeping her mentally off balance? What could be in it for them?

With a sudden leap of aggression, she leaned into his face and stared into his eyes. "I'm done talking. Now you. You tell me. What happened to you?"

He picked up his coffee cup. As he'd said, the grounds had settled. But the coffee was cold and thick and black and made him want to gag. He put it down. "I was in the military in high school. ROTC. Went to college on an ROTC scholarship, went professional as soon as I graduated. In all, I've dealt with the military for twelve years, and this Korean operation was the dumbest idea the brass ever came up with. That's saying something."

She stopped cutting and stepped around to lean against the table and watch him. "What'd they do?"

"The U.S. Army, in its infinite wisdom, decided to place a bunch of their high-IQ recruits in a South Korean research facility with orders to think outside the box. The theory was that if these kids got a look at a place that was officially at peace but where a real shooting war could break out at any minute, they'd come up with clever ideas for weapons or defense that no one else had ever imagined." In some remote corner of his mind, he noted that she had barely sipped her coffee. She'd made it, but she didn't like it.

"Why were *you* there?"

Obviously, it never occurred to her he was a genius, too. And he wasn't. But— "I've got a degree and a respectable IQ, so I was put in charge of them. It was like being a dorm mother with a bunch of brainiac Camp Fire kids. Six boys and two girls, all under the age of twenty-five, and bored out of their skulls."

"They got in trouble."

Yeah, Maddie, jump to conclusions. The right conclusions. "They invented and built a prototype of a small hovercraft that . . ." She was too easy to talk to. Not that he thought she was a North Korean spy. But still. "Theoretically, this hovercraft could fly low, carry soldiers and equipment while eluding the enemy. One night the kids were drinking. Doing shots. One of the girls—Mormon, she didn't drink—woke me up at zero two hundred. Her intoxicated comrades had decided to see how well their invention worked. They went over the border, into the DMZ. They hadn't returned. The North Koreans are never amused by anything or anyone attempting to invade their country by any means. So I went over the border looking for my kids. My responsibility plus I had combat experience. I found them. They'd managed to get past the DMZ before they crashed. I didn't have a chance to get them back across the border before the North Koreans captured us. One of the kids had to spout off about who we were. Then . . . the enemy took us . . . they drove us to . . . this building." Jacob had been talking like a normal person. But he was running out of steam, running out of words, running into trouble. Because pain was waiting out of sight, over his horizon, to take him and hold him hostage.

Those kids. His bright, careless, innocent, stupid brainiac kids.

"What happened?" Maddie whispered.

"By the time it was over, we knew the dead were the lucky ones."

"I am so sorry." She put her hand on his arm.

At her touch, the pain blasted him, blew him to pieces like a detonated grenade.

He flung off her hand, stood up, shouted, "No! No! I don't care. I don't want to hear. I don't want to feel. I don't want to . . . see." *He could see.* It wasn't fair. He could see a warm beach where palm trees waved and waves broke over warm sand . . . He would never forget the sight as long as he lived, and every time it lit up his mind, he wanted to kill someone.

He *had* killed someone.

But that wasn't enough.

He needed to kill himself.

He put his hands to his head, to the rough patch of cut hair and the grizzled length of matted hair. "I have to go. I have to . . ." He looked up at her. *"What have you done to me?"* Turning, he ran out, stumbling, through her door, down the street, over the barrier. At the edge of the cliff, he stood until dawn lit the sky.

He never noticed the slight, still figure that watched over him until he returned to his house.

CHAPTER SEVENTEEN

At dawn, Jacob stumbled his way back down the street, shut himself in his room, and blocked the door. He huddled in the corner, eyes wide, staring into darkness, willing back the words he had spoken.

Like all the mistakes he had made, he couldn't fix this one. Nothing he did—wishing, praying, ranting, swearing—could turn back time to a moment when he was strong, confident, and sure of himself. He knew. He had tried them all.

He sat like that, on the floor in the dark with his legs pulled up to his chest and his arms around his knees, for hours, days, an eternity of writhing in agony.

Yet life relentlessly marched on. For when the electricians fixed the power he discovered that the bedroom light switch had been flipped on. Without warning, the overhead blasted him with incandescence.

He went mad: screaming, shouting, rampaging around his room until he managed to turn it off. Then he went roaring out into the living room and screamed at the crew until the electricians fled, the framers retreated to the outside of the house, and only Moore and Web remained.

When Jacob had wound down and stood panting, Moore said, "Your refrigerator's working again, and so's your hot water heater. We're knocking off for the day, going to the bar for a beer. See you tomorrow."

In his slow, understated tone, Web said, "You should shave your head. Because right now, you look like a breaded veal cutlet."

Jacob stood, breathing hard, watching Moore and Web leave in separate pickups, knowing they were headed to a pleasant, normal evening the like of which he could not even remember. While he . . . he was going to take his razor and shave his head—and cut his own throat.

Except he didn't have the guts for that.

So instead he sat in the funky-smelling recliner and stared out into the night.

If he was lucky, Madeline Hewitson would try to walk off the cliff again.

This time he wouldn't stop her.

First thing in the morning, Kateri called a meeting of her law enforcement officers in the briefing room, and asked Ed Legbrandt that the city cops be there, too.

She didn't want to explain this kidnapping theory to these guys, not at all, and she definitely did not want to explain it twice. But it had to be done, so she sat on a high stool behind the podium and waited while the officers filed in, got coffee, grabbed folding chairs, and planted themselves.

Even when she added in the Virtue Falls cops, she only had thirty-one guys to cover the whole county: twenty-two guys here, nine off-shift, all males, all iffy about a girl boss. About half of them had been willing to listen to Garik Jacobsen and give her a chance, and even now with the election coming up, they were okay with her. The others . . . the others were like most guys in uniform, both in the Coast Guard and here. A woman was fine as long as she knew her place. Attitudes were changing. But not fast enough.

Bergen sat in the front row. Of course. The guy never said anything hostile. Never showed her less than respect. But he was always there, always watching.

Once the guys got shuffled around, Officer Bill Chippen called, "Sheriff, how's the campaign going?"

"Pretty good with you guys out there stumping for me."

Patronizing male chuckling. Some patting of Bergen's shoulder.

"A lot of people don't think you have enough experience to be sheriff." Officer Ernie Fitzwater had been in town and on the force his whole life. He prided himself on saying what he thought. He also wasn't offended when she answered him plainly, and that counted for a lot.

"I *am* sheriff," she said.

"Appointed," Officer Norm Knowles snapped back. Now *he* was easily offended.

So she answered to the whole group. "Guys, this is like being commander of the Virtue Falls Coast Guard unit. I was the only female there, too. All it required was that I prove myself twice as smart, skilled, and accomplished as the men." She raked them with a glance. "Luckily, that was never difficult."

Guffaws. Much elbow poking. Some frowns. At least one vote lost. But she supposed Knowles wasn't going to vote for her, anyway.

Bergen crossed his arms over his chest. "Guys, way to set her up for the punch line."

When they were done with their ritual razzing, she got serious. "Gentlemen, I called you in because—"

"Because someone put dog poop on Mrs. Butenschoen's front walk?" Rupert Moen asked.

Kateri tried to decide if she could ignore that.

She couldn't. "Please tell me you're joking."

Heads shook. Men grinned.

"She called the cops because someone put . . . ?" Kateri faltered.

"Twice." Moen held up two fingers. "She has had to remove dog poop from her front yard twice."

"I thought the dog couldn't get in her yard anymore," Kateri said.

"The dog next door would have to gain about one hundred pounds to produce that much poo," Moen assured her.

Now Kateri fought a grin. "So someone is gathering up dog bombs and decorating her yard with them?"

"*Strategically* decorating her yard." Moen managed a fair imitation of Mrs. Butenschoen's fussy indignation.

The officers guffawed.

When they had calmed and she had fought back her amusement, she gravely said, "This is an outrage. I am outraged. But sadly, the sheriff's office actually doesn't have the resources to have a patrol car sit outside her fence twenty-four hours a day."

"Mrs. Butenschoen told me to tell you she realizes that," Moen said.

Kateri raised her eyebrows. "Civilized of her."

Moen continued, "She has decided to get a security camera mounted on her front porch and point it at her yard to catch the culprit."

"Good." Kateri nodded. "Good." Finally. One problem fixed

without her having to do a damned thing. She looked down at her notes and once again saw the texts, and her humor failed her. When she looked up, the men had sobered, too. "Guys, I have reason to believe there's a kidnapper and someone who is being kept against their will somewhere in Virtue Falls or the general vicinity."

Bergen straightened in his chair. "Why do you think that?"

Trust him to think to ask. "Cordelia Markum has intercepted a series of texts over the past months that point to this conclusion."

Groans.

Moen hooted. "Crazy Cordelia?"

"I know," Kateri said. "She's odd. But I'd like to point out that the last time she reported threatening texts to law enforcement, somebody did die."

More chatter. "That was because—"

"As weird as that was—"

"Coldhearted and warped!"

Bergen's voice cut through the babble. "Sheriff, I assume you saw the texts. What makes you believe them?"

Kateri lifted the paper Cordelia had given her and read, *"The first night, she was cautious, checking every entrance. She doesn't realize I'm already in place. Then, I let her catch sight of me. She knows what's going to happen to her now. Then, Now I've got her. The electronics are set up. She'll never escape again."*

The talk in the room died. The guys exchanged intense *Oh, shit* glances that meant they heard the underlying menace in the words.

Kateri waved the paper. "There's more. I'd love to hear another theory about what this stuff means. But no matter what, I don't think it's good, and it's all creepy."

"Can you send us a scan?" Bergen asked.

"I could. But if I did, someone outside of law enforcement would see it. Our little newspaper would report it. Then we'd lose whoever's doing this. The girl, whoever she is, will be hurt, moved, or murdered."

The silence in the room was tomblike, the atmosphere wary.

Kateri continued, "I don't have to tell you this needs to be quiet and kept in the department. But I need you to look. Really look."

Heads nodded.

Bergen asked, "In town? Out of town?"

Kateri showed her empty hands. "Cordelia doesn't know. She only knows it's in our area of responsibility. Have any of you seen anything that, looking back, made you wonder?"

Heads shook.

"Isn't what Cordelia's doing illegal?" Moen asked.

"Yes, but I'm not arresting her," Kateri said, "and neither are you."

"I don't like being spied on by Crazy Cordelia," Officer Eli Weaver said.

Then stop cheating on your wife and you won't have anything to hide. Kateri didn't say that out loud. She simply thought it forcefully.

Bergen stood. "Sheriff Kwinault brought us something that needs investigation. Now that we know something is out there, we can watch for suspicious behavior. C'mon, guys, let's go."

Kateri was glad he'd stepped up, glad the guys respected him enough to accept his judgment on her judgment. Because today she didn't think she had it in her to enforce her authority. Wearily she got to her feet and groped for her walking stick.

"Where are you going?" Chippen asked.

"I've been on duty for about sixty hours, and I'm going home to bed."

Moen grinned. "I'll come and tuck you in."

She stopped. She turned on him. "Tell me you never say stuff like that to other women, because this sheriff's department doesn't need a sexual harassment suit."

"I don't. It's just you, and everyone knows you're not—" He stopped.

She looked at him.

He stepped back. He flushed, his fair skin turning the same color as his orange freckles and carroty hair.

The officers backed up, clumped together into a protective little group.

She looked them over, snorted derisively, and walked out, through the courthouse, out the front door, and down the street toward her apartment six blocks away.

Five minutes ago, she had been dragging. Now she was so mad she could walk to Japan.

Damn them. Damn them all! Did they really think she was no longer quite a woman? Sure, she had more artificial parts than a Barbie doll. And no, she couldn't have children. And yes, if she ever got the chance to have sex again, she hoped to hell she didn't pop an artificial joint out of place. But goddamn it, she was thirty-four years old, and that was too young to be declared a nonplayer.

Behind her, she heard running footsteps.

Bergen swung into place beside her. "Sheriff Kwinault, can I talk to you?"

"Yes. You can talk." Truth to tell, she thought he would be a good sheriff. She would vote for him except she'd be better. Let's face it: she had way more real-life experience than any one person needed—or wanted.

She'd grown up on the reservation, run wild with the other Native American kids, gone to school in Virtue Falls, discovered what prejudice was here . . . She'd seen the bigger world, too, faced prejudice on so many levels she had faced only one choice: grow strong or crumple.

She had grown strong. She'd worked and studied, been accepted to the Coast Guard Academy, been assigned to various U.S. facilities and finally brought back to Virtue Falls as commander.

God, that had been a great job—until the earthquake.

She didn't remember a time when she didn't know the legend of a monster frog god that crouched off the coast. The elders said that when it woke and hopped up to taste the sun, the earth broke apart. On that day of the frog god's leap, the ocean would rise to eat the land.

One summer day four years ago the frog god had jumped. The ocean rose. Kateri saved her men and two of the Coast Guard cutters.

And she had died. She had descended to the depths. She had seen *him,* the frog god, green and merciless. He had taken her in his claws and devoured her, made her a part of himself . . . given her gifts she didn't want. Then he brought her back to life and flung her toward the shore.

Months of surgeries, pain, and rehabilitation had followed, as well as a court-martial for the loss of the cutter. She had had to accept a medical discharge. She had learned to sit in a wheelchair, to accept the help of others. She, who had been the epitome of strength and beauty, had had to wait and ask and brood about the inequity of life. Finally she fought—to stand on her feet, to earn a living, to live alone and un-aided.

She had secured a job as the Virtue Falls librarian for less than min-imum wage. In the end, she liked the librarian gig—she learned to deal with situations as serious, scary, funny, and diverse as wife beat-ings, overdue books, and poopie diaper leaks. She had changed from a woman who had believed she controlled her own destiny to a woman who seized opportunity. That opportunity was the job of sheriff. She wanted it. She would be good at it. Hell, she *was* good at it. Plus it paid considerably better than town librarian.

She said to Bergen, her fellow officer and opponent, "Thank you for supporting me back there."

"That's what I want to talk about. You know a few of the guys joke about you being all woo-woo."

She came to a halt. The air around her chilled. "They joke? Do they?"

"After you walked out, they speculated on whether or not you had had a vision and that was why we were off on a wild goose chase."

She turned on him like a windup toy soldier. "They believe I would waste law enforcement resources on a wild goose chase?"

"It has occurred to me, too. So I guess my question is—are we doing this because logically you think that someone out there needs help, or because you have a gut feeling?"

Maybe he was oblivious to her irritation. Or maybe he was merely dogged in his pursuit of the truth. Or maybe . . . he was subtly undermining her. "Does your continued support depend on my answer?"

"No. You're in charge."

She could almost hear him think, *For the moment.* Her humiliation at being labeled asexual and her rage at having her motivation questioned made her temper slip and her judgment fail.

Sometimes the frog god's gifts made revenge all too easy.

She wrapped her fingers around Bergen's wrist, called on the frog god . . . and for the merest second, the earth shook.

CHAPTER EIGHTEEN

Bergen's eyes grew wide. He tore his wrist out of her grasp and he jumped, literally jumped, away from her.

"Woo-woo." She made another one of those toy soldier turns and marched away. Or she would have marched, except her knees were giving out and she had to lean heavily on her walking stick. She could feel Bergen staring at her back.

She'd only ever done that trick with one other person, and he'd ended up in an asylum being treated for insanity. Not that he hadn't deserved it. But Bergen did not. His question was—probably—well meant. A warning of the challenges she faced.

Now she would have to wait to see what he would do.

Two blocks down the street, Coast Guard Lieutenant Commander Luis Sanchez swung into place beside her. "Hi, Kateri. You cause that tremor?"

She lifted her free hand and looked heavenward.

"What?" he asked.

Luis was handsome, smart, an up-and-coming officer in the Coast Guard. He was also the guy who had wanted to sleep with her even after she'd been broken and put back together.

First she had rejected him. Then she'd changed her mind. By then it was too late. He was involved with another woman, the young, sweet, ambitious, and talented businesswoman Sienna Monahan. Proof positive a woman couldn't leave a good-looking guy alone for a single minute.

Now here he was, strolling along beside her not ten minutes after Moen had insulted her.

"So did you? Cause that tremor?" He caught Kateri's elbow and turned her to face him. "Never mind. I can see you did. Your hair is glossy, your skin is glowing, and your walk is jaunty. You don't feel a bit of pain, do you?"

"I'm fine."

"You're better than fine. You're a glorious Indian maiden."

That stung. "Native American and I'm not a maiden, thank you very much. I used to have a perfectly adequate sex life."

"*Chica,* if your sex life could be described as perfectly adequate— it wasn't."

She laughed and relaxed. She needed to remember that Luis was not Moen; even after the tsunami, Luis had pursued her. "Who knows? Maybe after being eaten by the frog god and reborn, I am a virgin again."

"You think?" Luis looked alarmed.

She laughed harder. "Anything is possible. Every time I make the earth move, more of me is mended."

"Then why don't you make it move all the time?"

She slowed and tried to articulate what she sensed. "A part of me is the frog god. A part of the frog god is me. Whenever I invoke him, whenever I bring him up from the depths, he owns a little more of me. He is a powerful deity and if I'm not careful I fear he could own . . . all of me." She looked straight at Luis.

He crossed himself and she knew that in her eyes he glimpsed the cold, green soul of the god.

"Anyway, that's why. So what are you doing? Walking me home?" She was kidding.

But he agreed. "Yes, but I didn't think you'd want me to hang around outside the courthouse so I sat in the park until I saw you come out and then I went the long way around to join you."

"Because you didn't want to be seen with me?" Moen had really gotten to her; she needed to knock off the sensitivity.

"Because I figured *you* didn't want to be seen with *me*. You're the one who's running for office. I didn't think having a boyfriend hanging around would be good for your tough sheriff image."

"You're my boyfriend?"

"I could be."

"No, you couldn't. You're living with Sienna."

"Not anymore, I'm not."

Oh, ho. No wonder Luis had put in an appearance, swaggering and cocky. "Look. If you need a shoulder to cry on, that's fine, but I don't appreciate you using me on the rebound."

"I'm not on the rebound. This has been coming on for quite a while, and I moved out a month ago."

Kateri stared at Luis. "What happened? She's gorgeous."

"She's also controlling. She schemes. She's got grand plans for what she wants to do in Virtue Falls and when I say I'm in the Coast Guard and I'll get transferred and we can't stay together, she says I should quit."

"But you've worked hard to take a command!"

"She doesn't care. She doesn't consider the Coast Guard to be a real branch of the military. She's . . ." He shook his head. "I don't know how else to say it. She wants me on her terms, and if I stick with her, she'll win. By any means, but she will win."

Kateri turned and started walking again. "Wow. I never saw sweet little Sienna in quite those terms."

Again Luis fell in beside her. "Since I left her, I feel like I can stand straight again, think straight again. I thought of you and how I'd like us to have a second chance."

Kateri opened her mouth with every intention of saying something wise, restrained, and mature.

But this was Luis. He'd stayed at the hospital when everyone thought she would die. He'd held her hand after the joint replacements. He'd pushed her in the wheelchair when the doctors said she would never walk again. Plus . . . it was Luis, and with black, close-cut, curly hair, dark eyes, brown complexion, movie star cheekbones, and a resolute chin. At one time they had kissed and she had wanted him. Now he was talking about a second chance. For them.

She needed to think about this. "Hang on, I have to pick up Lacey." Luis waited on the sidewalk, hands in pockets, while Kateri climbed the steps to Irene Golobovitch's tiny apartment, three doors down from hers, knocked, and listened to the ecstatic barking.

How Lacey knew Kateri's knock from any other, Kateri did not understand, but although the pretty blond cocker spaniel adored Mrs. Golobovitch, she was never quite content unless she was with Kateri. Kateri had rescued her; Lacey remembered, and every day, she repaid Kateri in love, loyalty, and a fiercely protective spirit that hid beneath a girlish charm. God bless her. When the elderly woman answered the door, Lacey raced out and danced around Kateri with exuberant joy.

"How was she?" Kateri leaned down, not too far or she would fall over, and dangled her fingers so Lacey could rub herself against them.

"She is always a sweetheart." Even after forty-five years in Virtue Falls, Mrs. Golobovitch sported a heavy eastern European accent.

"Thank you for caring for her. Can I bring her back tomorrow?"

Mrs. Golobovitch clasped her hands at her bosom. "She's always welcome. In fact, if you ever wish to leave her here permanently—"

Both Kateri and Lacey stopped and stared in horror.

Kateri recovered and straightened. "Thank you, Mrs. Golobovitch, but Lacey is my better half."

Mrs. Golobovitch gave Luis a good looking-over. She considered the dog. She smiled. "We shall have to find you a husband, yes? Every woman needs a man to take care of her." Apparently Mrs. Golobovitch also sported an Old World attitude toward romance. "I'm here for her when you want me."

"I appreciate that," Kateri said.

Lacey pressed close to her ankle and marched down to the street. She took a moment to greet Luis—he was always a favorite with every female, human or canine—before returning to Kateri and sticking close.

Kateri appreciated that. She needed to have some creature who treasured her above all others. Then she tried to decide what it meant, that she was more worried about her dog's affections than about Luis's. Probably Moen was right: while she was busy being stitched back together, her sexuality had died from lack of attention.

Luis stopped at the bottom of her steps. "What do you think?"

"About what?" She started to climb toward her door.

He caught her hand and stopped her. "About you and me and second chances?"

Right. "That I am too sleep-deprived to make important decisions, so I will go in and we'll discuss this another time."

"All right. But add this to your decision-making process." He stepped up and kissed her, a nice hands-off kiss of lips only. Turning, he walked away, whistling.

The kiss was nice. Not too intimate, yet clearly yearning. But she didn't like the whistling. That felt . . . cocky.

Later. She would worry about him later.

She headed inside. She fed Lacey. She brushed her dog and brushed her teeth. She collapsed on her bed and let Lacey snuggle close.

Kateri could change her clothes when she woke up. For now, a full night's sleep was all she needed. If only Virtue Falls would cooperate.

CHAPTER NINETEEN

Jacob lived like a vampire, rising after sundown to eat and drink, to sit in the recliner and look at his world through the narrow lens of his shattered shotgun house.

For the first three days, things got worse rather than better. Somebody—Web?—removed the plaster ceiling and insulation, exposing the roof trusses and the interior of the attic. Looking up, Jacob could see moonlight through the shingles.

Not surprisingly, the next day Moore insisted Jacob come out and sign off on a new roof.

Steel framing rose quickly, yet it offered no shield; without wallboard or siding, Jacob was still exposed to the world. The electricians returned; apparently their first efforts were nothing more than emergency measures, for now wires ran through the studs and the attic. Pipes arrived, and everywhere he looked, they moved like crooked mazes through the walls. A new water heater arrived and sat waiting to be put into place. His refrigerator filled and emptied seemingly by itself as the construction workers used it for their lunches and the grocery delivery boy placed Jacob's order inside rather than on the porch.

Jacob began to understand the nighttime rhythms of the neighborhood, too: who went to bed and when, who stayed up too late, which houses remained dark and empty, which houses burst with life.

He had seen no sign of Madeline Hewitson, nor could he watch her silhouette as she worked at her desk. She had bought a blackout shade and installed it.

If it was possible for anything to make him happy, that was it. Happy.

On night five, Jacob came out at zero twenty-one hundred hours. He sat. He stared. He breathed as the air turned fresh and sweet, as the earth exhaled the scent of grass and the asphalt cooled. He watched the ghosts dance across the broken porch and into his living room; he recognized their faces, and he grieved.

That felt good; his ghosts deserved his grief. He owed them his grief.

Midnight came and went, and at zero two hundred his solitude was broken by a man, middle-aged, tall, and broad-bellied, climbing up the makeshift steps and into the living room. The stranger didn't notice Jacob sitting immobile in the dark. He walked to the kitchen table and unrolled the construction plans. He spread them out, leaned over them, pulled a flashlight from his pocket, and shone it on the first page.

In exasperation, Jacob asked, "Who are *you*?"

Unperturbed, the man looked up over the top of his wire-frame reading glasses. "I'm Dr. Frownfelter, your neighbor."

Crap. A doctor. "Doesn't anyone on this street ever sleep?"

"I'm the physician here on the peninsula. I finished with a forty-eight-hour shift at the hospital and a stopover at the Honor Mountain Memory Care Facility. I'm just now getting home and I thought I'd come by to see what Berk has planned for your place." Frownfelter looked at his massive wristwatch. "It's two A.M. I should be the only one up. What's your excuse?"

Jacob figured what he was doing up was none of Frownfelter's business. He got up, rummaged in the refrigerator, brought out two white bread sandwiches, and offered one to Frownfelter.

Frownfelter grimaced, rolled up the plans, put them back on the table, and took the sandwich.

Jacob sank down into the piece-of-shit recliner. "Where do you live?"

"Next door." Dr. Frownfelter waved a vague hand toward the corner.

In an obnoxiously knowledgeable tone, Jacob said, "So your house is one of the two largest in the neighborhood and was built for a sawmill superintendent."

Dr. Frownfelter grinned, perched on the edge of the trunk, and placed the sandwich beside him. "You've been talking to Candy Butenschoen."

Jacob paused, his sandwich halfway to his mouth. *"Candy?"*

"I went to school with her. I promise that's her name. She hasn't changed much." With the edge of his right hand, he chopped at his left palm, and in a staccato voice, he said, "Clean house. Clean yard. Clean conscience."

"So she has a clean conscience?"

"Indeed."

"She's a bully."

"That, too. But she doesn't see it that way."

As if they had roused her with their conversation, her kitchen light flashed on, and Mrs. Butenschoen rushed to the cupboard beside her sink.

Jacob sat up straight. "That's not keeping with her schedule. She works in her yard until nine, goes inside, washes her hands at her kitchen sink, and right after the news, her lights go out."

"So, unlike other disreputable folks, she is never up in the middle of the night?" Dr. Frownfelter watched as she pulled a bottle out of the cabinet, shook out some pills, and swallowed them with a glass of water. "Hmmm."

"What does that mean?"

"Just hmmm." He unwrapped his sandwich and took a bite, but not once did he look away from Candy Butenschoen.

Clad in that atrocious pink robe, Mrs. Butenschoen stood looking out her window, unaware that two men watched her with very real interest. At one point she rubbed her forehead with both hands. Finally she put the bottle back in the cupboard and turned away from the window. The light went out.

All was quiet again.

Frownfelter stood, walked to the roll of paper towels and yanked a couple free, then came back and offered one to Jacob. "Napkins on a roll."

Jacob took it and almost smiled. That's what his dad used to call them.

"Have you seen our resident fashion model?" Frownfelter asked.

"Who?"

"Chantal Filips." Dr. Frownfelter flapped his paper towel toward the street. "She lives in the house next to Madeline Hewitson. She disappears on shoots for weeks at a time. When she comes back, she's not what you'd call friendly, but she's good to look at. She comes and goes late at night, too."

"Why late?"

"She dates. Remember dating?"

"Vaguely." From about a million years ago. Jacob looked toward Maddie's house. His most recent date had been a haircut at Maddie's house. Jacob eyed Maddie's blackout shades. He didn't want to talk about her. He didn't want to remember her.

"Have you met the Franklins?"

"No."

"Do you know who they are?"

"No."

"Young family, nice kids. Kids accidently broke my window with their baseball, tried to run away. Well, hell, I wasn't home when they did it, but of course Candy saw the whole thing. Kids had to come and apologize and they're working off the cost by weeding my yard."

"Under Candy's supervision?"

"God, no. I wouldn't do that to anyone. She'd have them out there with tweezers. Who else is up late?"

The good doctor was one nosy son of a bitch. . . . Was Dr. Frownfelter specifically asking about *her*? About Maddie? Or was Jacob being too suspicious?

Then Dayton Floren's car drove up, and Jacob was rescued. "Him. The guy who wanted me to sell my house."

Dr. Frownfelter did a double take worthy of another viewing. "He wants you to sell your house? That's interesting. He talked to me about selling my house, too. Seemed to think the doctor in town should own a fancy house."

Jacob examined Dr. Frownfelter. His clothes were rumpled and baggy. His white, thinning hair looked as if it had been styled by a nesting bird. The bags under his eyes drooped like a basset hound's. He finished his sandwich in two huge bites. Jacob couldn't see him living in high style. "Dude shows up occasionally, usually late, pulls a bag out of his car, goes in. But he's always gone when I come out the next night."

"So he doesn't really live here."

Jacob shrugged.

Dr. Frownfelter dug a bottle of Tums out of his pocket and shook a couple into his palm. "You want some?"

"I don't have heartburn."

"That's good. But you could probably use the calcium."

"I'll eat cottage cheese."

"See that you do."

Yeah, Frownfelter was a doctor, all right. Couldn't mind his own business. Had the formidable presence to make himself heard. Jacob moved to distract him. "Every night, a cop does a drive-past."

"Which cop?"

"Varies. Sometimes Sheriff Kwinault. She always waves like she sees me. Mostly it's the red-haired kid. He's oblivious." Oblivious to Jacob, anyway. He never took his gaze off Madeline Hewitson's house.

"Young Rupert Moen."

Drawing on his gut feeling, Jacob said, "He's not going to make it as a cop."

Dr. Frownfelter peered at him. "Very astute. His dad is a cop, so Rupert was expected to go into the profession, too. He's not happy. Whether he'll work up the nerve to try something different . . ." He shrugged. "I always see Madeline Hewitson's light on when I come home."

The two men gazed across the street at the window leaking light from the sides.

"She's awake at night," Jacob said. And, "She sleepwalks."

"Not surprising, after her kind of trauma."

"You her doctor?"

"Around here, I'm most people's doctor."

Which wasn't an answer, but probably was as much as Dr. Frownfelter could say. "Did she tell you about . . . what happened to her?"

"God, no. She's famous around town for being close-mouthed about her past. And her present, for that matter, although that's a matter of public record." Humor laced Frownfelter's voice. "Anyone who can make Candy Butenschoen fall out of her rut and into a frenzy is a friend of mine."

Right on cue, Maddie's front porch light flashed on, her door opened, and she came shooting out, her hair standing up, her eyes wide and cartoon-terrified. She was visibly trembling, and she slammed the door behind her as if to keep the nightmares at bay.

At the same time, Mrs. Nyback let Spike out. Spike went berserk, wiggling through the fence—true to Moore's prediction, Spike's entry to Mrs. Butenschoen's had been repaired—planting himself about three feet away from Maddie and barking furiously. Maddie stared at the puny excuse of a dog as if she weren't sure he was real. Then she sat down on the lawn and held out her hand. It took a while, but Spike finally stopped yapping and sniffed her fingers. She scratched under his chin.

Spike stuck out his head, as if in pleasure. Then in a reversal that surprised even Jacob, the little beast bit her.

She yelped and yanked her fingers away.

As if he were the one whose trust had been betrayed, Spike started barking again and only left when Mrs. Nyback called him.

Jacob passed judgment. "That's a ghastly little dog."

"It's all Mrs. Nyback has."

"I got it. We don't want to kill it."

"That's it in a nutshell."

Maddie stood up, climbed over her picket fence, and strolled down the street toward the ocean.

Jacob ignored the urge to follow her.

She wasn't sleepwalking. If the woman wanted to go for a walk at two thirty in the morning, who was he to stop her?

Besides, Dr. Frownfelter wandered to the front of the house and watched, then turned and came back.

"Did she head over the cliff?" Jacob asked.

"No, she took a right, headed toward town on the cliff walk." Frownfelter rubbed his hands over his red-rimmed eyes. "Madeline Hewitson's brother is an author. Have you read him?"

"No."

"Scared the hell out of me, but I was too wrapped up in the story to put it down. Andrew Hewitson must have been interviewing her for the info, because I can see the fingerprint of her terror on the pages."

"She told me she wrote books, too. Or she draws graphic novels. Or something."

"Maybe so, but Andrew is clearly the hand at the wheel. The books are written by a man. They look at horror without flinching. They are filled with dreadful anticipation, mutilation, and death. You ought to download one."

"I've seen mutilation and death. I don't need to read about it."

"Sometimes it helps to know the experience has been shared by others."

Jacob felt the rise of irritation. No, of fury. He knew better than to think he could have a normal conversation with a doctor. Nosy, all-knowing, interfering bastards, every one. "I don't have an e-reader."

"With the right app, you can read on your tablet or your computer."

"I don't have a tablet. I don't have a computer. I don't have an Internet connection."

Dr. Frownfelter could not have looked more appalled. "How do you live in the modern world?"

"I don't."

With a physician's assurance, Dr. Frownfelter said, "The time is now. You're not an old man. So start." He hefted himself off the trunk. "I'll bring over one of the hardcovers. You can read that. In the meantime—you're not dead. Act like it." He stomped off to get the book.

Jacob went into his bedroom, locked the door, and knelt in the corner in the dark.

The neighbor's dog bit her & she kept trying to pet it. She's pathetic in her need for affection.

Dog bit me. I drop-kicked that little fucker across the yard.

CHAPTER TWENTY

In his dream, Jacob heard sirens, softly at first, then louder, shrieking their message.

GET OUT GET OUT GET OUT GET OUT GET OUT

He sweated and groaned.

Dr. Kim is coming. He's coming.

He's here!

Jacob found himself on his feet, staring into the darkness of his bedroom, sweaty and anguished.

He had fallen asleep.

But he still heard sirens. On the street. Police sirens.

This was his home in Virtue Falls. He was at home. Not in Korea. Not . . .

My God, what had Maddie done now?

He didn't care. Unless she'd driven into his house again.

He knew she hadn't, she didn't have a car, but he opened the door and walked into his living room.

A different nightmare billowed toward him on a cloud of black smoke and orange flame. Something was on fire. His kitchen was on fire. His house plans. The wooden table . . .

The sirens screamed. Closer. Turning onto the street. Sirens flashing, red and blue and . . . not white. Not spinning white lights that looked so much like a death he welcomed.

Jacob clutched at his head.

The roof. They needed to get to the roof. His kids needed to get to the roof. Would they all make it? Would they survive? Would they be trapped and die?

A hulking figure appeared out of the smoke. "Sir, this way!"

No. He wanted to stay, to die here, to sacrifice himself for his kids.

"Sir, I'm Peyton Bailey, one of the Virtue Falls firefighters. Follow me!"

But Brandon was shot. Jacob had to get him out. Jacob had to save him.

The figure took off his mask, stuck it under his arm, and shouted, "Sir, please, your home is on fire. Let me help you!"

The smoke cleared for a second. Jacob saw a young man's face topped by wavy blond hair.

Brandon had black hair. Not blond. And no gear had protected him from the fire, the flames, the bullets that tore through his flesh.

Jacob snapped back to reality. "I can take care of myself." He inhaled smoke and paint fumes. He choked, coughed.

Bailey put his mask back on, took Jacob's arm, and led him toward the front of the house, to the porch, out of danger, and into the chaos of fire engines, shouting firefighters, surging hoses, flashing lights, sirens, and neighbors. Curiosity-seekers. A carnival atmosphere pervaded the air, an excitement brought by the danger of a fire and the daring of the men who fought it. From blocks around, Virtue Falls citizens were watching, gossiping, staring. At him.

What were they doing here? It was still dark. It was still night. Why weren't they in bed? Hadn't Jacob already played this scene?

Bailey said, "There you go, sir. Get some oxygen. Down there!" He pointed toward the ambulance parked at the curb.

"No." Jacob was not walking into the crowd.

"Move out of the way, sir, so we can save your house!" the fire chief shouted. "Bailey!"

The boy joined the other firemen.

Someone shone spotlights inside to give the firefighters illumination.

One caught Jacob and he blinked, momentarily blinded by the brightness.

Deliberately the firefighters dragged the hoses under Jacob's feet so that Jacob had to jump away, onto the ground.

Immediately an EMT took his arm. "Sir, are you hurt?"

"No."

"Let's give you some oxygen."

"No." Jacob was standing in his yard. On the grass. His sanctuary was burning. People stared. People crowded the street. Mrs. Butenschoen in her pink bathrobe. Dayton Floren in his suit. The Franklins and their two oldest children—the toddler must still be asleep. Across the street, Spike was barking and Jacob could see Mrs. Nyback's dim outline holding the tiny, hostile dog.

Jacob tugged at the saggy neckline of his T-shirt. Too many people. He couldn't *breathe*.

The EMT tugged him toward the ambulance. "Here's the oxygen," he said, placing a mask over Jacob's face.

Jacob pushed it off.

"Are you claustrophobic? Here, you hold it. Breathe, then take it away."

Jacob didn't want to. But it helped. It did. And he noticed that having the mask over his mouth meant he could hide.

Maddie was crazy. She really was Mad Maddie.

Lit by shifting spotlights and flickering flame, Sheriff Kwinault loomed out of the darkness. He stared. Tonight, her black hair was loose around her shoulders, her bronze skin absorbed the crowd's elation, and he saw her as she had been before the accident that had broken her body. Beauty and strength cloaked her; was he seeing her true form? Or was this an illusion of night and crisis?

She seemed unaware and she sounded normal as hell. "What happened?"

"I woke up and my house was on fire."

"Did you set it?"

Of course she would ask that. "No."

"Was it possibly set by faulty wiring? Maybe something the electricians did without the proper precautions?"

He thought back on his impressions as he had been rushed through the smoke. "Unlikely."

"Do you think someone deliberately set it?"

He knew who she meant. "Possible." *Maddie made me talk.* But even he knew that wasn't a crime.

Her red-haired deputy joined her. Rupert Moen.

Officer Moen nodded, spoke to him. "Hi, Mr. Denisov, sorry to see this happen. Man, you have the worst luck of anyone I know."

"Moen, shut up," Sheriff Kwinault said.

Officer Moen did.

"Who called it in?" Jacob asked.

More light flooded his yard; now he could see that weariness rimmed Sheriff Kwinault's eyes, and she leaned heavily on her stick. "Who do you think?"

"Mrs. Butenschoen."

"Right."

The neighbors were pressing closer.

This was worse than the first time, because now he knew them. They wanted to talk to him, exchange information, find out how he felt, what he was going to do.

"Madeline Hewitson is conspicuously absent." Sheriff Kwinault turned to Officer Moen. "Where's Maddie Hewitson?"

"In the house?" Moen seemed uncertain.

"You don't know?" Sheriff Kwinault sounded exasperated. "I thought you were parked at the end of the street *for a reason*."

Moen hung his head. "I don't know where she is. I fell asleep."

"Go to her house and see what you can discover!" Sheriff Kwinault turned back to Jacob. "Excuse me. Mrs. Butenschoen is summoning me." She stalked away, leaving Jacob alone by the ambulance. He groped for a seat on the bumper, put the oxygen mask over his face, and ignored the murmurs of curiosity and speculation. About him. About Mad Maddie. These people assumed she had done it. Just assumed. Probably she had. But it wasn't their business. They should go away.

Dr. Frownfelter wandered over, clad in a tattered navy blue robe and striped pajamas. "Damn it. I just got to sleep."

Me, too. And this is the price I pay. "Where did you leave the construction plans?"

"On the table. Held down by the book." Frownfelter leaped toward Jacob's house. "You set my book on fire? You could have simply not read it!"

Jacob laughed shortly. He coughed. He pressed the oxygen mask to his face.

So Mad Maddie wasn't the only suspect. How acute of Frownfelter.

Frownfelter took an audible breath, then cursed loudly enough that Mrs. Butenschoen's disapproval zoomed in on him. "Sorry, Denisov, that was uncalled for."

Jacob waved a dismissive hand and sucked in the oxygen.

The firemen had the fire contained now. The flames were dying and so was the excitement. The Franklins wandered back up the street to their house.

"Where are you going to go?" Frownfelter asked.

Jacob swung the mask away. "Go?"

"Your house was on fire. If nothing else, the place reeks of smoke. Surely you can't intend to stay!"

Jacob surveyed the interior of the house. The kitchen table was a charred pile of sticks. But except for the soot left behind by the smoke and maybe damage to the wooden floor, nothing else was harmed. Much. "I'm staying."

"My God, you people are stubborn." Dayton Floren arrived, looking remarkably fresh considering the hour. "It's like you're the Pilgrims and you've landed on Plymouth Rock."

Like an annoying, high-pitched mosquito, Mrs. Butenschoen buzzed up. "We like our neighborhood, Mr. Floren, and despite all the terrible things that have occurred lately, we will remain loyal to it. Isn't that right, Mr. Denisov?"

To shut out the sight of her, Jacob put the oxygen mask over his eyes.

"The neighborhood is full of old houses and weird people. Who could want to live here?" Dayton Floren asked.

"Once we find out who did this, we will have peace and quiet once more. I told Sheriff Kwinault who lit this fire," Mrs. Butenschoen said. "She needs look no farther than Madeline Hewitson!"

"You're sure of that, Candy?" Dr. Frownfelter sounded tired and sarcastic. "Because that's quite an accusation to make."

"Well, who else? The girl is crazy, we all know that, and—" Abruptly, Mrs. Butenschoen's voice failed her.

Having that female shut up was enough of a surprise to open Jacob's eyes.

A woman made her way through the crowd. Tall, gorgeous. In a short black dress that looked as if it had been sprayed on. Wearing platform heels that added three inches to her already formidable height.

This was the woman from across the street.

The firefighters stopped in midmotion.

Dr. Frownfelter almost drooled on his shoes.

Dayton Floren straightened his shoulders.

Mrs. Butenschoen was short and middle-aged, and standing in this woman's shadow, she seemed insignificant.

The magnificent female thrust her hand at Jacob. "I'm Chantal Filips."

The neighbor from across the street. The fashion model. He didn't like her. He ignored the hand, ignored her.

She moved closer, wrapped those fingers around his shoulder. She had a warm, firm grip and a warm, firm voice. "You've had bad luck, haven't you. First Mad Maddie drives into your house and now this arson. Do you know why she focused on you in particular? Do you think she's obsessed with you?"

Chantal fired questions as if they were weapons. Was she a reporter?

No, not a reporter, because she didn't wait for his answers. She kept talking. "Some people are like that. You're a celebrity and she's crazy. That's a dangerous combination."

This woman had Maddie tried and convicted before the fire was completely out. "Maybe you did it," he said.

Chantal reared back, insulted. "Me? I didn't drive into your house."

"Doesn't mean that you're not an arsonist."

She bent down to his level. In a calm voice that contained a stern threat, she said, "I would appreciate it if you didn't start that rumor."

He looked straight in her perfectly made-up smoky-lidded eyes. "If you can start a rumor, so can I."

Something caught his attention, a surreptitious movement at the edge of crowd. He forgot Chantal Filips and glared.

Rumpled and with her patented appearance of sleepy confusion, Maddie looked back at him. "What happened?"

Maddie's appearance gave Mrs. Butenschoen a target. The pink-bathrobed female stepped up to Maddie and pointed one finger in her face and with the other hand indicated the destruction. "You burned down his house!"

"What?" Maddie shook her head as if trying to knock wax from her ears. "I didn't burn down anyone's house! I wasn't even—"

"You did, too!" Mrs. Butenschoen was almost dancing with indignation. "Who else would have lit this poor brave veteran's house on fire?"

Her accusation of Maddie and her mixture of accolade and pity for him turned Jacob's stomach, and it seemed to him as if the atmosphere changed from the carnival of fire and excitement to an accusing mob.

Maddie looked around the circle of righteous faces. "I didn't. I wouldn't!" She looked at Jacob. "You know I wouldn't. I didn't kill you when I had the chance!"

When she was cutting his hair, she meant, but the way she phrased it didn't go down well with Chantal Filips, who said, "Wow, that's scary," or with Mrs. Butenschoen, who grasped Maddie's arm and caroled, "Sheriff Kwinault! Sheriff Kwinault! We have your arsonist right here!"

Jacob handed the oxygen mask to the EMT. Without thinking of the consequences, he prepared to stand, to intervene.

But Sheriff Kwinault had a way about her; the crowd opened to let her through. Behind her, an elderly couple followed on her heels.

Jacob sank back onto the bumper of the ambulance.

The old woman was Asian; she had once been beautiful and had easily topped five feet ten inches. Now osteoporosis and arthritis had taken its toll; her shoulders were curved, her hands warped, but her dark eyes sparked and her voice was strong when she said, "Candy, you were a bossy, obnoxious child and I am sorry to say you've grown into a bossy, obnoxious adult."

Mrs. Butenschoen tried to speak. "Mrs. Williamson, I—"

Mrs. Williamson stopped her with one raised and crooked finger. "I tried to improve your behavior in first grade, but unhappily, I do realize a child's personality is set at birth."

The old man was more frail than his wife, but like her, his voice carried. "Until we heard the sirens, Madeline was asleep on our porch swing."

As if she had a right, Mrs. Butenschoen demanded, "Why was she there so late?"

With awesome patience, Mrs. Williamson said, "Walter was up with heartburn—the man cannot eat ice cream before bedtime, but does he listen to me?"

Walter grumbled something inaudible.

Mrs. Williamson continued, "He saw her staggering along the cliff walk, half dead from fatigue. So I fetched her, we fed the poor child— she eats like she's starving!—and talked with her about her troubles until she fell asleep in the swing. Then we covered her with a blanket and left her. Not that that's any of your business, Candy."

Maddie stood on the sidelines with the tiniest of smiles on her face.

Mrs. Butenschoen glanced around, pulled herself up to her full height, which still wasn't close to Mrs. Williamson's, and said, "I think that is my business. She could have killed you!"

"I taught elementary school for forty-five years and Walter is a veteran of the Korean War. I hardly think a mere slip of a female could overpower us both." Mrs. Williamson turned to Sheriff Kwinault. "You're looking well, Kateri, dear. How are you doing?"

With that, the crisis was defused.

Dr. Frownfelter joined the conversation centered around Kateri's health.

Chantal Filips and Dayton Floren drifted away.

Mrs. Butenschoen stood as if she wanted to do something more, something to prove she had not been vanquished, but no one paid her any heed, so at last she vanished toward her house.

Officer Moen arrived to report that Madeline Hewitson was not at home. When he saw Maddie standing there, excitement lit him from the inside and he offered to walk her to her home and check it for monsters.

Maddie looked startled and wary.

Jacob wondered why the kid had suddenly become such a fan of Maddie's. Had he fallen in love? Was he like one of those people who for some sick reason offered to marry a convicted prisoner? Jacob half-way expected Maddie to appeal to him, but instead she grasped Moen's sleeve and allowed him to lead her across the street toward her house.

The EMT was putting his equipment away.

The firefighters were dousing any hot spots and writing their reports.

No one was paying any attention to Jacob. No one at all.

Silently he stood. He made his way through the dripping interior of his once-again ruined home and into his bedroom. He locked the door and figured the world could go to hell.

With or without him it always did just that.

CHAPTER TWENTY-ONE

Maddie walked into her house and turned to block the door. "Officer Moen, I appreciate you offering to check for monsters, but I'm not afraid tonight and—"

The big guy pushed his way in and headed right to her desk. He picked up one of her drawings. "You're a graphic artist, aren't you?"

She marched over and snatched it out of his hands. "Not exactly."

"Last time I was here, I saw your sketches on the desk. You're good."

She stacked the drawings and stuck them in the belly drawer. "Thank you." She didn't mean it. Officer Moen seemed like a big, bumbling, good-natured cop. But he had seen her sketches. He knew the monster that chased her. He was pushy and he had been at the end of her street, waiting to be called. . . . Was he her stalker, her tormentor? Was he one of those men who liked to frighten women?

She backed toward the front door, prepared to run.

"I want to be a graphic artist, too."

"I'm really not a graphic artist. I was just fooling around."

"Could you give me lessons?"

"No. I'm no good."

His face was flushing a mottled red. His blue eyes were bright and getting brighter. "You *are* good. That monster . . . I'll never forget what it looks like. If you won't give me lessons, would you look at my stuff? Give me advice?"

"I'm not a . . . No. Really."

"But if you looked at my drawings and you thought they were good, you could recommend me to your publishing company, right?"

"No! I don't have a publishing company! Officer Moen, are you going to check for . . . for monsters?"

"Sure." He rapidly walked the house.

She realized how well he knew the location of every room, every closet. He looked like a big, innocent kid, but she of all people knew better than to believe in appearances.

When he came back into the living room, he dug a card out of his wallet and presented it to her. "If you change your mind, you can call me anytime."

She took the card from his fingers, careful not to touch him. "I can't help you."

He opened the desk drawer and pulled out her drawings. "You can. You just won't!"

Kateri walked up Madeline Hewitson's front steps and paused outside the open door. Inside she heard two voices speaking simultaneously.

Moen was saying, "Please. Please, I promise it won't hurt and I would make it worth your while!"

Maddie was saying, "No. No, I can't. I can't do that."

Kateri stepped across the threshold, slammed her walking stick on the floor, and snapped, "Officer Rupert Moen, what are you doing?"

To her surprise and immense relief, he was standing by Maddie's desk and holding papers in his fist. He jumped, turned to face Kateri, and blushed as red as his hair.

At the sight of Kateri, Maddie closed her eyes in what looked like thankfulness, then opened them and in a bright voice said, "Thank you for escorting me home, Officer Moen. You can go now. Go *now*."

Kateri said, "Yes, Moen, go."

He looked wretched and if possible even more embarrassed, like a kid caught with his hand in the cookie jar. With one last pleading glance at Maddie, he started toward Kateri.

"Rupert, shouldn't you return those papers to Miss Hewitson?" Kateri asked.

He returned to her desk and placed the papers there, then stumbled out the door.

Whatever had been going on was probably not as bad as Kateri thought it initially sounded . . . but clearly it wasn't good. "Miss Hewitson, do you want to make a complaint about Officer Moen?"

"No. He's fine." Maddie made her statement firmly. She looked down at the business card in her hand, opened her desk drawer, and tossed the card in the far back.

That wasn't good enough. "If he's bothering you in any way, I'll take action. I won't allow him to behave in an inappropriate manner while on or off duty, and I do promise I recognize signs of guilt when I see them."

Maddie met Kateri's gaze, and for once she looked normal: mature, calm, balanced, as she always would have if terror and madness hadn't touched her life. "He just . . . he wants things and thinks I can help him. I wish I could, but I can't. I don't have the power."

That sounded very much like Moen had made an inappropriate proposition to Maddie Hewitson. But for whatever reason, Maddie was refusing to press charges, and Kateri couldn't take action until she did. "If you change your mind, call me anytime. I'll put my card on your desk." She started toward the desk, intent on leaving her card—and attempted to quickly glimpse the papers he had left behind.

Maddie hurried to intercept her and snatched the card from her fingers. "I won't change my mind. But I will call you if I need you."

So Maddie didn't want Kateri seeing what she kept on her desk. What could it be? Pornography? An accounting of drug sales? Maddie's sanity report? "Good. I look forward to hearing from you."

Maddie carefully propped Kateri's card up on her lamp. "The sun is coming up."

Kateri glanced out the window. "Yes. That happens at dawn."

Maddie grinned. "I'm going to bed."

Thinking of how little sleep she'd had in the past week, Kateri groaned and headed out the door. Behind her, she heard Maddie turn the lock. Kateri was scheduled for duty, and no matter what Maddie said, Officer Rupert Moen was about to have the facts of law enforcement life explained to him in a manner that would penetrate that thick young skull. Then, to give him some perspective on what was important in life, they would go looking for a kidnapped and abused child. God grant that they find the child before it was too late.

"For shit's sake, if I find the arsonist son of a bitch who did this, I'm going to clean his clock." Berk Moore flung up his arms and shouted, "That fucker! Do you know what kind of smoke damage we're looking at? Do you? Cleaning this place is going to suck big hairy dog dicks! Melted pipes. Melted! And look at the wiring in the attic. Compromised, every bit of it."

Electricians, plumbers, and carpenters stood staring in awe at their usually even-tempered boss.

Jacob had staggered out of his bedroom in time to witness Moore's tantrum. Wow. Just . . . wow. Good times. He hadn't seen a fit like that since . . . well, since his own last fit. He was enjoying it, so he yawned, scratched his belly, and said, "Mrs. Butenschoen won't be happy if this sets back the schedule."

"Sets back the schedule?" Moore almost frothed at the mouth. "Hell yes, it's going to set back the schedule! We're back at square one and I've got another job starting. East of town, total remodel, wealthy people who expect it done *now*. This schedule is fucked. Absolutely fucked. Might as well call Web to clean this shit up."

Web walked up off the lawn. "I'm here, Berk."

"About goddamn time. Clean all this crap up and haul it away, and start bringing in more shit to do everything over again that we already did." Moore kicked the blackened remnants of Jacob's table. "I need another set of plans printed out. Pronto!"

Unperturbed as always, Web nodded. "Will do."

"And shit son of a bitch, has anyone called that prick insurance agent Dennis Wodzicki and made a claim? Updated the claim? Whatever it is we have to do?" Moore looked at Jacob in inquiry.

Jacob shrugged. "Dunno. I went to bed." He had slept, too. Something about having his nightmares come true vanquished the worst of the terror for at least one night. He scratched again. "I've got nowhere to sit."

"No shit?" Moore was winding up again. "You might as well blow up every damned piece of furniture in here. There isn't a charity that would take any of it. Cleaners will never get the smell out. Go get a hotel, stay there until we get the worst of this scrubbed up."

"No."

"Is that all you know how to say? How about saying *yes* for a change? How about—" The house phone rang. Moore turned to stare at it; his voice got louder, if that was possible. "How the hell can every damned thing in this house fall apart and that damned phone still works?"

"They don't build 'em like they used to." Jacob would have been enjoying this more if it hadn't been ten o'clock in the morning. That was his mother calling. He wasn't going to pick up the phone.

Moore, good ol' pissed-off Moore, marched over and picked up the phone. "Mrs. Denisov, how are you?" He listened for about half a second before saying, "Someone set fire to Jacob's home last night. He's fine, but we've got blistered paint on the cheapo plywood kitchen cabinets, the whole goddamn kitchen has to be replaced, and he's standing there scratching his nuts like he's looking for gold."

Jacob opened his arms so his hands were extended far from his body. He glared meaningfully at Moore.

Moore grinned callously back at him. "So I guess he's done being depressed and he's on to being something else. Horny. Or maybe perverted. That's progress, right?" Moore watched a truck come around the corner—a truck advertising the New Age Furniture Store. "I've got to go. We've got a delivery coming. Next time you call, maybe Jacob will pull his fingers out of his sweatpants long enough to talk to you." He slammed down the phone.

"Thanks, Berk," Jacob said with a fair amount of irony.

"You're welcome, Jakie," Moore said with an equal amount of sarcasm.

The truck pulled up to the curb. Two guys got out, opened the back, unloaded a footstool and a black leather recliner—not just any leather recliner, one of those expensive Scandinavian recliners that rocked, had a drink holder in the arm and, if the right music was played, could line dance—and carried it up into the sooty living room. They put the new recliner down, moved the old recliner out of the house, moved the new recliner into its place.

One of the men—Leo, if the stitching on his overalls was to be believed—looked around until he located Jacob. "Mr. Denisov? Would you sign here, please?"

Jacob took the iPad and signed on the line.

Leo took the iPad, read the form, and recited, "This is for you, a gift from Mr. Wodzicki of Wodzicki Insurance, and he hopes you get many years of enjoyment from sitting in it."

Jacob's eyes narrowed on the small brass plaque attached to the back of the chair.

Leo pulled his phone out of his pocket and found his camera app. "Mr. Denisov, if you'd sit in the recliner, Mr. Wodzicki would like a picture for his collection." He held up his phone as if expecting Jacob to obey like a well-trained dog.

Instead, Jacob got on one knee and read the inscription: *A gift from insurance agent Dennis Wodzicki to our local military hero, Jacob Denisov. We will never forget.*

In a determinedly level voice, Jacob asked, "Has Mr. Wodzicki taken a photo of the plaque?"

"Yes, sir," Leo said. "He's going to frame it and the photo of you in the chair and put it on his wall."

Web groaned.

Moore snorted.

Jacob smiled. "I'm afraid that won't be possible."

Leo wasn't the brightest bulb in the box; he couldn't figure out why all the construction men took a step back. "Why not?"

Jacob sucked in a deep breath of fresh morning air. Standing, he grabbed the chair by the back and one arm and swung it up over his head. Walking to the edge of the makeshift porch, he roared like a berserker and flung it as hard as he could into the middle of the yard.

Leo's cohort stood there, wide-eyed, while Leo sputtered, "But . . . you . . . he . . . the chair . . . publicity . . ."

Jacob turned toward him, clenched his fists, flexed his shoulders, and roared again.

Leo's cohort broke and ran.

Leo shook his head and said, "I'm going to be in trouble."

Moore said, "Kid, if you don't get out of here, you're going to be dead."

Jacob stalked toward Leo.

Leo looked out at the chair, catawampus in the lawn. He looked at Jacob. He fled, jumping off the porch, and bounding toward the truck.

Jacob stopped, breathing hard.

As if nothing untoward had happened, Web wandered over. "You signed for that, right?"

"The chair?" Jacob nodded.

"So it's yours, right?"

Jacob lowered his head and glared evilly at Web.

Nothing ever seemed to perturb Web. Probably because he towered over everyone. "Here's what I'm thinkin'. The women's shelter could use something like that, a nice chair for nursing mothers and abused old ladies. What say I take it down there and donate it in your name?"

Jacob didn't even have to think about it. "And the footstool."

"And the footstool. On the way back, I'll stop by my mother-in-law's and grab the old recliner off her front porch. It's my dad-in-law's. The family got him a new recliner for Christmas. He put the new one in the living room and the old one out where he could sit in the summer, look through the window, see the TV, and watch baseball. He loves that thing. But he's the softest-hearted guy in the world. If I tell him the chair is for a veteran, he'll offer it gladly. And if you take it, you'll make my mother-in-law happy because that broken recliner sits there lopsided on her porch, and makes them look like white trash." Web's mouth twitched as if he wanted to grin. "Her words, not mine."

Jacob thought it over. Seemed like an honest proposition, one that screwed that pompous windbag Dennis Wodzicki, gave homeless women someplace to rest their weary bones, did a favor for Web's mother-in-law, and at the same time got him—Jacob—someplace to sit. "Yes."

"Good deal." Web grabbed the footstool and headed toward his truck.

"All right, everybody, we got another crisis solved." Moore sounded so reasonable anyone hearing him would think he didn't know a single curse word. "Let's repair the damage from last night before Mrs. Butenschoen comes over and gives us one of her famous pies. So to speak."

Laughter from the men.

"You!" Moore pointed at one of the framers. "Build us a kitchen table. Mr. Denisov might not give a damn, but we all use it for lunch and I want to be able to spread out the house plans that are going to be handed to me before the day is over."

Much nodding from the electricians, the plumbers, the framers, the drywall men.

Moore continued, "If anybody's got a lawn chair, Mr. Denisov can sit there and wait for his new used recliner."

More laughter.

Moore turned unexpectedly grim. "While he sits, he can work on figuring out who didn't want his house repaired and why. Because by God, this was most definitely a case of arson and I am one *slightly annoyed* construction manager."

The men nodded in agreement at Moore, then nodded sympathetically at Jacob and went to work.

They left Jacob standing in the remains of his blackened kitchen, feeling oddly like an accepted part of the community and even more oddly like a sleuth who owed them an explanation for the destruction of their hard labor.

Jacob hadn't thought about it before, but Moore was right—if Mad Maddie hadn't set fire to his house . . . who had?

CHAPTER TWENTY-TWO

One thing about being this tired—to Kateri's gaze, the world was skewed. The trees waved fingered branches; the wildflowers glowed with impossible colors; the houses, what few there were on this isolated county highway, tilted on their foundations; and the two lanes wavered from side to side. If she'd been driving, she would have put herself under arrest.

But she had commandeered Moen as her chauffeur, given him several firm and aggressive lectures about how he represented Virtue Falls's law enforcement and was not to harass Madeline Hewitson about anything ever again.

He nodded and agreed.

When she asked what he had been harassing Maddie about, he looked sheepish and chagrined, but other than assuring her it had not been sexual in nature, he would not talk. She believed him. But she wished she'd gotten a glimpse of the papers on Maddie's desk.

Now they scoured the county looking for anything they deemed unusual behavior, anywhere someone could be hiding an abused child.

"Since you told us about Cordelia's report, I've been viewing my neighbors differently." Moen sounded earnest, with an edge of desperation. "This evening at Starbucks, I waited in line and eavesdropped on conversations. Then at Bell Groceries, I pushed my cart through the aisles and I watched what people put in their carts, trying to judge if they were buying for a kid they don't officially have."

"That's good," she murmured. "Hear anything? See anything?"

"No! But I don't like being suspicious of people I have known my whole life."

"I hear you." He was right. Suspicion tainted everything.

"I said I would sit at the end of the street and watch Miss Hewitson's house, and I did, but first I cruised the streets, looking for windows with curtains that were never lifted, for sheds that were newly built, or for outbuildings with weird markings."

"Weird markings?"

His voice lowered to a whisper. "Like . . . if someone is performing dark magic."

She wished she could scoff at the idea. But he had a point. People who liked to inflict pain sometimes wanted blood and skin for rites better left in the Dark Ages.

Her eyelids drifted down. A dream started in her head, about a little girl in a cage. . . . Her head nodded. She jerked herself back into wakefulness, held her eyes wide and her back stiff.

"You can take a nap, you know," Moen said. "Everyone knows you're working too many hours, and I won't tell if you sleep on the job."

"I can't do it."

He slanted a look at her.

"I mean, I can, but I don't want to. I dream about that little girl . . . and I'm afraid law enforcement will never find the people who held that child captive, and she'll live out her days in darkness and abuse."

"We'll find her. We've just started looking. Give it some time."

Moen was a nice kid. She needed to remember that . . . when he was making her insane with his seemingly pointless inanities and wistful sighs. "I don't want to give it some time. The longer it takes, the more likely my officers would blab, and like all things in a small town, the news will spread like wildfire and the captor will move his victim."

"We won't talk," Moen said stoutly.

Now *she* looked sideways at *him*.

He squirmed. "Yes, it's a possibility. My dad says law enforcement is a gossip factory and if you're going to solve a crime, you have to do it fast."

"I remember your dad. He was a law officer and a good one."

"Until he was shot on the job. Now he's disabled and proud of me for doing what I'm doing." Moen did not glow with the filial gratification she would have expected. "He also says"—Moen swallowed—"that half of the officers aren't going to seriously look for an abused girl because the warnings came from a female everyone thinks is crazy."

"Me or Cordelia?" Kateri asked drily.

Moen looked alarmed. "No one thinks you're crazy!"

"Your dad doesn't think I'm crazy for listening to someone who's crazy?"

Moen was squirming now. "No. No! He thinks . . . he does think . . . he says that if you're going to win the election, you should stick with tried-and-true law enforcement techniques."

"Did your father never go with his gut?" It was a shrewd question; most officers had their occasional flashes of intuition.

"If he did, I've never heard him admit it."

"Is he always right?"

Moen looked wretched. "He is."

"Then I guess we ought to . . ." They cruised around a sharp corner, and Kateri focused her bleary eyes on the acreage surrounded by towering forest. Rusty cars cluttered an unkempt lawn. A ramshackle house sat at the end of a pitted gravel driveway . . . and at the back of the lot sat a new and suspiciously well-kept shop. "We ought to . . ."

"We ought to what?" Moen asked.

In a voice that was suddenly brisk, she said, "We ought to look closely at the Terrance place."

Moen focused on the home . . . and the shop. He slowed. "I know them. John Junior was two years ahead of me in school. Biggest bully in town. Beat me up until I got taller than him."

"Then?"

"Then I punched him out."

"Heh!" Kateri was glad to hear it.

"He whined to the principal and got me in big trouble."

"That figures. A bully and a coward." John Senior was a bully, too, and a single father whose legacy to his son was bad manners, a nasty attitude, and a predisposition to evil. Once upon a time, the two had fixed cars. Probably still did. Both men were the kind who, if they caught a woman's eyes, leered and adjusted their manly plumbing. Because if there was one thing that attracted a woman, it was a guy with jock itch. "Go past, then turn around," she said. "Park and I'll go check things out."

After the next curve, Moen made a U-turn. He pulled into a wide spot on the shoulder and prepared to unbuckle his seat belt. "I'll go with you."

Leaning over, she put her hand on Moen's arm and smiled into his face. "Rupert, there's a reason my people survived in the deep, dark forests of the New World. We have black hair that flies in the breeze. We have bronze skin that blends into the bark of the trees. We have dark eyes that watch—"

"Are you screwing with me?"

She straightened up. "Maybe a little. But for sure a man with red hair, white skin, and freckles can't skulk through the forest, so you have to stay here."

"If you're not back in fifteen minutes, I'm calling Bergen." The kid was good with a threat.

"Make it twenty." She took her walking stick and exited the car. She walked back along the side of the road, and when she reached the edge of the Terrance property, she skirted the forest and stopped beside an immense Douglas fir. Here she had a good view of the property—and of the hungry-looking Rottweiler that bounded out of the yard, barking furiously.

Poor dog. He never had a chance. Within seconds she had looked him in the eyes, fed him a treat, scratched his ears, then his belly, and told him her cocker spaniel Lacey would teach him a lesson or two about manners.

She knelt beside him; he whined and wiggled in ecstasy while she observed the property with a keen eye. To her surprise, a current-model black muscle car was parked behind the shop: a Dodge SRT Hellcat with air intakes cut into the engine hood. Clean and waxed, it gleamed in the sunlight. Was that a car John Senior and John Junior were fixing? Not likely. It was this year's top-of-the-line model. Nothing should be broken. Yet it must be, for how else could they afford it?

The possible answer made her feel sick.

The house's back door opened. The two Johns came out and headed toward the shop; they grinned like boys going for a treat. Kateri noted that, before they could enter, they had to deactivate an alarm and unlock the door. Most people in Virtue Falls didn't bother locking their doors, and as far out of town as these two were, she wouldn't have thought the Johns would have to bother. Perhaps they were paranoid about their tools. But locked doors in the middle of the day *and* an alarm system—that bumped her suspicions to a new level.

Before they opened the door, they looked around, searching for . . . what? Observers?

As she had promised Moen, they didn't see her, dressed in her khaki uniform and kneeling in the dirt in the shade. They hurriedly stepped inside and shut the door. If they turned on a light, she couldn't tell because . . . black paint covered the windows.

She distinctly heard the lock turn. She waited for another five minutes to see if they came out again. With two more treats to the hungry dog and a final rib scratch, she walked back to the cruiser and nodded to Moen's unspoken question. "We've found something," she said.

They drove toward town, and ten minutes down the road toward the coast a black car roared up behind them, John Senior at the wheel. As he passed, he flipped them off.

For him to be so bold, that car must really have muscle under the hood. Or perhaps it was his contempt for a female law officer. Or maybe he was high. She didn't care what his reason was. That behavior had given her another excuse to obtain a search warrant.

Which she did. With Rupert and ten of her officers, she raided the Terrance property. They had to break down the metal door to the shop to get in, and once they were in, they had to dodge bullets aimed from John Junior's pistol.

It was an ugly arrest.

Her officers dragged John Junior out of the lab while he shrieked insults and promises of violence directed at them and, when he saw Kateri, at her in particular. He would rape her, he promised, while she screamed and begged, and when he was finished with her, he would cut her up, piece by piece, and feed her to the fishes.

Her men hustled him away.

Bergen said, "Sheriff, please be careful. Meth has eaten his brain."

"It didn't have much to work with."

He didn't even crack a smile. "If he gets out on bail—"

"Let us hope the judge does not allow that to happen."

There was no female being held captive, but what they found there put Kateri on the front page of their tiny newspaper and made her a hero throughout western Washington.

They had discovered a large, efficient, fully functioning meth lab, the one that law had been seeking for more than a year.

CHAPTER TWENTY-THREE

The Coast Guard had been put on alert and captured John Senior on the coast, loading meth onto a small and beautiful schooner flying the Malaysian flag. The vessel tried to escape; the Coast Guard fired a warning shot, and when that didn't stop the schooner, they fired another shot to disable the vessel's power. While it foundered, they took command, arrested the five-man crew, and returned the schooner to port under auxiliary power.

Over the next few days, Kateri spent as much time as she could spare watching the men in the hazmat suits clean out the Terrances' shop. All the while she hoped fervently that they would find no captives, and even more important, no bodies. If they did, of course, that would wrap up the investigation, yet she cringed at the idea of a young woman subjected to a combination of brutal rape, torture, and those chemicals.

No persons or bodies were found. A relief, and yet . . .

She was filling out the paperwork when her administrative assistant knocked at her open door. "Sheriff, Lieutenant Commander Luis Sanchez is here to see you."

"Good. He can help me fill in the details on the Terrance case."

"I don't think that's what he's here for."

Kateri stared at Mona's knowing smirk. "Then what . . . ?"

Luis stepped into the doorway, holding a small bouquet of red roses.

Kateri wanted to drop her head onto her hands. The man had walked through city hall carrying red roses. Within a few hours, rumor would have her engaged, married, divorced, pregnant, and/or transferring with her new lover/husband out of Virtue Falls to some "exotic" locale such as the Texas Gulf Coast.

Luis strolled in as if he were quite at home, came around the desk, kissed her cheek, and pressed the flowers into her hand. "Hello, *chica*."

"What a pleasant surprise, Luis," Kateri said with patent insincerity. And, "Mona, would you find a vase for these flowers?"

"Of course!" Mona, predictably, didn't even bother to step away from the sidelight, but hung close, listening.

Kateri raised her voice. "Mona Coleman!"

The woman scurried away.

Luis perched one hip on the desk and smiled into Kateri's eyes. "May I take you to dinner tonight to celebrate your triumph?"

"What triumph is that, Luis?"

"You are too modest! The drug bust! You are the talk of the town, and you deserve a treat."

"That's very thoughtful of you, but—"

His smile dimmed. "Why but?"

Cordelia's texts were still unsolved—and still coming in. Someone was eagerly and cruelly tormenting a girl in this town. How to explain to Luis her need to rescue this child before another moment had passed?

Luis, being Luis, understood without explanation. "You cannot save the world all in one day. Tonight, we celebrate your triumph. Tomorrow . . . who knows what the hours will hold? You have chosen a task that will bring you heartache, trouble, and pain. Should you not revel in each success? Only in that way will you survive and flourish."

Damn. He was right. "When did you get so wise?"

He touched his chest and deepened his voice. "I am a man. You are a woman. Of course I am wiser than you."

She laughed and punched his leg. "Okay. What time tonight?"

"Our reservation is for seven at the Virtue Falls Resort."

There was that cockiness again, and it bugged her. "Were you so sure of me?"

"Reservations are easily canceled."

Again, he was right. But she still didn't like it.

He continued, "I will pick you up at six thirty at your home, yes?"

"Yes."

"I will depend on you."

"I'll do what I can, but first I must get this paperwork done. Sit— in a chair—and tell me exactly what happened on your end with the arrest."

CHAPTER TWENTY-FOUR

Maddie went to sleep in her bed with the blinds open and the morning sun blasting in, and woke eight hours later feeling refreshed and, by God, vindicated. For the first time since she had moved to Virtue Falls, someone had taken her side. Someone had borne witness to her innocence. The Williamsons, God bless them, had fed her and let her sleep on their porch and never once had they been afraid she would somehow murder them. Better yet, Mrs. Williamson had ripped into Mrs. Butenschoen so comprehensively that Mrs. Butenschoen had retreated in disarray.

The only other person who had shown her such trust was Jacob Denisov, and he hadn't so much trusted her as encouraged her to do the deadly deed of cutting his throat.

Of course, Maddie still had the problem of Deputy Moen to deal with, but a full day's sleep meant she could handle anything . . . even the drift of clouds that signaled the beginning of another sunset, another night. All that mattered was—right now, she was alive. All was well.

She fixed her dinner, toasted cheese on a pita and tomato soup out of a can, and took it out on the front porch. She sat in her rocker, ate, and observed the neighborhood.

The construction crew was long gone from Jacob's. He was no-where in sight. In his bedroom, she supposed, hiding.

The Franklin kids played ball in the street until their parents called them in.

Dr. Frownfelter's living room was dark, yet it flickered with the play of his TV. She would bet he was sitting in his easy chair, "watching" some documentary with his eyes closed and the sound muted.

Chantal Filips came out of her house in the shortest red skirt Maddie had ever seen. A low, fast, black Mercedes S-Class coupe driven by the ugliest man on earth pulled up. Chantal tossed an overnight bag into the backseat, tucked her long legs in the door, and as they roared away, she waved at Maddie and smiled smugly.

Maddie would be smug, too, if she had legs that long, a guy in a sports car, and a career that included traveling around the world look-ing gorgeous.

Across the street, Dayton Floren stood in the window of his dark-ened house and watched Chantal Filips leave.

Dang. Glamour, envy, and jealousy in Virtue Falls. Who would have thought it?

The neighbor on the other side of Jacob hadn't been home for a very long time; Maddie had heard rumors that Bernice was off on a three-week ocean cruise to Tahiti followed by another three weeks per-forming missionary work with the natives of Borneo. Having met Bernice—she was a copy of Mrs. Butenschoen—Maddie thought the natives didn't stand a chance.

Except for the damage to Jacob's house, it was as if last night had never happened. Idly Maddie wondered who had set fire to his house. Had the enemy who drove him to long for death somehow found him here in Virtue Falls? Or had he at last cracked up and tried to kill him-self?

A car turned onto the street and slowly drove the length to the end, to that spot where the pavement ended in the guardrail. The driver per-formed a three-point turn, and as he returned, Maddie could see him looking from side to side. He stopped at Dayton Floren's, then inched forward to park at Jacob's. If he was looking for Jacob, that made sense; she had knocked the house number right off the front of his house. In fact, she'd knocked the wall that held the house number right off the front of his house.

The guy parked at the curb, got out, and walked up to the make-shift front steps. From there he stared uncertainly into the empty living room.

He didn't look like a contractor. For one thing, he wore polished shoes, pressed slacks, and a starched shirt. For another, he limped and one arm had been amputated at the elbow.

Did Jacob have a visitor from his military days?

Since it was her fault the house was the wreck that it was, she should go over and introduce herself and offer such help as she could. Although, she supposed she could admit to the tiniest prod of curiosity. . . . She crossed the street and walked toward the fellow, who turned to face her. He was younger than Jacob, and handsome, with a scar down his cheek and across his chin.

"How do you do?" She offered her hand. "I'm Jacob's neighbor Madeline Hewitson. Can I help you?"

"Where's the front door?" His voice was soft, slow, and hoarse.

"Draped over the hood of my car."

Amusement blossomed on his face. "So, Madeline Hewitson, you drove your car into Jacob Denisov's house? I am privileged to meet you." He shook with his left hand. "How did he take that?"

"He was not pleased." An understatement.

The guy grinned. "No. Not our lieutenant. I'm one of the men he rescued. I'm Brandon LaFreniere."

"It's an honor, Brandon."

He made a face. "I'm not the hero."

"That's what he says, too, that he's not the hero."

Brandon studied her for a moment. "I'd like to see him, speak with him. Where is he living?"

"Here. He's inside somewhere."

Brandon did a double take that included her and the house. "In *there*?"

"In the bedroom. There's not many other places he could be. I can get him for you." She started up the stairs.

"Wait." Brandon hobbled after her. "How is he? I mean—do you know? Because all of us who returned with him have been worried. He won't reply to e-mails or answer the phone. We keep getting our mail back marked *Not at This Address*. In his handwriting."

She liked this guy. "So you came to check on him?"

"I work in Seattle now so I was the logical choice to come."

"I'm glad." She *was* glad. Glad to know someone cared about Jacob, someone who had been with him in his darkest days. "He's . . . angry. He blames himself for what happened in . . . Korea." Should she be talking about this? Jacob wouldn't like it, of course. This man had been badly wounded during his ordeal. Was he as angry as Jacob?

"Can we talk?" Brandon limped over and looked up the porch steps and shook his head. "Not today," he said. "Not without more assistance than you can give me. We can sit here, if that's okay. They shattered my femur and my kneecap, and I can't stand for long."

By "they" he meant the North Koreans.

"If you would put your hand under my part of an arm and steady me, I should be able to lower myself onto a step without too much damage to either of us." He grinned at her, but his complexion was waxy.

She did as instructed, and with much effort the two managed get him seated. She viewed him with concern. "Are you okay? Can I get you some water?"

He used a handkerchief to mop a sheen of sweat off his face. "I'm fine. I'm having another surgery in a few weeks. That should fix me one way or another." He patted the step beside him. "Sit." When she did he asked, "How much do you know?"

"I know what I read in the press, and I know what Jacob told me. That you were one of his brainiacs, that you built a hovercraft, got drunk, and took it across the border. That he went after you and you all were captured and . . . tortured."

He lifted his empty sleeve. "I entered the service with two working legs and two complete arms. And no nightmares. So yes, torture."

"Jacob said one of you told them who you were and what your assignment was."

"That was me." Brandon's face turned red, his voice cracked, and she caught a glimpse of the callow, untried youth he had been. "I thought it would help. Instead, it gave the doctor what he had been waiting for—a chance to perform experiments on intelligent human beings."

"Experiments. On humans." This wasn't exactly the way the news stories had been written. "So he was like a Nazi?"

"Exactly. Dr. Kim. Um . . . yeah. But he viewed the six of us brainiacs as collateral damage. He didn't care about us. It was Jacob he wanted. He wanted to own that disciplined mind, so he used us to break him." Brandon tried to smile, as if the memories didn't hurt. "We were held in a compound not far from the border, an old prison built of concrete, steel, pain, and fear. Two died the first week, Lydia Adelaide Jenkins and Nolan James Tanaka, tortured to death. They were the lucky ones."

"He said that. Jacob said that, used those exact words. That the ones who died right away were the lucky ones."

Brandon nodded. "They separated us. We weren't allowed to speak to each other, but in the time-honored method of all prisoners of war, we devised a code. It kept us alive, I think, being able to communicate with each other. It killed us, too, for we had depended on Denisov to rescue us, and instead he abandoned us."

Now it was her turn. *"What?"*

"He abandoned us," Brandon repeated. "Every day, one of us was taken from our cell to an interrogation room. It had a window. We could see into the control room. There was a guy at the control board—big control board, old technology. It ran the lights, the cell locks, the electric fences, the whole prison. We didn't know that then, but it did. He had his back to us. And a gun, of course. All the North Koreans had guns."

She put her hand on Brandon's shoulder again. "Why did you say Jacob abandoned you?"

"Because he was watching through the window as they tortured us. He watched, and all the while, Dr. Kim was whispering in his ear. Day after day, the same thing. He didn't care what they did to us. He never changed expression. He acted like we weren't even there."

She was shocked. She didn't believe it. She did *not* believe it. "Did you never get to speak to him?"

"No. After a few days of screaming in agony, calling his name, begging him to rescue us—he was so calm, so competent, we really thought he could rescue us—we just hated him. So much. Even more than the men who were breaking our bones and pulling out our fingernails. We hated Jacob Denisov."

"Something changed."

"We found out the truth. That day . . . started out to be a typical bad day. The soldiers came and got me out of my cell. They took me to the interrogation room. They asked me questions. I'd given all the answers the first time they tortured me. I told them everything." Brandon gave her a half smile. "I wasn't much of a soldier. I was never brave."

She looked at the evidence of his pain. "You have a different definition of brave than I do."

"No, really. I simply didn't want to suffer. There was nothing new to learn from me. But still they asked, and I tried new answers, anything to make them stop. They nailed my hand to the table. I was screaming in agony when all of a sudden—"

"Brandon." Jacob's voice sounded from behind them.

Maddie jumped in surprise and guilt.

Brandon jumped, too.

How long had Jacob been standing there? Long enough. He glared at them in a forbidding manner.

Brandon tried to leap to his feet and failed, tilting to one side.

Maddie steadied him.

Jacob hurried down the stairs, nudged her out of the way, and took over.

"Sorry, sir," Brandon said. "I'm still not completely used to the leg."

Jacob's expression eased. "And the arm?"

"As far as I'm concerned, it's there. But the docs insist it's only a phantom limb." Brandon looked keenly into Jacob's face. "I suspect you've experienced something similar with your situation."

What situation? Why had Jacob interrupted them precisely when she was so close to hearing Jacob's story?

"Different but the same." Jacob helped him up the first step. "Come in. I'm a little short on food, drink, and walls, but we can sit and talk."

Eager to make amends for the crime of curiosity, Maddie said, "If you like, I can make coffee. I bought filters."

"That would be kind of you. Thanks!" Brandon smiled at her as if trying to make up for Jacob's cold reception.

"Great! I'll bring it back." She glanced into Jacob's living room. "Oo! You got a new recliner. Nice!"

"Is it?" Jacob was deadpan.

Maybe not. The material was worn tan suede, the back tilted to the right, one of the arms had a tuft of cotton coming through the seam. She compromised. "It's better than the old one."

"Sure."

"The smoke must have ruined that one."

"Yes."

"You got some sofa pillows, too. Flowered. Really . . . big flowers. They look mostly good piled on the old steamer chest."

Jacob tilted his head and listened. "Your phone is ringing."

She groped for her cell phone in her pocket, pulled it out, and stared at it.

"Your landline," Jacob said.

In a panic now, she sprinted toward the house.

"Nice girl," Brandon said. "Pretty. Did she really drive into your house?"

"She really did."

"Some guys have all the luck."

"Isn't that the truth."

Well, excuuuuse me. We have a plan. It's working. Don't back
out now. She'll make us a fortune.

CHAPTER TWENTY-FIVE

Maddie knew who was calling.

Andrew. He was her only relative, the only person who had her phone number, and if he didn't reach her on her landline he would call her cell.

She ran inside and grabbed the phone. "Andrew!"

"Where were you?" he asked testily.

"Across at the neighbor's, the one I crashed into."

"What kind of damage did you do now?"

She hated Andrew's attitude, hated that she immediately felt defensive. "Nothing! I met one of his friends and entertained him until Jacob arrived."

"Jacob? Really. Now you're friends with Jacob Denisov?"

"I wouldn't say friends, exactly." What was wrong with being friends? "But we know each other. We have a lot in common."

Andrew sounded disbelieving. "*You* have a lot in common with a decorated military hero?"

She took a breath, let it out slowly, and in an even voice said, "We've both suffered pain and trauma, Andrew. Even you should be able to understand that."

That shut him up. For a moment. "You're right. I'm sorry. I'm testy and taking it out on you. But . . . you're supposed to be writing."

Oh. That was why he was disapproving. "I am."

"You don't want to be late for your deadline."

"I won't." As long as the monster stayed away. "I never am." But Andrew always acted as if she would be. As if she were unreliable.

She glanced out the window toward Jacob's, saw the two men sitting in the shadowy living room, talking.

Coffee. She had promised them coffee. She could make it while she talked. She hustled into the kitchen, tucked the phone under her chin, and got out the coffeemaker. "How are you? How is the money business?"

"Fine. Do you want to send me pages to read?"

"No. Do you have to go on book tour for *Sacrifice!*?"

"Yes. My promotions team has lined up autographings. Are you working on the graphic novel?"

"No." She had almost a whole book finished, but she couldn't tell him that. He would want to see the drawings, and she wasn't ready. Perhaps she was superstitious, thinking that every person who saw pictures of her monster fed him power. Perhaps she didn't want to hear Andrew's critique, have him talk to her about her characters as if he really was the author.

"The graphic novel would really add to my popularity. *Our* popularity. You haven't told anyone that you are the one writing the novels, have you?"

"No . . ." Although she had sort of told Jacob. She glanced out the window again. The two men looked tense. *In*tense.

"Because if that came out, it would cause all kinds of trouble with the publisher and the public."

"I know." Andrew had told her often enough. She opened the bag of gourmet coffee. It smelled good. "Will the autographings hurt your business? I don't want to take you away from work."

"Not a problem. I'm supporting you, aren't I?"

"Yes . . ." She remembered the coffee filter, found one, and arranged it carefully in the basket. She measured the way the directions said: eight tablespoons per four cups. "When can I have a new car?"

"Why do you need a car? Virtue Falls is a small town. You can walk to the grocery store, can't you?"

She didn't like the direction this conversation was going. "It's not a matter of getting there. It's a matter of coming back with the groceries."

"I'll send you one of those wheeled carts you can drag behind you."

"I would like a car."

"You can't have one. I'm not made of money. Publishing doesn't pay that well."

"I know." He'd told her that often enough, too. "But you have your other job, and the insurance will pay on the last one."

"You've had too many wrecks. Insurance doesn't want to cover you anymore."

"Oh." She hadn't thought of that. She hated being stranded in Virtue Falls. She liked the town, but sometimes she wanted to drive up the coast, to a place where no monsters lurked and the scenery offered sanctuary for her mind.

"This Jacob guy. You're not dating him, are you?"

"What? No! He's not even friendly." Although she had confessed almost everything to him, and he had behaved as if he were interested. After listening to Brandon, she was certainly interested in what drove Jacob to live in isolation and fear.

Carefully she poured water into the coffeemaker and pressed the *On* button. Coffee began to dribble into the pot. She'd done it! "Do you have a girlfriend?" she asked.

"Between being the front for your writing career and doing my job, I don't have time for a girlfriend."

"But you like having a girlfriend." When he had a girlfriend he wasn't as bossy and grumpy.

"Never mind me. I'm the normal one in the family, remember? It's you I'm concerned about and you don't have time for a social life."

"The only social life I have is calling the cops when things get too weird."

"So the monsters are still after you?"

"How did you know?"

"I've got a contact in Virtue Falls. I get reports."

She looked around as if she would see someone watching her. "From who?"

"Never mind." Andrew sounded as if he were sorry he'd said anything. "Just keep writing."

Andrew was overbearing, but he was her family, the one steady influence in her life, and he worried about her.

"I will."

"Eat right and get some exercise. Stop worrying about the monster. It's an illusion. It can't hurt you."

"They never found Easton's killer."

Andrew got that impatient tone in his voice. "Maddie, whoever that was is not going to chase you to Washington to make you miserable. Stop being such a coward and write!"

"Good-bye, Andrew." She gently put the phone into the cradle and sat with her hand on it.

It rang again immediately. Andrew was not used to having her hang up on him.

She picked it up. "What?"

"Kid, I love you."

He sounded like the brother who had cried with her at their parents' funeral, like the brother who had haunted her hospital room as she recovered from the wound to her belly and the infection that inevitably followed, the brother who, while she lingered in the sanitarium, encouraged her to write and who, when she got out, agreed to take her place in the public eye.

"I love you, too, Andrew, but you can't talk to me that way. I'm not an idiot, I'm not a child, I'm not a coward, and I am not crazy."

"If you'd come home, the monsters would go away."

"No. Colorado is not my home anymore. It hasn't been for a long, long time."

"I could take care of you. Watch over you."

She had wanted to say this for a long time. She needed to tell him. "I appreciate all you've done for me. I know you didn't sign on to raise me, and I'm sorry things went badly at the precise time when I should have been getting out on my own. But I'm an adult now. I don't need a babysitter. No one needs to watch over me."

It was like he didn't hear her. Or maybe he didn't want to hear her. "I don't understand you. If you'd come home, you could write another book a year."

"No. I can't." She didn't want to spend more time in the dark places of her soul. She wanted to live in the light. She walked over and looked out at Jacob's house, at the two men who now seemed relaxed, who had settled into some kind of camaraderie.

"Why can't you? It doesn't have to be long. You would make so much more money." Andrew's voice became coaxing. "Then you could have a car. Or a scooter. Wouldn't you like a scooter?"

"No. I'm not riding a scooter in Virtue Falls in the winter. Andrew, how's your business?"

"My business?" He sounded startled. "Why do you ask? You've never asked before."

She heard it again, that note of . . . panic? "You still have your firm, don't you?"

"Yes! I paid for the license the other day."

"You're still trading stocks, right? Is it going okay?"

"Some days are better than others." His voice grew eager. "It's like gambling. You have to pay attention all the time, read the signs, follow your gut. Sometimes you win, sometimes you lose. Do you understand, Maddie?"

"Have you ever lost everything?"

"Yes. But never fear. You're not going to starve."

"I'm not asking because of me. But you sound"—*desperate*—"concerned about money. Maybe worried."

"Honey, everybody's concerned about money these days."

"I thought the recession was over."

"Officially. But in the risky world of stock trading, there's always that fear that you'll lose and always the golden ring of winning big."

"How much could you get for a shorter story?"

"Maybe as much as five thousand dollars advance."

"I can't get a car for that."

"Used . . . I might be able to talk the publishers up to ten thousand advance."

"I'd like to see the contract this time."

"Sure, honey. Sure. I'll show you the contract." He sounded like a snake oil salesman, then he switched back to the eager boy. "When could you finish it?"

It depends on how many ghosts come to haunt me. "I'll have to think about it, figure out a plot."

"Make it short."

"Andrew, the books are as long as they are. I have a story. I tell it."

"If you would try the graphic novel idea—"

"No!" He was really hung up on that. "No."

"Are you sure you haven't started drawing?"

"I'm sure." *Sure that it's none of your business, and sure wondering why you sound as if you know something.*

"All right, but I don't know why I bothered to pay for those art classes for you."

"I thought it was because you wanted me to be happy."

"I do. No matter what happens, I hope you believe that."

She guessed she did, but as she hung up, she thought about what he'd said and the way he'd said it, and she wondered what Andrew was up to . . . and why he sounded frightened.

The coffee was finished.

She got two mugs out of the cupboard, poured them full, put them on a tray with some cookies from Sienna's Sandwiches, and headed out the door for Jacob's.

She walked slowly, taking care not to slosh the coffee out of the mugs, and as she crossed the street, she thought that perhaps it was time for her to tell the truth about her writing, to replace Andrew on the books' title pages.

Then she remembered why she had handed it off to him. After she came out of the institution and gave him her first book to review, he had said, *Maddie, you'd better let me handle this. The media is still fascinated with you. They would follow you to every book signing and harass you at every opportunity. You would hate that.*

That made sense to her. So he became the name on her books. He took care of the money that came in and gave her an allowance, and supplemented with his own income.

When Easton had discovered the deception, he had been most perturbed and wanted to look at the financials. But he'd been killed before he got the chance, and after that, she was content to continue with the relationship as it was.

Except . . . except things were changing. *She* was changing.

She stumbled as she got to the curb, looked up, and realized Brandon's car was gone and Jacob had disappeared. His bedroom door was once more closed, shutting out the world.

She glanced around. She stood here in broad daylight holding coffee and feeling foolish.

Then a cab—*the* Virtue Falls cab—screeched around the corner onto the street and parked in front of Mrs. Butenschoen's. There was a pause while the cabbie collected his fee. Then he leaped out as if his pants were on fire, opened the passenger door, and out stepped Mrs. Butenschoen, looking plump, sweet-faced, and well dressed. The cabbie handed her a small bag, leaped into the driver's seat, and roared away like all the hounds of hell were chasing him.

Poor guy. Mrs. Butenschoen had probably been telling him how to drive. And to clean up his cab. And—

Mrs. Butenschoen stood on the sidewalk across the street and looked across at her. "How are you, Madeline?"

Maddie froze. Mrs. Butenschoen never spoke to her except to complain or accuse. "I'm . . . fine?"

"That's good. I hope you have a pleasant evening."

"Yes. Thank you." Belatedly she said, "I hope you had a nice day."

"Thank you. It was interesting." Mrs. Butenschoen opened her gate, walked up to her front door, and went inside.

Huh. An agreeable Mrs. Butenschoen. That was different.

Maddie sat down on the curb, ate a cookie, sipped the coffee, and wondered—where had Mrs. Butenschoen gone all dressed up? And why hadn't she driven herself?

You hired me to do this. Stop trying to back out.

You're weak.

CHAPTER TWENTY-SIX

At five, on her way out of the police station, Kateri endured catcalls, well wishes, and a chant of *Kateri and Luis sittin' in a tree*.

So apparently Mona had returned with the vase in time to hear the juicy part.

"You guys are sooo mature," she told them. "Has Bergen checked in yet?"

"Haven't heard a word." Norm Knowles scowled.

"That's not like him." Kateri hesitated.

"He's probably in the mountains and can't make a call," Ernie Fitzwater said. "You've got your cell phone. You're in contact. Go on your date."

He was right. It wasn't like she was going to sleep with Luis . . . tonight. "Okay," she said. "Let me know if anyone really needs me. Otherwise . . . behave. All of you."

She got grins in return and a loud kissing sound from Moen.

Kateri supposed it didn't matter what they said or thought. The damage had been done. Truth to tell, she was looking forward to tonight's . . . get-together. She didn't want to call it a date. That made it official. She wasn't ready for official. But eating with a friend at Virtue Falls Resort was always a treat.

She gathered Lacey from Mrs. Golobovitch, took the dog for a long walk, then went home and dressed in record time in a long black sheath dress with gold buttons and a slit up each side. She consulted Lacey about how much makeup, then realized the ridiculousness of asking a stylish blond prom queen cocker spaniel about a grooming matter. Lacey's answer would always be *More!* So Kateri used foundation to mute her scars, blush to give color to her stark cheekbones, and mascara and eye shadow to create deep, dark, smoky eyes. When she put down her brushes, she surveyed herself in the mirror. "I look pretty good."

Lacey clearly agreed.

Luis arrived promptly at six thirty, looking pretty good himself in pressed black jeans, a nice tight T-shirt that proved he had worked out, and a black sport coat. At the sight of her he did a double take. He knelt to pet her dog, looked up, and said, "You're beautiful!"

Lacey barked and wagged her tail.

He cupped the dog's chin. "Yes, you, too." He stood, brushed Lacey's blond hair off his knees, and opened the door for Kateri.

She grabbed her red silk wrap.

He took it from her and placed it around her shoulders. *Nice.*

Her walking stick leaned against the wall by her front door. As she exited, she grasped it; somehow, tonight it seemed to fit in her hand.

It felt odd to be in the car with him. Not that he hadn't driven her back and forth to Seattle for her checkups. But this was different. No matter what she wanted to call it, it *was* a date, her first in four years.

He led the conversation with, "Your men are proud of you."

She thought back on the catcalls as she left, and asked, "How did you reach that conclusion?"

"They told me."

"Did they? I assume this was when you came in with the roses?"

"Yep, and they warned me to take care of you." He glanced at her, then back at the road. "Like I don't know how to do that."

"You've been such a good friend to me, Luis. I truly appreciate it."

He pulled into a viewpoint overlooking the ocean, turned to her, and placed his hand on her seat. "I don't want your appreciation. I want more. I want your hand in mine, your body against mine, your trust, your love."

Ack. "It's only a first . . . date."

"We've known each other for a long time. Why do we need to go through the formalities? I have half a mind to turn the car around, go to your place, and spend the night making love."

He was moving too fast. "Luis. I want the formalities."

He stroked the scar on her cheek. "You shall have them. But don't make me wait too long, please?"

"Those things you want . . . they take time."

He began again. "We've known each other—"

"Not in that way, we have not." She was right about this. She knew she was. "Formalities, Luis. That will allow us to be sure."

He looked sulky. Then he smiled, that flashing white smile he utilized with such success. "Let's go eat."

Virtue Falls Resort hadn't changed for more than a hundred years. At the turn of the nineteenth century, logs had been stacked four stories on the edge of a cliff overlooking the Pacific and now, despite earthquakes and tsunamis, the hotel held old-fashioned charm. The guest rooms were above. The ground floor hosted the reception area, the grand room, and the exclusive dining room. The staff knew Luis and Kateri by their names, their jobs, and their reputations. The hostess took Kateri's wrap and her walking stick. In the restaurant, the two were escorted to a table by the big glass windows. There Kateri found another bouquet of roses and a bottle of champagne chilling. "Luis, did you order this?"

He flashed a smile. "The staff were happy to arrange it."

She hated to, but she had to remind him, "I don't drink."

"A drop," he coaxed.

"Not even that." Never. Not with the ghost of her mother haunting her. "But thank you for the thought. It is generous of you."

He sent the champagne away and ordered a glass of red wine for himself and, for her, her usual sparkling water with lime. When they had their drinks in hand, he leaned forward. "I propose a toast."

She lifted her glass to his.

"To Kateri Kwinault, the future elected sheriff of Virtue Falls."

"From your mouth to God's ears."

When she would have clinked, he held up one finger. "And to me, who is at last commander of Virtue Falls station."

"Luis, such good news! And well deserved." She clinked glasses with him, then offered her hand across the table.

He took it and kissed her fingers.

"When did it become official?"

"This afternoon."

So he had invited her to dinner knowing full well he had good news, too. But that was all right. "By tomorrow morning the gossip will be in full bloom all over town."

His eyes glittered with high spirits. "Shall I call back the champagne?"

"Not even for you." She had to confess to disappointment that he had not remembered or believed in her no-alcohol rule.

He didn't press her again, and the dinner proved truly a celebration for them both. With excellent food before them, they easily fell back into the old camaraderie, exchanging stories of the Coast Guard and gossip from town, and they conducted a serious discussion about Kateri's chances for election. She told their waiter about Luis's promotion, which led to an announcement to the diners, who applauded and offered their congratulations.

Luis had never looked so handsome, and Kateri felt a fleeting pity for his girlfriend, Sienna. Her demands had made Luis flee; she must be crying every night.

The desserts had been served when Margaret Smith made her nightly appearance. At ninety-six, Margaret was tiny and frail, and in the past year, her walker had become her constant companion. But as the flesh failed, Kateri saw the spark of her soul burning ever brighter.

Luis and Kateri stood as she came to their table, and she kissed them both. "I heard the grand news about both of you! It is good to see you celebrating together." In the quavering voice, Kateri could hear a faint Irish brogue.

"We have a history," Luis said.

"So you do." Margaret looked into Kateri's face and with fragile fingers stroked Kateri's cheek. "You're looking well, child." When her maître d' tried to set a chair for her, she waved him away. "No, Harold, these children want to enjoy their celebration in peace." As she made her way through the dining room, men and women stood to speak to her. Of the people who dined there tonight she knew almost every one by name; once she met you, she never forgot.

"She's an extraordinary woman," Luis said.

"She directed my rescue from the ocean. Her people brought me to shore and notified Coast Guard rescue."

He took her hand in his. "I remember."

Their waiter arrived bearing a phone. "Sheriff Kwinault, apparently you're not answering your cell."

She pulled out her cell and looked. "No signal."

"It's the police. It's urgent." He handed her the receiver.

"Sheriff, it's Norm Knowles." The officer sounded grim—and excited. "We found the girl. The girl Cordelia's texts referenced. The kid is the Milhollands' foster child, held in the family room . . . in a dog crate."

"The Milhollands . . . the *dentists*?"

"Yes, ma'am."

"You are kidding." They were both, husband and wife, upstanding members of the community and parents of a popular son who played high school football. And they had been keeping their foster child in a *crate*? "Why?"

"They said she needed discipline."

Kateri waited for more. "That's it?"

"They seemed to think that explained everything. Bergen asked if they didn't think she needed to go to school, to get an education, to play in the sun, and they said no, she was already spoiled enough and—" Officer Knowles choked.

"Okay, Knowles. Sorry. I should have known that there wasn't a . . ." No explanation ever made sense. Not when this happened. Never in these circumstances. "How did you find her?"

"Bergen remembered they had had a foster child, wondered what happened to her, checked, and found out Social Services had lost track of her. He watched the house. Watched Mrs. Milholland shop and wondered why she bought dog food when they had no dog. Finally he stopped by to ask about the child. The girl heard him and screamed and screamed. He called for backup and went in." Officer Knowles's tone changed to one of helpless anger. "She's seven. She was filthy. Starving. We've arrested the Milhollands."

"I would hope to hell!"

"She won't come out of the crate. There's a belt there—every time when we try to get her to come out, she looks at it and shakes her head."

"They beat her."

"She's scared and cowering, and we don't know what to do with her."

Officer Knowles sounded as panicked as any man facing an emotional crisis of this magnitude. "Did you call Child Protection Services?"

"Yes, but it will take a couple of hours before anyone can get here."

"Right." Virtue Falls held little in the way of local human resources. "I'm at Virtue Falls Resort. Can someone come and get me?"

"Moen is already on his way."

"Good. Send someone to my house to pick up my dog."

"Your *dog*?"

"Her name is Lacey. Bring her to the Milhollands. She'll do us more good than anything."

He got it now. "Right."

She hung up, stood, and looked at Luis. "I'm sorry to cut this short, but I have to go."

Luis sighed and tapped impatient fingers on his glass. "Can't they take care of anything by themselves?"

"In every other circumstance, yes. Not in this case. I'm the one who can help." Because Kateri knew what it was to be taken from the place she loved, from the parent who loved her, and given into the hands of indifference and contempt.

Luis didn't know. Her past was her past, and she made no confessions. So he made his second mistake of the evening (the first being the champagne). "If you are going to be sheriff, you can't go every time the men think they need a woman's touch. They'll be calling you for every little thing."

She smiled at him, a fake smile that should have warned him how much his advice irritated her. She wanted to point out that she had been *his* commander, that she had helped train him to hold the exalted position he now held. But he was possibly a little drunk and tonight was his triumph, so she said only, "Thank you. I'll keep that in mind in the future."

"But not now?" He looked into her eyes. "I had plans for later this evening."

"We already discussed this."

"Kateri, this is our time, our chance. Don't you see? We're both celebrating our successes. Our lives are running on parallel lines."

"Yet a frightened girl needs help and I will provide it. Surely you understand compassion."

He visibly struggled, then leaned back in his chair and relaxed. "Of course. I know you. You must follow your conscience."

Leaning down, she pressed a kiss on his cheek. "You can have my dessert."

He laughed mockingly. "That will resign me to going home by myself."

Her irritation snapped back in place. "I'm sure the newly promoted Coast Guard commander could find companionship."

His dark eyes watched her mournfully. "But it wouldn't mean anything. I want only you."

Harold appeared at her side. "Your ride is here, Sheriff Kwinault."

With one last squeeze of the fingers, she left Luis alone.

He felt conspicuous sitting here by himself. He felt foolish and abandoned. He had wanted to celebrate his promotion with the one woman who could truly understand what this meant to him. And she had left him alone.

He took a bite of his cheesecake and sipped his espresso. He put down his fork and got to his feet. He thanked Margaret for her gracious hospitality, spoke to the diners who congratulated him on his promotion, went out to his car, and got in. He had enjoyed three glasses of wine. Probably he shouldn't be driving. Possibly he wasn't thinking clearly.

He drove to Sienna's home. He knocked on the door. She opened it to him, took him by the hand, led him inside, and shut the door.

CHAPTER TWENTY-SEVEN

At seven thirty in the morning, Kateri dragged up the stairs into city hall, planting her walking stick firmly on each step as she climbed. Beside her, Lacey trotted, her head down and her ears sad.

The night had been difficult for them both.

Inside the building, Kateri nodded at the cop at the counter and headed straight for the back and the coffeepot. She leaned her walking stick against the table and poured herself a cup. She sniffed the coffee; it smelled old and strong. She stirred in some sugar and a good dollop of cream, tasted it, and tossed it down the sink.

Moen had made the coffee again. Just for that, she'd send him to Best Beans for a double-shot espresso that would help her get through the next few hours. . . . She leaned against the counter and looked around.

Huh. Where was everybody?

She'd walked into a mostly empty patrol room, and after she arrived the few guys who had been sitting at their desks got up and drifted away. Like they were guilty. Or they knew something she didn't.

Well, well. An unexpected event was going on; time to find out what. "Where are they, Lacey?" she asked.

The dog trotted down the corridor toward the press room.

Kateri started to follow, came to a halt, returned for her walking stick, and gripped it firmly in one fist as she stalked after her dog.

She had her suspicions. She hoped she was wrong . . . but she knew she wasn't, and she knew she was totally pissed.

She could hear a male voice drifting down the corridor—Bergen's voice. Then another male voice, then Bergen.

She stepped into the doorway leading into the press room; she was looking at the side of the podium and Bergen's profile. Two dozen men filled the chairs, most of them her law enforcement officers. Bergen's wife, Sandra, sat in the back row. There was also one Seattle TV reporter and his cameraman, and Noah, her campaign manager. Mr. Caldwell, Bergen's campaign manager, stood at Bergen's side.

In Kateri's absence, that treacherous son of a bitch Bergen had called a press conference.

Kateri was exhausted, physically, mentally, emotionally, and every other way anyone could imagine, and right now, she did not need this crap.

Her cops spotted her first. They started moving restively.

Then Mr. Caldwell. His nasty grin was a direct challenge.

Noah saw her, but he kept taking notes. He was here for the *Virtue Falls Herald.*

The reporter from the Seattle TV station and his cameraman paid no attention to her.

Sandra Bergen stared fixedly at her husband, arms crossed over her chest.

Kateri walked in, thumping her stick on the old wooden floor with each step, headed for the podium.

Lacey trotted at her side.

Mr. Caldwell moved to intercept her.

One firm walking stick blow to the shin cleared him out of the way.

Bergen stopped talking.

She looked him right in the eyes. "Thank you, Deputy Bergen, for handling the press conference for me. Let me fill in the details, then you can finish up."

He hesitated. He looked at Sandra. He looked down. He moved aside.

Kateri stepped up to the microphone. Lacey joined her. Kateri thumped the tip of her walking stick hard on the top of Bergen's foot.

He flinched. But he didn't make a sound.

Speaking to the audience, she said, "I'm Sheriff Kateri Kwinault. As Deputy Bergen told you, yesterday he discovered the location of a foster child, a girl, seven years old, who was lost from the system and for the past three years had been systematically starved and abused. The Virtue Falls law enforcement team, led by Deputy Bergen, worked hard to quietly and safely extricate her from her situation without allowing her foster parents to do her further harm. Their natural child has also been removed from their custody." Kateri drew a breath. "Last night I spent six hours coaxing that child out of the dog crate that has been her home."

The room was abruptly quiet, as if each man held his breath in horror.

Kateri flicked a glance at Mrs. Bergen.

The woman had uncrossed her arms. Now she clutched the seat of her chair and leaned forward, her gaze fixed on Kateri.

Kateri continued, "The child was understandably reluctant, confused, and frightened by the changes in her environment. In short, she didn't trust us. Although she was starving and dehydrated, she did not respond to promises of food or drink, but rather to my dog, Lacey, who entered the crate and cuddled with her. She also listened to my assurance that I would remain with her while she was settled in a new home and, most sadly"—Kateri's voice quavered and her eyes filled with tears—"to the promise of a hug."

Mr. Caldwell grinned.

Noah covered his eyes with his hand.

She knew why. No one wanted an emotional sheriff. Those tears had just lost her the election.

So what the hell. Might as well go for broke. "The child is in the hospital for observation. She's been fed and bathed. When I left her, she was asleep. In the future, let's all watch out for each other a little more, be kinder to those who depend on us to shield them from the cruelties of life." Abruptly, she was done. "Now, if you'll excuse me, Deputy Bergen will handle your questions. I am going to get some sleep." She stepped away from the podium. She leaned heavily on the staff and limped toward the door.

Lacey followed.

Mr. Caldwell stepped aside.

She smacked him on the shin anyway.

Outside the conference room, she leaned against the wall. She took a few long breaths and heard someone ask, "Did your sheriff sustain an injury in the raid?"

"She wasn't at the raid." Mr. Caldwell spoke without the microphone, but loudly enough for everyone, especially Kateri, to hear. "She didn't know anything about it until the Milhollands had been arrested."

Bergen said, "That's Kateri Kwinault. You might remember her from a few years ago, when the tsunami swept through Virtue Falls. She was the Coast Guard commander who saved the Coast Guard cutters and almost lost her life in the process."

To give Bergen his due, he made her sound like a hero. On the other hand, that information would remind everyone that she had lost the cutter under her own command and been subjected to a court-martial, and that was never good publicity.

Time to go home. Definitely time to go home.

CHAPTER TWENTY-EIGHT

Taking care of that little girl had brought childhood moments bubbling up in Kateri's subconscious, and by late afternoon she was on her feet, fleeing vivid nightmares of dark and fear and being torn from her mother's arms. She visited Natalie in the hospital; the child was so pathetically grateful to see her, she reminded Kateri of what was important in this life. And it wasn't winning the sheriff's race.

Unfortunately, when she walked into the Oceanview Café, Noah was waiting at her table. He hadn't been reminded of *anything*. "Did you have to cry?" he asked.

She seated herself across from him. "I didn't cry."

"You were doing great. Took command like a pro. Made Bergen and his campaign manager look like the assholes they are. And I saw those strikes you laid on Bergen and his buddy with your walking stick. You don't even need that thing, do you?"

"On occasion." She leaned back in her chair, smugly remembering Mr. Caldwell's wince. "In high school, I took karate. Got good with a bamboo staff. I've retained it all."

"Then you had to cry." Noah rolled his eyes like a ten-year-old boy.

"I didn't cry."

"Girls cry."

"I can use the staff on you, too."

Noah grinned. "Okay. Damage is done. Since Bergen couldn't answer a lot of the important questions because he abandoned the kid after he rescued her—you made that abundantly clear—he wrapped up the press conference in a pretty big hurry. He left with Mrs. Bergen and she was mad about something."

Interesting. "How do you know?"

"She wasn't speaking to him. He looked scared, the big sissy."

"Good. I hope she gave him hell about . . . something." Anything.

"In the paper, he looked like a hero."

"*You* wrote the article."

"Gotta keep the paying job."

"Yesterday *I* was the hero."

"In the news, yesterday's a long time ago. Plus you only found drugs. He saved a kid." Noah looked hopeful. "I don't suppose you could save someone?"

Kateri looked at the table where Cordelia frowned at her computer. "I think we found the kid we had the tip on. In fact, I hope we did. I don't want to think there's another person out there suffering like that little girl." She shuddered.

Noah drooped despondently. "I suppose you're right."

Kateri laughed. "Oh, Noah."

"Never mind. I know you're right. I'm headed to the resort. Elizabeth and the baby are in town. Want to join me?"

"Thank you, I'd love to, but I'm ordering dinner to go, I need to check in at the office, and then I've *got* to get some more sleep."

"Sleep? Is that what we're calling it now?" He indicated the door. "Your boyfriend's here."

Kateri looked up to see Luis walking in. "He's not my boyfriend."

"Doesn't matter anymore. We've lost the election. You can have a boyfriend."

"Thank you, Mr. Campaign Manager." She pointed out the obvious.

"He's not my boyfriend, and even if he were, he's the Coast Guard commander. He's not a disreputable guy to date."

"Females running for office as sheriff can't date strong men because that makes them look weak, and they can't date weak men because that makes them look like ballbusters. But that doesn't matter, because—"

"I didn't cry."

"See you later." Noah kissed her forehead, then headed out the door.

Cordelia watched him hungrily.

Kateri wondered if Noah had even noticed, or if he was pretending to be oblivious.

Luis slid into the chair opposite and smiled with all that Latin charm. "Tell me you'll go to a movie with me tonight."

"See these bags under my eyes?" She pointed. "Not tonight."

"Tomorrow night then. A movie, popcorn, a Coke, and one box of Raisinets."

"I hate Raisinets."

"I know. That leaves them all for me."

"You're incorrigible."

"And cute. Don't forget cute."

He *was* cute. Damn him.

Rainbow put the cardboard container of food on the table. "After the week you've had, Sheriff, dinner's on us."

Kateri shook her head at Rainbow. "Does Dax know he's buying my dinner?"

"No, but he's glad to do it."

"You mean you'll tell him he's glad to do it."

"I mean he's so grateful to have me working here, he's glad to do anything I tell him." In the kitchen, Dax rang a bell and bellowed something about green cheese and loggers, whatever that meant. Rainbow rolled her eyes and headed back to pick up the chili cheese fries and deliver them to the latest group of sunburned tourists in from a hike.

Kateri grabbed her walking stick, prepared to get to her feet, and found Luis helping her with her chair and otherwise assisting her.

Sometimes he was so charming she forgot how incredibly supportive he was—and had been during her long recovery.

He tucked her hand into his elbow, smiled into her face, and led her toward the door. And stopped when Mr. Caldwell called, "Sheriff Kwinault, I stubbed my toe. Here's my handkerchief if you want to cry about it."

Luis abandoned Kateri. He stalked toward the table. He put his fists on the table, leaned forward, and in a voice both deadly and angry, he asked, "What kind of man does not cry to hear of cruelty to a child? Only a coward who does not admit to emotion . . . or a man who can perform such cruelty himself. Which are you, Mr. Caldwell?"

CHAPTER TWENTY-NINE

A blotchy red stain under the skin crawled up from under Mr. Caldwell's collar, up his face, and over his scalp, the flush shining brightly through his thinning hair.

Kateri was afraid he was going to have a stroke. She thought she should say something to defuse the situation.

Then she realized—nothing she said could fix this. This matter was between these two powerful men: between the elderly U.S. statesman and the new Coast Guard commander. And they would not welcome her interference.

Rainbow drifted behind her and whispered, "Strategic retreat advised!"

Right. Kateri sidled backward and out the door. She hurried into city hall and into the quiet patrol room. So quiet she realized the old camaraderie had vanished. Her drug bust, Bergen's rescue of the abused child, and most of all, the press conference had solidly divided the officers into two camps. Not that they probably hadn't all known for whom they were going to vote before, but now discreet disagreement had turned into stiff dissension. The department was uncomfortable—and silent.

She went into her office.

Kateri could do nothing about the cool atmosphere but deal with the day-to-day situations as she had always done. Every day the election loomed closer, and according to the polls, every day Bergen continued to pull ahead. Win some, lose some. Not that she didn't care, but she found that for her, it was less about the race and more about losing the job she did well and loved. And, of course, the specter of unemployment reared its ugly head. Maybe Bergen would hire her as . . . a psychological counselor to the police department. Or a psychic. In the novels, all the police departments had a psychic.

Cheered by the idea—because, after all, she had better psychic creds than anyone else she knew—she fired up her computer and pulled the first file folder across her desk.

Everyone agreed the downside of being a law officer was the paperwork.

The downside of being sheriff was reviewing everyone else's paperwork and making sure her own paperwork got done. She was going through the case files, one eye on the clock, and when Mona buzzed through on the antiquated intercom Kateri was almost relieved.

That lasted until Mona said, "Sheriff, Mrs. Butenschoen is on the phone and asking for you."

Forty-five minutes before Kateri intended to leave and Mrs. Butenschoen was calling to complain about dog poop or illegal rhododendron clipping.

"Thank you, Mona." Kateri picked up.

"Sheriff Kwinault, this is Mrs. Butenschoen on Dogwood Blossom Street."

Kateri would recognize that persnickety voice anywhere. "Yes, Mrs. Butenschoen, I know where you live."

"I don't know if you've heard, but I recently installed a video camera in my front yard."

"I did hear that." *And wasn't at all surprised.*

"It's not as easy to program as one might like, and well . . . would it be possible for you to come by and view something I saw? By accident?"

Oh, no, please, no . . . "Mrs. Butenschoen, if you have discovered who is placing dog bombs on your front walk, you can file a report and use your video as evidence—"

Mrs. Butenschoen interrupted. Of course. "I would like to speak to *you*. I would like *you* to see this." A hesitation. "Please."

Hm. *Please.* Mrs. Butenschoen being nice. Interesting. Maybe ominous. "I've got a few minutes left before I go off duty. Why don't I come by now?"

"That would be perfect. Thank you, Sheriff Kwinault."

Kateri stared at the phone before she put it back on the charger. *So close to going home . . .* Yet best to catch Mrs. Butenschoen in a good mood. Standing, Kateri fetched her walking stick and exited her office. "Mona, I'm going to visit Mrs. Butenschoen and then take off for the day."

"All right, Sheriff. See you tomorrow." Mona started shoving her work in her desk drawers. It was four thirty, she should put in another half hour, but with Kateri gone Mona would skip out. She was a crummy personal assistant, a malicious gossip, she wore enough perfume to set off every allergy in the patrol room, and Kateri itched to fire her. But Mona was in the throes of a hot affair with City Councilman Venegra, less than fondly known in the police department as Viagra Venegra, and until the flames cooled, the councilman lost an election, or Mrs. Venegra shot her, there was no getting rid of Mona.

In the patrol room, no one gave Kateri a bad time about leaving early to go on a date. No one said anything until she called, "I'm headed to Mrs. Butenschoen's. Anyone want to come with me?"

She got a chorus of moans and Moen's "Sucks to be you," and the arctic atmosphere warmed a few degrees.

No matter how slowly Kateri drove, she still reached Dogwood Blossom Street in less than ten minutes. She pulled up in front of Mrs. Butenschoen's, turned off the motor, and looked at the neat and tiny house. With a sigh, she climbed out and headed up the front walk, watching carefully for dog bombs.

She had to admit, it *would* be interesting to see who was willing to go through so much smelly trouble to give Mrs. Butenschoen a rough time.

The front door opened before Kateri put her foot on the first step; she found herself looking up at Mrs. Butenschoen and wondering how much hair spray it took to torture her hair into those immovable helmet-like waves.

"Thank you for coming so quickly, Sheriff. I do appreciate it." Mrs. Butenschoen swung open the screen door.

"Just doing my job," Kateri said, and wondered when she had descended into clichéland. They walked through the entry and into the neat kitchen decorated with formal English china teapots set on a corner shelf and formal teapots printed on the wallpaper. The round dining table held a steaming teapot clad in a knit yarn cozy, two delicate flowered cups, a plate of cookies—and a laptop.

Mrs. Butenschoen seated herself in the captain's chair and gestured for Kateri to seat herself. "Do you like tea, Sheriff? If not, I can make coffee for you. Or pour you a Coke."

"Tea is fine, thank you." Kateri asked for one lump of sugar and a dab of cream and watched as Mrs. Butenschoen poured it out. She sipped and ate a lemon cookie. She felt as if she had fallen into an alternate Mrs. Butenschoen universe.

"I can't think why I've never asked you in before. This is so much more civilized than having a row on the street."

Definitely an alternative universe. "It's lovely. Thank you. Now . . . you said you have video confirmation of your"—what to call him?—"'culprit'?"

"I do. But it gets even more interesting than you can imagine." Mrs. Butenschoen pulled her laptop toward her and opened it. "Once I determined to buy a surveillance camera, I researched the matter thoroughly, determined I could install the camera myself, and when I was last in Seattle I bought it at Costco for a good price."

"Of course." Kateri accepted another lemon cookie. "These are great."

"Thank you. I made them myself."

Kateri had never doubted it.

"Unfortunately, the software is not easily mastered and the manual is less than helpful, and rather than scan only my yard, the camera swings in wide circles." Mrs. Butenschoen nudged the laptop toward Kateri. "Sometimes I see my yard, sometimes across the street, sometimes next door, sometimes my rhododendrons or my siding. Which is how I missed the poop perpetrator the past two times."

Kateri angled her chair to see the screen. "That's rather dizzying."

"Yes. And frustrating. But last night I did at last catch the criminal in the act."

On the screen, Kateri saw a man in a dark suit walk up to the gate. He carried a shovel, and when he glanced around, she recognized him and did a double take. "Isn't that the neighbor from across the street?"

"Yes. Dayton Floren."

"Right." He opened the gate, placed a pile of dog poop on Mrs. Butenschoen's top step, and quickly left. Kateri sat back in her chair. "Law enforcement is one surprise after another."

"I didn't suspect him either. He dresses so well, seems so prosperous and well spoken. I was going to call as soon as I saw him, but then I had a thought. Because of the erratic behavior of the camera, I wondered if I could see who had set the fire at Mr. Denisov's home."

Kateri's respect for Mrs. Butenschoen's logic took a forward leap. "You would make a good detective."

Mrs. Butenschoen smiled. "Yes. I would."

"Did you succeed in catching the arsonist on camera?" Obviously she was or she wouldn't be sitting there all rosy-cheeked and smug.

Mrs. Butenschoen typed in a command, then turned the screen face toward Kateri.

Kateri's jaw dropped, and it took her more than a few moments to recover her power of speech. "But he . . . he . . . that's Dayton Floren again. Why . . . why . . . ?"

"Exactly my thought. Why him?" Clearly Mrs. Butenschoen had the answer, because she opened her browser and pointed.

There it was, a biography of Dayton Floren, disgraced son of Washington real estate developer Neil Floren. Before he was twenty-four, Dayton had been accused of real estate fraud. Nothing had been proved, and in the ensuing seven years he had developed subdivisions in Tacoma and the Tri-Cities area. One of those subdivisions had had to be abandoned before it was finished because of pesticides in the soil. Real estate fraud indeed. "But what is he doing *here*? What does he hope to accomplish?"

"I have thought deeply on this matter, and I believe he wants to chase us out of our beloved historical neighborhood, buy the houses on the cheap, and develop the area into horrid modern beach houses or, worse, duplexes." Mrs. Butenschoen was clearly offended to the depths of her soul.

"You may be right."

"Of course I'm right! He has been disparaging of our pristine neighborhood, offering to buy people's houses."

"That's hardly a crime." Although in Mrs. Butenschoen's eyes it was. "Putting poop on someone's front walk isn't exactly the act of a terrorist."

"I assure you, I felt afraid that the person who hated me so much as to defile my yard might proceed to other, more violent crimes against my person." Mrs. Butenschoen's voice quavered.

"Yes. You're right, of course, Mrs. Butenschoen." Just because the police department giggled at poop on the lawn didn't mean a single woman living alone would not feel alarmed by the malevolence of the act. "Arson, at least, is incredibly serious and could have led to the death of Mr. Denisov or a firefighter. Or both."

"I have also wondered whether . . ." Mrs. Butenschoen traced the edge of her teapot with her finger. "I'm somewhat ashamed of the way I accused Madeline Hewitson of setting the fire."

Wow. Yet another indication of the heretofore unsuspected human side of Mrs. Butenschoen. "Yes. But in all fairness, Maddie is quite . . . odd."

"She always thinks someone's after her. I was wondering if Dayton Floren had been tormenting her as he's been tormenting me."

Kateri didn't want Mrs. Butenschoen to make premature accusations, but she did have a point. "That's worth looking into. . . . Do you possibly have any video of him over there?"

"I would have to look. It does take time to review the recordings." Looking suddenly weary and blue around the mouth, Mrs. Butenschoen lifted her teacup.

Kateri noticed a slight tremor in her fingers. "I'm sorry you've been worried. Have you not been sleeping?"

"As I said—my conscience is not entirely clear in regard to Madeline Hewitson."

Which was an answer of sorts. "Do you know, is Dayton Floren at home?"

"Not now. I saw him drive away. Sometimes he's gone for days. Sometimes he comes home in the middle of the night and staggers up his walk. I suspect he goes to bars and drinks alcohol." Now she sounded like the prissy, disapproving Mrs. Butenschoen.

Kateri stood. "Mrs. Butenschoen, thank you so much for your help, and thanks for any future help you might give Virtue Falls law enforcement. Now—why don't you get some sleep?"

"I've got plenty of time to sleep." Mrs. Butenschoen used her hands to get herself to her feet. "No. I will keep watch and call when I see Mr. Floren arrive at his home."

"No need. I'll order extra patrols for the neighborhood." Obviously Mrs. Butenschoen would watch and call if she wished, so Kateri added, "When the arrest is made, I will give you full credit in the news story."

Mrs. Butenschoen folded her hands at her belt. "Thank you. I would like that. I hope his arrest will ease Madeline Hewitson's anxiety."

"I hope so, too."

CHAPTER THIRTY

Kateri stopped to pick up Lacey, then headed for home. As she fit her key into the door, Charlotte Lombardi came out of the next-door apartment looking young and disgustingly fit in her workout clothes. She carried a large, square cardboard box in her hands. "Sheriff Kwinault, Bill asked if I would sign for this and of course I was glad to."

Bill was their aptly named postal carrier. Charlotte was a physical trainer at Planet Granite, the local gym. And Kateri didn't remember ordering anything online. "What is it?"

"Registered mail from Baltimore!"

"Baltimore." Funny how the name of the place still had the ability to chill the blood and heat the face.

"From Neill Palmer. Do you know a Neill Palmer?"

"He . . . yes. I know him." Her father. Her uncaring, uninterested, unresponsive father. "I'm surprised to hear from him." They hadn't had contact since she had asked for help getting into the Coast Guard Academy and he had given it . . . after grinding her pride into the dust.

"Let me carry it inside for you. It's heavy!" Charlotte spoke in exclamation points, especially when she was nervous.

Kateri could see why. "The tape on the box has been ripped away." She opened the door.

Lacey raced inside, ears flapping like adorable pigtails.

Charlotte followed. "You know what they're like down at the post office. It was open when it got here!"

"Um-hum. Did you peek inside?"

"By accident!" Charlotte's face slid from perpetually perky to simply sad. "I couldn't see anything. There's another box inside. It's black."

Lacey sat next to her food bowl, scraping it across the kitchen floor with each nudge of her butt.

"Okay," Kateri said, "put it over there in the corner beside the couch."

"Black and with a lid that lifts off." Charlotte placed it on the coffee table. "A big, heavy, textured gift box!"

"Thank you for signing for it."

"Aren't you going to open it?" Charlotte shuffled from foot to foot like a kid waiting for Christmas. Obviously, *she'd* never received a gift she didn't want.

"Maybe after dinner." After next year's dinner. "Are you off to teach a class?"

"Yes, I'm taking the hot yoga class tonight because Archie pulled his hamstring. Is it your birthday?"

"No. Archie pulls a lot of muscles, doesn't he?"

At last Kateri had pried Charlotte's attention away from the delivery. She planted her hands on her skinny hips and said hotly, "I tell him and tell him not to overstretch in hot yoga, but when there's a handsome man there, he must show off!"

Lacey barked and nudged her bowl with her nose.

Good dog. "I've got to feed Lacey, and you'd better hurry or you'll be late."

Charlotte's gaze snapped back to the box. "But—"

Kateri used her walking stick to gently shoo Charlotte out. "Thanks again! Don't be late on my account! See you later!" When she got the door shut, she thankfully leaned against it. If she hung around that young woman for long, she'd be talking in all exclamation points, too.

She fed Lacey—for such a girly dog, Lacey had a good and insistent appetite—then poured a can of soup into a pan and put it on the stove. While it heated, she ignored the cardboard box, and when that didn't work, she removed it off the coffee table and placed it beside the couch, ripped the return label off, and tossed it into the garbage. Then she used her foot to nudge the box as far behind the couch as possible. Which wasn't enough, because it was still visible.

Charlotte was right, it was heavy, and Kateri felt certain she knew what it contained and what it meant. She didn't care. She did. Not. Care.

She tried to eat her soup and couldn't, tried to ignore the memories that whispered cruel things in a kind, overly patient tone.

The phone rang.

She jumped, glanced at the caller ID, picked up, and said, "Rainbow, I'm really tired and want to get ready for bed."

"It's not late," Rainbow said. "Do you know what that old fart Mr. Caldwell said to Luis?" Her voice made it clear she had the juiciest gossip ever.

No, no, no. I left so I wouldn't be involved.

"He said the only reason Luis got the position was because he's a Mexican."

Kateri thumped her head against the wall. "I didn't want to know."

"Then Luis said the only reason Mr. Caldwell was ever elected state senator was because he was white."

Kateri groaned. "Oh, Luis."

"The old guy threatened to beat Luis up."

"Luis is fifty years younger!"

"Didn't matter. Dax had to come out of the kitchen and tell them to take it outside. And they did. Now stay awake because I'm coming over."

"No, Rainbow! I really don't want to know."

The doorbell rang.

Lacey barked.

"Too late, I'm here," Rainbow said.

Kateri had been sucked into the maw of curiosity. She limped over, opened the door, looked at a grinning Rainbow, and hung up the phone. "Then what happened?"

Rainbow killed her phone, too. She petted Lacey and held up a pizza box. "Have you eaten?"

"Yes!"

"What? A can of soup?"

Kateri hadn't really eaten it, so she said, "Soup is very filling." At the smell of garlic, cheese, and basil, her stomach growled.

"Heh!" Rainbow pushed her way inside.

Lacey pranced after her. Like most people in Virtue Falls, she adored Rainbow.

Of course, Rainbow immediately spotted the shipping box. "What's that?"

"God, you're nosy." Kateri should have flung an afghan over it.

"That's how I know everyone's business. What did you get?"

"Maybe it's your birthday present."

Rainbow spun to face Kateri. "When's my birthday?"

Damn. "Um, August?"

"April." With great ceremony, Rainbow put the pizza and her beer down on the coffee table. "My birthday is in April."

Did Kateri get points for guessing an "A" month? "Did I miss it again? I mean, I'm a lousy friend and I wanted to make up for my negligence so I bought you this great . . ." she gestured at the package.

"Thank you, Kateri Kwinault, and I will open it now."

"No. Come on. I need to wrap it . . ." Kateri watched as Rainbow tromped—yes, tromped—over to the box, picked it up, and carried it to the breakfast bar. "Okay, it's not a present. It's something from—"

"Baltimore. Your father. I can read the postmark, you know. You'd think a high roller like him would send packages FedEx overnight."

"You'd think." Kateri watched morosely as Rainbow ripped all the tape away from the package, pulled out the textured black box, and raised the lid.

Lacey subsided on her bed, put her head on her paws, watched the two women as if puzzled by the tension.

Rainbow looked inside and gasped. "Wow. Wow, this is . . . gorgeous. I've never seen anything like it. You know what it is?"

"A raven, right?"

"A raven?" Rainbow sent an incredulous glance at Kateri. "A piece of art! Nineteenth-century black cast iron, eighteen inches tall, weighs"—she lifted it from the box, unwrapped it from the bubble wrap—"a hefty twenty pounds."

"Been watching *Antiques Roadshow*?"

"That. And my parents are artists. Textile artists, but they know their way around the field." Rainbow placed the statue on the counter and stepped back. "Look at those eyes. They watch. They know. This is brilliant."

Kateri remembered how the raven watched, what the raven knew. She remembered being transfixed by that fixed, beady-eyed gaze.

"Ravens are great Native American icons of magic and transformation. Your father must have sent it to you because—"

Kateri interrupted. "It's got nothing to do with Native American culture. This is Edgar Allan Poe's raven."

Hand on chest, Rainbow staggered back. "*The* raven?"

"Evermore." It was almost funny to see Rainbow's awe.

"So not just art. Art with a history. This thing must be worth—"

"A lot." Memory swamped her. *Don't touch that, Katherine. It's not a toy. It's valuable, it's been in this well-respected family for a hundred years, and you are . . . Just don't touch it.*

Rainbow checked the postage again. "At least he insured it. Generous gift. You going to call him and thank him?"

"No."

"Someday you're going to have to let go of your father issues."

"No."

"Hm." That single word held a world of judgment. Rainbow looked around Kateri's tiny living room. "Where are you going to put it?"

"Back in the box to send it back."

"Right." Kateri had never told Rainbow—had never told anyone—about her time in Baltimore, but Rainbow knew better than to argue. "What about the photo album?"

Kateri froze. Her lips barely moved. "What photo album?"

From the bottom of the box, Rainbow lifted an old-fashioned leather-bound photo album with black pages and stick-on photo corners. She opened to the first page. "Family photos. Wow. I took that picture. Your dad and your mother. At the beach. She looks so happy."

Disbelief. Anguish. Rage. Her father had sent Kateri *that*? The *bastard*. In a guttural tone, Kateri said, "Get rid of it."

Lacey lifted her head and growled.

Kateri's voice rose. "Get rid of the whole thing. The raven. The album!"

Hackles raised, Lacey raced to stand between Kateri and Rainbow, then looked between them, obviously bewildered. She knew Rainbow. She liked Rainbow. Why was she protecting Kateri from Rainbow?

"Don't you want to see . . . ?" Rainbow saw Kateri's expression. "No. You don't. So . . . send it back?"

Kateri's chest hurt. "Throw it away. Dump it."

Rainbow looked into the open album, then back up at Kateri. In obvious distress, she said, "Listen, I'll take it, keep it until you—"

"Leave it here." Kateri put on a pleasant face, moderated her voice, called her dog to her side, and leaned down to rub her ears. "I'll . . . deal with it."

"Right." Rainbow shut the photo album, plopped it in the bottom of the box, wrapped up the raven and placed it on top, put the lid back on. She took the box back to its spot beside the couch, grabbed the pizza and beer, and brought them to the kitchen counter. She managed to sound almost prosaic when she asked, "Want to hear what happened with Luis and Mr. Caldwell or not?"

That was Kateri's cue to be normal. And be normal she would. If she didn't, Rainbow would start talking about cleansing Kateri's aura with crystals to remove the poisonous hate that corroded her soul. There had been times when that hate had given her backbone, kept her alive. "Sure. Let me get the plates." She gave Lacey one last pet and urged her toward her cushion on the kitchen floor. "So Luis and Mr. Caldwell took it outside and . . . ?"

"Deputy Bergen came out of city hall and across the street at a run—"

"How did *he* hear about it?"

"I called him. Jeez, like we need your Coastie boyfriend in jail just when the affair is getting interesting."

Automatically Kateri said, "We're not having an affair."

"Whose fault is that? Anyway, Bergen towed Mr. Caldwell away. Mr. Caldwell was shouting at him."

Kateri began to relax and so did Lacey. "Poetic justice. I hope Bergen and his slimy campaign manager are at loggerheads."

"Luis didn't come out looking too well, either. Insulting people because they're white!" Rainbow stuck out her freckled arm. "Look at that. Certified white bread!"

"Me—I don't have to hate someone because of his language or his skin. There're always enough assholes around I can hate people individually."

"Truth. Get yourself something to drink." Rainbow opened up the pizza. The garlicky scent got stronger and Kateri could see what looked like the most delectable margarita pizza ever. "This is from Sienna's Sandwiches. She got a wood stone oven and now she's making dough and gourmet pizzas."

Kateri popped the top on a bottle of sparkling water and subsided on a bar stool. "Of course she is." Luis's former girlfriend hid gritty ambition behind a sunny disposition, a peaches-and-cream complexion, and a sweet smile.

"Hate isn't a healthy emotion," Rainbow warned.

"I don't hate her"—exactly—"I simply don't trust her."

"Me, either." Rainbow smirked. "I sure didn't tell her I was sharing the pizza with *you*."

One bite and Kateri admitted, "Good."

"Could you say it more grudgingly?" Rainbow leaned forward into her juicy gossip position. "Have you heard Stag Denali is back in town?"

That brought Kateri up short. "I thought he was in prison for . . . something."

"He was. For beating up some guy who insulted him. Or maybe for killing him." Rainbow waved an airy hand. "After a couple of years, his lawyers got him released. He's been out for a while, making money hand over fist."

Stag was Native American, tall with a build that was, ironically, rawboned John Wayne-esque, with broad shoulders, narrow hips, and long, long legs. Which was about all anyone knew about him for sure. Rumor claimed he was from Alaska. Rumor also claimed he started his career young, moving up from bouncer to enforcer to the guy who developed casinos on the reservations and had connections to the mob.

Kateri sipped her sparkling water. "I haven't seen him in years. Since I was a teen. Did I ever have a crush on him!"

"Join the club. Strip that man down to a loincloth, give him a hatchet, and he can scalp me anytime. . . . Was *that* racially insensitive?"

"Might have been, Miss Certified Pasty White."

"He still looks good. Real good."

"Glad you cleared that up." Kateri was possibly more glad than she wanted to admit. "Life being what it is, I figured he would develop a paunch."

"He came into the Oceanview Café for pie and coffee. He looks like a man who works out every day . . . by running naked through the forest."

"Insensitive again," Kateri warned.

Rainbow grinned. "He likes me that way."

"I don't think Stag Denali has ever met a woman he didn't like."

"Yes, he's one of the good ones. Do you *still* have a crush on him?"

"I don't know. I'd have to see him again . . . running naked through the forest."

Rainbow snorted beer out of her nose.

Kateri pumped her fist in victory and passed her a napkin.

When they settled down, they finished the pizza, and Kateri asked the question she hated to ask. "What's Stag Denali doing in Virtue Falls?"

"He didn't say."

"You didn't ask?"

"Of course I did. He just didn't say."

To Kateri, that sounded like trouble had come to town.

Her sense of disaster grew when she took a bathroom run, came out, and discovered Rainbow was gone—and so was the box from Baltimore.

Kateri felt as if an old bomb had started ticking toward detonation; perhaps it had always been there and she'd only now noticed.

Sunday, Luis took Kateri to the movies, bought her a box of Raisinets, and as promised, ate them all.

Monday they drove to the far end of town, grabbed food from

Birdie's Fish and Chips, climbed the sand dunes, and ate while watching Lacey chase the seagulls.

Tuesday after work he dropped by and took her and Lacey for a walk down to the marina, newly rebuilt since the tsunami and a burgeoning tourist attraction.

Wednesday it rained, which was okay because Natalie was released from the hospital and sent to a new foster home. Kateri found herself reassuring the terrified child; she promised to e-mail every day and call once a week forever or until Natalie no longer needed her. Then she went home and cried. When Luis showed up at her door she tried to send him away. He took one look at her tear-stained face, charged through the doorway, ordered pizza *not* from Sienna's, sat on the couch, and held her while she told him too much about her childhood . . . but not all. Not nearly all.

That night he thoroughly kissed her, but he didn't press for sex.

Thursday it rained again and it was her night on call, and she worked a fatal head-on collision. She was on the scene with ambulances and a cleanup crew until after ten, but she talked to Luis all the way home.

Friday evening he drove her and Rainbow to the resort, where they enjoyed a family dinner with Margaret and her granddaughter Patricia, Garik and Elizabeth, and their daughter. That night Luis wanted to come in and finish what they had started, and Kateri was tempted. So tempted. But she thought about the nosy neighbors, her race for sheriff, and the recent end of his relationship with Sienna, and she regretfully refused. He pointed out everyone in town knew they were dating. She agreed that was true. He said that if she kept holding him off, his reputation as a stud would suffer. She laughed, kissed him good night, and sent him on his way.

On Saturday, he called in the morning and chatted, suggested a few things they could do that evening, seemed perfectly at ease . . .

He never showed up. Kateri got angry, called Rainbow and complained that all he'd wanted from her was sex.

Rainbow was not sympathetic to Kateri's grievance.

On Sunday, he didn't call or appear. Kateri started to worry, but reasoned that if he'd been hurt, she was the sheriff and would be the first to know.

Monday she overslept; despite her own logic, all night she had been worried and wakeful. She walked into city hall and through an unusually silent and watchful patrol room and idly wondered if Bergen had called another press conference.

Mona was at her desk outside Kateri's office, and she had that expression on her face, the kind that meant she was about to explode with nasty gossip.

Kateri knew better than to try to hold her off. So she stopped by Mona's desk and waited.

Mona said nothing except a nervous, "Hi, Sheriff, hope you had a *real* good weekend."

"Yes. Thanks. It was fine."

"Good! Yep. Good. I'll have last week's reports typed up and sent to you before the morning is much older!"

Huh. It was Monday morning, and Mona was working. That could not be good.

"Is there more ugly news about the sheriff's race?" Kateri asked.

"Gosh no, Sheriff. In fact, I know Mrs. Bergen is mad because Deputy Bergen hired Mr. Caldwell. She doesn't like the old f . . . guy."

Fascinating. "But Mr. Caldwell seems to be effective."

"That's for sure. The deputy is miles ahead of you in the polls." Mona snapped her mouth shut as if even *she* had realized she'd been tactless.

Mona being worried about whether she hurt Kateri's feelings. *Definitely* not good.

Kateri walked into her office. At once her gaze fell on a brown envelope wrapped with a shiny blue ribbon tied in a bow. It had been meticulously propped against the photo of her with the men of her Coast Guard command. Picking up the envelope, she noted her name was written in calligraphy with sparkly blue ink.

The envelope, the ribbon, the calligraphy—to Kateri, they all said *Sienna*.

Kateri was pretty sure her week had taken a turn for the worse.

CHAPTER THIRTY-ONE

Someone was in the room with her.

In the middle of the night, Maddie woke and came to her feet. Her chair clattered and fell. Her heart raced and pounded. She spun in a circle, looking, seeking.

Nothing. The room was empty. No caped figure stalked her. No narrow eyes glinted in crazed pleasure. She was alone in her house.

She glanced at the clock. It was 1:15 A.M. She had been asleep two hours. More, maybe. Her butt hurt from sitting in that hard metal chair. Her arms had rested on the desk, her head cradled between them, and her shoulders ached from the awkward position. But she *was* alone. The trail of fingers across the nape of her neck was nothing but a terrifying dream.

Wait. At her dining room table. Who had turned that chair to face her? She hadn't done it. She knew she hadn't done it.

But maybe she had. She already knew that when she wrote, she was distracted. So maybe . . . maybe. Yes. She must have done it.

She stood and stretched. And saw a small piece of paper on the floor by the chair.

Reluctantly, she approached it. It looked like her drawing paper. Perhaps it had sailed off her desk and traveled on a wind current . . . although, of course, all the windows were shut and locked.

She picked it up, turned it over, and saw a sketch in pen and ink with a dark, menacing figure in a cape and hat.

But she had not drawn this. The style was primitive, the face had been painted with peach watercolor. And the eyes. Oh, God, the eyes. They glowed a sick, bright red.

With painful deliberation, she placed the paper on the dining table.

He had been in her house while she slept. *He* had been watching her. *He* had seen the monster she drew and he knew now she could identify him.

She sat down at the table and put her head in her hands. Why was he doing this? He could have killed her while she slept. Instead he cruelly tormented her. For what purpose? Why did he wish her to live in constant debilitating fear?

She wanted to call the police, to tell them, show them her evidence. But then everyone would know what her monster looked like, and she would be even more vulnerable.

She needed more sleep.

She couldn't have sleep.

So she needed to eat. Standing, she went to the refrigerator and pulled out a beribboned box from Sienna's Sandwiches. She had bought it earlier today. Right now, she wasn't hungry, but she knew a cookie waited inside; her favorite, apricot nut oatmeal.

She deserved that cookie.

Setting the box on the counter, she slowly untied the shimmering blue ribbon at the top. She loved doing that; she loved the ritual involved, knowing when she opened the box, she would see the careful arrangement of sandwich, salad, and cookie. She eased the tabs apart, pulled back the flaps, and exposed the . . .

Maggots.

Hundreds of white maggots writhing on the bread, the cookie. The top had popped off the salad, and maggots used the macaroni like an amusement park, crawling in and out and . . .

Maddie screamed. She *screamed.* She swept the box off the counter and screamed. Never taking her eyes off the maggots, she ran backward, bumped into the edge of the table, bruised her hip. Hit one of the chairs and knocked it over. Still staring, whimpering now, she wiped at herself.

Had she touched them? Did she have any maggots on her?

Turning, she ran into the bathroom and washed her arms to the elbow. She soaped again and again, trying to get the sensation of white, crawly things off her skin. Then she dried, scrubbing herself with the towel, tossing it into the garbage, and using another towel.

Going to the phone, she dialed 911.

The dispatcher said, as she always did, "Please state the nature of your emergency."

"Maggots. Maggots on my sandwich. And the chair turned wrong. And a sketch—someone was in my house!"

In a weary, patient voice, the dispatcher said, "So you're reporting an intruder, Madeline Hewitson? Again?"

"Yes. Yes!" Maddie could not take her gaze away from the spilled contents of the box. "Maggots. The chair. The sketch. He was here!"

"Would you like me to send out a law officer?"

"Yes. Yes! Why else would I be calling?"

"It will be a few minutes. Please don't disturb the crime scene."

"I'm not touching those maggots," Maddie fervently assured her.

"The officer should be there soon."

"Thank you." A knock on the door. "There he is now." She hoped. She dropped the phone, looked out the peephole.

Jacob. In the circle of her porch light, Jacob stood clad in cutoff khaki shorts and a stained and wrinkled T-shirt. He was staring at the peephole and he mouthed, *What's wrong?*

She yanked open the door. "How did you know to come?"

He was barefoot. "You screamed." He narrowed his eyes. "Louder than normal."

"Right. Thank you for coming." She pointed a shaking finger toward the kitchen. "They're in there."

"What's in there?"

"Maggots. Please take them away. I can't stand the thought of them crawling all over my kitchen."

Jacob went over to the spill. "Ew. How long have you had that sandwich?"

"I bought it today!"

"You must have had it longer than that. This is from Sienna's, right? The place you buy your sandwiches?"

"Yes." Her voice was squeaking.

"This food is rotten."

He wasn't going to believe her. No matter what she said, no matter if she dug out her receipt and showed him, he wouldn't believe her. "Get. Rid. Of it."

He got a handful of paper towels to protect his hands, scooped up the contents—the bread, the meat, the cookie, the salad—and placed it back in the box.

Maddie shuddered and shuddered, and wiped at tears that leaked from her eyes.

"Where's your garbage can?" Jacob asked.

"Out back. But I called the police. Shouldn't you save that as evidence?"

The wail of a siren. Another knock at the door.

Jacob paused, the box held in his hands. "Ask the cop."

She looked through the peephole at Officer Moen of the bright red hair and the raging ambitions. Opening the door, she pointed at Jacob. "*He* came. He helped me. Do you want us to save the maggots as evidence?"

Moen lost color, taking his complexion from pale to pasty white. "Maggots? Ew. No one said maggots. No, I don't want them!"

"I've seen worse. Hell, I've eaten worse." Jacob headed out the back door.

"Miss Hewitson, do you want me to come in? Protect you?" Moen asked.

"From who?"

"From, um, him. He's"—Moen lowered his voice—"a little crazy."

She remembered all too well what had happened the last time Moen was in her house. "No. No, thank you. I'm fine."

"Miss Hewitson, I don't know what the police department can do about these incidents, but I will continue to park close and hopefully that will make you feel safer."

Please, no. "That's not necessary. I know you have other duties."

"It's okay. I have to go somewhere on my lunch hour. Anytime you feel threatened, come out and wave at me and I'll be here ASAP."

"Sure. Thank you." She shut the door in his face. She peeked out the window and watched until Officer Moen pulled away. But he wouldn't go far, she knew. Not far enough.

Jacob came back, wiping at his hands. "Anything else?"

She pointed again. "That chair was not where I put it. There is a sketch I didn't draw."

"Maggots, chair, and sketch. Check."

She felt hostile. Scared. "You can doubt me all you want about the chair and the sketch, but those were maggots! In the large scheme of things, maybe they aren't so bad. *They* can't kill me." She stopped, swallowed, whispered, "Only when I'm dead of a slashed throat will they visit again."

With heavy mockery, Jacob asked, "Aren't you dramatic?"

How dare he? The guy—this man Moen labeled as "a little crazy"—was ridiculing her. "You were the last man I expected would make fun of me." Her voice broke. Then she fell apart, sobbing into her hands until she had to rush for the tissues on her desk. Handfuls of tissues, and never enough. She didn't see Jacob pacing toward her—how could she, with her eyes shut tightly against the tears?—but when he tried to wrap her in his arms, she shoved at him. "No!"

He paid no attention, pulling her gently against his chest and murmuring, "I'm sorry. I'm a jerk. Maggots are gross."

"They . . . they . . . they . . . eat dead people!" She tried not to think of her friends, sliced open by a maniac, of Easton, throat cut, bleeding, dying . . . and all of them locked in an eternal embrace with squirming death.

But how could she not think of them? Every day, she worked at her desk and saw that blood spatter. Every day, something stalked her, and for all her sorrow, she did not want to join her friends in their graves. She mourned Easton, but she wanted to live her life, enjoy the sunshine, and never fear the night. She sobbed harder, slurred her words, rained tears on Jacob's wrinkled T-shirt. "I want . . . I want to be normal. I can . . . can . . . can be normal!"

"Shhh."

"Live . . . live like everyone else."

"You can do it."

She yelled into his chest. "Yes! I can! Just . . . let me. Someone . . . let me!" Her own sobbing choked her. She couldn't breathe. Her knees collapsed.

He caught her, picked her up, carried her into the bedroom illuminated only by the light from the living room. He stood her on her feet and threw back the covers. "You need to sleep."

That piece of inanity stopped the tears, restored her breath. "You . . . idiot. I can't sleep! He's been . . . in my house. I don't know what . . . what else he has done to . . . me!"

Jacob wavered under the weight of his decision. "Fine. I'll stay with you." He collapsed onto the sheets, taking her with him.

"I don't want you," she said petulantly.

"I don't want to be here."

She couldn't stand to be alone. "Promise you won't leave."

"I'll be here when you wake up."

"I won't go to sleep."

"Neither will I."

They lay together, both staring at the ceiling in miserable silence, waiting for the morning.

They slept together. No sex. I figured he had no balls.

CHAPTER THIRTY-TWO

Jacob opened his eyes to a sunny room with yellow walls. An antique dresser with a pale blue silk dressing stool. A silver hairbrush. A collection of glass perfume bottles.

Where the hell was he?

He looked down at the person cuddled into his body.

Shit. Maddie. He was at Maddie's. He had slept. All night. At Maddie's.

Look at them now. She'd thrown her leg over his hip. He'd shoved his leg between hers. His arm was asleep because her head rested against his shoulder. And he held her boob in his hand. He hadn't touched a boob for a couple of years. Since he'd been in Korea. Amazing how right away he knew what it was.

She was snoring. *So much for not sleeping.*

God almighty, though. *He'd* been asleep, too. He'd *slept*. Slowly he turned his head to face the nightstand. The clock said ten thirty. The light said it was morning. He'd been here with Maddie for . . . hours. Sleeping. *Sleeping.* No nightmares. No phantoms. Just sleeping like a couple of exhausted . . .

No. Don't use the word "lovers."

He needed to get away before she woke up. He needed to get home before anyone saw him. Before Mrs. Butenschoen scolded him for lowering the moral tone of her beloved neighborhood. Because no matter what he said, no matter how much he denied having sex, Mrs. Butenschoen would think the worst. *Everyone* would think the worst.

Moving with great care, he slid his hand away from Maddie's very agreeable boob. *Good shape, nice size.* He eased his leg from between her legs. Since his morning erection had chosen this moment to make a stand, that was more of a struggle. Not to mention she moaned and flung her arm around his waist like she wanted him to stay put.

Oh, no. He was too smart for that. That way lay . . . so much trouble.

Now to ease his shoulder out from under her head.

He calculated the velocity he should move, the replacement of him with her pillow, how he would maneuver toward the edge of the bed and slide out of the room. . . .

If his arm hadn't been asleep, he would have made it. But at the most inopportune moment, his lifeless hand flopped on her chest—yes, on her boob again—and she came awake like a surprised cat, stiff as a board and claws out.

She recognized him and froze.

He saw the moment she realized what they had done.

She said, "Oh, my God. Oh, my God. We slept together!"

He clapped his hand over her mouth. "We did not. Don't say it like that."

She pushed his hand away. "Right. You're right. We didn't sleep together. We rested on the same bed." She sat up and shoved her hair out of her wide eyes. She looked warm, soft, startled, wary. "But I did . . . were you awake the whole time?"

He was going to lie. *Sure. I was awake.*

But she looked closely and said, "You look better. Less maniacal." She realized the truth and without a thought to diplomacy, she accused, *"You slept, too."*

He nodded grudgingly.

She grabbed the collar of his T-shirt. "We'll never tell anyone. Right? You promise. Right?"

"God, no. Never."

"No, really. You and me. In bed. The neighbors. *Mrs. Butenschoen.*" She shuddered. She edged off the mattress.

He began to feel insulted.

Then, so close they both jumped, a police siren started wailing. No, more than one, and some in the distance, too.

Next door at Mrs. Nyback's, Spike started yapping.

Maddie looked at Jacob, her eyes so wide and horrified that he was undeniably insulted. Irritated, he said, "No one is coming to arrest us for sleeping in your bed."

She took a quavering breath. "Right. You're right."

"No one cares."

"If you believe that, I've got a bridge to sell you."

Now, *she* was right. Not that Jacob would admit it. He stood up and walked into the living room.

"No!" Before he could open the blind, she scampered after him and caught the back of his shirt. "Let me." She peeked out. "Two police cruisers are out there with Moen, Sheriff Kwinault, some other officers. Another patrol car just came around the corner. They're all stopped at the neighbor's across the street."

"Dayton Floren?"

"I don't know. The guy in the suit, the one who's never home. He's standing on the sidewalk. Guns are pointed at him. He's talking fast. Everyone's looking at him." She faced Jacob. "You have to get out. This is the perfect time. Everyone's distracted. Get out."

She was right. "I'll leave the back way, go west down the alley, and come out down at the end of the street by the Pacific." It was broad daylight. He was going out *in broad daylight*.

She implored, "Don't let anybody see you. If anything happened to you, I would never forgive myself."

Now he understood. She was afraid her monster would hunt him down. He supposed that was marginally less insulting than her being embarrassed to be seen with him. But really. "I can take care of myself."

"You're skin and bones. Out of shape. A teenage girl could break you." She pushed him toward the back. "Now go. Go!"

He went out the back door. He tried to slide through her gate. She'd failed to mention she had padlocked it shut. So rather than making an inconspicuous exit, he had to jump the five-foot fence onto the hood of someone's black SUV.

Teach them to park there.

He glanced up and down the alley.

No one was in sight.

He ran to the end of the alley, turned onto the lonely path that wound its way along the cliffs overlooking the ocean, and when he reached the pavement that marked Dogwood Blossom Street, he headed for his home and the ruckus that surrounded Dayton Floren. By the time Jacob managed to reach the police action, he was winded. Skin and bones. Out of shape. *Damn you, Madeline Hewitson, for being right.*

He stopped running and walked up to the crowd.

Mrs. Nyback's damned dog was still yapping. Neighbors from two blocks around were assembled on his lawn. On *his* lawn. Evidently after so many crises they figured his lawn was the common assembly place. And his construction crew—the electricians, the plumbers, the framers—they were here, too, dawdling, fascinated by the unfolding drama.

Jacob glanced around, trying to judge how well he had eased into the scene.

He found Dr. Frownfelter watching him nonjudgmentally, but watching him nevertheless. Frownfelter knew Jacob had come from somewhere else. Still, as far as Jacob could tell, the doctor kept his own counsel, and he would not betray Jacob.

Maddie stood in the middle of the crowd, studiously ignoring him and clasping two books to her chest. Two hardbound books.

Really? On her way out the door, she'd stopped to grab books?

Mrs. Butenschoen arrived, all brisk sympathy and superficial friendliness. "Did they get him?"

The young father from down the street turned on her. "Him who?"

"That young man next door. My surveillance camera caught a man in Mr. Denisov's house looking at the construction plans. It was Dayton Floren. He crumpled them up, put them on the table, ran down the steps—and the flames leaped into the air."

Mr. Franklin turned to his wife. "Dayton Floren? We just sold our house to Dayton Floren!"

"What?" Mrs. Butenschoen arched up like a hooded cobra. "Why would you do that? Why would you leave our beloved historical neighborhood?"

"Every night the cops are here. Every day there's a new crisis. Some of the neighbors are danger—" Mrs. Franklin cut off her words, eyed first Maddie and then Jacob, then added primly, "The neighborhood no longer feels like a safe place to raise our children."

"Of course not. But obviously Dayton Floren is the one who has been making all the trouble." Mrs. Butenschoen moved closer to Maddie. "*All* the trouble."

Maddie edged away, still clutching the books to her chest.

"Not all of it," Mr. Franklin retorted.

"No." Jacob looked at his broken house and the construction crew taking their break on his lawn. "Not all of it."

"Nevertheless, I think we all owe Maddie an apology for our suspicions of her. I, for one, am sorry." Mrs. Butenschoen patted her arm.

Maddie flinched and said, "Thank you, but it's okay. The night of the fire, I got to meet the Williamsons and they kindly exonerated me."

Mrs. Butenschoen glanced around. "Too bad our neighbor Chantal isn't here to see this occurrence. She still seemed doubtful of our Maddie's innocence even after the Williamsons' testimony."

"Speak of the devil," Jacob said.

The low, fast, black Mercedes S-Class coupe drove up, parked at the curb in front of Chantal's house, and Chantal got out of the driver's seat dressed in another one of her short skirts, heels, and a tight black leather jacket. The ugliest man in the world was nowhere in sight.

"In her case, the wages of sin is a really great car," Dr. Frownfelter said.

Jacob did not laugh. But he must have grinned, because both men found themselves pinned under the stern gaze of Mrs. Butenschoen.

As if she had heard them, Chantal tossed her blond hair and went inside.

"Is she an actress?" Maddie asked.

"I heard she was a model," Dr. Frownfelter said.

"That must be why I thought I recognized her," Maddie said.

Moore and Web joined Jacob and Dr. Frownfelter. Moore said, "I have supervised the building of many projects that make me proud, but nothing has ever come as close to perfect architecture as that body."

Web nodded solemnly.

Chantal came back out and, shoulders back, stride long, walked down her sidewalk and across the street. She stopped on the sidewalk—

Jacob figured she didn't dare step into the grass or her stiletto heels would sink—and said, "Hi, neighbors. What's up this time?"

Jacob was a PTSD-plagued veteran so he didn't have to answer. Which was a good thing, since looking at those legs commandeered all his concentration.

Anyway, with Mrs. Butenschoen around, no one else had to say a word. "Mr. Floren has *wicked plans* for Dogwood Blossom Street, and with this fire in Mr. Denisov's home, he went too far."

"Wait. Wait." Chantal waved a long-fingered hand that sported one glittering diamond ring, and Jacob got a whoosh of expensive perfume. "Are you saying that guy set Mr. Denisov's house on fire? On purpose?"

"That is what Sheriff Kwinault is arresting him for." Turning to the Franklins, Mrs. Butenschoen asked, "Aren't you ashamed for selling to him?"

Mr. Franklin clearly did not appreciate being scolded. "Not at all. Dayton made the sale painless and he paid us a good price!"

"I wonder if the contract on the house will hold." Mrs. Franklin confided, "We made a down payment on another, larger home."

"So that guy is buying the houses on this street?" Chantal looked over at Dayton Floren, who was now glaring at Mrs. Butenschoen. "I wonder how much he'd give me for mine."

Mrs. Butenschoen shook her finger at Chantal. "Young lady, don't you sell to him!" She turned to Maddie. "Not you, either!"

Maddie's chin jutted out. "I'm not going anywhere."

"Yeah, well, I need a place with a better garage," Chantal said.

"For that car?" Web muttered. "You don't need a garage, you need a vault."

Chantal watched Dayton Floren through absurdly long lashes, and Jacob thought he detected a mercenary gleam. "Too bad about him getting caught," she said. "How did he get nailed?"

Mrs. Butenschoen leaped to take credit. "I caught him on my security camera and reported him."

Chantal's gaze flicked between Dayton Floren and Mrs. Butenschoen. In a jaded tone she said, "Wow. Just like a real detective."

"Yes. He was also the one placing dog poop in my front yard. I have tried to form a neighborhood watch, but people are so careless about their duties! They say they're busy or they don't care. So I take up the slack." Mrs. Butenschoen patted Jacob's arm. "Such good luck for our local hero! House fires rapidly get out of control, and with the paints, varnishes, and lumber available for fuel, his home would have been totally destroyed in no time."

Jacob's mother, in the form of his conscience, sat on his right shoulder, nagging him about his manners. "Thank you."

Mrs. Butenschoen patted Jacob's arm again. "No need for thanks. I did the neighborly thing."

God, but the woman was patronizing.

"Mr. Floren is a real estate developer who intends to buy our beautiful, traditional neighborhood, tear it down, and create a subdivision of soulless, modern houses. Maybe even . . . town houses." Mrs. Butenschoen's tone made it clear that, in her opinion, soulless housing was akin to the dog poop on her front walk.

"Sheriff Kwinault has finished reading him his rights," Jacob said. "She's taking him away in handcuffs. Maybe you should go spit on him."

"Spit? I do not spit. But I intend to give him a piece of my mind!" Like the Little Engine That Could, Mrs. Butenschoen puffed toward her intended target.

Jacob was now at the center of a cluster of people. He hated this. He would leave and go . . . somewhere. For a walk. He turned away, ready to head into his house and hide in his bedroom, and wonder what had happened last night and why Maddie had vanquished his nightmares and how to explain to his ghosts that he had not abandoned them.

Maddie stood with Dr. Frownfelter, offering one of the books.

Dr. Frownfelter took it with obvious gratitude and trekked back across his yard to his front door.

Maddie started back for her house. He understood. She had had enough of people. But wait—where was the second book?

He glanced into the half-reconstructed wreck of his house and saw the book sitting on the seat of his new old recliner.

She had given him one of her brother's novels.

Jacob didn't want to read the damned thing. Why would she think he would? Or should?

Deliberately he turned. He walked up the makeshift steps into his house. He passed the book—he did not care about it at all. He went into his bedroom and shut the door. He left the noise and the humanity behind and stepped into the embrace of his nightmares.

CHAPTER THIRTY-THREE

Trouble was, Jacob had slept the night before. He crouched on the floor of his dark room, waiting for hell to find him, and hell remained determinedly elusive. When at last his cramped knees drove him out into the kitchen, it was evening, he was alone, and he was hungry. Hungry. Two weeks ago he hadn't cared about hunger or thirst. Now he was heating soup in the microwave on his counter.

When had a microwave appeared on his counter? He hoped the construction guys had brought it. If Wodzicki had sent it over, on principle Jacob would have to throw it into the yard.

Bowl in hand, he walked over to his sideways-listing recliner and stared across the street.

Maddie was nowhere in sight. Maybe her nightmares had remained elusive, too.

He prepared to sit. Those maggots had been pretty gross and—what the hell? He sprang to his feet, turned, and looked. That book was still on the seat of his chair. Damn it. Why hadn't one of the construction men taken it? It would save him the trouble of tossing it. Picking it up, he put it on the floor, reseated himself, and slurped his soup.

When he had finished, he put the bowl in the sink, came back, and tripped on the damned book. It was as heavy as a doorstop and twice as thick. Whatever else A. M. Hewitson was, he was also a windbag. Although he was brief enough on the title; it was called *Sacrifice!*.

Jacob picked it up and leafed through it. He read the first sentence.

I was born in a whorehouse, and while I was still damp I was wrapped in rags and taken to the baby dealer, who sold me to priests for a ritual killing.

That was chilling. He started again.

I was born in a whorehouse, and while I was still damp I was wrapped in rags and taken to the baby dealer, who sold me to priests for a ritual killing. As you can see by the marks on my body, they succeeded in performing their ritual.

They were not so successful in killing me.

That was the first time I was helpless, at least briefly, at the hands of someone else.

Infant that I was, still I swore it would never happen again.

I was not so fortunate in keeping my vow . . .

Horror sucked Jacob in. He read until the light faded and he couldn't see the page. He went looking for a flashlight; he found a construction light with a hook and hung it on the open rafter over his chair. He kept reading until the small hours of the morning, when his eyes slammed shut and his chin hit his chest. Then he took the book into the bedroom—he no longer wanted the construction workers to remove it—and lay on the bed and slept. He expected to have nightmares. And he did. But the phantoms had changed. Dr. Kim no longer held sway; he was small and petty, foolish and cruel. A monster, but a lesser monster. Jacob's fear had morphed into something more than his usual helpless anguish; he now thirsted for revenge, fought for justice. He woke sweaty and afraid and yet . . . he took the book, went out into the daytime, and read.

Construction went on around him. Hammers. Air compressors. Swearing. Grunting. Welding. Lunch in the microwave. Questions he waved away.

Kids ran past. The garbage truck rumbled down the road. Neighbors waved. Police patrolled.

Jacob's eyes burned from overuse. He didn't care. He was enthralled. Transported.

When at last he finished, he looked up and realized the construction guys were gone, the neighbors had disappeared inside to eat dinner, and he was alone.

He shut the book and sat with his chest heaving, his heart racing, the breath caught in his throat. He stared at Maddie's house. It wasn't yet sunset, yet as he watched, the lights inside popped on one at a time until every room was brightly lit.

He hated this book. He *hated* it. And he had not been able to stop.

The story spoke to the dark corners of Jacob's soul, whispered of pain and false hope, shouted defiance and recognized *him*—his broken mind trapped in a life of desperate memories only death could end.

The story had proved two things.

One: the person who wrote this was a powerful, emotional writer who had stared terror in the face again and again.

And two: Maddie's worthless bastard of a brother claimed to write about helplessness, rebellion, unrelenting fear, and recovery. He was lying. Madeline Hewitson had written this.

This novel showed Jacob that he was not alone. At least one other human felt what he felt. The heroine of this book lived with guilt that parched her soul. Yet she had created life out of the desert. She bore scars, yet wore them proudly. She lived to honor her fallen dead.

He wanted, needed to talk to Maddie, to express his thanks for making him a part of the human race again. He stood, novel in hand, and walked to the edge of his makeshift porch—and there she was, looking up at him, dark hair disheveled, skinny legs sticking out of her shorts, T-shirt on crooked, eyes big and wide and wise.

She said, "You finished the book."

"I did. You were watching me."

"I was. What did you think?"

He was unprepared. He didn't know what to say. "It was good."

"You liked it."

"No. I . . . no." He shuddered. "No."

She watched him steadily. . . . Oh, God. She understood him.

"Why should I explain? Brandon told you everything about me." All Jacob's secrets . . . shame, pain, guilt, terror. Knowing she was privy to his secrets felt like a hot knife to his gut.

She advanced up the steps, onto the porch. "No, he didn't. You arrived before he could tell me the good stuff."

Jacob fell back like an army under siege. "The good stuff?"

"The stuff that drives you crazy. I don't know what was happening on your side of the glass. I don't know how you escaped, how you rescued your men." Without invitation, she walked into his house. "But I want to."

Mindlessly, he followed.

Maddie was only one person. But he feared her. He revered her. "You wrote this book."

"I told you I did."

She *had* told him. He hadn't believed her. Now he couldn't believe she had allowed her brother to appropriate her identity. "Why—"

"You know why."

He did. She didn't have to explain. This book had proved she understood him. But he understood her, too. They shared similar experiences. They were alike. He pointed at the recliner. "Sit down."

She did, perching on the edge and watching him.

"I've got stuff to eat," he said.

"Sure. As long as it's not a sandwich, macaroni salad, or a cookie." She pressed her hand to her stomach, then laughed at the look on his face. "I'd eat an apple."

He opened the refrigerator and scrounged around. "I've got grapes."

"Close enough." The grapes would give her something to do with her hands—and he wanted to feed her, to fortify her for his confession.

It would not do for them both to fall apart.

He doused the grapes under the kitchen faucet, placed them on a paper towel, and carried them over. He presented them with a bow that put him on Maddie's eye level. When she met his gaze, he said, "Do you remember everything that Brandon told you about being captured by the North Koreans?"

"Yes." She took the grapes. "The brainiacs you babysat took their hovercraft over the border. You went after them and you were all captured and kept at a research facility as guinea pigs."

"Yes. Guinea pigs. We were that." Jacob straightened. "Dr. Kim was an ophthalmologist, and he fancied himself a research scientist. He told me he had been waiting for the opportunity to try out his pet project, and we had thoughtfully provided him with his . . . yes. His guinea pigs. He kept us together for the first few days—I don't know how long, we had no windows, no natural light in our cell—so he could observe us, then he chose me as his subject. Because I was older, obviously the leader and, as he said, I had strength of will and a rigid moral code."

She ate a grape. She ate another. When he had gone to so much trouble to pretend all was normal, it seemed the hospitable thing to do. "What was he trying to do?"

"He wanted to see if he could break a man's mind without the use of drugs or torture." Jacob stopped, breathing hard. Then in a normal tone, he asked, "Do you want something to drink?"

"*What?*" Why had he changed the subject, she meant.

But he said, "Usually the guys leave bottled iced tea and Cokes. Beer, sometimes. Bottled water. They tell me to help myself."

"I . . . sure. Iced tea. Please."

Jacob headed back to the kitchen and rummaged in the cooler. "What Dr. Kim did first was a fairly simple operation for cataracts."

"You had cataracts?"

Jacob came back and loosened the lid. He offered the bottle. "No. My vision was perfect."

She put the grapes on the arm of the chair, took the tea, and sipped. "Then what—"

"As he told me when they were tying me down, it was an outpatient procedure, one he had performed many times. All that needed to be done was to remove the lens from my eyes and replace them with a different lens."

"To what purpose?"

"To make me blind."

The grapes and the tea soured in her stomach; she put the cool bottle against her forehead and took a long breath. "I don't understand."

"The good doctor inserted blackout lenses." Jacob took a careful step back, as if standing close would contaminate her. "I was blind, staring into endless darkness."

She wrote horror. She delved deep into pain, cruelty, indifference, and, yes, darkness. Yet not even in her most grotesque fantasies had she imagined this. Not this.

"After the surgery, while I was still under the influence of the tranquilizers, he explained his plan. One by one, he would take my kids to be tortured, and I would listen to their screams. I would listen to them beg. I would be unable to help them in any way. He understood how frustrated that would make me. How much I would hate him. That eventually the helplessness would tear at the fibers of my beliefs, my strengths, my being." Jacob picked up the hem of his ratty T-shirt, ducked his head, and wiped his forehead. "He succeeded in every step of his plan."

"Except the last one," she said.

"Why do you say that?"

"Because you're here. You're alive. Your mind is recovering."

Jacob turned his head and gazed at her, and his eyes looked as blind as they once had been. "Listen," he said. "Listen to the whole story."

She hoped it wouldn't get worse.

She knew that it would.

"Dr. Kim told me that when he was satisfied that my mind was pliable, he would fill it with a different reality."

Moving slowly, as if a single abrupt gesture would overbalance them both, she rolled the bottle between her two hands. "What? How? How could he—"

"At first we were in a soundproof room. Not that I knew that. I was shackled to a chair. I did know that. There was a monitor into the torture chamber. Not that I could see it. But Dr. Kim could. He would sit behind me on my left side and speak into my ear. I heard the sounds of the torture and in that soft, soothing, gentle voice of his, he would describe the procedure, what they were doing to my kids. If I cried or flinched or begged that they torture me instead—and at the beginning,

I did—he would get on the speaker and instruct his men on more brutal methods of torture." Jacob plucked one of the grapes from the
bunch at her elbow, tossed it in the air, caught it. Then, as hard as he
could, he threw it out of the wrecked house. "I learned to remain absolutely silent, to show no reaction to the brutality being delivered on
my kids."

She offered her hand, palm up, a gesture of comfort.

In a clear, flat voice, he said, "No, Maddie."

She nodded. She understood that sometimes the words had to
come from a place lonely and hidden or the soul would wither.

"My kids starved. They lived in constant fear and cold and pain.
But because I was the subject of Dr. Kim's experiment, his prize, he
treated me like his prize poodle. I ate well. I dressed well. I bathed
daily. When I tried to resist, to go on a hunger strike, Dr. Kim personally put a tube down my throat and force-fed me, and when the deed
was done, he told me that the only result of my resistance was the
knowledge that one of my brainiacs would die a horrible death, and
that that death would be on my conscience forever." As if he were still
under Dr. Kim's command, Jacob stood absolutely still, his hands
limp at his side. "It is. Joseph Waters Phillip's name is carved upon my
soul."

She wanted to tell him that wasn't true, that Dr. Kim was responsible for that death. But she understood survivor's guilt. She understood
the responsibility Jacob felt. She understood the frustration of helplessness.

"When I had demonstrated a thorough grasp of my role—those
were his words, 'a thorough grasp of your role'—we changed rooms. I
knew we had. I would feel the difference in the temperature and
humidity—we were now in the basement—and I could hear the beeps
and clicks of some machine behind. But I couldn't see and didn't realize that . . ." He faltered.

She remembered Brandon's story. "This was the room with the see-
through glass?"

Jacob seemed relieved not to explain that. "Exactly. My kids, my brainiacs, had a good view of me. Day after day as they were tortured, I sat and displayed no reaction. At first they called my name, begged me for help. Then they cursed me, swore that someday in this life or the next, they would get their revenge. Then I did surmise that they could somehow see me."

"That was the flaw in Dr. Kim's plan."

"Yes. I suspected a window between us and it wasn't hard to verify that. It was easy for a blind man to stumble when he walked; I did, and I was right. With the use of carefully orchestrated stumbles and the occasional wild groping, I began to build up a mental picture of the room."

"You were plotting the escape." She felt a bone-deep satisfaction at the knowledge.

"Yes. Plotting. I could *see* no escape for us all, yet still I plotted . . . hopelessly . . . plotted." Jacob's hands hung at his side. His fingertips twitched as if in his mind he was sketching plans for their getaway. "I ignored every shriek and moan and whimper. I pretended I could not hear their curses. They thought I was indifferently watching. Or worse, enjoying their agony."

"You were anything but indifferent."

The color washed from his face. "That is the dreadful part. The only way I could not move, not protest, not inflict more pain on them was to turn my mind away from the sounds coming from that room."

Sympathetic tears leaked from Maddie's eyes. So much guilt. It surrounded Jacob like a dark miasma. He breathed it, slept and ate and drowned in it.

"Dr. Kim knew he had trained me in silence and stillness, and, of course, I was blind. What could I do to harm him?" The corner of Jacob's mouth twitched in bitter amusement. "So after two days in the second room, I was not shackled."

"Foolish on his part, wasn't it?"

"In the end, yes. His arrogance killed him." Jacob's face was stark and proud. "But I assisted in his death." Then he seemed stuck, unable to continue his story.

So the worst was yet to come. She rolled the bottle back and forth, back and forth, the moisture cooling her sweating palms. "Tell me the rest of the story."

He shook his head.

She made her voice firm and mature. "Jacob, tell me."

He met her eyes, stared into them as if her authority kept him grounded in the *now* and allowed him to speak. "Dr. Kim moved to the next phase of his plan. Rather than describing the tortures, he began to describe paradise."

Outside, the sun had begun to set. The shadows in the house grew deeper. Yet she could still see Jacob, standing apart, chin lifted, face set, hands loose. He was a statue created of agony and memories.

She asked, "What paradise? Like heaven?"

"*My* paradise. He had done his research. He described my home here in Washington: the mountains, the ocean, the snowy winters, and the brief, warm summers. My family was worried about me. They didn't know where I was. So they posted online photos of me and my friends, the holidays, our traditions." Jacob's face twisted with longing. "That gave him everything he needed. He described my mother, my father, my sisters, my priest. Home was where I wanted to be and he exploited that. *My* longing. *My* need."

"While you could hear the screams, he talked to you about your *home*?" Maddie had witnessed madness. She had witnessed sadism. She had witnessed death. Never had she witnessed the kind of cold intent Dr. Kim had used to batter Jacob and his sanity.

"He told me I *was* home. He told me I could hear the waves, smell the salt air, feel the hot sand and the cold water. He told me all I had to do was look, and I would be transported. He would ask me what I saw . . . that voice in my ear, kind and sweet . . . We had been imprisoned two months. They were torturing Brandon when"—Jacob swung his arms so suddenly she jumped—"when I snapped."

CHAPTER THIRTY-FOUR

"You killed Dr. Kim." Maddie was glad. So glad.

"I stood up, picked him up by the scruff of the neck and the seat of his pants, and slammed him headfirst into the glass." Jacob moved, lifted, used what looked like a sledgehammer in a gruesome reenactment of his violence.

She put down the bottle, leaned forward eagerly. "How did you know what to do, how to reach him?"

"When we walked, I judged by his voice that he stood no higher than my shoulder, so I knew his height. In the torture room, he was always speaking into my right ear, close behind me, so I knew where he was. But . . . but mostly I didn't care where I grabbed him, only that I used his head to shatter the window, to destroy the window." Jacob stopped, breathing heavily, as if he were reliving that moment. "I couldn't do it; I didn't realize the glass was reinforced with metal mesh. He screamed and screamed, over and over, and kicked his feet, but I used him like a battering ram. Brandon said before I quit, the doctor's brains were oozing through the—"

She held up her hands. "Please. No."

More quietly, he said, "Luckily for me and Brandon, the two soldiers who worked the torture room were not armed. But the machine I could hear was the control center for the prison, and like so many things in North Korea, it was thirty years out of date. The soldier who manned it *was* armed, and when he realized I had gone berserk, he pulled his pistol and started shooting. Me."

"I saw your scars." Bullet holes, surgical scars.

"He hit me five times."

"You should have died."

"Later I almost did. But at that moment, I was invincible. All I knew was that something stung me—in my rage, it felt like a wasp— and I swung Kim's body around and flung it at the control panel. The soldier went down beneath the weight. The two men slammed into the panel, flipping switches, setting off alarms." Jacob's face lifted in exaltation. "I *liked* the noise. I *loved* the siren. I knew I had done something dire. So I stumbled to the panel and flipped every switch and pressed every button. I unlocked all the cells, released all the prisoners. The prison was in havoc. The guards didn't know what to do, where to run, what had happened. In the torture room, the two North Koreans escaped, leaving Brandon with his hand nailed to the table. He had seen it all. He was determined to help, so he tore his hand loose."

She closed her eyes against the image, but still she could see Brandon, the young man she had met, had helped sit and helped rise, had listened to and empathized with.

"He grabbed the iron bar the torturers used to break bones. He had to get through an army of soldiers to get to me. He eliminated them. Not bad for a brainiac."

She opened her eyes. "An enraged brainiac."

"Exactly." Jacob smiled at her, a savage delighting in the defeat of his enemies. "I groped around and found an old-fashioned corded phone connected to the control panel. I picked it up and tried to figure out how to make an announcement. But I hadn't killed the soldier with the pistol. Brandon arrived in time to save me from a gunshot to the head. He confiscated all the weapons in the room, handed one to me, told me to shoot as necessary. He still hadn't snapped to my problem."

She could imagine the anger and anguish Brandon had felt—hating the man who had been impervious to his pain, beholden that Jacob had at last acted.

Jacob continued, "Then he saw my eyes from up close. My eyes had no color, no pupil. They were shiny black. I must have looked . . . grotesque. He realized that somehow I had been mutilated. I'm surprised he didn't run from me."

That idiocy incensed her. "You do him an injustice. He came to get you even when he thought you had abandoned them!"

Jacob turned his head stiffly to look down at her. "I'm sorry. I am descending into self-pity."

"In this case, it is acceptable," she said formally.

He frowned, concentrating on the story. "Brandon told me to hold the gun and use it to threaten. He set the emergency beacon to flash red, white, and blue. At once a call came in from the Americans—"

"A call? What kind of call?"

"The phone rang." Jacob laughed, a dreadful splinter of amusement. "I told you. Primitive technology. Turns out we were being held in a bunker not far from the border. Since our disappearance, the Americans had been watching the facility. They told us to get to the roof. Brandon got on the PA system and announced to my men to rendezvous with us for pickup."

"Didn't any of the Koreans speak English?"

"Some. But the guards had bigger fish to fry. As soon as the locks on the prison cells clicked open, my men were out, and they were angry. They had all been tortured. Because of their injuries, they had to help each other up to the roof." Jacob stood like a commanding general, shoulders back, chin up, hands clasped at the base of his spine. "Please remember, they were the brainiac squad. While they ran, they set fires. They visited the armory and cleared the way with grenades and tear gas. They had lived through hell and they left hell behind."

His words sent a chill through her. A thrill through her. "You're proud of them."

"On that day, they became warriors. Yes. I'm proud of them." His expression defied the world's condemnation.

But she—she understood how much it meant to fight back. "Brandon led you to the roof to join your soldiers."

"He did. He led a blind man through leaping flames and up smoke-filled stairwells. We were almost to the top—almost—when a shot from below hit him, taking his leg out from under him." Jacob whispered, "So close."

Enthralled by the story, she wrung her hands. "What happened? What did you do?"

"He collapsed." Jacob's voice rose as he remembered the action. "I used a fireman's carry to transport him the rest of the way. He remained conscious long enough to tell me of upcoming obstacles. When I stepped onto the roof, we were the last Americans to arrive. I could hear the helicopters coming in. I asked if they were U.S. choppers, if we were really going to be saved. The others wouldn't answer me. They wouldn't speak to me. They hated me. I didn't blame them. I hated me, too."

"Why didn't Brandon tell them—"

"Brandon was now unconscious. I loaded him into a basket and waved him up. I sent the others ahead, too. I didn't want to come. I wanted to stay behind, to put down enough fire to allow the helicopters to escape. But someone—one of the rescuing Americans—grabbed me, harnessed me, and pulled me up, and we were away. By the time the choppers got safely over the border, my men had seen my eyes. They knew I had not willfully abandoned them." Jacob drew a quivering breath. "That meant everything to me."

Silence fell between them, but the story wasn't finished. She could tell that it wasn't. But he didn't want to continue, and she had to know . . . had to know what drove him out of his mind. "Did the helicopters make it across the border?" A stupid question, but it drove him to talk again.

"Of course. Our pilots were the first to see the pain and torture the North Koreans had inflicted on us. Failure was not an option." He turned and stared out into the oncoming night as if he could see the agony they had suffered. "Two months of hell . . . then suddenly we were home where soldiers guarded us and doctors mended us and nurses cared for us. Such an odd contrast . . ."

"Did you tell them what had happened?"

"I gave my report, of course, before I went into surgery the first time."

"To fix your eyes?"

"To remove the bullets. And my spleen and one kidney."

"Of course. The bullets." For all her horror at Dr. Kim's cruelty, the doctors had to save his life first.

"I didn't want the care. I wanted to die. No one understood, because Brandon's report praised me, exalted me, gave me credit, and was responsible for awarding me military honors." With a bone-deep hostility, he said, "Honors for doing nothing but sitting there listening to my kids being tortured."

"You *did* get them out."

"By accident. I could as easily have killed them all."

"Isn't it enough that you were blind and wounded?"

"I still hear their screams in my head. I still hear Dr. Kim in my nightmares. I wake up rigid with terror. I am a coward."

He shied away from the final revelation. And she had to know. "How long until the doctors fixed your eyes?"

"With the bullets, the organs, the blood, and the anguish . . . infection set in. I was in the hospital for two months. At week four, the medical team determined I would live, and performed the operation that gave me my sight back. They seemed to think it was a gift. But . . ." Jacob looked down at her. In the dim light, his eyes looked as black as they must have in the depths of his blindness. "I can't tell you the whole truth. Not here. I want the dark."

CHAPTER THIRTY-FIVE

Candy Butenschoen stood in her kitchen, lights off, watching the drama in Jacob's house. And it was drama, she could tell. Jacob was telling a story and he stood so stiff and straight; she recognized pain when she saw it, and he was a man in pain.

Madeline leaned forward, occasionally spoke and gestured, but mostly she listened, and Candy saw her wipe her eyes against her shirt-sleeve.

Drama. Tragedy. The two of them were enthralled by their conversation, oblivious to anything and anyone.

How Candy would love to hear their words!

Jacob began to gesture wildly and Candy flinched, thinking he was going to strike Madeline. But no, he was explaining more of his story while Madeline questioned and commented. These two—they shared a bond. Candy didn't know what, but it was fascinating to watch as their empathy grew.

Suddenly everything stopped.

No motion. No speaking.

Madeline stood, took Jacob's hand, and led him back toward the bedroom. Toward the bedroom!

That was it, then. They were going to have carnal relations.

"No!" Candy hated to see poor Jacob Denisov trapped with a combination of compassion and sex by the neighborhood crazy woman.

But Candy reminded herself she had resolved to be more charitable toward Madeline Hewitson. That woman had also suffered through dreadful trials. So she tucked her lips tightly together—she prided herself on barely showing her disapproval—and flipped on the undercounter lighting. She returned to her kitchen table and her half-eaten meal.

The doctors had warned her to keep her strength up, but the dinner that had enticed her an hour before now made her feel vaguely ill. She took one last bite and a sip of tepid coffee and pushed the remains away. She shook a pill out of her loaded pill case and washed the pill down with water.

Captivated by the drama across the street, she had delayed too long, and now she had to sit, holding tightly to the edge of her table, waiting for her pain to subside.

Finally it did. She pulled her laptop close. She opened the security video and pushed *Play*.

She had at last discovered how to program and slow her security camera and at the same time discovered a better way to spy on the neighbors. With the dog poop malefactor in jail, she felt free to allow the lens to roam up and down the street. The camera was equipped with a motion sensor; motion attracted it, and it focused on each man, woman, child—and pet—as they walked, ran, skateboarded, drove through her historic neighborhood. She understood that none of the neighbors appreciated her diligence. But she did what she did not as spying but as a community service. After all, look at the good she'd done by unmasking the arsonist Floren. Why, she deserved a public service medal!

Not that she would get one. People were so ungrateful.

She sipped her water and observed first the early morning's action as her neighbors left for work and school. She fast-forwarded through the lull in the early afternoon, then slowed to watch the neighbors' returns. The action was lively all the way through the long, late daylight hours. . . . She again saw Madeline cross the street, saw her ascend Jacob's steps . . . then the camera moved to follow Mrs. Nyback's obnoxious dog as he trotted out into the front yard, raised his leg, and piddled on the picket fence next to Candy's house. The little beast did that every day, and Mrs. Nyback did nothing to stop him. In fact, Candy had heard Mrs. Nyback praise him. Which made Candy so angry . . . but in the big scheme of things, it wasn't important. She needed to remember that. Mrs. Nyback and her urine-laden dog could not interrupt her serenity.

The doctors told her it was important to maintain her serenity.

On the monitor, she watched the sun set—that had been less than an hour ago—and the camera went into nighttime mode. That is, it switched back and forth between infrared in the dark patches and regular under the streetlights. Candy didn't like that; it was hard to watch and gave her a headache. If it were up to her, she would flood the neighborhood with light all night for everyone's security. Her eyes began to burn and she moved to shut down the computer—and paused.

What was that? In infrared mode, she'd caught a flash of someone who had jumped over her fence—she checked the time stamp—ten minutes ago. She hitched her chair forward and played those brief moments again. The camera tracked the person, but she couldn't tell who it was. Male, she guessed, someone young, tall, and strong, by the way he vaulted the fence. And in a costume? With a hat and a cape . . . ?

Candy remembered Madeline's babblings, her own worry that she had misjudged Madeline, and her fleeting thought that if someone was actually tormenting Madeline, that person would be very dangerous. . . . She pushed back her chair and prepared to stand. "I must call the police!"

A broad, strong hand clamped onto her shoulder and pushed her back down.

She turned and looked up into a familiar face, and heard a familiar voice say, "No you don't, Mrs. Butenschoen. You've seen— and said—too much already."

CHAPTER THIRTY-SIX

Jacob said he needed the dark. "All right." Standing, Maddie took his hand and led him through the kitchen, through the bathroom, and into the bedroom.

He followed obediently. *Blindly.*

She shut the door behind them. Profound darkness pressed like a weight on her eyeballs and her own fear sprang to life.

Monsters lurked in the dark.

But he wrapped his arm around her shoulders and led her to stand against the wall. He tugged her hand and the two slid down until they sat on the floor, shoulder to shoulder, staring into nothingness. She could feel his body struggling for breath, reaching for speech, and she pressed herself harder against him, trying to lend him strength. "Tell me," she said.

"After the medical team performed the operation that gave me my sight back, everyone congratulated me and celebrated . . . for me. They seemed to think I would be . . . happy. But I didn't deserve the gift because . . . I could already see."

She didn't understand. "See . . . what?"

"A beach, crashing waves, sunshine, and salt air. Snowcapped mountains. My family running toward me to embrace me."

Now she was glad of the darkness, for it hid her horror.

"I saw what Dr. Kim told me to see. That was why I snapped, why I risked everything to kill him." Jacob's voice grew hoarse with torment and memory. "He had done as he vowed. He won. He took possession of my mind. He broke me." Putting his head in his hands, Jacob cried, great, ugly, wrenching sobs, a primitive whirlpool of anguish that swept Maddie into the depths with him.

She put her arms around him, pulled him toward her.

He resisted, rigid with anguish.

But she wouldn't let him go. She held him, never wanting him to ever be alone again. Not when sorrow held him in its grip and unceasing cries broke from his throat. This was more than hurt. This was shame.

And yet practicality ruled; he was crying. He needed to wipe his nose. He needed tissues.

She couldn't stand to leave him alone, not for a second. Gently she pushed him away, stripped off her T-shirt, and shoved it into his hands.

He muffled his sobs with the cloth, rocking as misery came tearing out of him.

She petted his head, ran her hands through his hair. She kissed his forehead, rubbed his back, kept her arms around him until they ached. She did for him what she had longed for in her own despair.

At last he lifted his head to say, "I'm selfish."

Maddie smacked him on the shoulder. "Selfish? You're not selfish. You're broken."

He caught his breath. "Broken. Yes." He cried again.

She understood. He had held it in for so long, never confessing his great dishonor, and his hell-bound soul gave vent to its torment.

When at last his sobs had eased, she said, "Look. I've seen ruined minds. At the asylum. Really ruined. Insane for God knows what reason. Or hurt by a parent for terrible reasons. Or cut down by disease that takes a brain and makes it a wasteland. *Those* people are ruined. They cannot be cured. They cannot fight their way back." She couldn't see him, but she felt him lift his head. He was listening. That was more than she expected and all she wanted. "You and me—we can fight. We can win. We have hurt parts, parts in our brains that our whole lives will never get better. Sometimes somehow we'll brush up against those parts and cry. Sometimes those parts will come back in nightmares. But in real life, we can put those parts away."

A metal grater couldn't have made his voice more rough. "I can't ignore what happened."

"No. Not ignore. Move the memories to a separate place where they are safe while you continue with your life."

"Sure." He moved away from her and leaned against the wall. "That's what the experts tell me. According to them, it's been two years. I should be recovering from the trauma."

She gave one brief, mocking laugh. "The experts? What do they know? It's a rare and wonderful therapist who can view each individual's behavior as his or her own. They don't want to think they don't understand. They want to put everyone in a box. They give you a list of how you should recover from grief, from pain, from broken hearts and broken dreams and a mind so shattered by what you've seen you can never forget it."

"I didn't see anything. I only . . . heard. I only . . . imagined."

"Whatever. About this I am the expert, and right now I tell you—*you* recover when and how *you* can." She was a warrior in the same deadly battle, and she recognized his reality. She spoke to his reality. "You have guilt for the young lives lost. If you weren't a good man, you would tell yourself it wasn't your fault. Not your responsibility. But it *was* your responsibility. You know that."

"You're the first person to admit that. To admit that what I feel is valid."

"They are your feelings. Of course they're valid. Now you have to find a way to live with them."

His voice firmed. "There is no way."

"There has to be a way. Your comrades are dead in horrible conditions, tortured to entertain a psychopath. You owe it to those young men and women to continue in your course to become a better man, a charitable man, a kind man. It's up to you to make the loss of their lives worth something. No one else can do it." She caught her breath. "Wait! That's not right. *No one else owes it to them.*"

He choked up again, and when he could speak he asked, "What if I can't? What if I can't move on and become that better man?"

"Then you are truly beyond repair. You are ruined."

CHAPTER THIRTY-SEVEN

Jacob cried again, but for a different reason. This woman who everyone believed to be mad . . . she had listened to his confession, comprehended his emotions, and saw what he could not see, that he owed his kids not his death but his life.

He had to live? With his shame, his grief, his memories? He had to use them to build character, to help others, to be a shining example in the eyes of God?

He used the cloth in his hand to muffle his sobs.

He knew now that when he stood on the precipice above the ocean preparing to leap, he would remember that Maddie in a few words changed his guilt to obligation—and that deep in his heart, he agreed with her.

No one else owed his kids for the losses of their lives and their innocence. Only him.

But he was too weak. Life was too painful. He couldn't stand it. He couldn't do it.

Yet Maddie leaned against him, warm-woman-scented and soft textured, running her hands through his hair and murmuring nonsense about his strength and courage and her belief in him. . . .

When he slowed down with the pathetic crying, she took his hand and put it on her breast.

Just like that. On her breast. Which was bare.

It was at that moment he realized the cloth he'd been sobbing into was her T-shirt, and although he'd had little experience with boobs since his return from Korea, he recognized that small, plump, soft flesh and the thrust of a nipple.

She pressed her fingers over his fingers and acted as if holding this boob were the one thing in the world he needed and wanted.

Women! How did they know these things?

Later, Jacob would be embarrassed to remember how he reacted. Because he launched himself at her, frantic, reckless, wild with wanting.

He had needed more than her understanding. He had needed sex: hot, sweaty, desperate sex. He knocked her over on his floor. All because of her breast.

She clawed at his T-shirt.

He fumbled for the zipper on her jeans and at the same time worked to get her naked from the waist down. He needed more than two hands, but he made do with what he had.

When he wouldn't lift his arms to let her pull the T-shirt over his head—c'mon, priorities!—she dug her fingers into the material of his shirt and ripped the cloth to bare his chest. He heard her mutter something about "So old you could see through it." He guessed she was casting aspersions on his favorite T-shirt. But he didn't care because she put her mouth on his nipple.

Good idea! He did the same to her *and* simultaneously managed to strip her pants off completely. Took both hands and one leg, but by God, he did it.

And this was all in the dark. Took damn near a miracle to find and remove those garments with no injuries to either of them.

When Jacob suckled on Maddie, she moaned and made a move on his shorts.

He was so skinny they slid right off his hips, and his underwear with them.

With one hand she found his erection. He would have come right then, but she giggled.

Wrong!

She said, "Let's do this thing, big boy."

Big boy. *Right.* They would do this thing.

And they did.

Fast. Too fast.

When he was sprawled on top of her, trying to recover his breath, he was dimly aware he should apologize. For everything. Blubbering. Jumping her bones. Coming like a teenager on his first time and leaving her behind.

But she was hugging him and touching him like she still liked him.

So he blurted, "I'll be ready again in a few minutes."

"Then I'd better make the bed, because this carpet is thin and hard on my butt. Come on." She wiggled out from underneath him. She groped for his hand and pulled him to his feet. She pushed at him. "Go shower. And hurry."

That phrase—"And hurry"—motivated him as nothing else could. He groped to the door. He opened it and glanced back.

She was peeling back the aluminum foil on his window to let in the feeble glow of light from the alley.

He supposed she could do that.

He broke speed records getting naked (he had to remove the shreds of his T-shirt). He leaped into the shower, washed everything once and the important parts twice, and jumped out. He toweled off and quickly discovered there was a thin line between drying himself and stimulating himself, so he hung the towel on the rack—military training was hard to break—and took a breath. He vowed, "I will go slower this time. I will make her happy." He hustled back into the bedroom.

She had found sheets and made the bed. She reclined in the middle of the mattress, her head on the one pillow. Her arm was behind her. The top sheet draped her. She smiled when she saw him, and smiled wider when she saw his erection. She said, "You weren't kidding. You *are* ready in a few minutes. . . . I like a man who keeps his promises."

CHAPTER THIRTY-EIGHT

Jacob woke up. *He woke up.*

He had slept.

Now he woke up. In his bed, in his bedroom with a window that was open and uncovered. He felt . . . *normal?*

It was very weird to feel normal.

No. Good. He felt good.

Because . . . last night he had confessed. He had admitted to

Maddie that because of his fundamental flaw, his ultimate failure, his brainiac kids had died.

Yet Maddie hadn't been repulsed.

He had burst into tears like the world's biggest tittybaby.

She hadn't laughed at him.

He had cried for what felt like hours, loud, snorting, gasping sobs. Tears and guilt had flowed in torrents.

She had hugged him. She had given him her T-shirt to cry into.

He'd had sex.

Maddie had made it a celebration of life.

This morning, he was proud to recall he had kept his vow to go slow. The second time, and the third time, too, he had spent long moments and hot kisses making sure she was satisfied. If he remembered anything about women—and that part of his memory seemed to be intact—he was pretty sure he had succeeded. He guessed making love was like riding a bike. Once you knew how, you never forgot.

Making love to Maddie was like riding a bike . . . down a steep hill, pedaling hard, wind in his face, grinning madly, and screaming with terror and exaltation.

Of course . . . she wasn't in bed with him now.

He leaped up, started out the door, caught a glimpse of sunshine streaming into his wrecked house, ducked back, grabbed a pair of shorts and pulled them on, decided they were going to fall off if he wasn't careful, scrounged around on the floor until he found a belt, cinched it around his waist, and headed out.

Maddie was bending over, rummaging through his refrigerator.

Nice ass. She had put her clothes back on, but still . . . very, very nice ass.

He didn't think she knew he was behind her, but she said, "I was going to fix you breakfast, but you don't have much in here."

His gaze traveled around his empty living room. The construction crew wasn't here yet, therefore . . . "It's Monday morning. Grocery delivery tomorrow."

"Oh." She straightened. She turned and came right over to him, slid her arms around his waist, and hugged him. Turning her face up to his, she asked, "How are you?"

When most people asked that question, it was perfunctory. With Maddie, *How are you?* was a solid inquiry with concern and affection behind it, and she truly wanted to know the answer.

Since he truly wanted to see her form more words with that sinful mouth, he said, "I might live. I might . . . want to live."

She watched him still, waiting for him to expound.

So he did. "I feel empty, like I had been filled with horrible things and now only the stains are left."

"You cried. You washed the bad things away."

She had beautiful eyes and she watched him as if she liked him, understood him. He didn't deserve her . . . but he kissed her anyway.

She kissed him back.

He started walking backward toward the bedroom.

She dragged her feet. "Jacob, I can't."

"Why not?"

"I have a deadline. I have to go work."

"This won't take long."

Maddie laughed. "Is that supposed to entice me?"

"No, this is." He kissed her again, deeply, lovingly, putting all his heart and soul into telling her without words how much he—

The damn phone rang.

She pulled her head away.

He murmured, "No, no, no. It's not important."

"Not important? How do you know until you answer?"

"It's my mother."

"How do you *know*?"

"She's the only person with my phone number. I don't know how she got it. She has connections." He paused. "Or she blackmailed someone."

"You don't want to talk to your mother?" Maddie seemed shocked. She eased out of his arms.

"Mother is a difficult woman. Opinionated. If I talked to her, she'd tell me what to do. It's better if I don't—" He got distracted watching Maddie's ass as she walked away.

She said, "I'll take care of it," and answered the phone.

"No!" He made a lunge for the receiver.

Maddie avoided him. "Jacob's place. He's busy right now. May I take a message?"

Jacob flopped into the recliner and covered his eyes. His mother was accustomed to talking to Moore. He could only imagine the look on her face now.

"My name is Maddie." She kept her voice bright and cheerful. "I'm Jacob's neighbor. I ran into him a few weeks ago in his house."

Jacob uncovered one eye. *I ran into him a few weeks ago in his house? Really, Maddie?*

Maddie continued, "He's great. He's a little thin, but he liked my cookies."

He uncovered the other eye and glared. *Her cookies?*

"Just last night. He was having a moment, so I stayed. I'll have him call you when he gets out of bed. . . . Um-hm . . . Um-hm . . . Okay, I'll tell him. Nice to talk to you, Mrs. Denisov. I hope to meet you someday soon!" Maddie hung up the phone and put it on the cradle. "There!" she said to Jacob. "I helped." She turned to go.

He sat up straight. "Wait a minute! What did she say?"

"Oh." Maddie turned back, faking surprise that he cared. Or maybe she *was* surprised that he cared. "Your mother said not to worry about calling her, to just enjoy yourself."

"She thinks we're sleeping together."

"We *are* sleeping together. And she sounds very relieved."

Jacob stood and wandered toward her. "I'm relieved, too."

"Relieved?" Maddie didn't know whether to laugh or be insulted. "Is that what you are?"

"Rejoiced? Reborn? Reinvigorated?" He smiled at her. Simply smiled at her. And he was right. He was reborn; all the bitter, troubled lines of his face had somehow been rearranged to show interest and delight . . . in Maddie Hewitson. He offered his hand. "Come with me?"

She extended her hand, then curled her fingers into her palm.

When monsters disrupted the night and sad ghosts haunted the day, discipline became the lodestone of Maddie's life. Two thousand words a day, every day; that schedule ruled her life. "I've got to get in my words."

"Words? How about these?" He deepened his voice. "Come live with me and be my love—"

"Oh, not poetry." How did he know she loved poetry?

"And we will all the pleasures prove—"

She put her hand over his mouth. "Stop that right now."

His eyes pleaded and cajoled. He kissed her palm, took her hand away, and laced his fingers through hers.

Life rewarded the disciplined.

Yet Jacob stood there skinny, barefoot, and bare-chested, his head recently shaved and his cheekbones taut against his skin, and all she wanted to do was go live with him and be his love. For the first time since Easton had been murdered, she had connected with another human being.

No, more important, she had helped another human being. That alone had given her satisfaction and a sense of worth, and those emotions would have been enough. But Jacob had amply rewarded her with passion and pleasure. . . .

Temptation beckoned, and for this moment, she knew she would yield.

He watched her too closely, knew her too well, saw her surrender, and moved quickly to take advantage. He led her into the bedroom and she shut the door behind them. He scooped up a blanket and guided her onto the enclosed back porch.

She glanced around at the ancient washing machine and the plastic pots of dead violets on the windowsill. "Um, Jacob?"

He opened the back door and walked down the rickety wooden steps into the narrow, fenced backyard. He turned to look up at her; the green, sunlit grass grew as high as his knees. He said, "Mrs. Butenschoen insinuated my yard is an overgrown disgrace."

"She did, did she?"

"I believe if there's one thing that would annoy and perturb Mrs. Butenschoen more than an overgrown lawn, it's illicit pleasure enjoyed in broad daylight on the overgrown lawn."

A smile tugged at Maddie's lips. She looked around; unless a neighbor actually looked over the fence—and the chance of that was tiny—she and Jacob could make love out here unobserved. Of course, even that small chance added a piquant element to the idea, and the thought of Mrs. Butenschoen's horror made the concept almost irresistible. Or perhaps merely . . . irresistible. "Are you sweet-talking me?"

"I hope so."

"Then I've heard enough." She launched herself off the porch into his arms.

He caught her, fell backward, and rolled.

She wrestled with him, laughing, the scent of grass wild with summertime and with love.

Skinny though he was, he was still stronger. She landed flat on her back. The blanket was gone, lost in the tussle. The tall, damp grass closed in around them and the whole world was nothing but blue sky, green grass, and Jacob Denisov warm and strong above her.

That was enough.

Jacob brushed at the green stain on Maddie's bottom. "When will you come back?"

"When I get my words written," she said firmly. "The sooner I start, the sooner I can return."

He gave her a gentle push. "Then go."

She pouted over her shoulder at him.

Pulling her back, he kissed her, then pushed her again.

She walked down the stairs, across the street, and into her house, dropping grass seed like Hansel and Gretel dropped bread crumbs.

He stared into space and thought about his mother, about her very real concern for him, about how much she must be worried. Then he thought about her talking to Maddie and realizing he'd been doing the wild thing with his neighbor. He thought about the struggle his mother must be facing between her Old World morals and her belief that men were so shallow, sex cured their every problem.

He imagined the look on her face when she spoke to Maddie.

And he laughed. A single, loud, hoarse bark of laughter.

The sound surprised him. The urge surprised him. The emotion . . . surprised him. He hadn't laughed in . . . he didn't remember the last time he had really laughed. And what was more . . . he laughed again. Out loud. That stark bark of laughter grew into a long, donkey-like bray that shook his whole body. He picked up one of those ugly flowered sofa pillows, placed it over his face, and laughed until his belly muscles hurt. He collapsed into the recliner, pillow still pressed to his face, and laughed, and at some point he stopped laughing and simply sat, and thought about Maddie, his family, his life, and most of all his kids, his brainiacs, living and dead. Because really, it all came down to them.

Three of his brainiacs had forgiven him. Brandon had told him that. Repeatedly, he had said that three of them had forgiven him.

One would never forgive him.

Two did not live long enough to have the chance to forgive him.

For two years, Jacob had been determined on one course—penance while looking for peace. Then when peace proved elusive . . . suicide.

Maddie had called on him to live for his fallen comrades and his wounded friends.

He had wanted to die for them.

But was Maddie right? Did he owe his brainiacs a sacrifice? Or did he owe them a celebration of life, a greater life, a life lived more fully to make up for the time they had forever lost?

And was that nothing but his own cowardice speaking, urging him to stay on this earth when he should leap to his death?

Because whether he sacrificed himself or lived for tomorrow, Maddie was definitely right about one thing—no one else owed his kids this debt.

Only him.

Only Jacob.

He himself had to make that decision. And he had to make it soon.

She fucked him!

I can tell. Bc she's happy.

I'll make her sorry.

CHAPTER THIRTY-NINE

As soon as Kateri drove her police cruiser up to Norway Hall, she knew she was in the right place. Shiny blue ribbons decorated lampposts, the same kind of ribbons that decorated Sienna's box lunches.

Cute. Pretty decorations and subliminal advertising at the same time. Sienna never missed a trick.

And Kateri reeked of bitchy cynicism.

Also, the sign outside proclaimed, LUIS AND SIENNA'S ENGAGEMENT PARTY! COME ON IN!

Two exclamation points. Adorable.

Kateri was late. One of the tourists had done her the favor of smoking shit and steering his rental ever so slowly into a ditch, and by the time she finished arresting him for driving while impaired and arranging to have his car towed, she considered not going to the two-exclamation-point engagement party. After all, who could blame her?

She had to go, of course. Had to show up with a smile on her face, a gift in her hand, and congratulations on her tongue. She wished she were a better actress, because somebody—everybody—in this town was going to gossip about her and Luis, and the entertainment for the evening would be scrutinizing the Native American female candidate for sheriff for immanent breakdown, or at least cracks in her façade. She had puttied those cracks, but a too-close examination might reveal that her toothy smile was wide and fixed.

She grabbed the gift bag—she'd picked up a blue Fiesta dinnerware gravy boat from one of the shops downtown—then hesitated about taking her walking stick. With her sometimes unsteady balance, the stick was useful in a crowd. Yet for no good reason she didn't want to carry it. It wasn't vanity, exactly, more her desire to appear healthy, strong, and confident.

Okay, that was vanity. But surely vanity for a good reason.

Taking a deep breath, she joined the crowd streaming toward the hall.

Some people sneered in her direction—the ones who intended to vote against her, she supposed—but most greeted her with smiles and waves. The prospect of free food and drink fueled the party atmosphere, and none of the guests seemed aware that Kateri had reason to feel betrayed by the guy who had been her best friend.

She didn't have a reason, really. Luis hadn't made Kateri any promises. If he wanted to marry Sienna, he could.

But damn him, he could have told her face-to-face. That Sienna-wrapped invitation had been humiliating and distasteful.

On the porch Cordelia sat on the concrete step, alone and intently eating herring salad off a paper plate.

Kateri stopped beside her. "Hello, Cordelia. Are you enjoying the party?"

Without lifting her head, Cordelia said, "They tried to put more than one kind of food on my plate at a time."

"The hostesses? The Ladies of Norway?" Kateri clarified.

"Yes. They don't know how to properly serve me, and Rainbow is busy dancing with the hot firefighter."

"Which hot firefighter?" In Kateri's opinion, Virtue Falls boasted several.

For the first time, Cordelia lifted her gaze. "The handsome one. *Hot* is another adjective for *handsome*. Sheriff Kwinault, I didn't realize it was you. Why did you tell me you'd found and rescued the little girl who was being held hostage?"

Pause. "We did." Natalie was a hundred miles from here and safe as part of a loving family. Kateri knew that was true; that morning she had talked to her.

"You didn't get the girl I was tracking."

A warning bell rang in Kateri's head. "Do you have more texts?"

"Yes."

Cordelia was reporting another captive child. Two abused girls in Virtue Falls? Anything was possible, but this was so unlikely . . . surely Cordelia with her off-the-beaten-track mind had misunderstood. "Would you send the texts to me?" Kateri asked.

"Yes. After I eat."

"Later?"

"Tomorrow." Cordelia dove back into her herring salad.

Kateri tapped her fingers against her leg. She couldn't force Cordelia to send the texts now. She wouldn't be able to judge the menace until she read them. And right now, like it or not, she had an engagement party to attend.

She followed the aromas wafting out the door and walked into the large room with pillars decorated with those same damn glittery blue ribbons. Come to think of it, the blue matched Sienna's eyes. More subliminal advertising, Kateri supposed.

In here, the crowd was dense, probably more than the occupant limit for the hall. But the fire chief wasn't going to shut them down, especially since he was standing not far away with a grin and a plate laden with every goodie the Ladies of Norway could dish up.

The town had turned out for Luis and Sienna's engagement party. The Coast Guard attended en masse. The mayor was there, the councilmen, Kateri's law enforcement officers. Young people Sienna's age and old people Margaret's age. Kateri could hear everyone exclaiming ecstatically about the food. If she was a bitch, she would say they had merely come to eat.

But she knew it wasn't true. Everyone liked and respected Luis, and everyone adored Sienna. She was one of those pretty women who always smiled, who was always successful, who never seemed to struggle and yet always won . . . and she'd won this one, too. She had Luis. Somehow she'd caught Luis.

Kateri was almost grateful when Deputy Bergen and his wife walked up. "Quite a do, isn't it?" Bergen asked.

"It is. The food smells great." The odors turned Kateri's stomach.

"Very good food," Bergen said. "As usual, the Ladies of Norway outdid themselves, and I understand Sienna had a hand in some of the traditional specialties."

Sandra Bergen said, "Which explains why Mrs. Erikson, who runs the kitchen, wears such a sour, pinched expression."

Kateri laughed. "Oh, dear. Sienna had better watch herself. We've had enough incidents in Virtue Falls." She thought about the suspicious texts Cordelia claimed to have. "We don't want another poisoning, too."

"How are you?" Sandra hugged Kateri rather forcibly. "You haven't been by the house for a while."

"It's summertime and the tourists provide us with lots to do." *And what with the election rivalry, visiting is awkward.* Kateri gestured to Bergen, who had lately turned in as many late nights as she had. "As you well know."

"Yes, he's busy, too." Sandra patted her husband's arm. "I never know when he's going to be home for dinner."

"Yes, well . . . how are your daughters?"

Sandra smiled fondly. "Good. Summers are my busy time, too, with them off school and doing every activity you can imagine. I live in my car."

Pretty soon we'll be discussing the weather. Kateri hated this: the stilted conversation with a woman she once would have called a friend, the strained relationship with the deputy she admired, the knowledge the three of them were being watched and their demeanor judged by every Virtue Falls citizen. It really couldn't get worse. . . .

Then it did.

From behind her, a light female voice said, "Sheriff Kwinault! I'm so glad you could come to our celebration."

Kateri swiveled to face Sienna, who was glowing in a blue silk maxi dress and sequined sandals. And Luis, standing beside and behind her and devastatingly handsome in his Coast Guard dress blues.

"Thank you for inviting me. You have a wonderful turnout." Kateri smiled until it hurt.

Sienna did the double cheek kiss with such expertise she never touched Kateri's arms or face. "We invited everybody we could think of to celebrate our joy with us."

Translation: *You're nothing special.*

Kateri kept smiling hard. "When is the special day?"

"As soon as Luis can get time off, we're eloping to Reno! Isn't that right, Luis?" Sienna hugged Luis's arm.

"Yes." Luis's gaze collided with Kateri's.

They both looked away.

"Since it's the first wedding for you both, I had hoped for a church ceremony," Sandra said. Sandra was a traditionalist.

"In situations like this, well—the sooner the better!" Sienna pressed her hand to her belly.

Kateri noted that the air in Norway Hall was suddenly hot as hell and twice as smelly.

Luis looked embarrassed and pained, like a man who had his pecker in a wringer. As he should.

Sienna was pregnant. *Luis and Sienna were having a baby.*

Luis had been dating Kateri and sleeping with Sienna. The *bastard.*

The only saving grace was—Bergen and Sandra looked as stunned as Kateri felt. So everybody *didn't* know!

Sandra blurted, "You're expecting a blessed event! Oh, my, I never thought . . ." Now she glanced at Kateri, at Luis, then back at Sienna.

Bergen rescued them all. "Congratulations!" He offered his hand to Luis, then Sienna, and shook heartily.

"We're not telling anyone yet," Sienna said.

"I'm sure everyone will be discreet." Luis sounded annoyed.

"No point in that. She'll be showing soon." Kateri no longer gave a damn about appearances. As soon as this hellish conversation concluded, she was out of here.

But because she'd apparently been evil in her former life, bad stuff kept coming.

Noah stepped up and said, "What a great shot for the newspaper. Both candidates for sheriff and the happy couple. Gather close and say cheese."

"Cheese" was not what Kateri wanted to say.

At once Sienna began to orchestrate matters. "What a wonderful idea! We'll stand in the middle. Deputy and Mrs. Bergen, you stand to our right. Sheriff Kwinault, you stand to our left." Sienna tugged Luis around where she wanted him, which was close to the Bergens and far from Kateri. That left Kateri in her rumpled police uniform and her tall, broken body standing next to petite, beautifully dressed, widely smiling Sienna.

Nothing could rescue this moment. . . .

From behind them, a man's deep voice intruded. "Just a minute. Let me get into the picture, too." A large hand settled intimately on the base of Kateri's spine.

She straightened in shock.

A man's lips touched her cheek and a flute of something sparkly was thrust in front of her. Close to her ear, yet loud enough for everyone to hear, he said, "Darling, as soon as I saw you had arrived I fetched us both a glass of Cascade Ice and I almost missed the photo op."

Even without turning, without looking, she knew who it was. She recognized the voice, the confidence, the height, the assured line of bullshit. "Stag Denali," she said, and smiled at the camera. "I was wondering where you were."

CHAPTER FORTY

That wasn't a lie. Since Rainbow had told Kateri Stag Denali was in town, Kateri had been wondering when she would run into him. Now he had come to her rescue in a way that made that tight knot of irritation and humiliation loosen and become relaxed amusement.

"Are we ready now?" Noah lifted the camera and snapped several shots. "There. That should give us at least one shot with everyone's eyes open." He stepped close to Kateri and transformed himself from newspaper reporter to campaign manager. "You should work the room."

Normally she would feel rebellious about campaigning at a celebration. Now with Bergen and Sandra and Luis and Sienna staring agog at her and Stag, working the room seemed exactly the right thing to do. "I've got my marching orders." She lifted her glass toward Luis and Sienna. "Congratulations again!" And toward Bergen and Sandra. "Only a few days until the election and we'll be back to normal. Thank God, huh?"

Heads nodded.

Sienna's white, cap-toothed smile wavered and widened. And wavered.

How nice. The hussy didn't know whether to be glad or horrified.

Kateri didn't even glance at Luis. "I'd better get something to eat before it's all gone!" She marched toward the food line.

Stag followed.

When he caught up, she knew exactly what to say. "Thank you so much."

He chuckled deep in his chest. "I had to do it. You looked like a field mouse being dive-bombed by a hunting hawk. That Sienna person is a piece of work." Putting his hand on Kateri's elbow, he brought her to a halt and turned her to face him. "Let me look at you."

She stood still under his scrutiny and took the opportunity to look him over, too.

In the ten years since she had seen him, he had grown more tan, more spare, older, tougher. He had a scar on his throat and a ruby on his finger that glimmered like a spill of blood. He wore tailored black jeans that hugged his long legs and a crisp white dress shirt that hugged his broad shoulders. His thick black hair tumbled across his forehead so stylishly she suspected a weekly trim. He really should have smelled like money, but no—as always, he wafted testosterone like an expensive perfume, and as they walked by, women did a double take.

His dark eyes scrutinized the rings under her eyes and her long hair held back with an elastic band and he said, "You've changed."

Since she'd always tended toward a lack of elegance with a touch of dishevelment, she assumed he was talking about her scars. "Being eaten by the frog god will do that."

Being Stag, he didn't doubt her for a minute. "I heard he'd had you for dinner. That bastard is damn scary."

She glanced around. "Don't insult him. Not here. He has good ears and a vengeful disposition."

Stag's dark eyes got darker and deeper like a wishing well that would deliver on its promises. "I'll remember. You used to be pretty. Now you bear a warrior's scars and have a warrior's power, and you're beautiful."

How like him to focus not on her disfigurement, but how her injuries had made her stronger. She smiled at him. "And you're still full of shit. What are you doing in Virtue Falls?"

"Would you believe me if I told you I came for you?"

"No."

"Okay then. I'm going to install a casino on the reservation."

She exhaled slowly. "I like the first reason better. Come on, Stag, don't do it! There'll be more of everything. More drunk driving, more suicides, more prostitution, more people stranded here because they're broke—"

"More tourists. More employment and more money for the Native Americans." He squeezed her shoulder. "More work for the new sheriff."

"Good thing I'm behind in the polls." She didn't really mean it, but damn. A casino was going to change the complexion of the county and probably not for the better.

"When's the election?"

"Tuesday. I hear mail-in ballets are already rolling in."

"Okay then. Drink your water. It'll help you make campaign promises."

"Do I have to? Make campaign promises?" She sipped the water.

"Do you love the job?"

She had never been so sincere. "It's what I was born to do."

"Then yes. Campaign promises are part of being elected sheriff. It's not like you're going to tell people lies. You are going to say that you'll keep them safe and put the bad guys in jail and protect the innocent." He made it sound so straightforward. "Isn't that what you do?"

"To the best of my ability."

"There you are." With his warm hand placed intimately on her lower spine, he steered her toward a table of senior citizens. "Go suck up. The elderly vote."

He was pretty fresh for a guy she hadn't seen in ten years, and too knowledgeable about the important people in town.

But she had always liked him; his powerful aura kept the Mr. Caldwells of this world civil, and his wicked, potent charm fascinated the nice members of the populace. He helped her forget the stinging humiliation of attending Luis's engagement party and made campaigning almost a pleasure. When, at the end of the evening, he offered to take her home, she handed her keys to Moen with instructions to take her cruiser to the police lot, and she left with Stag.

She enjoyed Luis's chagrin, Rainbow's astonishment, and she could almost hear the swell of gossip behind her. But what difference did it make? The voters needed to remember how she performed as sheriff, and regardless of what everyone always said, an election would never be won or lost on a single vote.

CHAPTER FORTY-ONE

All morning while construction went on around him, Jacob sat in his chair and mutely stared across the street. Plywood was going up on the sidewalls. Double-pane windows were being framed in. The crew were intent on their work, yet occasionally they chatted and joked, believing Jacob had returned to normal. Or at least he was less crazy.

Was he less crazy?

If anything, he thought he was crazier.

Because—he was no longer concentrating on right and wrong, his sorrow or his guilt. Instead, he was thinking about sex. All the time. Sex.

When weariness from the long night overtook him and he found himself napping in his chair, he didn't dream about Dr. Kim whispering in his ear while his brainiacs screamed and died.

No, he dreamed of a slight, welcoming body, warm, embracing arms, and the scent of a woman aroused and then satisfied.

Awake he concentrated on those dark moments in North Korea when his soldiers begged for mercy and when helplessness robbed him of his self-respect.

Then his mind would wander, and before he knew it, he was contemplating making love with Maddie. How soon could they do it again?

And where? In the bed? In the yard? In his car he had parked in the garage and forgotten?

Was he really so shallow that the act of animal passion cured his angst?

Or did the advice she gave him make sense? Was he finally learning to live again?

Good advice from a woman. What a concept. His mother would faint that he even acknowledged the possibility.

The construction crew worked late, trying to get back on schedule, and at 7:00 P.M. they closed in the front of his house. The windows were covered with plywood. It was dark. The sound was muted. He didn't have to come out and face life anymore. He was happy. Except he couldn't see what was happening on his street.

The crew packed up their gear and headed out.

Jacob was alone. He waited for night to fall. He would take a couple of sandwiches and something to drink. He would sneak across the street and knock on Maddie's door. She would open it, take his hand, draw him inside, they would—

From across the street, Maddie shrieked with such volume and terror he found himself on his feet and trembling, in the grip of a brutal flashback.

If he reacted, Dr. Kim would increase the torture.

But no. Jacob wasn't in Korea. He was in Virtue Falls. He wasn't bound by shackles or cruelty. He could move. He could help.

He jumped off the porch and hit the ground running. He sprinted across the street and slammed his shoulder into the door. "Maddie. Let me in. It's Jacob. Let me in. Maddie!" He heard the crash of furniture, the shatter of glass. "Maddie, damn it!" *Damn it* was right. He needed to get a key to her house.

The screaming went on.

He was ready to break a window when the lock clicked. She peered around the door but kept the chain on. "Are you really here?" she whispered. "Or are you an illusion?"

"I'm really here." He reached out to touch her.

She shrank back. The door started to close.

He stopped, hand extended. "Touch me."

As she reached out to him, her fingers shook. They paused directly above his skin, then in a rush she clasped his fingers. "You're real." She undid the chain, flung open the door, and pulled him inside, talking all the while. "Jacob, I was so afraid. First I heard the back door open and close and heard a man's voice call, *I'm home!* It was Easton. Easton called me."

Never taking his eyes off her, Jacob shut the front door behind him. "Were you asleep?"

"Yes!" She paced in tight circles. "I lifted my head off my desk and realized I'd been asleep."

She looked it; her dark hair was tousled, her oversize white shirt was wrinkled, the right side of her face appeared to have been resting on a pencil.

"Hang on." Jacob headed into the kitchen.

She followed. "What are you doing?"

He opened the back door and felt the metal handle. No, it had none of the scratches associated with picking the lock. "Does anyone besides you have your house key?"

Fierce and annoyed, she said, "Why does everyone ask me that? *No!*"

"All right." He shut the door. "Go on. You heard Easton."

As if she couldn't keep still, she started pacing again. "I sat up and there he was, standing in the kitchen, a ghost in a gray suit. He smiled at me. Then I saw blood on the tile floor, running in slow, red rivers along the grout lines."

He looked at the hardwood floor. "You don't have tile."

"I know." She stopped to wring her hands, then started those circles again, each getting tighter and tighter until she was almost meeting herself when she turned.

He avoided her, wandered to her desk, looked at the drawings there.

The ones at the bottom were spare black-and-white pen-and-ink. Then they became wild, sprawling across the paper, with black blotches where her pen had stuttered and sudden assaults of color—red pencil mostly, but some bright, hot yellow and a blip of purple. These were works of disturbing madness.

He advanced on Maddie, taking his time, trying not to alarm her. Reaching out a slow hand, he brushed her arm.

She jumped and looked at him, her face flushed, her blue eyes wild and big and black, as if the pupil had expanded to swallow the iris.

Startled, he leaned back. He took her by the arms, held her in place, and stared. "Have you been taking drugs?"

"No! Why?"

"Prescription drugs? Maybe something the doctor gave you?"

"No, I . . . After I left the asylum I wouldn't take drugs anymore. They made me . . . I don't react well. I screamed and screamed when they stuck the needles in me, and they laughed. I tried to scream when they shoved the pills in my mouth and held my nose and mouth shut until I swallowed. Finally they put them in my food. All the food, drugged to make me crazy." She shivered convulsively. "They laughed."

"Who laughed?"

"Them. Barbara and Gary. Nursing assistants. It wasn't fair." One by one she removed his hands from her arm and started pacing again. "I don't like drugs."

He didn't believe her. She was too vehement, with a slight slur to her voice. And those eyes . . . This explained so much. The outbursts, the hallucinations—he should have realized it sooner. She needed help. She *could* be helped . . . when she stopped lying about her problem.

For now, she needed something to do to keep her busy, stop that awful pacing, wear off some of the drugs. "Maddie, I'd like coffee. Could you make some coffee?"

She stopped pacing and stared at him through those wide black eyes. "Yes. Coffee! You like coffee. *I'll make coffee.*" As if her pacing had wound her like a spring, she turned in two circles in the opposite direction. Stopping, she took a breath, then hurried into the kitchen. She moved fast, burning so much energy she left a virtual heat trail behind her.

He followed more slowly, watching, not understanding, not wanting this to be true. For if it was, if she truly was a drug addict, how had she remained with him all last night without withdrawal symptoms? Last night, she had seemed so kind and loving, generous to a lost man groping for meaning in a life blasted by avid cruelty. She had seen no ghosts, no visions of murder and death. She had remained in his arms, sane and intelligent, keeping him safe from his nightmares.

Now she rattled around in her cupboards, muttering all the while. "Coffeemaker. Filters. Coffee. I can do this. Coffee will help. Coffee bonds people together. Coffee takes away the need to sleep. I don't want to sleep. I can make coffee." She shoveled too many grounds into the filter and poured in the water, frowning as if it took effort to remember the process. Her hands shook, her breath caught, and she pushed the button to start the brewing, announcing in a bright tone, "Maddie, this will help!"

He eased into a kitchen chair. "Tonight—what else did you see?"

She flung herself around and stared at him as if she had forgotten he was there. "My God, look at this mess. Did I do that?" She got the broom and dustpan and hustled toward her broken lamp. She began to sweep and said, "Maddie, be careful not to cut yourself." She was avoiding him.

So there had been another hallucination. "What else did you see, Maddie?"

She stopped suddenly, as if she were a puppet and somebody had cut her strings. "On the wall over my desk, I saw the scene from my dorm room. All the girls sprawled there in their own blood. Ragnor the Avenger dead, too. Of them all, only I am missing . . ."

"That's because you're still alive." Tonight he had come to make love, to find and give comfort. Now he was experiencing a totally different Maddie, the original Mad Maddie of legend.

She put her hand over her heart. "I am, aren't I? For now." With a clatter, she dropped the broom and the dustpan. The glass she'd swept up spread once again all over the floor. "The coffee's ready."

The machine hadn't beeped yet, but she pulled mugs out of the cupboard, spoons out of the drawer, and put the canister of sugar on the table. By the time she got done fussing, the coffee *was* ready, and she poured the mugs full. She stared at them for a few minutes, then whirled to face him. "Do you want milk?"

"No. I take my coffee black."

"I have to have milk. And sugar. I can't stand the taste otherwise."

"You do that. Milk and sugar will do you good."

She put his mug in front of him and headed for the refrigerator. She leaned down and rummaged inside.

He remembered this morning when he'd caught her leaning into his refrigerator. Same nice ass, but now she jiggled one foot as she looked for the milk . . . which he could see from here on the top shelf. Absentmindedly, he lifted the mug. A split second before he took a sip, an off smell hit his nose. Too late. He had hot coffee in his mouth—hot poisoned coffee.

He spit it across the table, leaped up, and ran to the sink. Flipping on the water, he leaned down and rinsed his mouth over and over, trying to rid himself of the taste of rat poison.

When he straightened, she stood beside him, staring. "What's wrong? I know it tastes awful, but I thought you liked it."

"Damn you, woman! You tried to kill me. *You* drink it!"

She frowned as if she couldn't make sense of this scene. Lifting the mug, she took a sip and grimaced, then took another sip.

He knocked the mug out of her hand and across the counter. Coffee splattered the backsplash and the cupboards. "You're crazy, you know that?"

Her face crumpled into tears. "Why did you do that?"

"You're crazy and on drugs."

"What's wrong with you?" She bunched her fists and put them to her mouth. She backed away.

"What's wrong with *you*? You tried to poison me and you tried to poison yourself." He poured the pot of coffee down the drain. He picked up the bag of ground coffee and took a sniff. Yep. Rat poison. "You're sick. You're crazy sick."

"I am not!" she shouted. "I have a certificate saying I'm sane!"

"You'd better burn it then." He stalked toward the door. He heard the patter of feet behind him. He turned quickly, hands up, prepared to defend himself.

But she held no weapon, nothing but her wild eyes and pretense of concern. "Jacob . . . I adore you."

"You pick a funny way of showing it." He went out the door and across the street, confused, angry, unhappy. And stopped short at the outer edge of his lawn.

Someone was there, watching in the shadows beside his porch.

CHAPTER FORTY-TWO

"Hello?" Jacob said. "May I help you?"

A woman stepped forward, coming to meet him, and in the streetlight's glow he saw that she was older, perhaps fifty, attractive, with a ramrod stiff military posture. And angry. By her body language he could see she was angry.

He could relate to angry.

"Are you Jacob Denisov? I assume you are. You look totally healthy." The words were civil enough, but her low voice vibrated with resentment.

Was this another crazy lady? He didn't think he could face two in one night. "I am Jacob Denisov. I'm fine, thank you."

"Of course you are. My name is Vera LaFreniere."

He tensed. "Brandon's mother." Why was she here at his house? Why so late?

"Yes. I'm Brandon's mother. I brought you a letter." She thrust a legal-size white envelope into his hand. "Take it."

He did, held it firmly, lifted it to the light, read his name printed awkwardly on the front.

"Sorry about the lousy handwriting, but Brandon . . . he insisted on writing that himself." She wasn't really apologizing. She was snapping. "He never did learn to write well with his left hand."

Jacob knew he did not want to hear the answer, but he asked anyway, "Why are you bringing me a letter?"

Bleakly she said, "Because Brandon made me promise I would . . . if he died . . . in surgery."

Jacob was suddenly aware the air had grown too thin to breathe. "Brandon's dead."

She smiled a terrible smile. "Didn't he tell you? He didn't have a real good chance of surviving. No more than fifty-fifty."

"He didn't tell me he was having surgery."

"Of course he didn't. I'm sure he didn't want to worry *you,* his hero. But he couldn't stand the idea of being maimed and paralyzed, and that was what was coming up next. So he rolled the dice. That's what he said before he went in. *I'm going to roll the dice, Mom. Surely I'm due to win.* But he didn't. After Korea, he could never win. He couldn't have children. He was missing an arm and a leg. Now he's dead because the surgeons couldn't remove that piece of shrapnel beside his spine without killing him." She must have thought the air was thin, too, because she stopped to breathe hard. "He said to tell you not to feel guilty. So I'm telling you he didn't want you to feel guilty."

She wasn't subtle; he got the unspoken message. "*You* want me to."

"Because your job was to watch a bunch of bright kids and make sure they didn't do anything stupid, and you were *asleep?*"

Yes. He had been asleep. So what? A man had to sleep. But this time . . .

South Korea . . . day after day, crappy weather all the time, nothing to do but watch his brainiacs build dumb projects that never worked. Their top-secret mission kept them effectively isolated from the rest of the base. The base commander was a bully and the only one who knew what they were doing there; he despised them for not being real military, begrudged them every resource, and hated Jacob in particular for standing between him and the brainiacs. The brainiacs had banded together, but Jacob had no one to talk to. No one who knew a thing about real life in the military or real civilian life or just . . . life.

He was bored.

That night . . . that night, those kids were all heads together, giggling, playing some stupid drinking game. He had known something was going on. But he was bored and tired and he'd gone to bed. He'd gone to sleep. He had neglected his duty and someone had to pay the price.

Vera LaFreniere said, "From the day they were born, those young men and women were privileged because they were brilliant. They thought the world was their playground. That they would always be cosseted. And the Koreans treated them like pieces of meat. Your fault."

"Yes." He should have paid the price.

"All your fault."

"Yes." He *would* pay the price.

She seemed to grope for a way to blame him again, to make the words new and sharp and painful. At last she put her fist to her breast-bone. "I don't care. Feel guilty. Feel good. Feel nothing. All I care is what *I* feel. Pain. So much pain. And resentment that your mother has a living son. It's not fair."

"No, it isn't."

They stared at each other.

"Read the letter," she said.

He did as he was ordered; tore the envelope, pulled out the thin piece of paper, read the painfully written message. He closed his eyes, seeking composure, then opened them and asked, "Do you know what he wants from me?"

"He wants you to deliver his eulogy."

"Yes." Why had Brandon asked him? Did he imagine Jacob's presence would soothe his mother, his relatives, his friends?

She said, "Although he hoped you would never see the contents, he worked hard on that letter."

"I am honored." Jacob knew what he would say. He would talk about his esteem for Brandon . . . and it was true. He did admire him. He wished he would emulate him, but now the darkness possessed his soul and he was . . . truly ruined. "I'm sorry for your loss." Words. In-adequate words.

"Thank you." Now that Vera LaFreniere had delivered her mes-sage, she was crumpling like a demolished building; her shoulders slumping, her head drooping, her whole body losing that formal stiff-ness. "I hear you never leave the house, but I see that's not true—you certainly feel free to visit your neighbor—so if you care to attend, Brandon's funeral is Friday at three. He would be honored by your attendance." Her voice cracked.

He had no choice. No choice. "I'll be there. I will do my best for him. I will . . . stand for him."

She nodded wearily and walked away toward the car parked at the curb. She opened the driver's door, paused, shut it, and came back. "I'm sorry. What I said to you—that was unfair. I had no right to complain that your mother has a living son. But Brandon was my only child and I'm so . . . I encouraged him to go into the service. He was a smart kid, a wild kid, and I thought it would help him grow up. Now he's dead and I encouraged him . . . I simply wanted him to be a man. Not like his father, not some Peter Pan flitting around without purpose, but a real man. I helped kill him."

"It's not your fault. It's my fault. I was asleep when they flew off. And when I went to get them, I failed . . . for too long. I didn't get them—him—out soon enough."

Vera LaFreniere laughed, and the sound was like dry leaves on the wind. "Brandon always said it wasn't my fault or your fault, it was that freak show of a doctor's fault. I guess we both need to remember that." This time she made it into the car and drove away.

Jacob mounted the steps and sat in his recliner, numb with shock and horror.

Brandon was dead.

Across the street, Maddie shrieked and screamed. Glass shattered.

She had rescued him only to send him back to hell.

On Friday, after Brandon's funeral, Jacob would come home, and when the sunlight was gone, he would jump off that cliff and see if hell's flames burned as hot as they said. It was no more than he deserved.

CHAPTER FORTY-THREE

The next morning, Kateri wasn't surprised to hear her doorbell ring.

She *was* surprised when she looked through the peephole and saw who stood on her step.

She tightened the belt of her robe.

She opened the door.

Without preamble, Luis crowded his way past her. "She lied."

Kateri flattened herself against the wall, held onto the doorknob, and kept the door wide open. "Um, Luis, you shouldn't be here at this time of the morning. Not after your engagement party."

Forcefully he said, "There is no engagement. Didn't you hear me? She lied. About the pregnancy. Sienna's not pregnant. She lied."

Kateri thought of several answers. *Tell me one reason I should care. Sucks to be you.* Instead she chose the neutral, "Sienna lied?"

His dark, curly hair was disheveled. His shirt was buttoned crooked. His eyes were indignant. "Who else claimed to be pregnant to get me to marry her?"

Not me, that's for sure. "How did you find that out?"

"After the party, she got sick and was throwing up so much I got worried she would get dehydrated and lose the baby. I wanted to take her to the hospital. Told her our baby's health was more important than anything else. She got mad, said I didn't love *her,* and finally threw it in my face that she wasn't pregnant."

Kateri tried to decide which part of this story she wanted to address. . . .

None of them.

So she said, "It was a great party."

He viewed her as if she were nuts.

Which she did not appreciate. "Luis, I don't know what you want me to do with this information."

"Take me back!"

Oh, really. She stalked toward him. "I never had you."

Eyes lit with purpose, he advanced. The guy was packing attitude. She reversed, hoping to keep this civil and hands-off.

He backed her against the wall. He put his elbow by her head and leaned into her. He fixed her with his melting brown eyes. He fluttered his curly long dark lashes. He lowered his voice to a sexy growl. "We could fix that right now."

She slipped under his arm and tied her robe again, tighter and with a knot that was large, complicated, and very Coast Guard. "No, thank you."

"Kateri—"

"Luis, let's be clear." She bit the words off. "Sienna may have lied, but you believed it was possible. Which means while you and I were dating, you were sleeping with Sienna."

"Once!"

"Only once." Sarcasm weighed her voice. "That makes it all better."

He spread his hands. "I drank. I was celebrating. You left me at the resort."

Her temper rose and her blood cooled. "Don't try to blame this on *me*. You're not a child. You're responsible for your actions."

He thought. He answered, "I love you."

Ah. The words of a desperate man who had betrayed her and knew it. "Thank you. I'm honored. You're a good man. But the fact is, I didn't sleep with you because I wasn't certain it was the right thing to do. I was right. I listened to my gut, and I was right."

"No. Hear me!" He flung himself at her. "We could do so much together. Be the perfect couple. You'll be the sheriff of Virtue Falls. I'm the Coast Guard commander."

"*There* are two really good reasons to have sex." The sarcasm was getting heavier, her irritation more acute. "Predictions are I'm going to lose the election. What happens if I don't hold up my end of the deal?"

"Sooner or later the Coast Guard will move me to my next assignment and it won't matter what you do for a living. You'll come with me."

She made a sound like a buzzer. "Wrong answer!"

Luis got annoyed. "What's the right answer?"

"I don't know what the right answer is—for you. For me, it's to chug along on this particular track until—"

From the bedroom, Stag called, "Honey, I used your razor on my chin. I don't have much facial hair but I still probably ruined the blade—" He stepped into the living room while holding a towel around his waist. A hand towel. A small towel.

Luis froze.

Kateri sighed.

Stag did an elaborate double take. Performance art at its finest. "Sorry! Sweetheart, I didn't realize you had company. Hello, Luis, didn't expect to see you here this morning. All well on the domestic front?"

Luis came to life slowly, his fists clenching, his brow lowering, his eyes narrowing. He swiveled slowly toward Kateri. "You wouldn't sleep with me."

"No, I wouldn't. Gut instinct saved me again."

"You slept with him."

"Obviously," Stag drawled.

Luis glared at Stag, then turned his attention back to Kateri. "Sienna said you were faking it. She said you'd probably hired him to act as your date so you wouldn't feel so self-conscious at our party."

As if he were ready to charge, Stag came up on the balls of his feet. "Kateri didn't hire me. I caught her in a weak moment, recognized my advantage, and swept her off her feet."

"Down, boy," Kateri said to him. Turning to Luis, she said, "Good news for you. Sienna doesn't always get to be right." She moved smoothly toward the door, took the knob again, and held it while she gestured toward the street.

With every appearance of a betrayed lover, Luis stalked past her and out of her apartment. "My heart is broken."

"Dang," she said. "Maybe you can take comfort in Sienna's arms." She slammed the door, leaned her forehead against it, and laughed in dismay and rueful amusement. "That was awkward." She turned—and Stag was right there, a foot away and naked.

At some point on his trip across the room, he'd dropped the towel.

She still smiled, amused and aroused and relieved he had rescued her from a potentially explosive situation. "You are absolutely appalling. What were you thinking?"

He stepped close, slid his arm around her waist, lifted her onto her toes, and pulled her against his body. "I was thinking that I've waited for years for you to grow up and way too long for the moment for us to be right, and I wasn't letting your half-tempting lover lay a claim on you for any reason." His chest heaved. His eyes burned. He slid his hands between her legs, lifted her, and pressed her against the door—and in one smooth, strong motion, he nudged his way inside her body and laid his claim. . . .

Never once during the whole orgasmic experience did she worry that he would hurt her; not her artificial joints, not her fragile emotions, not her future in Virtue Falls. She knew she was being foolish . . . but Stag made her feel safe.

CHAPTER FORTY-FOUR

Less than two hours since a disillusioned Luis had stopped by and had left disillusioned by Kateri, too.

Less than thirty-six hours until the start of Election Day.

A few hours of quiet Sunday morning peace. Or so Kateri hoped.

Right now, as she walked into the Oceanview Café, walking stick in hand, she knew Noah would say she should shake hands and kiss babies and campaign to win the election.

She was willing. Last night with Stag had given her a confidence she hadn't experienced before; Stag knew how to influence people, and in only a few hours he had taught her a lot. About campaigning . . . yes. He'd taught her a lot about campaigning. Afterward, he'd taught her a few other things, too, but no more than she'd taught him.

She smiled at the memories.

She started toward the back of the diner—and stopped. She looked around at the mostly empty tables. She stared unhappily at the spot where a computer nerd should sit. She intercepted Rainbow, who was headed toward the seniors' table, coffeepot in hand. "Where is everybody? Hungover? Where's Cordelia? I thought she always came in for Sunday breakfast."

Rainbow chuckled manically. "Didn't you hear? Everyone who ate the herring salad at Luis and Sienna's engagement party has food poisoning."

"My God!" Kateri covered her mouth in horror and shock.

"Cordelia ate a *lot* of herring salad. She's in the hospital."

"Is she going to be okay?"

"She'll be fine. Cordelia is strong as an ox." Rainbow stepped around Kateri, filled Mr. Harcourt's cup—he sat alone, reading his tablet—and came back to the counter. She poured a mugful and shoved it across to Kateri.

Kateri scooted onto a stool. "The Ladies of Norway poisoned the party?"

Rainbow smirked. "No. The Ladies of Norway didn't prepare *all* the food. This morning, Mrs. Eriksen came in to make the announcement—Sienna read their time-honored recipe and thought it sounded icky, so she insisted on making the herring salad all by herself. Sienna poisoned her own guests."

An unexpected chuckle caught Kateri by surprise.

Rainbow stood with her hands on her hips. "Half the town's sick and you're laughing. You're going straight to hell."

"I'm not laughing because people are sick. I'm laughing because Sienna . . ." Sienna the seductress. Sienna the liar. Sienna the earth goddess and chef worshipped by all . . . had spread food poisoning throughout the town. Kateri chuckled again. "You're right. I'm going to hell." She waved at Mr. Harcourt.

He waved back and called, "Hi, Sheriff Kwinault. I guess you're lucky enough to dislike herring salad, too?"

"Can't stand it."

He gave her a thumbs-up and went back to his reading.

Kateri asked Rainbow, "Are the other seniors sick?"

"Yep. Mr. Setzer is in the hospital, too. According to Mr. Harcourt, Mr. Caldwell's too stubborn to go to the hospital. So he's home tossing his cookies. Quiet morning at the ol' Oceanview Café." Rainbow leaned over the counter. "Now dish."

"About what?" As if Kateri didn't know.

"Last night, you left with Stag Denali."

Kateri sipped her coffee. "So?"

"So did you get to see him running through the forest naked? So to speak?"

Kateri did not smirk. She did not. "I don't know what you mean."

Apparently that wasn't enigmatic enough, because Rainbow slapped Kateri's shoulder. "You did! I worried you were celibate for so long you were going to dry up and blow away, and now you're involved with Stag Denali. The way I hear it, he's not named *Stag* for nothing!"

"Could you say it a little louder?" Kateri glanced around.

Mr. Harcourt was peering over his glasses at them.

In a piercing whisper, Rainbow repeated, "Now you're involved with Stag Denali!"

"Yeah, that's better. Don't tell everybody, okay? I don't know if he's going to stick around." Although from what he said, he'd had the hots for her for years. Which was flattering and weird at the same time, and not a topic of discussion. "I really need to see Cordelia. She was going to give me more texts she . . . found."

Rainbow stopped grinning. "What kind of texts?"

"She thinks we didn't rescue the right girl. Or there's another girl out there."

Rainbow grew still and grim. "What is it with people? The ones who are only happy when they hurt someone?"

"I don't know. I don't understand it. But I sure see enough of it." Kateri thought about the Terrance boys, still in jail, thank God, and still threatening to break out and hurt her in ways that would, quote, "leave you more deformed than you already are."

"If that's true about the girl, if there is another abused child . . . kudos to Cordelia. It's a good thing to know."

"Yes, but I wish she could figure out who's sending the texts. Not knowing makes this so frustrating."

Rainbow fetched a frosted doughnut out of the case, placed it on a plate, and slid it across to Kateri. "You might as well eat it. Today we don't have enough customers to finish them up."

"If you're going to put it that way . . ." Kateri took a bite.

"You know who Cordelia is for you? You know how in the books the police detective always has a secret psychic who warns him of upcoming trouble, but the warning's so vague he can't do anything to stop it?"

Kateri thought about it and nodded. "You're right. That is so Cordelia." Her phone rang. She looked at it, muttered, "This is never good," and answered. "What's up, Dr. Frownfelter?" She listened, stiffened in shock. "I don't believe it."

"What is it?" Rainbow asked.

"No, I really don't believe *that*."

Rainbow leaned over the counter again. "What?"

"Did you call the ambulance? Or the . . . morgue?"

Rainbow gripped Kateri's wrist. "Who's dead?"

"I'll be there as soon as I can." Kateri ended the call. "Dr. Frownfelter went to check on Mrs. Butenschoen; she's missed some doctors' appointments and that's not like her. He knocked, no answer, got her key out from under the fake rock by the front door, went in, and discovered Mrs. Butenschoen's body in her kitchen"—she met Rainbow's incredulous gaze—"hanging from her light fixture."

Give me another week & she'll have come back on her own.

Or they'll commit her.

CHAPTER FORTY-FIVE

Jacob sat in his broken recliner in the dark living room with aluminum foil over his windows, waiting for Friday, when he would put on his military uniform, go out to Brandon's funeral, and present the eulogy for a man who had died too soon.

Fitting that this would be his last act on this earth.

Outside, sirens wailed, but he did not care.

They came closer and closer. He did not care.

They stopped on the street. He did not care. He did not wonder who had run the stop sign at the end of the block or if Madeline Hewitson had poisoned someone . . . or poisoned herself.

But if he truly didn't care, why was he standing and walking to the door? Why was he opening it and looking out into the morning sunlight?

As always, the neighbors had gathered on his lawn. Web was there, too, although why he'd come by on a Sunday, Jacob did not know. But rather than the usual circus atmosphere brought on by disaster and flashing emergency lights, the crowd stood silent, their arms crossed over their bellies, their faces grim, and when they spoke, they spoke in whispers. They stared across the street at Mrs. Butenschoen's house, where an ambulance waited, lights flashing, siren now silent.

Jacob did not care about Mrs. Butenschoen.

He didn't care if she was ill.

He didn't care if she'd had an accident.

He looked over the heads of the crowd toward Maddie's house.

Across the street, Mrs. Nyback and Maddie stood each in her own yard, yet close against the fence that divided them. Their body language was the same as that of the other neighbors: closed, distressed, uncertain. Mrs. Nyback clutched her dog tight in her arms. Spike responded to her desperate embrace with a display of teeth and aggression, wiggling madly and fighting Mrs. Nyback's embrace.

Nasty little dog.

At Mrs. Butenschoen's house, the front door opened.

The neighbors shuffled forward, straining to see.

The EMTs came out the front door and down the stairs. They carried a body bag on a stretcher.

What the hell had happened?

Dr. Frownfelter followed the stretcher. As always, he looked tired, but now he looked aggrieved and distressed, too. Sheriff Kwinault walked with him, and he was talking to her, shaking his head, gesturing, his body language rejecting . . . something. Mrs. Butenschoen's death?

How? Why? Maybe Jacob was paranoid—or possibly more paranoid—but this was one horror too many.

He came to the edge of his porch, caught Mrs. Franklin's eye, and gestured her over. "What happened?"

In a faint voice, she said, "Mrs. Butenschoen killed herself."

What? Bullshit. "Mrs. Butenschoen—"

"Committed suicide."

Now Jacob knew why Dr. Frownfelter was shaking his head. No way Mrs. Butenschoen would commit suicide. "What makes anyone think she took her own life?"

"She hung herself on the light fixture in her kitchen. She wrote a note on her computer and left it open on the table. Rumor is she had cancer and that's why . . ." But even as Mrs. Franklin spoke, she didn't sound convinced.

"When did this happen?"

"She's been hanging there for days. A couple of days, anyway. I didn't notice she wasn't around. I mean, I did, because she wasn't complaining about my kids playing in the street. But I was relieved, you know?"

"I know."

"What's happening here on this street is spooky. Everything about it is spooky." She glared at the house next to his.

Jacob's gaze followed hers.

Dayton Floren stood in his own yard, hands in his pockets, wearing a faint smile as, with Dr. Frownfelter and Sheriff Kwinault as honor guard, the EMTs loaded the body into the ambulance.

"Floren posted bail," Mrs. Franklin said. "He's a proven arsonist. Now none of us is safe in our beds."

She sounded more than a little agitated. "I thought you were moving," he said.

"Floren reneged on the contract, too."

Jacob thought she considered that a greater crime than arson. On the other hand, in his kitchen the faint odor of smoke still lingered, so he held a grudge, too. He put all his strength of will into his glare, and in seconds Floren glanced his way.

The real estate man jumped, ducked his head, and hurried into his house.

Jacob's attention returned to the scene across the street and, inevitably, to Maddie.

She was looking at him, but as soon as their gazes met, she looked away, as if she were ashamed. Which she should be; for all the misery he had suffered, no one had ever tried to poison him before.

She appeared to be in control of herself, no longer drugged and hyperactive. Yet she looked sad and weary, too, and he found his heartstrings unwillingly tugged. What was it with the woman that she could try to kill him one day and he felt sorry for her the next?

She reached across to the dog in Mrs. Nyback's arms and rubbed his head, and for a moment the dog leaned into her touch. Then Maddie yelped and pulled her fingers back.

Spike had bitten her. Again. Didn't the woman ever learn?

Maddie disappeared into her house. She came back with a plastic canister, popped the top, and offered a treat to Spike.

The little shit snatched the treat.

With another yelp, Maddie pulled her hand back, examined her fingers, and wrapped them in her T-shirt, he supposed to stop the bleeding.

Mrs. Nyback smiled apologetically and petted Spike's head, oblivious to the fact that her darling boy was a monster.

Which made it even more startling when Spike started frothing at the mouth.

For the first few seconds, the two women stared as if they did not understand what was happening.

But Jacob knew what was happening. He knew immediately. *Poison. Again. Damn you, Madeline Hewitson.* He started down the stairs.

This was going to get ugly.

Mrs. Nyback patted Spike's back in a fast, frenetic beat.

Spike went into convulsions.

Maddie tried to pry Spike's teeth apart, but the dog had them clenched as it strained and jerked.

Jacob saw the moment Mrs. Nyback figured it out. She looked at Maddie in horror, pulled the dog away, pointed, and in loud, high hysteria she screamed, "Murderer! Murderer!"

Maddie backed up, shaking her head.

At the shouts, Dr. Frownfelter turned, observed, and in long strides got to Mrs. Nyback and the dog.

Sheriff Kwinault slapped the ambulance as a signal for it to go, and followed Dr. Frownfelter.

The doctor took one look at the convulsing dog, pulled a small brown bottle from his capacious coat pocket, flipped Spike upside down, and shook a drop into the dog's mouth.

At once the dog threw up the contents of its stomach.

Dr. Frownfelter shook the dog like a rat, cleaning it out.

Mrs. Nyback shrieked in wild hysterics.

The sheriff tried to talk to Maddie, but Maddie cried piteously and shook her head. *No. No. No.*

Sheriff Kwinault looked across the street to the neighbors assembled on Jacob's lawn, all riveted by the drama. She frowned. Pulling out her cell, she made a call.

As Jacob strode through the crowd, the muttering started. In an instant, they changed from decent individuals to a mob with a goal and a target. They were ready to attack—ready to attack Maddie.

Jacob got to the sidewalk in front of his house, faced them, and in his command voice said, "The law will handle this."

Like Mrs. Nyback, Mr. Franklin pointed an accusing finger at Maddie. "No, sir. No, sir! This woman has made our lives hell and now she killed an old lady's dog. Maybe she killed Mrs. Butenschoen, too. Madeline Hewitson deserves to hang!"

"You're not the one who gets to decide she's guilty."

"She *is* guilty," Mrs. Franklin said. "I saw her poison that dog!"

Hard to argue with that. Yet Jacob couldn't let them lynch Maddie. "The police will handle this. Listen. Hear the sirens? Reinforcements are on their way." He headed across the street in time to meet two patrol cars as they pulled up in front of Maddie's house.

Deputy Bergen, Officer Moen, and two other officers climbed out. Bergen went at once to Sheriff Kwinault. Moen headed for Maddie and offered his handkerchief. The other officers moved to halt the advance of the crowd, yelling for them to stand back.

Jacob also stopped, observing everything with a keen eye.

Dr. Frownfelter handed the once again snarling dog back to Mrs. Nyback.

She cradled the little beast like a baby, petting him and crooning.

Dr. Frownfelter called Officer Moen over and spoke to him.

Moen clearly objected, looked toward Maddie, and objected again. Then at the sight of the trembling, tearful Mrs. Nyback, he yielded. Taking her arm, Moen led her toward the patrol car.

Jacob walked to Frownfelter's side. "You sent them to the veterinarian's?"

Frownfelter pushed his fingers through his rumpled white hair, rumpling it even more. "The dog should be all right, but I don't know how much poison she gave it and with little beasts like that, it's best to be thorough." The two men watched as Deputy Bergen handcuffed Maddie, still crying, and put her into the car's backseat. The doctor mumbled quietly, "There is something seriously wrong here."

Sheriff Kwinault walked up in time to hear the comment. "Yes. Dr. Frownfelter, I want your opinion." To Jacob she said, "I understand you used to be military police."

"That's right."

"Your opinion, too." She tapped Bergen gently on the thigh with her stick. "Bergen, let's have a confab."

Bergen left the door open to allow Maddie some air, gestured Officer Knowles to stand guard, and along with Dr. Frownfelter and Jacob, followed Kateri to the shelter of Maddie's front porch.

She put her back to the street, perched one hip on the railing, and in a quiet voice that carried plainly to Jacob's ears, she asked, "What do you say when in the space of a few weeks on one street in one small town, someone drives a car into a house, a house is set on fire, a man is reported holding a screaming, struggling woman in the middle of the street in the middle of the night, one neighbor commits suicide, and a dog is poisoned?"

Jacob said, "I'd say you'd better do an autopsy on the neighbor."

Sheriff Kwinault nodded. "That's my opinion, too."

"I don't understand," Bergen said. "Do you believe Mrs. Butenschoen was killed?"

Sheriff Kwinault bent her gaze on her deputy. "When a seemingly healthy woman who spies on her neighbors dies suddenly, I'd call it suspicious."

Bergen promptly answered, "The note on the computer said she had cancer and couldn't face the treatment."

"I've known that woman my whole life," Dr. Frownfelter said. "She went to church, she obeyed the rules, she made sure everyone else did, too. And one of the first rules is, 'Thou shalt not kill.' Most especially not yourself."

"Makes you think," Sheriff Kwinault said to Bergen.

Bergen frowned. "Who would kill her?"

"Yes, Sheriff." Jacob grinned in a twisted way. "Who's your suspect? Me or Maddie?"

Sheriff Kwinault opened her mouth, shut it, and shook her head.

Jacob said, "You don't really think it's me or you wouldn't have told me."

Sheriff Kwinault met his gaze straight on. "It's not that I don't think you're dangerous. I think you're probably the most dangerous creature on this block. I know PTSD can exhibit as violence. But you're so locked in the horror of the past, you can barely function."

He was functioning now. His brain was working again. She merely hadn't realized it.

She continued, "I simply can't see you sneaking around. Maybe you've got me fooled, but if you ask me, you're not underhanded, not a guy who plots and schemes." She finished and leaned back.

"You mean you don't think I'd murder a dog and a nosy neighbor."

"That's right."

"*There's* a compliment."

Sheriff Kwinault smiled. "I'm keeping an open mind. Could be you or Maddie or both of you. Could be Dayton Floren. He has motive, he's all lawyered up, and he's over there peering out the window. Could be someone else entirely, although I don't know why."

"Could be coincidence," Bergen said.

"Could be," Kateri acknowledged. "Which brings me to my current question. Do you believe Mad Maddie Hewitson poisoned that dog?"

Jacob and the two other men turned to look at Maddie weeping quietly in the back of the patrol car.

"No!" Kateri's voice lashed at them. "Don't look at her. Look at me. Tell me whether you think she poisoned that dog."

Jacob would never forget the smell of that coffee, the bitter poison that permeated each drop. "Yes. She did it."

"You seem very sure, Mr. Denisov. Are you telling me what you know with your mind?"

"Yes."

"What does your gut say?"

He knew what she meant. Facts change. Truth is eternal. And a mind only interested in facts made a poor judge of character.

"Mind and gut," Dr. Frownfelter said, "Madeline Hewitson is innocent."

Jacob wanted to object, to point out that Dr. Frownfelter was a basically decent guy who believed in the goodness of humanity. Usually Jacob blamed that on innocence. But in Dr. Frownfelter's case, that wasn't possible. Physicians saw the worst of people. They saw the suffering caused by those people. If Dr. Frownfelter believed the best of everyone, that was his choice. Jacob simply didn't know how valid that made his opinion.

But Kateri nodded and pointed at Deputy Bergen. "What do you think? Guilty or innocent?"

"Guilty as all heck." Bergen looked disgusted with the whole interrogation. "After seeing poor old Mrs. Nyback crying over that stupid little dog, how can you even ask?"

"That doesn't mean Madeline Hewitson did it," Dr. Frownfelter said.

"Who else could?" Bergen replied.

Jacob contemplated Maddie's house. He didn't mean to say it. It sounded too stupid. But the words popped out of his mouth. "She's being gaslighted."

CHAPTER FORTY-SIX

"Gaslighted? Like in the old movie?" Dr. Frownfelter rumpled his hair again. "Yes. I like that. Smart deduction. In the circumstances, it makes sense."

"What are you talking about?" Bergen shifted impatiently, straining to understand.

Sheriff Kwinault said, "*Gaslight*. It's an old movie with Ingrid Bergman and Charles Boyer. He's the husband trying to put her into a mental institution by convincing her she's crazy."

"What?" Bergen clearly thought someone was crazy. Probably all of them.

Yet now that Sheriff Kwinault had explained, now that the words were out, Jacob felt sure he was right. "Gaslighting explains everything. The illusions, the paranoia, the moves to isolate Maddie." He started toward the patrol car.

Sheriff Kwinault blocked his way with her walking stick. "Why do you think that? Have you seen something?"

"I've seen plenty." Jacob gestured to his house. "Until yesterday I haven't had a front door or, for that matter, a front wall."

Sheriff Kwinault pulled her stick back to her side. "All the incidents could also be explained by the fact Maddie's nuts."

"If she's being gaslighted, why poison the dog treats?" Deputy Bergen sounded reasonable, a man explaining the obvious to the oblivious.

"To isolate her from the people who could be her friends, who might provide support for her." Jacob had it figured out now.

Why poison her coffee?

Because she didn't drink coffee, but if she had a guest, she would serve it and poison them—not fatally, but enough to make them sick—contributing to her seclusion and the legend of her madness. "I have wondered if someone had the key to her house. Someone does. Someone must have. Someone has access."

"That's stupid." Deputy Bergen was clearly exasperated. "What reason would someone have to gaslight Madeline Hewitson?"

"The usual." In Jacob's mind—*Kaching! Kaching!*—it was adding up. "Money."

Bergen's exasperation grew. "How are you going to get money out of gaslighting Madeline Hewitson, the woman who depends on her brother to support her?"

Kateri viewed Jacob with an intuitive gaze. "I believe Mr. Denisov is saying there's something about Madeline Hewitson that we don't know."

"I guess I am." Jacob wasn't going to tell them about Maddie's writing, not until he looked up a few things, such as how well her books were doing. If a lot of money was involved, and Jacob guessed there was, then her brother was guilty of terrifying Maddie because . . . he wanted her to return to Denver and live close, where he could control her.

But would her brother torment her like this? Maddie thought he loved her. Was she wrong? Was Andrew driven by jealousy? Did he truly hate her so much? "Sheriff, you said you wanted me to vote with my gut. Here you go. Maddie's innocent."

Kateri surveyed the three men. "So guilty, not guilty, not guilty." She pointed to herself. "Not guilty."

Bergen clearly didn't care what Dr. Frownfelter and Jacob thought. But he just as clearly thought Sheriff Kwinault needed to be brought back to reality. In the sharp tone of an annoyed father, he asked, "May I remind you of her overall history of murder and madness?"

"Nothing was ever proved," Dr. Frownfelter said. "If she is innocent, she has been much maligned."

"And if she's guilty, she's gotten away with murder!" Bergen waved at them all to let him finish. "That aside, let's examine her history here in Virtue Falls. Madeline Hewitson has been nothing but trouble from the moment she moved here."

"That's not true," Sheriff Kwinault said. "For months after she arrived, she caused no trouble and I didn't know who she was."

Bergen put his hand on his service pistol. "You know now."

Jacob wondered if the man knew how hostile he appeared, and he wondered, too, if this overt display of manly domination was prompted by a real belief in Maddie's guilt . . . or by his intent to dominate in the upcoming election.

"She's trouble. That doesn't mean she's a killer." Kateri got to her feet. "Bergen, it's getting ugly in the street. Better get her out of here, take her to the station, book her on charges of cruelty to animals. Put her in a cell overnight and put a watch on her. If anything happens to Mad Maddie Hewitson while she's in our custody, I'll hold you personally responsible. At this point, we have to save her from the mob of angry Virtue Falls citizens and their flaming torches."

Everyone looked toward the incensed Dogwood Blossom Historical Neighborhood residents. Word had spread about Mrs. Butenschoen and about the dog, and citizens from surrounding neighborhoods now also milled around on the street, muttering angrily.

"We also need to save her from whoever would kill a little dog in pursuit of"—Sheriff Kwinault turned to Jacob—"money? Really?"

"Money," Jacob confirmed. To Bergen he said, "Check her for drugs."

"We always do," Bergen said acerbically.

"Do a thorough screening." Jacob stood and faced the deputy. He was—had been—Bergen's equal, an officer in charge of enforcing military law, a man responsible for lives and rescue. "Look for hallucinogens. Drugs that would amplify illusions. Drugs that cause anxiety and hyperactivity."

At once Dr. Frownfelter displayed his expertise. "Good. Yes. That makes sense. Look for Haldol. Old school, but still used. Stelazine, Thorazine, Navane. Lithium. Alone and in combination, all of these drugs, if injected into a patient without mental issues, could actually cause hallucinations, both visual and auditory."

Bergen considered them as if he could not believe they were serious. "You can't inject someone and they not know it. She would have to inject them in herself!"

"She fights sleep. When she finally goes down, she sleeps hard. And let's face it, if I'm right, if someone has access to her, they could feed her the drug orally or inject her and then sit back and watch the fun." Jacob surveyed the scene, and for the first time, he felt like himself again. He couldn't, he realized, stuff himself back into the black hole where he had been hiding. Life was here, demanding to be lived. Maddie was here, needing to be helped.

Who was Jacob Denisov?

All his life, he had been the man who helped people find their path.

Despite Dr. Kim's best efforts to twist and subvert him, he remained Jacob Denisov, and the bedrock of his nature remained unchanged.

"I'll post bail for her," he said.

"Or I will," Dr. Frownfelter agreed.

"Gentlemen, while I appreciate the sentiments, we'll need a court hearing before she's released. She's going to spend the night in jail." Sheriff Kwinault started down the stairs toward her vehicle.

Deputy Bergen ran past her and worked his way through the crowd, speaking to each angry individual, shaking hands when he could, campaigning even now.

Jacob jumped off the porch, swerved around Sheriff Kwinault and Deputy Bergen, and got to the patrol car. With one hand on the roof, he leaned into the backseat.

Officer Knowles caught his arm. "I'm sorry, sir, I can't permit you to speak to the prisoner."

Jacob looked at him. Just looked at him.

Knowles released him and moved out of the way.

Jacob stuck his head into the car. "Maddie, listen to me."

Her relentless sobs tore at his heart.

"Damn." He slid into the seat beside her. As she had once done for him, he stripped off his T-shirt and blotted her face, held it to her nose, and said, "Blow."

She did. She turned tear-filled eyes to him. "They're going to put me in a cell like last time, like in the mental hospital, and I can't stand it. I . . . can't . . . stand it."

"Yes, you can. You're the strongest person I know."

"No, I'm not. I'm a coward afraid of shadows."

"They're not shadows. They're projections—"

Beside him, Deputy Bergen said, "For Pete's sake, Mr. Denisov, you cannot do this!"

"Right." Jacob heard the crowd's increasingly loud hostility and spoke more quickly. "Maddie, my mother always told me—when you're having a nightmare and the monster is chasing you, you have to turn and face it. That was the only way to triumph. You have a lot of monsters chasing you. Promise me you'll face them bravely."

"I can't!"

"You will." Gently he wiped her face one last time, climbed out of the car, nodded to Bergen, and stepped away.

Bergen shut the door on Maddie and climbed into the passenger seat.

Officer Knowles got into the driver's seat. He put the car in gear and carefully maneuvered through the people.

Maddie turned to look behind her.

Jacob stood still and waved, then gave her two thumbs up.

Did his gesture give her the encouragement she needed to survive the trial of disapproval and outrage she would face?

He could only hope.

CHAPTER FORTY-SEVEN

That afternoon, for the first time since he had moved in, Jacob deliberately turned on the overhead light in his bedroom.

In here he had suffered his most terrible nightmares. Yet it didn't look like a torture chamber. It was merely small and dusty, decorated with starched, crocheted doilies created by the lady who had lived and died in this house. He fingered one. The stiff lace reminded him of his great-grandmother.

In his tiny walk-in closet, he pulled the chain that turned on that light. He looked around at the chaos of clothes and bags. He extricated his overnight case and in a return to his military training, he precisely folded and packed a change of clothes. He found his cell phone. The battery was dead; he hadn't charged it in months. So he plugged it in. Going out to the living room, he picked up the old push-button phone and put the receiver to his ear. The dial tone hummed in his ear, waiting for instruction. He pushed zero and waited.

Did directory assistance still exist?

To his amazement, an operator answered, albeit an automated electronic operator. He got the number for Alaska Air, called, and made his reservations.

That evening he visited Dr. Frownfelter and borrowed his computer, joined him for pizza and beer, and went home to bed. He climbed between the sheets and slept the sleep of the righteous.

In the morning, he shaved, showered, and dressed in travel clothes. He opened the top drawer and pulled out his revolver. He checked it, made sure it was clean and loaded and the safety was on. He slid it in the leather holster, strapped the holster around his chest, and shrugged into his jacket. With one call to the police department, he discovered that early this morning Dr. Frownfelter had posted bail and Maddie had been released. Jacob walked across the street, knocked on the door, and called, "Maddie, it's Jacob. Let me in."

No answer.

In his firmest command voice, he said, "Madeline Hewitson, if you don't let me in, I will break down the door."

He heard the rattle of the chain. The door opened a few inches. She peeked out.

Her eyes and nose were red. She had been crying, probably in jail, probably all night.

He gently pushed the door the rest of the way open, shoving her back far enough to slip in. Shutting the door behind him, he looked around.

Packing boxes filled the house. Books and belongings were strewn everywhere. "What are you doing?"

"Moving out. Moving back. Giving up. I had to promise the judge I would commit myself to a mental asylum within seven days. It was the only way she would release me. And I . . . I guess I'll be in there forever." Maddie's voice wobbled.

He took her in his arms. "Honey, don't beat on yourself like this."

She burst into tears. "I l-liked that dog. He was such a gr-rumpy old thing. Now he's half dead and everyone thinks it's . . . it's *me*, and I don't know how the poison got in the dog treat! Poor Mrs. Nyback is so hurt. She was n-nice to me and I guess I killed Easton . . ." Frantically she shook her head. She grabbed Jacob's collar and gripped it hard, and she talked faster and faster. "I don't remember killing him. I don't remember . . . I remember being afraid. I remember seeing him dead, seeing the man in the hat and coat. But then, I don't remember buying poison, but I tried to poison you and me and the dog is sick so . . ."

He walked her to her desk chair and pushed her into it, got her a handful of tissues, and pushed them into her hands. "You didn't poison the dog."

She pushed him away, stood up, and with her shoulders hunched, went back to her packing. "I didn't? Really? I saw myself. How is it you missed it? Apparently the rest of Virtue Falls saw it."

"Let me check." He looked under the kitchen sink first, then the bathroom sink, then did a search of all her cupboards. Then he went out in back to her garage and glanced around at the empty shelves. He rummaged through her recycling—glass, paper, and plastic carefully placed in separate bins—and at her garbage can he pulled out the lone bag of trash and sorted through it. He came back in and washed his hands, turned to her, and said, "You don't have any poison here. If you did the poisoning, what happened to the package?"

"I . . . threw it into the ocean?"

"Yes. Ruthless recycler that you are, you sullied the environment and killed fish by tossing a container of poison into the sea." He scanned the walls.

She stood with a pile of office supplies in her hands and a box in the other and watched him. "What are you doing?"

"I'm looking for cameras that spy on you, and projectors that could produce an illusion of something attacking you." He was disgusted that he hadn't searched before.

She blinked at him. "I never installed anything like that."

"I didn't suppose you did."

Maddie might be mad, but she wasn't stupid. "You think someone is picking on me."

"Picking on you?" His voice rose. Carefully, he lowered it. "No, I think someone is torturing you. Creating ghosts . . . spying on your nightmares and creating monsters to match. Someone knows far too much about you."

"Why? And who?"

"Who do you think?"

She stood and thought, and answered slowly. "My brother was unhappy when I moved to Virtue Falls. He said he wanted to keep me close where he could watch over me, protect me. He thinks I could write more if I didn't have to worry about, you know, life." She put down the box and loaded it with books and pictures. "Maybe . . . maybe he . . . but no. He wouldn't do that to me. He loves me."

How telling. When asked for a suspect, she immediately thought of Andrew. "When did you last talk to your brother?"

She shrugged one shoulder, picked up her house phone, and made a call.

Jacob came over and pushed the button for speakerphone.

It rang five times; the answering machine picked up. *This is Andrew Hewitson. I'm not available right now, please leave a message.*

Jacob already didn't like that cheerful, smarmy voice.

"The new book is out. He's probably at an autographing." With more confidence, Maddie hung up. "That's why he took over as the author. Because I can't . . . I'm too scared to go out and see people."

Jacob took her hands and looked into her eyes. "Maddie, once this torture is stopped, your confidence will rebound. Then you can decide whether you want to make appearances. You don't have to, you know."

"Andrew said the publishers pressure you."

"You're an adult. You don't have to do anything you don't want to."

Clearly she was troubled. "He *couldn't* do what you think he's doing to me. He could never dream up a scheme like the one you're describing. He has no imagination at all. And he does love me!"

This is where it got sticky, where she had to weigh her brother's greed against his love. "He wants you close so he can keep you working to support him."

"I'm not supporting him! He owns a firm. He trades stocks." She fetched another box and began to fill it with the contents of her desk.

"Stock trading is an iffy proposition, and your books make a lot of money."

Her packing got faster, more frantic. "But they don't. He told me—"

"Dr. Frownfelter loaned me the use of his computer so I could look up A. M. Hewitson." Last evening had been both busy and revealing. "Your publishing contracts are very profitable."

"How much?"

"Millions."

She flung the last of her drawing pens in the box. "Of dollars?"

She looked around at her little house. In the voice of an author who recognized a plot when she saw it, she said, "Money is always motive."

"Yes. Did you never think to check?"

"No, I . . . I don't read reviews, either. I used to and if they were bad I'd cry, so Andrew forbade me to look up my books online . . ." Her voice faded as evidence piled up against her brother.

Jacob ran his hand along the bottom of kitchen cabinets, found a small lens of some kind, and detached it. He showed her the miniature piece of electronics. "Wireless. I suspect someone placed this and occasionally activates a program that projects your boogie man into the room with you."

She put her hand to her throat. "No one could set that up. I keep my house locked."

"Locks can be picked. Keys can be copied. Does your brother have your house key?"

"Yes." Wearing a truculent expression, Maddie called Andrew's cell. Still no answer.

"He's not home. But he's not in Virtue Falls. He can't be doing this to me. He loves me," she said. "I know he does."

"This torture was designed to keep you frightened and dependent. But perhaps he hired someone for this job and doesn't realize how terribly you are being persecuted." Jacob made excuses to ease Maddie into the truth. Yet even if Andrew wasn't personally putting her through this ordeal—and Jacob judged that Andrew would never dirty his hands with the menial labor involved—he was sure no one else could know her well enough to pick apart her fears and play into them so successfully. And no matter how much money was involved, no reason was good enough to justify the maggots, the poison, and this program that projected horror into Maddie's front room. This persecution showed a malice Jacob had glimpsed only once before in his life. . . . At least Dr. Kim had not been a relative. "I'm going to pay your brother a visit."

"You *cannot* go to beat him up."

"You said I'm skin and bones. Out of shape. A teenage girl could break me."

"Yes, but you're a soldier. Andrew never exercises and the only time he ever fought anybody was in middle school and he got his glasses crunched."

Jacob grinned. "I'm flattered. But I intend to find out who's behind this, and if Andrew is indeed ignorant, enlist his help."

"You're going to Colorado Springs to talk to Andrew?" She mulled that over. "But you're a hermit."

"That's a life choice I'm choosing to abandon."

"You are turning to face your nightmare monster."

Her insights sometimes struck him as almost too acute, too personal. And yet, who else could have dragged him from his self-imposed hell and back to life? Only someone who had lived in hell herself. Only someone he could rescue in return. "With luck I'll be back late tonight. I'll call Sheriff Kwinault, see if she can find you somewhere safe to stay."

Maddie frantically shook her head.

"You don't want to stay here, knowing someone can watch you, listen to you." Again he started scanning her little house, looking for more electronics. "With my cursory search, I can't be sure I've found all the electronics used to create these illusions and spy on you."

She hugged herself. "I love my house. This is my sanctuary."

"Right now, someone could be listening to us talk." He pulled a tiny wireless microphone out from underneath her desk and showed her. "Whoever this is will try different and more desperate ways to torment you."

"But if I know what's going on—"

He took the microphone into the bathroom and flushed it. When he came back, she was huddled in her desk chair with her legs pulled up to her chest and her arms hugging them.

He knelt beside her. "There's an element of madness about this campaign. I'm afraid of escalation. I'm afraid that when whoever is doing this realizes you have escaped from the terror they are imposing, they'll try to do you physical harm."

"All this stuff reminds me of the things that used to happen in the mental institution. Sometimes the attendants weren't . . . kind. Sometimes they liked to pick on the patients, make them crazier. This is . . .

like that." She hugged her knees tighter. "Do you think this person killed Mrs. Butenschoen?"

"I think it probable. Someone who is entering your house to drug you, plant poison in your coffee and your dog treats, and perform unspeakable cruelties would not appreciate a busybody like Mrs. Butenschoen."

Maddie shivered and lowered her chin onto her knees.

"I'm sorry I didn't believe you sooner. I could have saved you so much suffering." Leaning in, he kissed her.

Her lips clung to his, her arms loosened around her knees and wrapped around his shoulders. "I'm sorry I didn't think to look for . . . I'm sorry I was gullible." She looked ashamed.

Then Jacob *did* want to beat up the brother who had so destroyed her confidence. "If you won't stay in police custody, will you at least stay at my house? It's closed in now. The doors lock. The construction crew will be there soon and they'll be another layer of safety for you. You've slept there overnight so you should be comfortable. Will you do that for me?"

She looked relieved. "I can do that." Then she flinched. "I don't want the crew to know I'm there, though. Last night I saw the look on Web's face." Emotion closed her throat again, and she barely managed to squeak, "He thought I'd poisoned the dog, too."

He squeezed her again. "Stay in the bedroom, then. And one last thing." He took off his jacket.

Her eyes widened at the sight of his holster.

He unstrapped it and adjusted the buckles. "Do you know how to use a revolver?"

"Yes. When I met Easton, he thought it would give me confidence if I learned to shoot."

"God bless Easton." Jacob slipped the holster on her; even at the smallest setting, it was too big for her. The woman was *skinny*.

She slipped it off over her head. "Why don't I use this?" Going to her bookcase, she removed half a shelf of books and from behind them pulled a Smith & Wesson 642 revolver in a snapped leather holster.

"Wow." He took the weapon from her, admired it, checked to see that it was loaded and the safety was on. "Why, when you were so frightened, did you put this out of reach?"

"The first time I saw an illusion, I shot it."

"Ah. I remember the story now." He had heard it from Officer Moen on the day Maddie had driven into his house.

"The bullets went right through that . . . mirage . . . and buried themselves in the wall. After I was arrested and charged with shooting a firearm in the city and a few other things, I lost my license to carry." Maddie's color was high; she was embarrassed or incensed or both. "I was kind of okay with that. I mean, it made sense in light of the fact no one else saw what I saw. Plus I was afraid I might accidently kill someone in the neighborhood. I couldn't take that chance."

"Now you know the illusions are not in your mind, so if someone comes at you, you know what to do." He helped her strap on her holster; this one fit.

"Point and shoot."

"Right." Belatedly it occurred to him: Maddie was in a fragile mental state. "Be careful not to hurt yourself, and only use the revolver as the last possible resort."

"As the last possible resort," she repeated, "and only for someone who has physically threatened me and proved to be real."

Her fierceness gave him comfort. "Have you got a sweater or a jacket you can use to cover this?" He gestured at the holster and gun.

"I'll figure something out."

He pulled the key off his ring and pressed it into her hand. "I have to go or I'll miss the plane. Can you get over there by yourself?"

"Yes."

"Promise me you'll go. I won't worry quite so much."

"I promise."

He started to stand.

But she caught his arm. "Jacob, if what you say is true . . . that means when Easton demanded to see my publishing financials, Andrew hired someone to kill him. Is that what you believe?"

"It's not important what I believe. What do you believe?"

She looked at him, her blue eyes hot. "I believe I am getting angry."

Wait. What? You can't be serious. What happened to the money?

CHAPTER FORTY-EIGHT

Jacob presented himself at the gate of Andrew Hewitson's upscale condominium development and considered the call box. Pressing the button for Andrew's place, he waited while it rang five times. The answering machine picked up, and a warm, pleasing man's voice said, *This is Andrew Hewitson. I'm not available right now, please leave a message.*

That got Jacob nowhere, but another car drove up, and in the rearview mirror, he saw the driver lift a remote control. The gate opened and Jacob followed that car in. The GPS sent him through the winding streets to an all-brick patio home; he parked in front and surveyed the property. The house was large, prosperous, but the yard looked ragged, while all around it, the lawns and flower beds were pristine. He got out, stood at the picket fence, hands in his pockets, and looked around. Nice neighborhood. Nice place. Really nice place. Andrew must do really well as an investment consultant. Or, if Jacob's suspicions were correct, Andrew was nothing without his sister.

But A. M. Hewitson novels were selling briskly. Andrew should be rolling in money. What reason did he have for the disintegration of the yard?

Jacob walked up the sidewalk and rang the doorbell.

No answer.

He leaned on the doorbell.

No answer.

A window from the house next door creaked open, an elderly gentleman leaned out, and in the loud tones of the deaf, he said, "They're not home."

They?

Jacob matched him in volume. "My name is Jacob Denisov, and—"

"Are you a bill collector?"

"No, sir."

"Who are you, then?"

Jacob gave the story he'd planned before he arrived. "I'm Maddie Hewitson's husband."

The elderly gentleman lit up. "Maddie's married? At last!"

"Yes, sir." Jacob observed the old man's posture and took a chance. "I'm retired U.S. Army, back from a tour of South Korea. I met Maddie in Virtue Falls, where she lives, and convinced her to marry me."

"She's an odd one, our Maddie. You sure you can handle her?"

"I'm a little odd myself, sir—spent time as a North Korean POW, didn't come out so well."

The old man studied Jacob. "I didn't know North Korea still took POWs. Wait there." He pulled his head in and shut the window, then came out the front door and down the ramp for the handicapped, using his walker. "I spent some time in Korea myself, back in '52. Didn't love it." He offered his hand. "Cyrus Caron, first lieutenant."

Jacob shook. "Good to meet you, sir. I came to meet Andrew, talk to him about Maddie. Do you know where he went?"

"Nope. I was up real early one morning—I can't sleep sometimes, need a hip replacement, but they don't dare put me under for fear I won't wake up—and I saw them. They loaded their bags into a cab and headed off, I figured for the airport. Haven't seen them since."

"They?"

"Andrew and his girlfriend."

"He told Maddie he didn't have a girlfriend."

"That female's been visiting him for a couple of years. I think she's some kind of businesswoman. She wears black suits and carries a brief-case. Shows up a couple of times a month for a little poontang, then she's off again. Nice-looking. Tall. Built."

"Damn. I was hoping to take care of this now." Jacob glanced at the blank windows, wondering if he could break in without setting off an alarm.

"After he locked himself out once, Andy gave me a key. Let me get it." At his own stately pace, Mr. Caron returned to his house and went inside.

Jacob blessed his luck.

Still moving slowly, Mr. Caron exited his home, came down the walk, out the gate, down the sidewalk, into the gate at Andrew's house. . . . He started talking before he reached Jacob. "So . . . Korea, huh?"

"Yes. Korea."

"Suckhole of a frozen wasteland. I couldn't wait to see the back of it."

"Me, too, sir."

"You wouldn't happen to be that young man who helped those smart kids escape that North Korean hellhole, would you?"

"That would be me."

Mr. Caron looked at him sharply. "It's a hard thing coming back to real life. Spent a couple of years on the streets after I got stateside. Then my wife got fed up and came and got me." He glanced toward the house. "She's a firecracker, that one is. She'll be after me to tell her all about Maddie's man."

"Tell her I'll keep Maddie safe."

"That'll be what she wants to hear." Mr. Caron fitted the key in the lock. "Let's go in and see if Andrew left a note for his housekeeper. Not that I've seen her around lately. Andrew has gotten very sloppy about his home maintenance. He's in trouble with the neighborhood association."

"Do you know why he's getting sloppy?"

"He's been holed up in the house a lot, and when I do see him and ask what he's been up to, he says working. On his computer—I see the light from his office all night sometimes." Mr. Caron stepped inside and disarmed the alarm. "Here you are . . . My God, he really has let the place go."

Jacob followed Mr. Caron into the dim house. The smell struck him first—musty, moldy, a house neglected. The home had originally been beautifully decorated and probably well kept, but now the floors were filthy, strewn with papers covered with calculations. Dust sat thick on the furniture, and if Mr. Caron hadn't seen Andrew leave, Jacob would have worried he was going to find Andrew upstairs on the bed dead of a heart attack or an overdose.

Mr. Caron watched Jacob wander into the living room. "I wonder what his problem is. Got money. Got a beautiful girlfriend. Got a sister he doesn't appreciate. Something must have gone sour."

Jacob picked up a glass that might once have held milk, looked inside, looked up at Mr. Caron, and nodded. "Definitely sour." He picked up a piece of paper and studied the calculations that covered it. They made no sense, but Jacob wasn't an investment adviser.

Mr. Caron wandered down the hall, pieces of paper crinkling as the wheels of his walker ran over them. "Here's his office," he announced. "Used to be a nice place."

Jacob walked into the room. A minimalist desk sat against the wall, an open file cabinet had spewed its guts on the floor, and more of those scribbled papers hung on the walls, pierced by colored stickpins.

"People say Maddie is crazy. Maybe they have the wrong sibling." Going to the answering machine, Mr. Caron pushed the blinking button.

You have four new calls.

Beep.

Andrew, this is your editor. Where are you? You're supposed to be starting your book tour with an interview on Denver Today *and they called in a panic. Don't do this, Andrew. You know how important this kind of local exposure is for book sales. Andrew? Pick up!*

Beep.

Mr. Hewitson, this is the station manager at KDPG, Jean Majure at Denver Today. *I made a place on the show for you today. Could you please let me know when you're going to arrive?*

Beep.

Mr. Hewitson, this is Latest Greatest Murder Bookstore. We've got your books and a line of devoted fans waiting to have them autographed. Can you tell us when you're going to show up?

Beep.

Andrew, this is your editor. You're a feckless beast but I'm starting to get worried. You didn't show up for Denver Today *and you didn't show up for your book signing. If you don't answer the phone soon, I'm sending the police over to check on you.*

Beep.

Jacob looked at Mr. Caron. "Did she?"

Mr. Caron shook his head. "Never saw them."

Jacob went to the computer and turned it on. He opened Andrew's writing program. He had no files labeled with the current book; the program wasn't updated to the current version. Jacob could barely contain his sarcasm. "Doesn't look like he was getting much done on his book."

Mr. Caron pulled out the seat on his walker, sat down, and squinted at the screen. "My wife never did believe that story about him writing the books. She said he was too pretty and smooth to write scary stuff."

"Who did she think was writing it?"

"Why are you asking? You know who is doing it. Our little Maddie."

Jacob was impressed. "No one else has figured it out."

"The Hewitsons, the parents, were our neighbors. We lived here when Maddie was born. We saw those kids grow up. We know her, and we know Andrew. He's got a good heart, but the man's as weak as ditchwater."

Jacob opened the browser. The home page came up—to a gambling Web site. He checked the history: more gambling sites.

Mr. Caron was reading over Jacob's shoulder and right away he knew what he was seeing. "I had friends like this in the service. Got paid, went to the poker tables, were broke before midnight. The card sharks raked it in."

"I knew those guys, too." Tucked among the online loan sites, Jacob found a United Airlines reservations page. Following a hunch, he opened the mail program and looked for a confirmation e-mail. He found it: two tickets to Las Vegas, one for Andrew Hewitson and one for Barbara Ulrich, leaving two days ago at 6:20 A.M.

Mr. Caron said, "Looks like Miss Ulrich wanted to get in on the action, too."

A bad feeling stirred in Jacob's gut. "First-class return tickets for Wednesday."

Mr. Caron pointed a shaky finger at the screen. "Five nights at the Bellagio for a monster-size suite. Andrew must have had some luck."

Jacob popped up another few e-mails. "It looks like he's run through a lot of money already. Careless of him to leave his bank account unencrypted. Anybody in the house could snoop and find out that he . . . wow! He blew over one hundred grand in the past month."

Mr. Caron put his hand on his chest and started wheezing. "My God, boy. Don't tell me that stuff. At my age, I could be dead of shock in a blink of an eye."

Jacob shot him a glance. "I'd guess it's going to take more than that to kill you."

The aged veteran stopped faking it. "Probably." He pointed a shaky finger at the screen. "Although if you open that e-mail, that may finish me off."

Jacob opened the e-mail from the White Shoulders Wedding Chapel with the subject line *Reservations Confirmed*.

There it was: a date and time, twenty-four hours ago, for a wedding to be performed for Andrew Hewitson and Barbara Ulrich. "It *does* look as if Miss Ulrich wanted to get in on the action."

"Looks like. But why would any woman want a husband with an out-of-control gambling habit and a mound of debt?"

"For the book royalties." Jacob pulled out his newly charged cell phone. "Looks like I'm traveling to Vegas."

It's not hard to kill a human being. I've done it before.

No, I don't mean I intend to kill her. Don't read things into my words.
You don't understand me.

You have never appreciated my efforts on your behalf.

CHAPTER FORTY-NINE

As soon as Jacob disembarked in Las Vegas, the noise and lights of slot machines assaulted him. They jangled and shouted as he walked down the concourse, gripping his duffel bag. As soon as he got outside, it was 4:00 P.M. and dry heat and bright desert sunshine blasted him. He fumbled for Moore's sunglasses, slid them on his nose, and got in the cab line.

This was a return to modern life with a vengeance.

He called the Bellagio and asked for Andrew Hewitson's room. He was informed they had no guest registered under that name.

Of course not. That would make this too easy.

He called Maddie and asked if she'd heard from her brother.

She hadn't, and she hadn't been able to get ahold of him. Jacob told her nothing except that he thought Andrew had gone to Vegas on business. She already sounded worried and scared and there wasn't much he could do to reassure her except to tell her he was on the case and hoped to find out exactly what was going on.

Hell, *he* was worried and scared. Maddie was alone, someone had it in for her, her miserable piece-of-shit gambling manipulative brother had acquired a wife, and the two of them had disappeared. Perhaps they had gone on a honeymoon. Perhaps they had returned to Colorado Springs while Jacob flew to Las Vegas. Perhaps they had fled the country. If he could find Andrew, he would put a stop to this systematic exploitation and harassment of Maddie . . . but he was starting to think that when Andrew had hired someone to kill Maddie's fiancé, he had tapped into bigger problems than he could handle.

In the cab, he gave the name of the wedding chapel and said, "Hurry."

The cabbie whipped into traffic. He glanced at Jacob, grinned, and asked, "Meeting her there?"

"Trying to stop a friend from making a bad mistake."

"Good way to get yourself killed."

"True. But I'm not worried about him. It's all about the bride."
Bride of Frankenstein.

"Women are the deadliest sex." The cabbie looked in the rearview mirror. "It *is* a woman?"

"I think so," Jacob said cautiously.

"Oh, it's like that." The cabbie hit light speed down the Strip, slammed on his brakes in front of the chapel, took Jacob's cash, leaped out, and opened Jacob's door. "Want me to wait in case you need to make a fast getaway?"

"Sure. Do that." Jacob suspected this wouldn't take long.

Inside he leaned across the counter to the elderly receptionist. He thought how best to get information out of—he glanced at the nameplate—Betty. He looked pitiful and asked, "Did I miss my friend's wedding?"

"Who's your friend?"

"Andrew Hewitson."

Betty smirked. "Boy, are you in trouble. We married him and his bride two days ago at three in the afternoon."

"I *am* in trouble. I was supposed to be the best man. Was it a beautiful wedding?"

"It was! Want to see the pictures?" She turned the monitor around so he could see a line of photos for "Andrew and Barbara's Wedding." The bride was tall, taller than Andrew, and by the style of her dress and sweater, rather frumpy. In every shot she was looking at Andrew or hiding behind her bouquet or twirling in ecstasy while Andrew grinned stupidly.

Jacob stared at her. Squinted and scrutinized and wondered—who was she? Why was she hiding from the camera? And why, oh, why, did Andrew look as if he were intoxicated/on drugs/had taken enough Viagra to rob his brain of blood? "Andrew was . . . drunk?"

"Well." Betty widened her eyes as if the thought had just occurred to her. "Perhaps he celebrated prematurely . . . with different substances. Many people do, you know."

"I know . . ." *Weak as ditchwater,* Mr. Caron had said. "Barbara's a healthy-looking girl."

"A handsome woman." Emphasis on *handsome.*

Jacob wasn't quite sure she wasn't a man. Apparently Betty had the same doubts. "Did Barbara change her last name to his?"

"She insisted on it." With the bright tone of a high school cheerleader, Betty said, "Isn't that refreshing to find a modern bride who isn't hyphenating or keeping her own last name?"

"Refreshing." Or a good way to conceal your identity. Everything was getting frightening and complicated. More frightening. More complicated. "I know they were staying at the Bellagio."

"I believe so. He was quite the high roller."

Jacob smiled winningly. "How long were they going to stay to celebrate their honeymoon? Do you think I can catch them and take them out to an 'I'm sorry I was late' dinner?"

"My, yes. They were going to stay for three more days. Just call before you knock on their door." She winked. "While they were here, he was trying to rip her clothes off. She was very forceful and pushed him away."

"Did she?" He looked right at Betty. "Anything else you want to share?"

Betty shook her head. Stopped. Glanced around. Wet her lips. "She dodged the camera. What kind of bride doesn't want her picture taken?"

So Betty had realized how *off* Barbara's behavior had been. "That is odd."

"She had a knife with her. In her bag. Sharp. Pointed." Betty measured the size with her fingers.

Oh, shit. Exactly what he feared. "Betty, you've been a lot of help."

"You won't repeat what I said?"

"Never. Let me catch my cab before it gets away." He stepped outside into the blast of heat, hurried down the sidewalk, and climbed in the backseat. "The morgue," he said.

"That must have been one disaster of a wedding," the cabbie said.

"I think we can safely say it was."

You're gone. She's alone. She's finished the book. Now I can do the job without you whining. Andrew, your sister will be with you soon.

CHAPTER FIFTY

On Monday, Maddie spent hours in Jacob's bedroom, sitting on his bed and working on her laptop, while out in the living room construction workers sawed and sanded and nailed and cursed. She snuck out once when they were at lunch, to use the restroom, but if they knew she was there, they never acknowledged it.

They left at 7:00 P.M. She raced out to use the restroom again—six hours between potty breaks was too much—then tiptoed out to the living room. She checked the locks to make sure they were secure, heated up a frozen dinner, and then got the highlight of her tense and lonely day; a call from Jacob. He had met Mr. Caron and together they were searching Andrew's empty home. He would call again when he made contact with Andrew, and he asked her to remain at his house. He sounded tired, and worried about her, and although she badly wanted to go home, she promised. She returned to his bedroom, shoved furniture around to block the door, reclined on the bed in her clothes and waited for morning. She slept in increments, jerking herself awake at every creak and groan of the old house, and rose before dawn to shower and change, eat breakfast and work on her story.

The construction workers arrived at 9:00 A.M. Their presence made Tuesday a repeat of Monday, except that when Madeline nodded off the noise and the knowledge that they were out there allowed her sleep hard for three hours. Again the workers left at 7:00 P.M., and again she raced out to use the bathroom. But this time, she didn't return to the bedroom. Instead, she strapped on her pistol. She pulled on her denim bomber jacket and buttoned it at the waist to ensure coverage. She hesitated over her computer, but with no Wi-Fi, no thumb drive, no way of backing up the contents, and a solid suspicion that her tormentor could follow her to the ends of the earth to hurt her, she didn't dare leave it. She tucked the laptop under her arm, got her house keys, and peeked out the front door.

She needed to go home. Just for a second, long enough to grab the work on her graphic novel. This morning, in her hurry to get to safety, she had rashly abandoned her painfully drawn sketches, and she couldn't leave them to be burned. Or otherwise destroyed. Or seen.

Tattered clouds slipped up over the horizon, and the breeze off the ocean smelled like incoming rain. The street was eerily empty; the neighborhood seemed to have died with Mrs. Butenschoen. Maddie crept across the porch, then hesitated in the shadows.

Dr. Frownfelter's house was dark. The Franklins had their windows open; the kids were playing a game, shrieking with laughter. If Dayton Floren was home, he was hiding like her, but hey—*he* was guilty of his crimes. She glared across at his house. Damn him; he had made her life more difficult. She was innocent, and today it had seemed as if knowing that let her breathe more easily.

With a last look around, she scampered across the street, unlocked her door, and swung it open. She looked inside; with boxes and belongings strewn everywhere, the living room looked dim and battered, but no different from when she had left.

She didn't trust that. She didn't trust what she saw or heard.

She did trust Jacob. She trusted his warnings, his concern, and his earlier cautious call that assured her he was tracking Andrew to Las Vegas.

Why Las Vegas? That worried her. Andrew and Las Vegas . . . that could not be a good combination.

Pulling the revolver from the holster, she felt the click as she eased the safety off. Holding it in her right hand, she rested the butt on her left palm. Arms extended, she let the barrel lead the way the first few steps into the living room. With her foot, she shut the door behind her and walked the house, checking each room, each closet, until she was satisfied she was alone. Only then did she lock herself in, return the revolver to safe, holster it, and go to her desk.

The drawings lay untouched in the drawer. With fierce delight, she gathered them together, stacked them carefully—and jumped when her cell vibrated in her pocket.

She dropped the drawings and the computer on the desk, grabbed the phone, and saw it was Jacob. At last. She answered. "Jacob? What did you find out?"

His voice was preternaturally calm and very quiet. "Maddie, I'm sorry to do this to you, but I'm sending you a photo of a body and I need a positive ID."

She sank into her desk chair. "Who is it?"

"Maddie . . ."

Of course she knew who it was. "Andrew."

"Yes."

"Where did you find him?"

"In the morgue in Las Vegas."

"How was he killed?"

"Stabbed and dumped in a backstreet."

"By who?"

"There have been no arrests. Have you got the photo yet?"

Her phone vibrated in her hand. "Yes, it just came in."

"Is it Andrew?"

I don't want to look. But she did. She looked at the picture of her brother's still, white, stern face. "That's him."

"I'm sorry, honey. So sorry."

"Um . . ." Her voice shook. "Um, why was he in Las Vegas?"

"He had a gambling problem."

"Gambling?" *No.* "He . . . years ago, he got in trouble because of his gambling. But he told me he had quit."

"Also he was in Vegas because . . . he got married."

Maddie felt as if she were being punched over and over with one truth after another. "Married? To who?"

"To his girlfriend, Barbara Ulrich. Do you know her?"

"I never heard of her. He told me he wasn't with anyone."

With an edge to his voice, Jacob said, "Andrew has told you a lot of lies."

She swallowed. "I got that. But *why*?"

"For the money. You make a great deal of money with your writing. He spent it."

"All of it?"

"He's in debt." With his tone, Jacob condemned him. "Where are you now?"

"At my house. I needed my sketches." She braced herself for anger or disappointment.

But Jacob surprised her. "I know you want to get more of your things, but not now. Listen. I'm on the plane. In a few minutes, we're going to take off for Seattle. From there, I'll get to Virtue Falls as fast as I can. But you need to get to safety."

"What do you think is going to happen?"

Again Jacob lowered his voice. "Andrew's wife murdered him. She's going to try to murder you, too."

"Why? Why kill me?"

"Because when you're out of the way, she's Andrew's heir. The royalties for your books are substantial and she could live well on them."

Maddie felt almost dizzy with the assault of information. "I'll go back to your house and lock the doors."

"No, Maddie, call the police."

"I've got my gun."

"You don't want to shoot anybody."

That was true. She didn't.

"Besides, I don't even know whether to tell you to watch out for a tall woman or a feminine-looking man."

"Andrew married a man? No, he would never . . ." But she had thought he would never deliberately harm her, never steal from her or lie to her. So what did she really know about her brother?

"In the wedding pictures, there were no good shots of her. She was the bride, which means she deliberately hid from the camera." Jacob sounded troubled. "But her hands on the bouquet looked large and muscular. Call the police. Ask them to come and get you and take you into protective custody."

She stiffened. She had been in protective custody before, in the mental hospital after Easton's murder and twice here in Virtue Falls. The police thought she was crazy, shooting at a phantom. They thought she was venal, poisoning a dog. They treated her the way they would treat a serial killer: watchfully and with an unpleasant edge. She wouldn't call them. She wouldn't take the chance they would put her back in jail. And Moen would try to take the call, and he was a sort of a stalker himself. "No."

Jacob started talking faster. "You have to. The coroner gave me Andrew's effects, including his phone. The battery was dead, so when I got to the airport I charged it. When I turned it on"—he took an audible breath—"a text came in from Barbara."

That did *not* make sense. "You said she killed him."

"She did. No doubt."

"What did the text say?"

"You're gone. She's alone. She's finished the book. Now I can do the job without you whining. Andrew, your sister will be with you soon."

"She sent him that text—and he's dead? She's happy to . . . to hurt me? Kill me?" Maddie took a frightened breath. "She's crazy."

"No doubt about that, either. She's ahead of me, she's had time to get to Virtue Falls, and she's been observing you. She knows you, Maddie, and I'm afraid for you."

In the background, she heard the flight attendant start the announcement.

Jacob said, "They're shutting the cabin doors. I've got to go. Maddie, it's all up to you. Get yourself to safety."

"Okay. I will. Right now."

"Maddie, call Sheriff Kwinault. She'll keep you safe."

"Jacob . . . I love you."

She heard a strangling sound, then quite loudly he said, "I love you, too."

"You be safe, Jacob. I will be, too." She hung up. She supposed distracting him with her first *I love you* wasn't fair, but if she was in danger—and that text clearly said she was—she needed him to know how she felt. Plus it had served its purpose.

Now he was on his way to her and she was on her way out the door. She glanced out the window.

The clouds skittered across the sky, masking the setting sun, revealing it, then masking it once more.

To get to town before dark, she would have to hurry.

Her nerves tightened. *Maddie, it's all up to you.* She gathered her computer and her drawings. She needed her computer case, stored in the bedroom walk-in closet. She went in, flipped on the light—and nothing happened. Was the lightbulb burned out?

She walked to the bedside, checked the lamp. It clicked. No light. Night was coming.

The electricity was off.

She returned to the closet, stood in the doorway, struggled with the onset of panic that tightened her chest and restricted her breathing.

But she wanted her laptop and her sketches, and to carry them safely she *needed* that case. She rushed to the dark closet, grabbed the bag strap, and pulled the bag off the top shelf. A pillow and blanket fell on top of her.

Panic bit harder. Her skin prickled. Was someone in the house with her?

Giving in to what some would say was good sense, she called 911.

The operator answered and, as always, they knew who it was. "Yes, Miss Hewitson. Please state the nature of your concern."

"Can I speak to Sheriff Kwinault?"

"She's left for the day."

"Can you reach her? Tell her I need to talk to her?"

"Miss Hewitson, we have many capable police officers who are on duty and able to take your call."

"But Sheriff Kwinault—"

"Had a difficult day. It is, in fact, Election Day, and Sheriff Kwinault deserves to spend the evening as she wishes."

Maddie persisted. "Do you know where she is?"

"I believe she went to the Oceanview Café. Why? Do you want to poison *her,* too?"

Maddie felt as if her face and her insides had shriveled.

Before she could reply, the operator said, "I'm sorry. That was unprofessional. Nevertheless, if you feel in danger, I suggest you allow me to send one of our on-duty officers to help."

"No. Thank you." Maddie hung up. Tears prickled her eyes, but more than ever before, she knew Jacob was right. *Maddie, it's all up to you.*

On the bed, she slid her laptop into the padded pocket, stuffed the drawings beside it, all the while glancing around her, watching, waiting for the terror to return.

Out of the corner of her eye, she saw it. Movement, dark and stealthy. She froze, unable to move, until at last she turned her stiff neck enough to see . . . a man's dark shadow slithering across her white wall toward her. Instantly she swiveled and swung her bag at it.

He was here. The monster was back.

But no. Her bag slid through it. This monster was nothing but a projection created by electronics. It was not an illusion created in her mind. She didn't have to cower. She didn't have to fear.

Except whoever was tormenting her was somewhere close. Too close. Watching. Andrew's wife.

Andrew's executioner.

Barbara Ulrich, who knew Maddie better than she knew herself.

Who could this Barbara person be?

Maddie slung the bag over her shoulder. She started toward the front door. And stopped.

No. Not the front door. When she went into town, she always took the same route through the streets. She shouldn't do that now. Barbara had been studying her. She would expect Maddie to follow the familiar pattern.

Maddie turned toward her back door, veered back to her desk, and picked up the baseball bat. She scurried through the back door, through her backyard, unlocked the gate, and slipped into the alley. She slunk past backyards, garbage cans, and fences, making her way toward the ocean and the wide-open horizon. When she passed the last house and the last wooden fence on the block, she looked both ways at the path that wound its way along the cliffs. It was empty. Had she escaped Andrew's killer?

She had moved quickly; it was only a mile to the cutoff that led into downtown Virtue Falls . . . a lonely mile marked by nothing more than a few remote houses, a beach access, and a single windswept tree known as the Bear.

Out on the ocean, a storm brewed in a swirl of ragged, bloody clouds. The setting sun turned the light gray and gold.

The shadows grew longer, the coarse sea grass waved like taunting fingers, and the ocean waves rolled through their own unceasing, uncaring eternity.

Maybe she should call the police to come and get her. Surely she could stand protective custody for a few hours.

She inched in the direction of the dead end of Dogwood Blossom Street and peeked around the fence.

No monster lurked there. Instead, as he had so many times before, Moen had backed his police cruiser up to the guardrail. He sat drinking coffee from an insulated cup and staring up the street toward her house.

No. No police. No Moen. He wanted too much from her. She could not save him from his fate.

Maddie ducked back and crouched down. Somehow she had to get past him. Pulling out her phone, she called 911.

The same operator answered. "Yes, Miss Hewitson. Please state the nature of your concern."

"I need a policeman at my house right away. Can you do that?" Whoops. She may have sounded a little too sure of herself.

"Can you state the nature of your problem?" The operator sounded patient. Hugely, mightily patient.

This time Maddie put a quaver in her voice. "My lights have gone out and I'm afraid."

"Our officers are not electricians."

Maddie felt as if she were reciting the lines to a well-rehearsed play. "Someone did it on purpose. Someone is after me!"

The operator sighed heavily. "All right. I'll send one of the on-duty officers. Not Sheriff Kwinault!"

"That's fine." Maddie hung up. She watched Moen's silhouette, saw him dip his head as he heard the call, saw him reply and start the car. She waited until he pulled up to the curb and opened the door. Then she scampered across the end of the street and onto the well-trod dirt path that led into Virtue Falls.

The fresh wind off the ocean moved the rough sea grasses and buffeted Maddie as she hurried, almost running, along the path. She *had* to get to town, to lights and the Oceanview Café and Sheriff Kwinault. She

needed to escape Barbara—Barbara, who had married and murdered Andrew and, according to Jacob, had been tormenting Maddie for months.
She had enjoyed tormenting Maddie, had preyed on her bloodiest memories and her deepest fears. And why? Why? What was there to gain from
such cruelty? Money, yes, but this harassment bore all the hallmarks of a
personal vendetta. Had Andrew's wife hoped to drive Maddie to suicide?
Or into a nervous breakdown and back into the mental institution?

Abruptly, Maddie stopped.

Damn it. Since age eleven, when her parents died, she had been a
victim. The victim of tragedy, of mania, of senseless murder . . . and
now of illusion.

She started walking more slowly.

Why? She had done nothing to deserve any of this. She had never
had the chance to become an adult. Not because she wasn't capable,
but because her growth had been stunted by bearing the constant bur-
den of fear.

She put her hand on the grip of the revolver, pulled it from the holster, released the safety, and immediately felt the potential power contained in the small, precise piece of metal. That bolstered her courage,
and with the revolver held low at her side, she continued down the
path with renewed confidence.

Courage and confidence; it had been a long time since she had encountered either of those emotions, and she liked them—a lot.

She passed the Williamsons' clapboard house, built to face the
ocean and battered by salt and rain. Mrs. Williamson sat in her porch
swing, huddled under an afghan, watching the sunset.

Maddie raised the hand holding the bat.

Mrs. Williamson waved back and called, "Are you taking up baseball?"

"Not . . . really." Thank God Maddie hadn't waved the hand with
the gun. She suspected that not even Mrs. Williamson wanted to see
Mad Maddie brandishing a weapon. That made Maddie remember
Jacob's warning—*use your revolver only as a last resort.* Carrying it provided her with courage, but it was false courage. Real courage came
from within, and she had to nourish it by facing her fears.

Careful not to show her hand, she clicked the safety and holstered the weapon.

Mrs. Williamson came to the porch rail. "Want to come in and sit a spell? Walter fell, hurt himself; he's in bed and feeling sorry for himself. He'd welcome the company."

For a moment Maddie wavered. She could go to the Williamsons and ask for sanctuary. She knew they would provide it. They would call the police and Maddie would bet if *they* asked for Sheriff Kwinault, they wouldn't be denied.

Yet their home was isolated and not easy to reach, and Mr. Williamson was hurt. The monster who hunted Maddie was not a figment cast up by her tortured mind, but a person who was in truth fearsome, tricky, large, and dangerous. She couldn't involve Mr. and Mrs. Williamson in this battle; they were good people who had been kind to her. And in her life, enough good people had been killed. She would not risk the elderly couple.

Maddie, it's all up to you.

She was alone. And she would survive.

CHAPTER FIFTY-ONE

Kateri supposed that some candidates spent Election Day shaking hands and kissing babies.

Some candidates were not sheriff of Virtue Falls, a town where two of the men running for a vacant seat on the school board got into a shouting match in the city park in the town square. That started a fairly polite riot among all the school board members; highlights included pushing, shoving, and name calling. Kateri and her officers had it under control until the city council members, who had come out of city hall to watch, found it in their hearts to step in to smooth things over. Within three minutes Stefanie Westerholm had slapped Councilman Venegra and, in front of his wife, accused him of screwing that slut Mona Coleman.

Mrs. Venegra slapped Stefanie first. Then she gut-punched her own husband.

While he was wheezing on the ground, Mona slapped Mrs. Venegra and called her frigid.

That's when the real riot started.

Arresting the city council, the school board, and her administrative assistant in front of the cheering Virtue Falls citizens involved more tact than Kateri knew she contained.

She took pride in the fact that she never once laughed.

Then, while she was writing up the reports, Officer Chippen came in looking grim and as if he'd lost the coin toss.

He had.

The Terrances—John Senior and John Junior—had been in the Virtue Falls jail waiting to be conducted to a federal prison, and in the confusion of placing respected politicians, angry wives, and indignant mistresses in their cells, the Terrances had escaped.

Kateri put her head in her hands, bade a final farewell to the election results—no one was going to vote for a sheriff who couldn't properly contain violent drug-dealing prisoners—then told Officer Chippen to get the bloodhounds in here because they had a manhunt to conduct.

Officer Chippen suggested that, because of the Terrances' proclaimed threats, she enter protective custody.

"In my spare time," she replied testily.

"Really, Sheriff, the guys and I talked it over and we agree it's a good idea." Chippen looked honestly worried.

"Chippen, tomorrow I won't be sheriff anymore, and as a private citizen I can accept protective custody. Right now I'm the sheriff and I've got a job to do, which now includes whatever Mona did around here. Thank God she did pretty much nothing!" Kateri took a calming breath. "Also, the Coast Guard just called with a report of a stolen speedboat, so let's assume that right now the Terrances are racing away from Virtue Falls toward China."

"Okay. Yeah, that makes sense. I mean, that they would have stolen the speedboat, not that they're going to China. I'll tell the guys to watch the nearby inlets for activity."

"Thank you, Chippen. That's a good idea."

Chippen lingered in her doorway. "We really are worried about you, Sheriff."

Translation: they might not be voting for her, but they liked her. "I know, Chippen, and I appreciate that."

That concern sustained her when she hit the road to answer a call about an aggressive black bear holding a carload of tourists hostage. Next she dealt with an abandoned and starving dog that had to be coaxed into a crate, a campaign manager shrieking because she had missed a speech at the Eagles lodge, and a fire in the library set by two eight-year-olds hiding in the bathroom to smoke their first cigarettes. It was almost 8:00 P.M. when Kateri walked into the Ocean-view Café.

Rainbow had left for the day.

Llewellyn covered the evening shift.

And Cordelia sat at her usual table, staring at her computer, frowning fiercely.

Never in a million years did Kateri expect to find Cordelia still at work. She walked over, pulled up a chair, and prepared to wait until Cordelia deemed it the proper moment to speak.

But Cordelia surprised her. She promptly put her work aside and, eyes sparkling, said, "You're late."

"I know. I'm sorry. I was here yesterday."

Cordelia folded her hands on the table. "I was sick. Throwing up is very inconvenient."

"I imagine it is."

"When accompanied by diarrhea, it causes dehydration and—"

Kateri interrupted. "Thank you for waiting for me. May I see your texts?"

"I got a new one today." Cordelia shoved her iPad across the table.

Kateri read, *"You're gone. She's alone. She's finished the book. Now I can do the job without you whining. Andrew, your sister will be with you soon."*

Revelation brought Kateri to her feet.

"It's that odd girl, isn't it?" Cordelia started packing her equipment into her briefcase. "The one everyone talks about. The one who calls the cops all the time. That's who is being threatened."

"Her brother is the writer."

Cordelia blinked myopically at Kateri. "Obviously not."

Kateri thought back to what she'd seen in Maddie's house: the desk set up with a laptop; the box filled with A. M. Hewitson's next book; the pens and paper; and, more important, Maddie's glow when Kateri praised the stories. Kateri had thought she was proud of her brother. But Maddie's appreciation had been personal; Madeline Hewitson was bestselling author A. M. Hewitson. "You're right. Obviously not."

"Once one has the right clue, it's easy to arrive at the right conclusion." One by one, Cordelia stuck her arms in her white sweater, the one with the yellowing collar.

Kateri called Moen. When he answered, she snapped, "Where are you?"

"I'm outside Maddie's front door. She called for an officer, but she's not answering. I'm worried." He *sounded* worried.

Thank God for Moen. Kateri was starting to suspect the boy had good law enforcement instincts. "Can you get inside? See that she's not hurt?"

"Sure, but—"

Someone beeped in. Kateri glanced at the ID; Deputy Bergen was calling. "Hang on," she told Moen, and answered.

"Sheriff Kwinault, Mrs. Williamson called me. She saw Madeline Hewitson go past on the cliff path and a few minutes later some guy in a costume followed her." Deputy Bergen sounded surprised and befuddled.

"What kind of costume?" As if Kateri didn't know.

"Cap, hat, white face, bizarre makeup."

"Her monster. Did this guy notice Mrs. Williamson?"

"Yes, and she's scared. Mr. Williamson took a fall yesterday and he's confined to bed. She's getting her rifle."

"Can't blame her." But in the right circumstances, a determined woman out to defend her man would certainly lead to bloodshed. Hopefully the police could get there in time to forestall that. "What's your closest access to the cliff path? Can you get there to help the William-sons?"

"I'm headed there now."

"Moen is at Maddie's house now. I'll send him to help Maddie from there. I'll access the path from Ocean Avenue. Listen, Bergen, that guy in the costume is a maniac and he's out to kill Mad Maddie. So let's get this bastard." She clicked over and spoke to Moen.

He had picked the lock and was inside the empty house.

She ordered him down the cliff path as fast as he could go.

He was out the door before she finished her command.

Kateri reached across and pressed Cordelia's hand. "Thank you, Cordelia. You did it. You gave us the break we needed."

Cordelia looked annoyed. "I know." She picked up her briefcase. "Now, do you mind? I'm going home."

CHAPTER FIFTY-TWO

Whether or not Maddie liked it, she had been trained to fear darkness as a presence that absorbed breath and blood and safety and confidence.

Darkness was swiftly coming, looming high behind the high roiling black clouds. Isolation walked with her down the lonely path, depriving her of human contact.

But in the distance, she could see the path turn onto Front Street, and that led into downtown Virtue Falls. She had her cell phone in her pocket, her revolver in her holster, her computer on her shoulder, and her trusty baseball bat in her hand. In a few minutes she would be hurrying toward the town square, toward the Oceanview Café filled with lights, warmth, the smell of coffee, and Sheriff Kwinault. She could relax, order pasta primavera made with zucchini noodles and lots of Parmesan cheese and at last explain exactly what was hunting her.

The incoming storm oppressed the day's last rays of sunshine.

Maddie hitched the computer bag farther up on her shoulder,

tightened her grip on the bat, and jogged until she reached the spot where the cliff sloped down toward the beach, toward sand dunes and driftwood.

There a human monster might lurk.

She slowed. She scanned the area. Nothing moved.

She hurried on. The cliff rose again, passed a modern house of glass and concrete with a privacy fence and a stern warning on the gate that this was private property. No lights shone here; whoever owned it was not home.

Not too much farther. She could see the tree they called the Bear. Its windswept branches marked the place where she would take a turn onto the street and into civilization. She was going to make it. She was almost there—

Behind her at the empty house, the fence gate slammed.

She whirled around and glimpsed a tall figure in a black, broad-brimmed hat and swirling black cape. The grotesquely painted white face held wide, dark eyes lit red by the setting sun. The large gloved hands held a thin knife that looked uncannily like the pointed finger-nail that had, so long ago, eviscerated her friends.

In grim and intent silence, the monster of her nightmares charged her.

Icy fear blocked Maddie's throat . . . then melted as hot anger blasted her. This person had killed her brother. This monster had terror-ized her. She wanted revenge. She wanted justice. She wanted to live.

She would not tolerate this horror anymore.

She didn't have time to pull her gun and click the safety. She was shorter, thinner, weaker. She had to be crafty.

So she stood as if paralyzed with fear. Stood and waited until the thing was almost upon her. Then she leaped aside, raised her bat, and as the monster rushed past, she smashed its head.

The monster didn't swoop away unscathed. Instead it grunted and stumbled sideways. Its hat fell off.

At the back of the neck, a rubber band held long blond hair in a tight bun.

How unmonster-like. How vulnerable.

How *human*.

The monster righted itself, turned and charged like a freight train, a freight train that was bleeding from the ear and whose white makeup was smudged.

Maddie liked that. She swung the bat again.

With a loud smack, the monster caught it in one large hand and tried to wrestle it from her.

Maddie screamed in fury and kicked out, hard, connecting at the knee.

The monster yelped and let go.

Maddie stumbled backward, alive and triumphant. She reached under her jacket, grabbed her holster, and unsnapped it.

And the woman in the costume shouted, "You little bitch!"

A woman. A blond woman, tall with broad shoulders.

"Barbara," Maddie said. Only she didn't say it, she shouted. Then, in recognition, "Chantal!"

This woman, this model with the short skirt and the long legs, this scheming neighbor, had been Andrew's secret girlfriend. She had married and murdered Andrew. This excuse for a human being had tried to drive Maddie mad.

At last, Barbara had succeeded; Maddie was crazed with rage.

Barbara rushed toward Maddie.

Maddie gripped the end of the bat like a battering ram and ran, not away, but at her.

Barbara's eyes grew wide. She tried to get out of the way. But Maddie, who had done nothing but whimper and flee from every cruelty through all the months of malicious tricks and clever illusions . . . Maddie rammed the end of the bat into Barbara's stomach.

With a whoosh, Barbara doubled over, wrenching the bat from Maddie's hand.

Maddie should flee, get to town, to safety. She should. She knew it. She should pull her revolver and shoot Barbara through the heart. This was the last resort Jacob spoke of, wasn't it?

But her legs were short and Barbara's were long. She would lose the race. . . .

The truth was, she was so *angry* and beating on Barbara was so *satisfying.*

Pulling the computer bag off her shoulder, she swung it by the strap, slamming the edge into Barbara's shoulder, then smashing it onto her downbent head.

Barbara grunted and staggered.

Then luck and Maddie's advantage of surprise ran out.

Still bent at the waist, Barbara slashed out with the knife, caught Maddie on the thigh, cutting through her jeans and into the muscle.

Maddie screamed with pain and fury.

Barbara slashed again, cutting Maddie open at the ribs.

Maddie jumped onto Barbara's back, knocking her to her knees. She grabbed at Barbara's hair, her eyes, her ears, anywhere she could reach to pull and rend, and she kept screaming, loud, long, enraged shrieks.

The voluminous cape inhibited Barbara's motion; she managed to wrestle her arm free and used her knife to stab repeatedly at Maddie's hands. She sliced between Maddie's fingers and pierced her palms.

The pain brought Maddie's shrieks to a new high pitch; she took care to do her screaming into Barbara's ear.

Barbara rolled, knocking Maddie beneath her.

Barbara's monster makeup was ruined, washed away in sweat and blood. She dripped crimson from her ear and her cheek, where with her own knife she had slashed her own face. She was no longer a phantom, but a real person—a creature Maddie recognized from her distant past when, for the first time, death and terror had united to create madness.

Not Chantal. Not Barbara Ulrich. But Barbara Magnusson, the nursing assistant in the mental institution, a woman who nightly used her knowledge of their fears to taunt the patients.

She slapped Maddie's cheek in a swift, familiar gesture.

Maddie's ear rang from the blow.

She wrapped her long fingers around Maddie's throat and tightened her grip.

Maddie struggled for air. She kicked out. Blood pounded in her ears. Colors exploded in her vision.

"Do you know who I am? Do you?" Barbara loosened her hold.

Maddie didn't waste her breath with replying. Instead she nodded and groped at her side for the holster.

Barbara tightened her grip again. "I'm the poor CNA from the nuthouse who had to listen to your whimpering about your poor friends. I'm the woman who came up with the plot to kill your beloved Easton and hired the hit man. I'm the woman who romanced and married and killed your goddamned gambling weak-willed brother." She let Maddie breathe again.

"You killed Mrs. Butenschoen." Maddie touched the revolver's cool metal, pulled it free of the leather.

"That nosy old bitch. She had a camera. She spied on me."

"*You* spied on *me*!"

Barbara shook Maddie by the throat; she shook so hard Maddie thought her spine would break. "You are mine. Anyway, someone had to watch you, poor, stupid weakling that you are! Now you're going to die, you ungrateful wimp. You're going to bleed to death in the dirt and I'm going to collect Andrew's life insurance and all your royalties, and live like a queen for the rest of my life." She loosened her grip again and she smiled a terrible smile. "What do you think of that?"

Maddie took two good, hard breaths and did what she should have done in the first place. She pushed her revolver into Barbara's side and clicked off the safety. "Not going to happen."

She pulled the trigger.

CHAPTER FIFTY-THREE

Kateri heard the report of a gun. "No. No!" She broke into a listing run, using her walking stick, favoring her artificial knee, yet setting a good pace. She rounded the corner onto the path and saw Moen racing from the opposite direction.

A still, black-caped figure sprawled on the ground.

Kateri got closer.

Someone was underneath, fighting to get out from under the weight.

Deadweight? Limp, unmoving, boneless. Yes, the caped figure was dead or unconscious and Madeline Hewitson was clawing her way free.

For the first time since Kateri had spoken with Cordelia, she took a deep breath.

Maddie was alive. Thank God, she was alive.

Moen arrived first at the scene.

But before he could reach down and assist Maddie, she got loose of the cape's voluminous folds and leaped to her feet.

Rich, red blood smeared her from head to toe.

Whose? Hers?

Maybe not. She held a gun in her shaking hand. . . . Mad Maddie with a gun. Not good.

Kateri and Moen froze midstep.

In a soft, coaxing tone, Moen said, "Miss Hewitson, please put the weapon on the ground."

Maddie tilted her head and dubiously considered him.

All of Kateri's doubts about Moen returned in full force. He'd done *something* to frighten Maddie.

Kateri again eased toward the crime scene. "Maddie, please put the weapon down."

Maddie looked around and met Kateri's eyes. She sagged in relief, nodded, and in slow, painful increments, she knelt and placed the weapon on the ground.

In the same polite tone, Kateri asked, "Maddie, would you please move away from the gun?"

Maddie nodded again, got one foot under her, and tried to stand. She couldn't. She swayed as if the wind off the ocean might knock her over.

Now Kateri was close enough to see that blood welled from Maddie's thigh, belly, and hands. Purpling bruises circled her throat, and a welt rose on her cheek. "Moen, call for medical assistance." Kateri took off her jacket, stepped close to Maddie, and put it around her shoulders.

Moen was already on his phone. Kneeling beside the black-caped figure, he pressed his fingers to the carotid artery. "No assistance needed for him."

"Her." Maddie's voice was hoarse. "Barbara. She was going to stab me. So I shot her."

"It looks as if she *did* stab you." Blood welled from the open wound on Maddie's thigh and dribbled from under her T-shirt.

Maddie looked down at herself. "Slash. She chased me and she slashed me. But I hit her with my baseball bat and my computer." As if she couldn't remain upright another moment, she lay back on the grass.

"We need a first-aid kit." Kateri straightened and started to walk away.

Maddie grabbed her ankle. "Don't leave me."

What had *Moen done?* Kateri turned back. "I won't."

Moen finished his call. "EMTs will be here in ten. Sheriff, want me to get a first-aid kit?"

"Right away. My car's close." Kateri called after him. "And the camera!"

Moen was younger, faster, and stronger; he got back and forth from her car in record time. He would have helped Kateri stanch the bleeding; she knew Maddie would not like that. "Take photos of the crime scene," she told him.

He sprang into motion. "Do you realize how jealous the guys at the precinct will be that we got here first?"

Kateri sighed.

Eyes slitted narrowly, Maddie watched him. "He's just a kid, isn't he?"

"He's getting better," Kateri assured her. "Anyway, he can't be much younger than you."

"I'm pretty mature. I've been through a lot," Maddie said.

"That you have." Kateri applied a tourniquet to Maddie's thigh, pressed a sterile pad to her belly, and wrapped linen around the lacerations on Maddie's hands. "How did you fight that woman? She's six feet tall if she's an inch."

"She made me angry," Mad Maddie said simply.

"Remind me not to piss you off," Moen muttered.

All too rapidly, blood soaked all of the bandages, and even as Kateri worked, Maddie's face turned whiter and whiter. Kateri asked, "Maddie, one thing I don't understand"—*When would the EMTs arrive?*—"If you kept that revolver, why didn't you shoot Barbara as soon as she threatened you?"

"I had to make sure she was real."

Kateri nodded. She understood that.

Maddie continued, "And when Jacob left this morning, he told me to shoot only as the last possible resort."

"I don't think he meant . . ." Kateri realized an explanation would be a waste of time. Maddie thought literally, and in the matter of killing people, Kateri approved. Far too many people shot impulsively and without thought for the consequences.

Moen lowered the camera. "Okay, Sheriff Kwinault, I've got the crime scene photos."

"Then turn that body over. *Her* body?" Still scarcely believing, Kateri looked inquiringly at Maddie.

Maddie nodded. "Definitely female."

Moen rolled the body faceup. "Yep. Female. Tall and . . ." He picked up the camera and took more photos of the body, concentrating on the face. "Creepy makeup, but Maddie, isn't this your next-door neighbor, the model?"

"Yes . . ." For a moment, Maddie seemed to drift, then she snapped back. "When I saw her on the street, I didn't recognize her, but she was one of the nursing staff when I was at the mental institution. She didn't look like that before."

"What did she look like?" Moen asked.

"Dark, short hair. Overweight." Maddie breathed deeply. Her words slurred.

Moen got out his phone and called emergency again.

"When I was in the . . . the mental hospital . . . I didn't dare stare at her because she would say I thought she was ugly and slap me. If I glanced at her when the doctor was in the room, afterward she'd slap me twice. Hard." Maddie sounded like a recording slowing down . . . and down.

"Why did she hate you so much?" Kateri asked.

"She hated everyone. Especially her patients. Especially me. She hated having to take care of me. She hated weakness. She said I was crazy-faking it. . . . She didn't understand why I would cry for my friends." Tears dribbled out of Maddie's eyes and into her hair. "I don't know how she met my brother."

"Your *brother*?" This monster knew Maddie's brother.

"My brother and . . . her." The sun's last rays stabbed at the scene. Maddie moaned and shut her eyes. "She hoped to scare me so I would return to Colorado Springs, close to him, where he could . . . he hoped to make me more dependent on him, get me to write faster."

"Why would he want that?"

"He was afraid that if I was independent, I would want control of my assets and someday reveal that I was the real author of the A. M. Hewitson novels."

Moen crowed. "I knew it. I knew you were. I figured it out!" He looked at Kateri and his face fell. "You knew, too."

"Yes." Kateri didn't feel the need to tell him she had figured it out less than an hour ago. "In a horrible way, that plan makes sense."

"But they didn't win. She killed him and I'm still here." Maddie opened her eyes and smiled. "I'm sorry, but I'm going to faint." And she did.

CHAPTER FIFTY-FOUR

As soon as the plane touched down at Sea-Tac Airport, Jacob called Maddie's cell. When Maddie answered, something relaxed in him. "You're okay?"

"I am." She sounded almost chipper. "I killed the woman who married and murdered Andrew."

He sat straight up in his cramped seat on the plane and shouted, "What? What?"

The flight attendants looked around. The passengers in the seats next to him leaned away.

More quietly he asked, "How? Where?"

"To be safe I headed toward town. She followed me in her costume. She thought she would chase me down and kill me. But I fought her. I shot her with my gun." Maddie's voice turned anxious. "But I didn't use it until it was the last possible resort!"

"Good." Not really; he didn't care when she had used it as long as she was alive. "Where are you now?"

"I'm in the hospital. They're keeping me for a few days."

"You're hurt?" How hurt?

As if it explained everything, Maddie said, "She had a knife."

On the plane, the chimes sounded. All around him seat belts clicked. He opened his and jumped up, bumped his head on the overhead bin, and cursed. "I'll be there as soon as I can."

"I know." Now she sounded a little woozy. "They gave me a shot for the pain. I'll probably be asleep. But wake me when you get here."

Jacob broke land speed records getting to the county hospital. It was after midnight when he parked, raced across the parking lot and into the quiet lobby. He leaned across the desk to the security guard. "Can you tell me where I'll find Madeline Hewitson?"

The guard had a badge—Jerry—and Jerry folded his arms. "I'm not to allow any reporters anywhere near her."

"Reporters?" Jacob glanced around. "There are reporters?"

"She was famous as a killer and now she's vindicated. Sure there are reporters. *Other* reporters. And *you're* not getting in."

Jacob drew himself up to his full height, stared at Jerry, and said in his commanding officer tone, "I am not a reporter. I am her fiancé."

In a bored tone, Jerry said, "Someone already tried that."

Dr. Frownfelter trudged around the corner. "It's okay, Jerry. I'll take him up."

"You mean he really is her fiancé?" Jerry peered at Jacob's departing form and called, "Sorry, man."

Jacob waved a hand.

Dr. Frownfelter led Jacob down a wide corridor. "I've been watching for you."

Jacob chafed at Dr. Frownfelter's steady pace; he wanted to run. "How badly is she injured?"

Dr. Frownfelter turned the corner to the wing with the patients' rooms. "That woman pretty effectively used a knife on her. If Maddie hadn't been so angry, she probably would have been killed. But as I understand it, Maddie moved in close enough to beat on her with her baseball bat—"

Jacob raised a fist.

Dr. Frownfelter continued, "And Barbara couldn't do the deliberately painful damage she wanted to inflict."

Jacob knew immediately what the doctor meant, and the slow anger curled like smoke in his gut. "She intended to kill Maddie, but she wanted to terrorize her first. Like all the other times, only this time with a fatal finish."

"After what Maddie's been through—the slaughter in the dorm room, her fiancé's murder, this constant harassment—it's a miracle that girl *is* sane."

"Woman," Jacob corrected fiercely. "Maddie deserves to be called a woman."

"You're right. She does." They stopped in front of room 116 and Dr. Frownfelter put his hand on Jacob's arm to bring him to a halt. "You can see her now. She's asleep. Be careful how you touch her. She fought a much bigger and stronger assailant. She's lost a lot of blood, she has a lot of stitches, a lot of bruises."

"But she won."

Dr. Frownfelter grinned. "Yeah. She won. Come on. Just be prepared."

"Whatever it is, I've seen worse."

"I know. Somehow, when it's a loved one, that never helps." Dr. Frownfelter pushed open the door and led Jacob into a dim hospital room with a hospital bed occupied by a small, crumpled form.

A cot had been set up against the wall; as soon as the door opened, the form on the cot half rose, gun in hand.

Sheriff Kwinault slept in Maddie's room. Seeing Jacob, she nodded an acknowledgment. She flopped down again and for all intents and purposes went right back to sleep.

"Does she think Maddie's in danger?" Jacob whispered.

"The sheriff wanted to make sure Maddie wasn't harassed. She could have left someone else to guard her, but she said she felt guilty for not realizing sooner what was going on." Dr. Frownfelter scratched the day-old prickles of beard on his face. "Welcome to the club."

"I'm a card-carrying member myself." Jacob approached Maddie. He tried to look her over with a judicious eye. A welter of bandages and bruises, fluids in bottles and beeping machines, and beneath it all, his Maddie, dark, tangled hair against the white pillow, dark, smeared bruises against her white skin. Dr. Frownfelter was right. Seeing her like this . . . Jacob wanted to gather her close. He wanted to hug her forever. He wanted to avenge her. He wanted once more to hear her say she loved him.

His fingers hovered over her face, her shoulders, but he didn't quite dare to touch her. Quietly he said, "I got into Andrew Hewitson's computer. I figured out everything, but I could not figure out how that woman got her claws in him."

Dr. Frownfelter took him by the arm and moved him toward the foot of the bed. "Maddie said after she witnessed the stabbings in her dorm she was placed in a mental recovery facility. The deceased worked as a nursing assistant there."

Jacob inhaled harshly.

"That information set off all kinds of bells and whistles for me, so I did a little digging, talked to the physician in charge of the facility." Dr. Frownfelter lowered his voice to a barely audible rumble. "Barbara Magnusson—"

"Magnusson?"

"She's been married a couple of times."

"And widowed?" Jacob asked.

"At least once." The two men exchanged significant glances, then Dr. Frownfelter continued, "According to the physician, Barbara Magnusson was dismissed from her position for tormenting the patients, specifically Maddie. Barbara disappeared for a couple of years, then she returned to the facility as a patient for . . . never mind the medical jargon, she was a violent psychotic bitch with control issues. Her family avoided her, but they did support her financially . . . for a while. Then they moved and left no forwarding address." Jacob's shock seemed to grimly amuse the doctor. "It happens more than you might imagine. The facility had funding problems, so they determined Barbara was stable enough to be released."

"How could they release something like her into the world?"

"Indigent medical funding is a problem everywhere, especially at mental facilities."

Jacob returned to Maddie's side and hovered again, in retrospect even more terrified for her. Returning to Dr. Frownfelter, he said, "That's how Barbara knew Maddie's history of mental illness and recovery. She knew specifically how to destroy her."

"Exactly. When Sheriff Kwinault searched Barbara's house, she found all kinds of eye-popping electronics Barbara used to play her tricks on Maddie—poisons, drugs, needles. . . . When Maddie was asleep, Barbara must have injected her with hallucinogens, or perhaps she laced Maddie's food with them." Dr. Frownfelter flushed an angry red. "I should have paid closer attention. I should have realized. . . ."

They all, every one of them, felt guilty. "No, you shouldn't have. I looked at Andrew Hewitson's computer. Barbara was the mastermind behind the scheme to frighten and coerce Maddie. Maddie's own brother didn't realize the woman was crazy until he was in far too deep, and he . . ." Jacob shook his head. "He was a gambler. He used Maddie's money to support his habit. He betrayed Maddie in every way and she deserves so much more."

The two men returned to Maddie's side.

"You'll give it to her," Dr. Frownfelter said.

Jacob leaned over her, touched her gently: her lips, her forehead, her poor bandaged hands. "Yes. I will."

"I know you do. I love you, too." This time she wasn't using the words to distract him or saying them because she might never see him again. She said those words from the fullness of her heart and the knowledge that they could now plan a future.

"You faced your monster." He was proud of her, irate with himself for not being there for her, angry that that bitch had tried to kill Maddie, and proud all over again. His Maddie was a fighter, and never again would she fight alone. "You defeated your monster."

She smiled, smug and pleased. "Yes. I did. She's dead, and I will never let another monster into my life." Her eyes narrowed. "No one had better ever pick on our kids, or I will take them down."

Their kids. Sure. Why not? They loved each other, and more important, they liked each other. They understood each other. They might not always agree—in fact, they would not—but when the world judged them unfairly, they would face that world together. "Children. I like children. But I won't live in sin. We have to be married."

She waved an airy, white-bandaged hand. "That's easy enough."

He laughed out loud, a comfortable laughter that lifted all his burdens. "You don't know my family. We're Greek Orthodox, we're close, there are a lot of us, my mother loves to plan get-togethers, she loves to cook. I'm the prodigal son returned from the brink of death and madness."

Maddie looked troubled. "Are you trying to say we have to have a *wedding*?" She made it sound like torture.

He didn't so much laugh now. He chortled. "Such a wedding!"

Her eyes got big with horror, then timid with hope. "But I don't have any family and you said Andrew left me in debt. The bride's parents are supposed to pay."

He brushed that away. "You're alone in the world, so of course my family will take you to their collective bosoms and treat you as their own. Which they would do whether or not you are marrying into the family, but marrying me makes you special. Did I mention I'm the only son? And the youngest child?"

She examined him out of the corners of her eyes. "Are you serious? Is that a big deal?"

CHAPTER FIFTY-FIVE

The click of the hospital door woke Maddie, and she watched as Sheriff Kwinault slipped out into the corridor and shut the door behind her.

Maddie's throat and lips were parched, her body ached in ugly ways. But fast on the heels of her own discomfort she remembered—she had killed the monster. It was morning, the sun was shining, she had all her body parts, and Jacob was coming home.

No, he was home. There he sat, slumped in the chair beside her bed, his head dropped to his chest while he snored heavily. He looked worn out, but in a good way—not as thin, not as grim, less like a man on the brink of death and more like a guy who had traveled the country in search of clues that would save her sanity . . . and her life.

She was glad. She'd had enough of death and fear and nightmares. She hated to wake him, but she needed water. "Jacob," she whispered.

At once, he was on his feet. "Maddie! You're awake!" He blinked in that manic way people did when they want to look attentive. He got his eyes really open, smiled, and leaned over her. He stroked her hair back from her forehead and whispered, "You're alive."

"I am." She touched his cheek with her bandaged fingers. "How am I?"

"Early this morning, before he went off duty, Dr. Frownfelter examined you and said you're doing surprisingly well for someone who got into a knife fight and lost a lot of blood in the process. How do you feel?"

"Like someone stabbed me too many times. And once is too many." She felt proud. She had made a joke.

Jacob didn't seem to think it was funny. He got a pucker between his brows and asked, "What do you need? What can I get you?"

His concern made her forget her thirst. "You. Just you."

Cautiously he pressed his lips to hers. Not hard. It hurt a little. But enough to let her taste him and let him taste her. He seemed to need that. As did she. "I love you so much," he said.

"In a politically correct world—not at all. For my mother and older sisters—oh, yes. But don't worry. All you'll have to do is pick out the china pattern and show up in a white dress." Actually Maddie was going to be up to her eyebrows in wedding decisions. But she was weak from loss of blood and he wanted her to marry him. So, being a sensible man, he lied. Or rather, prevaricated. Yes. That sounded so much better. He prevaricated.

"If I have to, but"—she put her bruised fingertips on his arm—"before the wedding, can we enjoy some occasional moments of sin?"

"Sure. We can do that." He would have had a rough time resisting.

"That's very sweet of you." Her lashes fluttered.

"Damn it, woman!" He put out his palm as if to hold her away. "Not now. Not here. Not until you're better."

"Of course. You don't think I'd suggest anything as improper as a romp in the hospital bed?" Clearly she was making fun of him.

He broke a sweat anyway. "Tease."

"Me? No, you're the one standing over me, all manly and handsome."

She made him feel manly and handsome, and he wondered uncomfortably if that was why his father worshipped and indulged his mother. Perhaps Jacob suffered from the Denisov genetic defect of being happiest when pussy-whipped.

Maddie said, "With you distracting me, I forgot. My mouth is dry. Please may I have some water?"

He offered an ice chip.

She patted the mattress next to her hip.

He seated himself gingerly, trying not to jar the bed. Again he offered an ice chip.

She took it eagerly, and with an expression of ecstasy, let it melt in her mouth.

He reminded himself she was severely injured and the ecstasy involved frozen water. He offered another chip.

"How soon can I go home?" She took the chip and sucked on it.

Severely injured. "Three to five days, barring complications."

"Could be worse, I guess. I could have lost the fight." He must have flinched, because she gently patted his chest. "It's okay. Everything came out perfectly. Remember what I said about being ruined?"

"I'll never forget it."

"I'm not ruined anymore."

He thought about it—about the trip, his conversation with Mr. Caron, his successful detective work. "You're right. And neither am I."

An hour later, Maddie had been given water and food, insisted on having her hair brushed, had her bandages changed, cried about her brother, chatted animatedly about killing the monster, and passed out cold in the middle of having her face washed.

God, Jacob loved her so much.

When he was sure she was sleeping and would be for a while, he wandered out into the corridor. He stood in the bright glare of fluorescent hospital lights, pulled out his cell phone, and called his parents' house.

His mother answered.

He said, "Hi, Ma, it's—"

"Jacob," she said, and burst into tears.

Oh, crap. His mother was crying.

His father was going to kill him.

CHAPTER FIFTY-SIX

When Kateri knocked on the door of Mrs. Golobovitch's apartment, she heard Lacey barking, an insistent demand that Mrs. Golobovitch open the door. Mrs. Golobovitch did so and Lacey danced around on two paws, expressing her pleasure so exuberantly that Kateri experienced an upswell of love. With the Madeline Hewitson case solved and the election behind her, she could spend time with her dog, she could somehow figure out her love life, and she could look for a job. After the past few days, that agenda seemed like a snap.

"Come on, sweetheart, let's go to work." She opened the passenger door for Lacey.

The dog jumped in.

Kateri gave Mrs. Golobovitch a grateful wave, took a long time to thoroughly indulge her dog with petting while explaining the events that had kept her away overnight. "It's all good. This morning when I left Maddie's hospital room, I checked in with the nursing staff on Maddie's condition—satisfactory!"

Lacey gave an approving bark.

Kateri continued, "I told Jerry at the security desk to continue to keep the reporters at bay!"

Lacey got positively ecstatic about that.

"And I got into my patrol car and came to get you, the sweetest, smartest dog in the world!"

Lacey cuddled close, put her head on Kateri's lap, and closed her eyes with the pleasure of their reunion.

Kateri carefully drove to city hall and with Lacey at her side, walked into the patrol room. She lifted a weary hand at the guys and headed back for the coffee. *Coffee.* She really needed coffee.

When her officers began to clap, first one, then another, then the whole room, Kateri stopped, stood, and considered them. "What?"

They grinned and kept clapping.

Lacey barked and danced with delight.

Okay . . . what with yesterday's busy afternoon, Kateri hadn't had time to worry about the election results. But . . . "Are the ballots counted?" she asked.

The guys laughed. The applause got louder.

"I won?"

Nods all around.

"I *won*?" She put her hand on her chest, trying to still the sudden wild beat of her heart. "How . . . ? How much . . . ?"

The applause petered out.

Knowles was the first to quit clapping and rather sourly he said, "You didn't exactly sweep the county. You won by two votes."

"Two votes?" She laughed out loud. "And one of them was mine." She laughed again and groped for the coffeepot. "How did it even happen? We lost the Terrances yesterday. No word on them yet?"

"If you want to call it that," Ernie Fitzwater said. "They stole their Dodge SRT Hellcat out of impound and got away clean."

"I thought they stole a boat?"

"Multitalented," Fitzwater said.

Kateri put her hands to her forehead. "We're doing great. We'll never catch up with those bastards. No leads?"

Heads shook.

"We've put out a bulletin to the State Patrol to be on the lookout, an alert to the citizens, and we're ready to take them out," Fitzwater said.

Kateri struggled between concentrated horror at the Terrance situation and confusion, astonishment, and delight at the election results. "I figured losing them right out of jail cinched the results against me."

"Voters didn't *see* you lose the prisoners," Chippen said. "They saw you arrest a bunch of politicians and they loved it."

"Didn't we all?" Kateri murmured. More loudly, she asked, "Where's Bergen?"

"Here." He stepped out of his office. "You don't want that coffee. Moen made it. Come on, I'll treat you at the Oceanview Café." He didn't look irked or angry . . . that was a good thing.

"You don't have to do that!" She shouldn't be grinning in his face like this, either, but she couldn't seem to stop.

"You don't have to come to my house for dinner to celebrate your victory, either, but Sandra will be insulted if you don't." He offered his arm.

"I'd love to come." She glanced at Lacey. "But—"

"Bring her along to the café. She's becoming the town mascot."

Kateri placed her hand on Bergen's elbow, and with Lacey in tow, they went out the door.

The police officers clapped again, approving the détente, aware that having their sheriff and their deputy work together would make their jobs not only easier but also a lot more pleasant.

Outside, the morning was fresh and clear, the sun beamed on the park, and Kateri didn't know how to read the expression on Bergen's face.

He looked placid. Almost . . . pleased.

"Thank you for being so gracious," she said.

"Since only one of us could have the job, it was inevitable *someone* would have to be." He looked at her sideways. "I'm better at it than you are."

She laughed. "True. But two votes. *Two votes.* That's nothing!"

"The election is a simple majority, so two votes are enough."

A thought struck her. "You can challenge the election."

"I'm not."

"Why not? Two votes! You know a recount could change the results. Or a few late votes."

With a fair amount of humor, he asked, "Are you trying to talk me into it?"

"No. I'm just . . . I thought everyone fought an election until the last dog was hung." She glanced down. "Nothing personal, Lacey."

Unconcerned, Lacey trotted beside her, sniffing the air.

In a tone of absolute practicality, Bergen said, "A challenge would waste taxpayer money. The recount would be contentious, and if it was close enough, you could challenge the challenge. That could go on forever. Besides, for an officer with no experience, you're a fine sheriff and you'll do a good job over the next four years."

Kateri appreciated his confidence in her. "Then you'll run again?"

"No. Once was enough." He pulled the door of the Oceanview Café open and held it for Kateri and Lacey.

Alarmed, Kateri asked, "You're not going to leave? You'll stay and work for the department?"

He smiled. "I would like that. We make a good team."

"We do, don't we?" She walked in, Lacey on her heels, and once again was treated to a round of applause, a lot of smiles, and a scowl from Cordelia.

The noise was interrupting her work.

Kateri beamed. She never expected this: to win, to be lauded, to get approval. But she liked it. She felt at one with Virtue Falls. Of course, they were also applauding because they liked Bergen. But so did she.

Rainbow indicated the table against the wall.

Kateri pantomimed coffee.

Rainbow rolled her eyes; as if she had ever had a doubt.

Bergen held the chair for Kateri. She faced the diner and the door; here she could keep an eye on the comings and goings. Lacey took her place under the table, where she could watch the patrons with a keen eye.

A glance at the old-codger table showed Kateri one empty spot. "Mr. Caldwell is not here today."

"Now, *he* took the loss badly." Bergen seated himself at the end of the table, where he could keep an eye on the street outside.

Rainbow showed up with two coffee mugs and a pot of coffee. "Congratulations, Sheriff Kwinault! I never had a doubt."

Kateri laughed. "You're the only one, then."

As Rainbow poured the coffee, Kateri took a moment to appreciate today's outfit: white ruffled bloomers, a red-and-white-striped skirt, a blue cotton shirt with white stars, cowboy boots, and a fur collar. Rainbow had shaved the sides of her head, dyed the remaining hair a brilliant blue, and sprinkled it with glitter.

"The colors are in honor of . . . Election Day?" Kateri guessed.

"Right. And the fur is in honor of you and your Native American heritage."

Kateri raised inquiring eyebrows.

Rainbow explained, "During the Ice Age, Native Americans came across the land bridge from Asia through Alaska and spread across the continents."

Solemnly, Bergen explained, "The fur represents the Native American attire as they trekked through the frozen wasteland."

Kateri gave Rainbow the thumbs-up. "A thoughtful combination of patriotism and ethnic pride."

"Exactly. And *this* is a combination of deep-fried dough and celebration!" From her big apron pocket, Rainbow produced a large plate and a greasy bag that smelled like heaven. She shook the bag, poured the contents on the plate, and with great ceremony placed it on the table. "Dax's hot homemade doughnuts doused with cinnamon sugar. He decided to make them today for the winner . . . whichever one of you it was." She produced two small lidded plastic containers and put them beside the doughnuts. "Served with mascarpone and the first batch of his homemade strawberry jam. The berries are small this year, but sweet and flavor-dense."

Kateri lifted one of the small, round, crusty brown nuggets. She smeared it with rich mascarpone and ruby-red jam, popped it in her mouth, and moaned at the blend of spice, cheese, and berries. "Thank Dax. He's the best."

"It was my idea."

Kateri could never say Rainbow's hints were subtle. "Thank you, Rainbow."

Bergen sipped his coffee.

Kateri shoved the plate at him. "Come on, I can't eat all these. Or I could, but I shouldn't. Celebrate with me!"

Rainbow knelt by the table and from the same capacious apron pocket she produced a heart-shaped organic dog treat she had made with her own hands. With the best of intentions, she offered it to Lacey.

Lacey took it politely and waited until Rainbow stood to receive Bergen's groans of appreciation. Then sweet, tactful Lacey sneaked into the dim corner against the wall and spit out the treat. Kateri didn't know what Rainbow baked into that thing, but she knew Lacey would eat anything . . . except that.

Rainbow basked in Bergen's lavish praise, then headed off to take more doughnut orders.

The door opened. Noah strutted in and over to the table. He opened his arms wide. "I'm so glad I told you to cry during that press conference!"

Kateri laughed so hard tears leaked from her eyes.

"Yes! That's good! Keep it up with the tears and we'll win the next election, too!" Noah kissed the top of her head and strutted off, out the door, and down the street.

Cordelia watched hungrily, then once more bent her head to her computer.

For Kateri, something about Bergen's behavior seemed off. He was too relaxed, too laconic, like he knew a secret she didn't know or he'd found the Holy Grail and had it hidden under his shirt. Leaning back, she studied him. "What are you so smug about?"

"Smug? Me?" He pretended astonishment, then laughed. "I'm thinking two votes *was* scary close, especially when you were the first vote . . . and I was the second."

"I—what? The second vote? What do you mean . . . ?" It took her a moment to grasp the concept. Her voice rose incredulously. "Are you saying *you* voted for me?"

He put his finger to his lips. "More quietly, please." He popped another doughnut in his mouth.

She whispered, "You voted for me? Why? Why? Why? You were a good opponent. If I hadn't been running, I would have voted for you. What were you *thinking*?"

He got serious fast. "I was thinking I wanted to stay married. I was thinking my wife was right and running for office brought out the worst in me. I was thinking I have two kids and I want to be there for their soccer games and their school plays and their music recitals regardless of what crime has been committed." His voice grew softer. "I was thinking I went looking for that poor little girl so I could win the election. Not because I was concerned for a child. Not because I wanted her to live and grow in the sunshine. Not even because I wanted justice to prevail. But to win the darned election."

Kateri winced to hear it.

"I didn't like the man I had become. By the time I realized that, it was late in the campaign. I backed off on the hand-shaking and ass-kissing and worked full time for the police force again. And when I went into the voting booth, I voted for you."

"Wow." She put mascarpone and jam on a doughnut and offered it to him. "You win the lottery for being a really good guy."

Bergen accepted his prize and ate it. "Depends on who you talk to. When I told Mr. Caldwell what I'd done, he about choked. Me." He slid his sunglasses down his nose and peered over the top of them.

Bergen had a black eye.

"Mr. Caldwell hit you?" Kateri's voice rose.

Bergen put his hand over arm and squeezed warningly. "Shh!"

She glanced around. People were watching out of the corners of their eyes. "No wonder you're wearing sunglasses!"

Bergen pushed them back up. "He packs a pretty good punch."

"I guess!" Kateri started laughing. "You didn't arrest him for assaulting an officer?"

"No, and don't you dare tell the other guys. It's bad enough having them commiserate with me over losing the election. I don't need to get into trouble about getting my ass kicked by an octogenarian." But a smile played around Bergen's mouth. "You cause earthquakes."

It was stupid, but she blushed. "Hardly ever!"

"Glad to hear it. They mostly make our jobs harder. But I think maybe whatever power you have has given you a solid intuition for the job. I would have arrested Maddie Hewitson and done everything in my power to put her away for a thousand years. You realized something else was going on. Because of you, justice was done."

"Gut instinct." Speaking of gut, it was time for another doughnut.

"I don't have that instinct. But I'm logical to a fault. Or so Sandra tells me. We'll make a good team for Virtue Falls." He offered his hand.

She extended hers.

He groped for it, but he wasn't looking. Something outside the window had caught his attention.

Kateri turned to see.

Stag Denali strolled down the street in his designer jeans and his white button-up shirt, looking too suave for Virtue Falls and yet . . . right at home. He gazed through the window at her and smiled. Then his head wrenched around. He looked up the street—and dove toward the ground.

What the hell . . . ? Kateri heard the screech of a car tearing up the asphalt.

In a violent motion, Bergen yanked Kateri to the floor.

As she fell, something slammed into her ribs. She landed flat on her back. Hit her head. Heard a series of blasts accompanied by the sound of shattering glass. Heard a screaming in her ears.

She opened her eyes. The world blurred and spun.

Lacey stood over her, kissing her face and growling at Bergen.

Bergen knelt beside Kateri, yelling into his radio. "Officer down! Officer down at the Oceanview Café!"

Blood. There was blood on the floor.

Dazed, Kateri put her hand to her side, lifted it, and stared at her palm. *Her* blood. "Damn!" She'd been shot. She took a breath. She was in *pain.* She looked toward the large window beside their table. The glass had shattered under the impact of . . . something.

Bullets. A lot of bullets.

The café was a freak show of shrieking tourists, seniors who huddled under the tables and shouted instructions at Bergen and Kateri, and a confused Dax, who appeared out of the kitchen, holding a plate with a Monte Cristo sandwich and a metal spatula like a weapon.

He threw everything. He dropped to his knees.

Bergen ripped at Kateri's shirt, opened it, and looked. "Not life-threatening." He grabbed the napkins off the table. "Hold those. Apply pressure."

She did, and at the same time soothed Lacey. "It's all right. I'm all right. Bergen is one of the good guys."

Lacey eyed him, kissed Kateri one more time, jumped over the top of her, and raced into the chaos of the café.

Bergen again shouted into his radio. "Drive-by shooting. Black Dodge SRT Hellcat. Suspect not apprehended. Last seen heading out of town north. Proceed with caution. Sheriff wounded! More wounded at the Oceanview Café. More wounded! Assistance required!" Keeping low, he crawled away. Crawled toward . . .

Blood rolled in a widening puddle across the linoleum.

Not Kateri's. Whose . . . ?

By the counter. Lacey guarded an unmoving body sprawled gracelessly on the hard floor.

Dax knelt beside Lacey, moaning and rocking.

"Oh, no." Ignoring the pain, Kateri pushed herself over and onto her knees. Keeping the napkins pressed against her ribs, she crawled after Bergen.

Rainbow. Rainbow was unconscious, shot once through the lung and once through the abdomen.

Two hours later, Kateri sat outside the hospital, on the top concrete step, holding Lacey in her lap.

The dog pressed her head into Kateri's chest.

Kateri ignored the pain from her broken ribs and cuddled her traumatized pet. Lacey had protected Rainbow until the moment the ambulance had taken her away. Then she crept into the dim corner of the café, and as reparation, ate the despised dog treat.

No stiff-necked minister could ever convince Kateri that this dog did not have a soul.

A black Cadillac SRX crossover pulled into the parking lot; she wasn't a bit surprised to see Stag Denali get out and head toward her. She had to give the man bonus points for good psychology; as soon as he got close, he sat on the bottom step and stared up at her.

"Should you be sitting out here unprotected?" His voice was warm and concerned.

She wished she believed he was worried. But over and over again in her mind, she remembered him diving to the ground before she heard the screech of the killer car, and remembered, too, he was a gambler, a bouncer, a mobster. He was a violent man who had gone to prison for the death of a peace officer. In answer to his question, she pointed vaguely around the parking lot. "My men are guarding the hospital."

He nodded as if relieved.

She added, "Most of them, of course, are out hunting John Terrance Senior and John Junior."

"How is Rainbow?"

"She's in surgery, not expected to live." The woman who had been the midwife on the day Kateri was born, the woman who had borne witness to Kateri's life, who had given advice, support, and encouragement . . . was not expected to live.

CHAPTER FIFTY-SEVEN

On Thursday, Sheriff Kwinault came into Maddie's room to fill out the police report on Barbara's attack the day before.

If Jacob hadn't known about the attack at the Oceanview Café, he would have said that, although Sheriff Kwinault walked stiffly and turned as if she were in pain, still she behaved in a normal manner.

Clearly Maddie did not agree. Almost immediately she asked what was wrong, and she kept asking until Sheriff Kwinault told her about the drive-by shooting, about how the Terrances still evaded capture, and that Rainbow hovered on the brink of death.

When Sheriff Kwinault broke down in tears, Jacob escaped from the room to pace the corridor and fret. He had moved to Virtue Falls, closed himself in, and never gone to the Oceanview Café. He didn't know Rainbow, but all around him the medical professionals, the hospital security guards, the police, and the patients agonized and hoped. From what he could understand, this Rainbow person could have manipulated world events. Instead, she had chosen to be the kingpin of a much smaller universe, the universe of Virtue Falls, and Virtue Falls prayed for her recovery.

For Sheriff Kwinault and for Maddie, he hoped God listened to their prayers.

On Friday, Jacob first went to see Maddie at the hospital. Then he returned home. He dressed in his military uniform, drove to Seattle to the funeral home, and gave the eulogy for Brandon LaFreniere. He spoke of Brandon's intelligence, his strength under torture, and his bravery under fire. He spoke of the spirit of a man who faced the rest of his life in pain, without an arm and a leg, and who yet declared he *would* be happy, for nothing could ever be as bad as the cruelty and terror he had already faced. Jacob spoke of the lessons Brandon had taught them all, the inspiration Jacob himself had derived from simply knowing him. He paid tribute to his fallen comrade, and when he was done, Vera

LaFreniere pressed his hand between hers, and with tears in her eyes, she thanked him.

Perhaps he couldn't truly live for his brainiacs. But he had given comfort to Brandon's mother, and today, for Jacob, that was enough.

On Sunday, Jacob drove up to the hospital entrance, got out, and hovered while one of the nurses wheeled Maddie out and helped her into the passenger seat. Jacob felt as secure as he could, assuming the care of a victim convalescing from multiple stab wounds: he had her medications, he had written instructions on her care, he had phone numbers to call, and best of all, he had Dr. Frownfelter next door.

As Jacob put the car in gear, Dr. Frownfelter rushed out of the hospital.

Maddie opened the window.

Frownfelter put his big hand on the door, leaned down, looked her in the eyes, and said, "Young lady, I give patients one of two lectures. I either tell them that they must begin activity or they will atrophy, or I tell them to take it easy. You are to take it easy. Jacob, you're in charge. Remember, Maddie, if you feel like overdoing, I live next door. I will find out."

Maddie smiled and promised not to overdo it.

Jacob promised to make sure she didn't.

Dr. Frownfelter slapped the door and waved them on.

As Jacob and Maddie drove away, she smiled drowsily, leaned her head against the headrest, and closed her eyes. Not until they turned onto Dogwood Blossom Street did she rouse and look around.

An orange moving truck was parked in front of Mrs. Butenschoen's house. A stream of people—relatives, Jacob assumed—trekked back and forth carrying boxes and furniture. An older gentleman— Mrs. Butenschoen's brother?—was speaking to the local yard service, and while Jacob and Maddie watched, a real estate salesman pulled up to the curb.

A FOR SALE sign already decorated Dayton Floren's front yard.

Another FOR SALE sign stood in the Franklins' front yard; different real estate firm.

They already knew Dr. Frownfelter wasn't home.

In her front yard, Mrs. Nyback stood guard over Spike as the little dog wandered around, thoroughly marking his territory. He seemed unchanged by his ordeal; Mrs. Nyback gave Jacob and Maddie a timid wave.

Maddie waved back at once.

God bless Maddie. She didn't hold a grudge.

Jacob helped Maddie out of the car and walked with her up his walk. Step by step he helped her up onto his porch, where a huge, hand-lettered sign proclaimed:

WELCOME HOME, MADDIE!
YOUR CONSTRUCTION CREW

She stopped and read it. "I love those guys."

"They've worked hard over the past few days trying to get the house ready for you. Everything's done. Almost."

She turned and looked across the street. "When I get better, I'll have to finish packing my house."

Something in him relaxed. Her home was larger, nicer than his. He had been afraid she would want to live there again. But as far as he was concerned, that place would always be haunted by specters, poison, and the hovering threat of murder. "I can do the packing."

"Okay." She laughed at his dismayed expression. "You didn't think I'd argue with you, did you? I *hate* to pack."

"I hate to unpack." He opened the door.

"I have to unpack all by myself?" She stepped carefully over the threshold. "But I'm wounded, slashed by a fiend masquerading as a human being. Dr. Frownfelter told me not to overdo—"

"Remember to go slowly. We have all the time in the world." He followed her in and shut the door in the face of the world.

They were home.

Read on for a sneak preview of

The Woman Who Couldn't Scream,

the next novel from Christina Dodd

CHAPTER ONE

Benedict Howard was used to having women *look* at him. He had money. He had power. People saw that. Women looked at him. As they always told him, they found him *interesting*.

Now, the most beautiful woman in the world looked through him. Not over him. Not around him. *Through* him.

The *Eagle's Flight*, the largest sailing yacht in the Birdwing line, cut through the waves with an authority that spoke well of the ships as well as the captain and his crew. As the new owner of the high-end cruise line, that gratified Benedict; his decision to buy had been sound.

But at three days into the two-week transatlantic crossing, his whole attention was focused on the world's most beautiful woman.

Her skillfully tinted blond hair was styled in an upsweep with short tendrils that curled around her softly rounded face. Her nose was short and without freckles. Her neck was long and graceful. Her figure was without flaw, Barbie doll–like in its architectural magnificence. Unlike the other determinedly casual passengers, she wore a designer dress with matching jacket and one-inch heels. Her wide blue eyes were set deep in an artfully tended peaches-and-cream complexion . . . but they were blank, blind, indifferent. To him.

If she was trying to attract his attention by ignoring him, she had succeeded. But only for as long as it took him to recognize her machination. As he began to turn away, she looked toward a table set under the awning. She waved and she smiled.

Benedict was transfixed by her smile. He knew her. He was sure he knew her. From . . . somewhere. Business? No. Pleasure? No. In passing? Absurd. How could he forget the most beautiful woman in the world?

Stepping forward, he caught her elbow. "We've met."

She turned her head toward him, but as if his impertinence offended her, she took her time and moved stiffly. She shook her head.

"I'm sure we've met." He searched her face, searched his mind, seeking the time, the place. "You must remember. I'm Benedict Howard."

She wore a leather purse over one shoulder. With elaborate patience, she pulled it around, reached inside, and pulled out a tablet computer. She brought up the keyboard and swiftly, so swiftly, she typed onto the screen. And showed it to him. It said, "How do you do, Mr. Howard. My name is Helen Brassard. I am a mute, unable to speak. DO NOT SHOUT. I am not deaf. I certainly recognize you. You're quite famous in the world of finance. But you don't know me."

"I don't believe you."

She gave him a look, the exasperated kind that without words called him an idiot.

And he realized he had instinctively raised his voice.

She typed again and showed him the tablet. "I'm sure we'll run into each other again. It is a relatively small ship and an intimate passenger list. Now if you'll excuse me, I don't like to keep my husband waiting."

Benedict wanted to insist, but he glanced at the small, dapper gentleman who glared at him with imperious fury, the gentleman who was old enough to be her grandfather. But wasn't her grandfather. Benedict recognized him; that was French billionaire Nauplius Brassard. That was the husband.

Trophy wife. Helen was a trophy wife: head-turningly beautiful, no doubt accomplished in bed . . . and mute. Perfect for the short, thin, elderly gentleman who had no doubt purchased her services for the long term.

Benedict let her go and turned away.

She was right. He didn't know her.

Helen Brassard seated herself next to her husband and used her hands to sign, "You look heated and I suspect you're ready for your afternoon cocktail. Shall I order you a sidecar?"

Nauplius flipped his bony fingers around, grasped her wrist, and squeezed. "I saw him speak to you."

She groped for her purse and her tablet.

"No! That's how you communicate with everyone else. Sign to me."

She shook her captured wrist, trying to free herself, to make it easier.

"Sign with one hand."

Of course she did. "Benedict did speak to me." She kept that gentle smile on her lips. Ignored the pain as the delicate bones ground together.

"He's lost his looks."

Signing: "He was never handsome." Although that was the truth, when she had known him before, Benedict's awkward arrangement of facial features had been offset by his youth and charisma. Now he looked . . . harsh, like a man who had tasted too much bitterness.

Nauplius adjusted his red bow tie. "What did he say?"

"He thought he knew me."

"Impossible."

Apparently not.

Nauplius was selfish to the point of psychosis, but his skill at observing and interpreting others had brought him wealth, power, and control. Now he must have read her thought, for his grip tightened again. "You look . . . not at all like the woman you were when he knew you." Menacingly, "Do you?"

There was the paranoia she knew so well.

"I have not been in communication with him either on the ship or off. You know that."

He *did* know that. He knew what she said and to whom, what she

did and when. He owned her, and she knew from experience that he was
infuriated by this unforeseen intrusion in the quality of his life. Especially *this* intrusion. During their nine-year marriage, they had lived in
France and Italy, Greece and Spain and Morocco, anywhere she was
isolated by language barriers, utterly dependent on him, and very, very
unlikely to run into anyone she had known before.

Like the old man that he was, Brassard moved his jaw and chewed
at nothing. "I didn't know Howard would be on this cruise. What is
he doing here?"

Signing: "I don't know."

"He didn't tell you?"

She took a steadying breath before she signed, "All he said was that
he knew me."

"What did you tell him?"

"That he didn't."

"I'll get us off this ship."

She glanced out at the turbulent blue Atlantic, then up at the
half-furled sails that caught the prevailing eastern winds, and signed,
"How?"

"Helicopter. They can come out this far."

"As you wish." She bowed her head and waited.

His voice rasped with irritation. "But the helicopter—it's very expensive and usually only used in case of emergency."

She signed, "That is my concern. A helicopter could cost possibly
one hundred thousand dollars." Which Brassard could well afford. But
wealthy as he was, he counted every cent and made sure she knew exactly
how much she cost him.

He said, "I can call it in. I'm doing it for you."

She looked into his brown, deceptively soft eyes and signed, "You
have no need. When I see Benedict, I feel nothing."

Brassard's grip tightened. "You never feel anything."

"Not true. Right now, you're hurting me."

In a swift, petty gesture, he tossed her wrist away from him.

As always, she was the perfect wife. In flowing, graceful movements, she asked, "Shall I order your cocktail?" and gestured to the hovering waiter.

For two days Benedict toured the working areas of the ship. He discussed meal preparation with the terrified chef and his equally terrified staff, inspected the lifeboats and their ongoing maintenance, and gave orders to improve the air-conditioning in the stifling laundry area.

Then Benedict moved into the public areas, stalking the ship's photographer as she recorded the voyage for later purchase by the passengers. The invariably pleasant Abigail photographed passengers as they toured the bridge, arranged flowers, played bridge, ate and drank.

It was when he was with Abigail that he saw her again, the most beautiful woman in the world, in the midship lounge at the line dancing class. Helen Brassard looked the same, tastefully dressed and in matching heels, and she frowned as she concentrated on the prescribed steps, placing each foot with a calm precision that created an anchor in the turbulently undisciplined line. She pulled the other dancers along, encouraging them with admiring gestures and warm touches to their shoulders. When the line completed the simplest dance step in unison, she smiled.

The most beautiful woman in the world had the most beautiful smile in the world, and he was transfixed, enthralled, in need.

"That's Mrs. Brassard," Abigail said. "She is married to Mr. Brassard, who is wealthy, possessive, and quite . . . demanding." Her voice held a distinct note of warning.

Benedict turned his cool gaze on her.

She respectfully lowered her eyes.

Abigail was afraid of him; all the staff were afraid of him. Yet she wanted him to know his interest would not be appreciated by a paying customer.

A good employee. A brave employee, one with guts and intelligence. He knew how rare those qualities were, and how valuable to the cruise line. He would see to it that she moved up in the ship's hierarchy, and if she continued to do well, she would be sent to college and consequently she would move into his family's company. "Thank you for the warning." Which he wouldn't heed, but that was of no consequence to her. He indicated a burly black man with massive shoulders and a calm demeanor. "That's Carl Klineman, right? I always see him lurking near the Brassards. What is he to them?"

"He never speaks to them, and they never even glance at him," Abigail said. "For the most part, he keeps to himself."

"And yet?"

She lowered her voice. "Speculation among the staff is that he's their bodyguard. Or an assassin. But no one really believes that Mr. Brassard would be oblivious to an assassin. He is a very astute man."

Benedict sensed she had more to say. "And . . . ?"

He had to lean close to hear her say, "Very astute and very . . . dangerous. He is dangerous. We, the staff, take care never to displease him."

A man could learn a lot from his employees, especially in these circumstances, and Abigail was genuinely frightened. "Thank you for your insight. I will take care to tread carefully around Nauplius Brassard." He gave her a moment to recover, then in a brisk tone asked, "What do you photograph next?"

"Musical bingo in the Bistro Bar starts in a half hour."

"Let's go."

Benedict despised trophy wives. He always had. And that name: *Helen.*

Helen of Troy.

The most beautiful woman in the ancient world, the woman whose face launched a thousand ships. He could hardly believe she had been born with it. Probably she had chosen it when she created her persona to trap a wealthy man. . . .

So Benedict did his research and online he found out all about her.

Yes, Helen was the name she'd been given at birth. Her beginnings were humble; she had grown up in Nepal as the daughter of missionaries. When she was a teenager, her parents were killed in a rockfall and she was sent to the United States to live with her family in the South. She finished high school at sixteen and began college at Duke

University, where her unusual beauty attracted Nauplius Brassard's attention. After a brief courtship, she graciously consented to be his wife and dedicated herself to him and his well-being. She did not work, did not express independent opinions, and during the days when he worked or during the evenings when he made appearances at government functions and glittering parties, she never left his side.

Very neat. Very pat. But nowhere did any source explain why she could not speak. And that single fact made Benedict doubt the whole story—although the numerous politically incorrect among the online community suggested that an inability to speak made her the perfect wife for Nauplius Brassard.

The world abounded with jackasses.

And Benedict's curiosity was piqued.

Before the voyage had even begun, the crew had studied the ship's manifest and passenger list, memorizing every face and name. Now Benedict did the same, and when he was satisfied with his research and his ability to greet the guests, he joined the convivial table that nightly gathered after dinner at the bar at the aft of the ship, a table that included five retired Southern high school teachers making their annual pilgrimage to Europe, two university professors on sabbatical, a group of Spanish and Portuguese wine merchants, a skinny eighty-year-old corporate lawyer—and Nauplius Brassard and his wife Helen.

Benedict turned a chair from another table and dragged it over. "May I join you?"

For a mere second, conversation faltered.

One of the middle-aged females scooted over. "We are all friends. Sit next to me." She placed her hand on her husband's arm. "We're Juan Carlos and Carmen Mendoza, wine merchants from Barcelona . . . and you are Benedict Howard."

Apparently he wasn't the only one who had studied the roster. "That's right, from Baltimore, Maryland, USA. I buy and sell things."

"On a grand scale," Juan Carlos said drily. "The Howard family is known for its business . . . acumen."

A nice way to say *ruthlessness*. "Yes." Benedict looked toward the opposite end of the long table. "But I interrupted the conversation.

Please, continue while I sit here and absorb the bonhomie." In fact, he had interrupted Helen Brassard, who had been animated and flushed as she recounted some story by signing while Nauplius Brassard translated in his faintly accented voice.

Cool and calm, she sipped her champagne and looked him in the eyes. She nodded. She put down her champagne, lifted her hands, and signed, "Of course. I was telling this illustrious company about the surprise party my husband threw for me for my twenty-seventh birthday."

"Fascinating," he murmured.

With a turn of the head, she dismissed Benedict and spoke to the assemblage. "On the banks of the Loire in the month of June . . . he scheduled the Osiris String Quartet to play chamber music and had a catered picnic flown in from Vienna and laid on blankets on the grass. He hired a film crew to record each precious moment and he surprised me with a custom-made gift of polished amber stones set in a magnificent gold setting."

Benedict had trouble knowing who to look at—Helen, who was speaking, or Nauplius, who was interpreting. He glanced around and saw that the others at the table seemed similarly stricken by uncertainty, and he wondered if they also found it odd to hear Nauplius Brassard praise himself so effusively . . . in her words. Certainly Brassard looked smug as he spoke.

But Helen gazed at her husband as if she adored him, placed one palm flat on her chest, and with the other spelled, "The memory is engraved on my heart."

The wide-bellied, rumpled academic nodded and, in an accomplishment Benedict appreciated, at the same time sneered. Dawkins Cipre didn't want to offend Nauplius Brassard, a generous donor to European universities. Yet as a professor of literature he could hardly approve such a romantic gesture; it might reflect badly on his pretentiousness.

Elsa Cipre, the academic's thin, nervous, carefully unmade-up wife and a professor in her own right, said, "Nauplius has studied the inner workings of a woman's heart."

One of the school teachers rolled her eyes. Another said, "Bless his heart." Apparently the self-important academics had not impressed anyone.

Then Elsa said, "Dawkins is an expert on classic medieval French romance literature. Perhaps, Helen, for your twenty-eighth birthday he could consult with Nauplius and bring the full weight of French literature to bear."

Faintly Benedict heard Carmen Mendoza moan under her breath.

Dawkins took the opportunity to launch into a college-level literature lecture in which he cited his years at Oxford and the Sorbonne. His pontificating encouraged low buzzing conversations to start and swell, and Nauplius Brassard flushed with irritation—he did not enjoy losing his place in the spotlight or being told what to do—and tried to interrupt.

Dawkins rambled on, oblivious.

Without asking, the bar staff delivered another round of stiff drinks.

The band came in; the musician played guitar and keyboard, the singer was thin, young, attractive, and handled the microphone with an expertise that spoke of long experience. They began the first set.

Dawkins rattled on until his wife touched his hand and they left to find the dessert buffet.

With a pretty smile, Helen pushed Brassard's drink toward him.

Brassard folded his arms over his chest, transferring his irritation to her.

She tried to sign to her husband, to cajole him into a better mood.

He turned his head away.

When she persisted, he whipped around to face her, caught her wrists, and effectively rendered her mute.

At once she stopped her attempt, and when he released her, she contemplated the champagne in her flute and drank.

An interesting scene, Benedict thought. Helen was Brassard's whipping boy. What kind of greed made a woman put up with that kind of abuse?

Carmen Mendoza began to hum and then to sing in a warm

contralto, and in five minutes she had kicked off her shoes and stood before the band, dancing. Before another minute had passed Juan Carlos had taken the female high school teachers onto the floor and the male high school teachers had joined them on the fringes, gyrating sheepishly.

Reginald Bardzecki, the eighty-year-old corporate lawyer, stood and offered his hand to Helen. She glanced at the still fuming Brassard, smiled defiantly, kicked off her shoes, and joined Reginald.

Unlike anyone else on the floor, they danced like experts. He led, she followed, the two of them staging a series of ballroom moves that only two people who loved the music could perform.

The musicians played. The staff and dancers stopped and watched.

Benedict leaned back in his chair and appreciated the sight. Then instinct led him to glance toward the other end of the table.

Nauplius Brassard sat glaring at the elderly man who spun his youthful, smiling wife across the floor.

And Benedict remembered what Abigail had said about Nauplius Brassard: *He is dangerous. We take care never to displease him . . .* Benedict thought Helen would suffer for her insubordination.

The song ended. The dancers came back to the table, flushed and laughing. They ordered drinks and complimented Reginald and Helen on their skill.

Helen seated herself next to her husband, keeping a few careful inches away from his simmering resentment.

The next song started. Carmen pulled Benedict to the dance floor and taught him flamenco. When he felt he'd made a fool of himself for long enough, Benedict started back toward the table.

The Brassards were gone.

The next morning, a helicopter arrived and lifted Nauplius Brassard and his wife off the ship.

Thirteen months later, Nauplius Brassard died of a brain aneurysm.

His children, all in their forties, moved swiftly to eject his young wife, Helen, from the Brassard Paris home.

They discovered her designer wardrobe, her jewels, and all the furnishings intact. But the fortune Brassard had set aside in her name had vanished—and so had she.

Less than forty-eight hours later, one of Nauplius Brassard's legal team was found murdered during working hours, slashed to death in her office.

The police feared a copycat killer, one imitating the serial killer who, two years before, had died in a Canadian prison.

To their relief, no further murders followed.

CHAPTER TWO

In the mountains on Washington's Olympic Peninsula

Officer Rupert Moen steered the speeding patrol car around sharp corners, up steep rises, and through washouts caused by spring rains. Sweat stained his shirt, ruddy blotches lit his cheeks and the middle of his forehead. He was young, a member of the sheriff's department for only a couple of years, shy, and never the brightest bulb in the chandelier.

But damn, put that kid behind the wheel and he could *drive*.

Sheriff Kateri Kwinault's only jobs were to lean with the curves and to keep him calm. In the soothing voice she had perfected during her time as the regional Coast Guard commander, she said, "Four wheels on the ground. All you have to do is keep 'em in sight. We've got a helicopter on its way and every law enforcement officer on the Peninsula moving into position."

Like a Celtic warrior, Moen was all wild red hair and savage grins. "This road is a real bitch, isn't it?"

"It's . . . interesting." Kateri kept her gaze away the almost vertical plunge on her side of the car, away from the equally vertical rise on the other side.

"Goddamn interesting." Moen harried the black Dodge SRT Hellcat with flashing lights and a blast of the electronic air horn. "This time we'd better catch those bastards."

"Yes." The Terrances, father and son, were bastards and worse: drug dealers, meth cookers, jail escapees, drive-by shooters . . . and murderers.

Kateri corrected herself. *Attempted* murderers. "I hope the roadblock stopped any nonofficial vehicles. We don't want to meet someone in a head-on."

"Not much traffic up here this spring. Too much runoff. Good thing, considering."

Considering the width of the road, considering the speed, considering no civilian wanted to encounter John Senior and John Junior.

All the things that made the Olympic Peninsula a hiker's and boater's paradise also made it an ideal hiding place for two fugitives. For three intensive days, the hunt had pulled in county, city, and state police to patrol the roads, and the Coast Guard to cruise the Pacific Ocean and the coastal inlets. After Pauline Nitz had spotted the black Dodge SRT Hellcat speeding along one of the narrow forest roads and called in the report, the chase was on.

Now, spitting gravel and raising dust, Kateri and Moen led the Virtue Falls Police Department in hot pursuit.

Moen's white knuckles gripped the wheel. "Hold on." He steered them over a series of washboards that rattled everything in the car and made Kateri moan and press her hand to her side. He glanced at her. "Sorry, Sheriff."

"Not your fault," she said. Four days ago, while Kateri sat in the window of the Oceanview Café celebrating her surprise election to the exalted office of sheriff, the Terrances had sprayed bullets through the windows. Their bullet had skipped off her ribs like a flat stone off the rippled surface of a river, leaving her broken and bloody but not seriously wounded.

Instead, they'd put two bullets into Virtue Falls's beloved waitress, busybody, and local wise woman, Rainbow Breezewing, and now she lay in the hospital in a coma, hooked to ventilators and drips. The doctors told Kateri that Rainbow didn't have a chance. They said Rainbow was dying. Dying . . .

"They're slowing down." Moen moved closer to the Hellcat's bumper.

"Maybe they're out of gas." That would be too wonderful—and too lucky, since as far as Kateri could tell, the Terrances had stashed fuel and food in hiding places in the mountains and up and down the coast. "But I don't believe it. Back off."

Moen sighed but did as he was told.

She leaned forward, watching, trying to figure out what they were up to. "Be care—"

John Terrance, Junior or Senior, goosed the black Dodge SRT and threw it into a skid that sent the car sideways, passenger side toward the pursuers.

"Don't T-bone him!" Kateri shouted.

Moen slipped it into second gear, eased off the gas, and in the excessively patient tone of the very young for the very old (Kateri was thirty-four), he said, "I know what I'm doing, Sheriff."

The SRT's passenger door flew open. Something tumbled out.

Someone tumbled out.

Moen screamed, "Shit son of a bitch!"

Kateri yelled, "Don't hit him. Don't run over him!"

Moen mashed on his brakes, skidded.

No way to avoid the collision.

The left tire caught the body. The front of the car went airborne.

"The tree!" Moen shouted.

They rammed it, a giant Douglas fir, square on.

The air bags exploded.

Kateri was slammed against the back of her seat. She couldn't breathe. She couldn't see. *She was drowning.*

No. Not drowning. Not again.

She fought the hot white plastic out of her face. The air bag was already deflating . . . She tore off the sunglasses. White dust covered them, covered the interior of the car. The siren blared. She needed to catch her breath—

Moen looked in the rearview mirror and yelled, "They can't stop. They're going to nail us!"

"Who?"

"Cops!"

Another collision rammed the right rear fender. Metal scraped. Fir needles rained down. The impact pushed the patrol car sideways, wrenched the stitches over Kateri's ribs. The wound opened, one torn stitch at a time. Icy-hot pain slithered up her nerves. Warm blood trickled down her side.

Moen opened his door.

Kateri heard sirens. The roar of an engine. Was another vehicle going to hit them? Or worse—had John Senior escaped?

Moen unbuckled his seat belt. "You okay, Sheriff?"

"Yes." She pressed the pad of her bandage. "Go."

He leaped out and ran toward the unmoving body in the middle of the road.

Had they inadvertently killed a hostage?

Someone yanked open her door. "Sorry, Sheriff, when you fishtailed, we couldn't stop." A moment, then a face thrust into hers. "You okay, Sheriff?"

Kateri blinked at the star-pattern of pain before her eyes.

The face belonged to Deputy Sheriff Gunder Bergen. Good guy. Good law officer. Second-in-command. He knew stuff.

"Who did we hit?" she asked. "Did we kill him?"

"Moen's coming."

Moen stuck his head in the driver's door. He leaned a hand on the steering wheel and one on the seat and spoke to her. "The body was John Junior. He was already dead. Like . . . there was rigor mortis, so a few days ago, right?"

Bergen inched farther in, leaned a hand on the dashboard. "We're getting the coroner out here, but yeah. What killed him?"

Moen switched his attention to Bergen. "Gunshot wound."

"Close range? His father shot him?" Bergen asked.

The two men were talking over the top of her. Which was as annoying as hell. "He shot his son so he could use the body as a diversion?" Kateri clicked her seat belt and let go.

The buckle smacked Bergen on the thigh.

He jumped back, bumped his head on the roof, looked surprised as the dog who ate the bumblebee.

"No. I mean, maybe, but the shot was long range, entered the right side at about the liver. He bled out." Moen looked hard at Kateri and did a double take. "Sheriff, you don't look much better than the corpse."

Bergen nodded. "Ambulance just pulled up. We'll send her to the hospital."

Kateri said the obvious. "Don't be silly. I'm fine."

"You sound just like my wife right before she collapsed with a ruptured appendix," Bergen said.

"I'm fine," she repeated. "Did we get John Senior?"

Moen clearly didn't want to give this report. "The diversion worked. He gunned it. No one could get past us. He's gone."